THE
CHOICE
OF
MEN

SAMANTHA WALTZ

Samantha Waltz

Paths of Thought

Library of Congress cataloging-in-publication data

The Choice of Men / Samantha Waltz

p. cm.

ISBN: 978-1-7355604-0-3 (paperback)
ISBN: 978-1-7355604-1-0 (electronic)

1. Literary fiction
2. Gay fiction
3. Historical

Library of Congress Control Number: 2020917840

Cover design by Wendy Bouis Creative <wendybouis.com>

Printed in the United States of America

THE
CHOICE
OF
MEN

To everyone forced to choose between who they are and what society wants them to be.

1

Paris, France, August 1939

Heber froze in front of President Hays' office door. What would the president do when he found out where Heber had been last night? His mission for the Mormon Church here in France would be over and he'd be ripped away from the French language and culture he'd grown to love. Would he ever again see the French friends who had welcomed him to their country? He'd be sent home to Utah for sure; home to a humiliated family and neighbors that would spit on him as he walked by.

He had to confess. What he'd done was an anathema to the Lord and a betrayal of President Hays' trust.

His hands shaking, Heber tried to straighten his tie and smooth the rumples in his suit jacket. Did he still reek of the Orléans train station? Or put on too much Burma-Shave to try to cover the smell? He wished he'd had time to shower and to starch and iron his clothes, but President Hays would be wondering where he'd been.

"Come in." President Hays' voice boomed a hearty welcome.

Heber stepped into the office of the Paris, France Mission and blinked away threatening tears.

"*Frère* Averil. So glad to see you." The president looked up from his desk, a grin splitting his broad face. "We were worried. You were supposed to be back in Paris last night. Everything all right?"

Heber studied the geometric pattern of the wool carpet. No, everything wasn't all right. He'd done what no good Mormon would ever do, let alone a missionary.

Strange how last night he'd felt more joy than he'd ever known. This morning all that was left of the evening was cold remorse.

His stomach growled and he flushed with embarrassment. He usually loved the crusty French rolls served for breakfast at the mission home, but today he couldn't eat a bite. He needed to fast and pray for forgiveness anyway.

President Hays motioned him to a straight-backed chair facing his desk. "You look awfully pale, son. You caught *Frère* Monroe's stomach flu?"

He wished. If only President Hays hadn't trusted him to go alone to Orléans when his missionary companion got sick. The branch there would have survived another week without their supplies from the mission home if he'd stayed in Paris. Then he never would have met André, and he wouldn't need to make this confession.

"What can I do for you, *Frère*?" The president waited, expectant.

Heber opened his mouth, but no sound came out. He crossed his legs, straightened them, crossed them again.

The clock on the desk ticked loudly.

"What is it, *Frère*? You're as nervous as a young colt."

"I'm not a good man." Heber pushed out the words, his voice breaking.

"What's that?" President Hays leaned toward him.

"I'm not a good man," Heber repeated, louder.

The president frowned. "What do you mean? Of course, you are! On your mission just over a year and already the best mission secretary I've had. It might help that you're a bit older. Twenty-three, right?"

Heber nodded.

"You make a real difference around here. The missionaries get a lot out of the newsletter you created. Especially since you've added the poems and stories. Very inspiring. And the way you can play any hymn on the piano or teach any Sunday School class. Amazing."

Heber looked up, squinting in the sunlight that poured through the tall window behind President Hays. How he'd miss this elegant villa that housed the president and his family, the president's office, and the missionaries who helped with mission business. His family's ramshackle farmhouse on the outskirts of Ogden, Utah was in so many ways a world away from this sacred and serene place.

"I'm glad to help," he murmured, dropping his eyes again. President Hays wouldn't sing his praises for a minute if he knew why Heber's senior companion in Blois had requested Heber's immediate transfer. It wasn't a "personality conflict." Not the kind President Hays assumed, anyway. Or if he knew what had happened in Orléans last night.

The president moved to a chair beside Heber and put a hand on his shoulder. "Tell me, son. What is it?"

When Heber met his gaze, he saw wide eyes soft with kindness and bushy grey brows furrowed in concern. He'd let down this man who'd respected him enough to make him his secretary at the mission home and treated him with far more kindness than Heber's own father had ever shown. Heber's tears overflowed and coursed down his cheeks. "I think about men." He mumbled the awful words.

"What? I didn't get that."

Sweat prickled the back of Heber's neck. He cleared his throat. "I think about men."

President Hays' eyes widened. "Surely you aren't saying …"

Heber nodded.

The president rose to his feet and towered over Heber. "Impossible. I know you. You aren't that kind."

"I don't want to be." Heber wiped his eyes on his shirtsleeve. "A man at church in Orléans …" He fought for a steady voice. "He wanted to learn about the Book of Mormon."

"So, you referred him to the missionaries there."

Heber's face flushed with shame. "I should have referred him, but he wanted *me* to teach him. I had to go. I … I wanted to see him."

President Hays drew in his breath. "And then?"

Heber didn't know how he could speak of what had happened next. "I gave a lesson. He'd prepared dinner for us. He … um …" He *must* confess it all. Take responsibility for the thing he'd allowed to happen. "I knew it was wrong. I got out of there. I missed the last train and slept at the station." Surely President Hays could fill in the blanks.

The president turned and paced the length of the room for several minutes.

Heber waited, not breathing.

"Ah," the president said at last and returned to his desk. "I see exactly what happened."

Heber slunk lower in his chair.

"That man was one of Satan's helpers. His job was to make you believe you're one of those."

What? Heber sat up straighter.

The clock ticked louder.

President Hays' eyes bored into Heber's soul. "*Frère* Averil, you wanted to preach the gospel to that man.

Nothing more. I tell you; you are not like that." His voice rang with authority.

Heber struggled to make sense of President Hays' words. Was the president absolving him? What if it really was André's fault and nothing was wrong with him? No. There was that time in Blois. Heber had told himself then that it would never happen again, and it had.

"You would not ask for eternal damnation," the president continued, wagging a finger at Heber.

A chill swept through Heber's body. "No, sir."

"You have more than a year left of your mission. Fill it honorably."

"I will, sir." With this promise came hope, rising in his chest.

"When you are released, go straight home and find a worthy woman to take through the temple. Get a good job. Raise a family."

"Yes, sir." Heber's actions from this moment forward would prove President Hays right.

"Accept all the church assignments given you and ask for more. Get involved in sports. Read your scriptures."

"Every day."

"The Lord is counting on you. I'm counting on you. Not another word about last night."

"Yes, sir."

"Now, tell me what music you've lined up for our mission conference next month."

Heber inhaled and let his breath out slowly. President Hays was called by God to guide the missionaries and had insisted Heber wasn't like that. *Please, Heavenly Father, let it be true.*

After his meeting with President Hays, Heber wandered onto the streets of the Ville d'Avray, buffeted by a swirl of emotions. Thrilled that he was allowed to stay on his mission, not sent home in shame to face the questions of friends and family, he vowed to work even harder sharing the message of the Gospel and proving that he was a righteous man.

He grew so hot under the summer sun that he paused to peel off his suit jacket and loosen his tie. When he came to a little church, Église Saint-Nicolas-et-Saint-Marc, he impulsively stopped at its heavy wooden door, pulled it open and slipped inside, his footsteps echoing on the stone floor.

Grateful for the cool solitude, Heber sank onto one of the wooden chairs making up neat rows the length of the church. The sweet aroma of incense, an exotic treat, filled his nostrils as he looked around. The church was like a jewelry box, simple on the outside but holding exquisite gems: an intricately decorated arched ceiling, stunning statuary, and the first frescoes he'd ever seen. He recognized paintings by Corot, an artist whose work he'd seen in art books in the Ogden library. President Hays encouraged the missionaries to take in all the culture they could while serving the Lord in France. Insightful advice. Although Heber had been taught as a child that the Catholic church was the great and abominable church, he felt God here as much as in a Mormon chapel.

Heber let the beauty wash over him, stilling his mind and allowing the worries of his meeting with President Hays to fade. He felt the same thrill he'd experienced when he first caught sight of the French shore. He hadn't believed his good luck receiving a mission call to France. The eight-day Atlantic crossing in the company of a group of young tourists as well as other missionaries headed to Europe had been a romp. He'd fit in better with this crowd than he ever did at home, finding them more like-minded — interested in travel, history, and the arts.

The two days lodged at the mission home in the Ville d'Avray, a hilly suburb of Paris, had given him an opportunity to wander some of Paris' tree-lined boulevards and encounter sites he'd read about in books — the Opera, Notre Dame, the Eiffel Tower, all of them more magnificent in person. When he met President Hays, an older man who guided the missionaries like a loving father, he knew serving under him would be the best two-and-a-half years of his life.

On his third day in France, Heber received his assignment to serve in Blois with Alan Richards who'd been on his mission for a year.

Heber shifted on the chair. A mental image of his first missionary companion swept him back to his time in Blois.

2

Blois, France, August 1938

"Welcome to Blois." Alan greeted Heber with a hearty handshake when he met him at the train station. "So much to show you. Kings lived here in the fifteenth century, in the Chateau de Blois right in the center of town. Sure is different from Boise, Idaho where I grew up."

Heber gawked at the stately, slate-roofed homes now turned into apartments, and the gardens bursting with sunflowers and gladiolas, as they followed winding cobblestone streets to their rented rooms. He'd never seen a building a hundred years old, much less many centuries old, and the sight conjured in his imagination a bustling medieval town. His body tingled with excitement.

For the next three days, he and *Frère* Richards—Alan to him—focused on setting up street meetings around town in locations where curious people might gather and listen to a short speech or pick up a pamphlet about the Mormon church. Afterward they dipped into small *cafés* for a *limonade* and talked about what might be added to their presentations to garner more interest. One late afternoon they went for a bath in the huge copper cauldrons of Vienne.

Heber sensed the seething unrest across the country with the military buildup in Germany and the Spanish civil war.

He'd arrived at the perfect time. These folks in Blois needed the hopeful message he brought of God's love for them and their salvation through the death and resurrection of His son, Jesus Christ. The Catholic church didn't understand God the same way the Mormon church did. Who could get their head around a Holy Trinity with the Father, Son and Holy Spirit as one substance? Mormons knew the truth. Heavenly Father was a real, glorified being. A literal father in heaven with whom they could have a personal relationship. Jesus was His son and Savior of the world. The Holy Ghost, to Catholics the Holy Spirit, was the third member of the Godhead, bringing inspiration and peace to the hearts of those who invited it into their lives.

He would do his best to share this message with everyone who would listen. This morning, only his fourth in Blois, held the possibility of his first success. Despite some Catholic priests warning their parishioners to avoid the Mormon missionaries whose message would lead straight to damnation, a woman and her eighteen-year-old daughter had attended a street meeting. After the meeting, they invited Heber and Alan to come to their home and teach them more about the Gospel.

As he prepared for the visit, Heber cobbled together the French he remembered from high school language classes, the French phonetics he'd studied during nine intense days in the mission home in Salt Lake City, and what he'd learned at the street meetings listening to Alan. He'd always been an "A" student, but here in France he stumbled to make himself understood. He hoped the Romrielles were patient.

Young Natalie Romrielle, gold earrings and black eyes flashing, apparently had a plan of her own to introduce the missionaries to her local culture. "I will read your palms, yes?" she said in slow, careful French as soon as they were seated at the sun-lit kitchen table.

Mme. Romrielle sat beside her, nodding her assent to her daughter's plan.

"Sure," Heber agreed, promptly removing his cufflinks and pushing up his shirtsleeves.

Alan frowned. "*Règles mission*, mission rules," he whispered to Heber.

Heber paused. He imagined the brethren in Salt Lake had more important concerns than two of their young men getting their fortunes told. Besides, President Hays, in his frequent talks to the missionaries, stressed that they learn about and honor the cultures of the people they taught. Alan sounded so rigid. Still, Heber liked his companion a lot, his easy grin, the laugh wrinkles around his eyes, his quick sense of humor. In fact, he liked him the best of the missionaries he'd met so far and hated to cross him.

"Do you want to please this man or me?" Natalie teased, winking at Heber.

Heber extended his arms across the table, shrugging when he caught Alan's eye.

"*Eh bien*," Natalie murmured as she took Heber's left hand.

"*Vous voyez quelque chose?* You see something?" Heber watched her trace each line of his palm with a slender, bejeweled finger.

Natalie rotated Heber's hand palm up, her touch cool and light. "We are having fun, yes? I see a long life."

Heber grinned. "Swell. What else?"

"Money. Not a lot, but enough."

Heber glanced at his threadbare slacks. Money would definitely be nice. His family's farm was small, and his father had gone from job to job trying to feed a family of eight children. Growing up they'd often been hungry. With the Depression adding to his family's woes, he could never have afforded the forty-dollar a month cost of his French mission without the help of the church members back home. He had big plans to change all that. Break into Hollywood or become a famous writer. Maybe Natalie could foresee his name in lights on a movie theater marquee or on the cover of a book. That would be real money. He could help his family and pay more than the standard ten percent tithe to the church with plenty left over to pursue his dreams.

"You have a strong heart line." Natalie's eyes glinted mischievously as she followed an explosion of lines starting between Heber's first and second fingers and wandering off the side of his hand. "*Ooo la la*, see *Maman*." Natalie turned Heber's hand toward her mother. "It is the heart of an artichoke with a leaf for every love."

Mme. Romrielle looked at his hand. "*Ah, oui.*"

"Every love?" Alan snorted. "He hasn't mentioned a girl since he arrived."

Natalie ignored him. "You are so tall, so slim," she cooed to Heber. "That wavy hair and those eyes the color of the sea. Many girls in your Utah must miss you." She put her hand to her heart and feigned a swoon.

Heber blushed.

She took his right hand, sighing dramatically as she studied it. "The left hand is the hand of possibility. The right is the hand of reality. Here, too, I see an artichoke. Many loves can be a good thing, *non*?"

"Maybe." Heber shrugged. He'd never even had a girlfriend, nor had he wanted one; too busy for much social life with his studies at Weber College and work to help out at home. He flicked a thumb at Alan. "His turn now."

Natalie held out a hand to Alan.

"*Pas moi*. Not me." Alan folded his arms across his chest.

"Dare you. Double dare you," Heber prodded.

"You are afraid?" Natalie challenged with an impish grin.

"*D'accord.*" Alan unfolded his arms, removed his cufflinks, and stretched his left hand across the table.

Natalie pressed her lips together, studying it. "You Americans are very strong," she intoned. "You, too, will have a long life. And you will have a lot of money."

"This isn't so bad." Alan's forehead smoothed and his mouth curved into a smile.

"You will marry and have many children."

His smile grew.

Heber knew Alan would be thinking about Lydia. He studied his fiancé's picture taped to the ceiling above the big, square couch that doubled as their bed at night as often as he studied the Book of Mormon.

"Oh, *Frère* Richards ..." Natalie's voice trailed off and she set Alan's hand gently on the table. "*Maman?*"

Mme. Romrielle looked at his hand. "*Ah, oui.*" She, too, looked sad.

"What is it? Tell me."

Heber winced at Alan's sharp tone.

"Life will teach you this thing." Natalie patted Alan's hand.

Mme. Romrielle pushed back her chair and stood. "Now we will eat," she announced. "Soup. And *cavaillon*, a sweet melon I know you will like."

"*Bonne idée. Merci.*" Heber had noticed a pot of vegetable soup simmering on the wood stove. He hadn't expected lunch and his stomach growled in anticipation of the savory meal.

"We have to go. Got a report due." Alan rose, shook his shirtsleeves over his wrists, and refastened his cufflinks. He glared at Heber. "You better not have forgotten."

"I... I remember," Heber stammered, swallowing his objection. "I'll offer a prayer and then we'll go." Reports weren't due until the end of the month, and their hasty departure would seem disrespectful. But Alan was awfully upset for some reason.

Heber bowed his head and prayed for blessings on the Romrielle household, then pressed the women's hands and mumbled a goodbye. He took his hat and suit jacket from the mahogany rack in the entry, required apparel even on warm summer days when doing the Lord's work.

"That was rude," Heber grumbled as they clattered down the three flights of stairs.

"Her hocus-pocus ..."

Heber heard a catch in Alan's voice and turned to him. Alan's shoulders slumped in a way Heber had never seen. This wasn't the man who always cracked jokes during their walks through town, jostling him as they drooled over window displays in the *patisserie* and *chocolatier*.

He touched Alan's arm. "You okay?"

Alan held his silence as he and Heber strode side-by-side past a *pharmacie* with its big, green cross, and a *charcuterie* with a full side of beef and several chickens hanging in the window.

"Not a word from Lydia this week," Alan finally said.

"She's just busy. You'll get a letter."

"Her last few ... so different from before." Alan's voice broke.

"I bet there'll be a good one today." Heber followed him into a *boulangerie* where Alan gave the clerk sixty *centimes* for a *baguette*. "Lunch is on me," Alan said. "Guess I owe the Romrielles an apology."

Again, that catch in Alan's voice. He must really love Lydia. A jolt of jealousy surprised Heber, and he was instantly ashamed. At a flower cart loaded with pungent snapdragons and lilies as well as more delicate roses in a rainbow of colors, he pulled a *franc* from his slacks pocket, selected a yellow rose, and held it out. "To you and Lydia."

"Sorry for being such a grouch." Alan took the flower and breathed in its fragrance. His face brightened. "You getting interested in Natalie?" He elbowed Heber. "That why you were so eager to have your palm read?"

"She's gorgeous. Isn't everybody interested in her?" Heber answered to be agreeable, although he felt no attraction to her.

"Lydia's the one and only for me." Alan kicked at a loose stone in the road. "Tell you what, Averil, let's go swimming. I know we haven't put in our hours today, but I can't face anyone right now. Tomorrow we'll work twice as hard. Set up a street meeting near the chateau. Put up posters over by the university."

"Sounds fun." Heber had learned to swim in the irrigation ditches back home and paddled awkwardly, barely keeping his head above water, but he enjoyed it. He started whistling "Wrap Your Troubles in Dreams." Alan looked at him the way someone looks at a goofy pet puppy, shaking his head with a slight smile, then punching him in the arm.

Back at the apartment, Heber went into the kitchen. As he took a tomato from the windowsill over the sink, he paused to watch a woman wrapped in a black cloak rummage through what seemed to be a pile of garbage in the alley next to the convent. The order was sworn to poverty, dependent on the community for their food, and he'd seen the nuns scavenge before. Times were hard for a lot of folks, although the proud French kept their neediness hidden behind closed doors. The *franc* had been devalued over and over. He was glad he brought them a message of hope.

Heber halved the tomato, tore chunks of bread from one of the baguettes, and cut two slices of cheese, their standard lunch fare. Heber enjoyed the different sharp cheeses they bought in the local *fromagerie,* but *Mme.* Romrielle's soup would have been a welcome change. He shrugged aside the regret and focused on the afternoon ahead. Joining him in the kitchen, Alan said a quick blessing on the food, and they ate everything in a few hungry bites.

Then they stood back-to-back in a shadowed corner of the living room and removed their *garments,* one-piece silk underwear resembling jumpsuits covering them from neck to knees. The underwear bore embroidered symbols to remind them of their temple covenants with the Lord that they'd made just before they came on their missions. They put on swim trunks under casual slacks and buttoned shirts over sleeveless wool swimming tops.

Shoulder to shoulder they tromped through the busy downtown district to Quai St. Jean, a tranquil public park that ran along the Loire River upstream from a huge stone bridge, le Pont Jacques Gabriel. Beyond the formal gardens and clipped trees of the park, a swimming area had been cordoned off. Warning ropes stretching out into the current marked the limits of safety. Barefoot children played in the sand at the water's edge, watched by two older women in dark, shapeless dresses.

The two men stripped to their swimsuits, stowed their street clothes at the foot of an elm tree, and walked to the shoreline. Heber couldn't keep his eyes off the way Alan's chest made a strong triangle, while his hips curved in muscular bands to firm legs. Feeling like a scrawny plucked chicken beside him, Heber feigned brushing sand off his feet before Alan could notice his skinny physique.

"Last one in is an artichoke!" Alan called over his shoulder as he ran past the women and children and dove from shore in a shallow, graceful arc, smoothly slicing the silver-gray water. When he surfaced, he struck out through the swim zone, his arms extending rhythmically, his body turning from side to side.

Heber stood entranced by Alan's beauty and the sun glinting off the water around him as he swam. A gentle breeze stirred the warm afternoon air. Then, bracing himself for the shock of the cold water, Heber splashed in and paddled furiously toward his companion. Soon Alan doubled back and came to his side, swimming slow circles around him.

"See that sand dredge?" Alan pointed sixty yards upstream. "Let's swim to it. There isn't much current today."

Before Heber could answer, Alan again cut through the swim zone, dove under the boundary ropes, and swam toward the dredge.

Heber treaded water, watching him. Could he ever catch this man? Would the currents be too strong? He counted to three and ducked under the rope.

When Alan reached the dredge, he turned back toward Heber and shouted encouragement. Heber reached the cable anchoring the machine and clung to it, panting, as the river played against his torso and legs.

"Race you back," Alan challenged.

"Some contest."

"The current will carry you. Keep working toward the shore. I'll give you a head start."

Heber's chest heaved from the swim out, but he let go of the cable and started working his way toward the swim zone. Within minutes, Alan reached the shore, turned around and returned to his side. "You're doing great. Angle more toward the embankment."

Alan stayed with Heber as they passed the swim zone and touched shore at a place where the river's bank was a jumble of tall, wild grasses sloping gently up to the park. After climbing out, he offered Heber a hand. Heber grasped it and scrambled up the muddy bank.

"Thanks," Heber said when they reached the top. "You saved me. I swear I could never get out by myself."

"Sure, you could. You're in good shape." Alan led the way to the elm and shrugged into his clothes.

"Another twenty yards and I'd have washed under the bridge."

Alan slapped his behind. "Nah. Kick hard with those legs."

Hot pleasure coursed through Heber. Singing "Anything Goes" under his breath, he danced more than walked up the hill to their apartment.

When they reached their door, Alan stooped and picked up a handful of letters left for them. At the kitchen table he sorted the mail — three letters for him and one for Heber, the usual allotment.

Heber sat across from Alan and opened his letter, his mother's weekly epistle of family news. He tried to read the carefully printed lines, but his gaze kept roaming to Alan's face; the thatch of blond hair spilling onto his forehead, and the quick smile that lit his eyes and played with the corners of his mouth.

Desire stirred in Heber's body. Resolutely he pushed it down. He'd felt something akin to a crush on his math teacher in high school, who often touched Heber's hand as he returned a paper. At Weber College he was warmed by the attention of a boy who'd sat in front of him in his theater class, his silky black hair curling over his collar and his eyes catching Heber's when he turned around. Heber imagined other men must have similar sinful stirrings at times and keep them in check. He did so by turning his attention to a book or a chore. Those feelings had no place in his life, especially not on his mission where he'd be spending every day and night with a male missionary companion.

As Heber watched, Alan's smile turned to a frown, a slight *V* between his eyes drawing his brow into furrows. What could be wrong?

"No! It can't be!" Alan cried and erupted from his chair. Fists balled at his sides, he paced back and forth, his breath harsh gasps.

"What is it?" Heber matched Alan's stride.

"Lydia! She's marrying someone else." Alan dropped into a chair, exhaling like a spent balloon.

"No way."

"Saturday." Alan buried his face in his hands.

Alan wasn't marrying Lydia. That must be what Natalie saw in his hand. Heber fought down a moment of dizzy joy and reached out to pat Alan's shoulder.

Alan grabbed Heber by the collar and, forehead to forehead, searched his face. "Three days! In three days! How could she do this to me? How?"

"She's crazy not to marry you," Heber sputtered.

Alan released him. "Could I send her a telegram?" He sank onto the chair. "No time."

Heber willed his racing heart to slow. "Do you want to be alone? I could go for a walk."

"No, I need you here."

Alan dropped to his knees, hands folded on the chair where he'd sat, and prayed silently. Heber knelt beside him, intending to pray for Alan to be comforted. The words "I need you here" echoed in his mind, drowning out all other thoughts. Finally, Alan lifted his head, pulled a handkerchief from his slacks pocket, and blew his nose. "Let's make supper," he said.

Alan's voice was husky as they ate and made plans for the next day. That evening he prayed longer than usual. Then he got out paper and pen and began to write. He was still writing furiously when Heber undressed, pulled the duvet onto the couch, and laid down.

Heber scrunched a pillow under his head, shut his eyes tight, and tried unsuccessfully to turn his thoughts away from Alan—his quirky grin, the sprinkling of golden hair on his chest, the forbidden territory.

Alan finally came to bed, his back to Heber's, as usual. He tossed and turned for a long time, then settled into a deep sleep on his back, his leg lightly touching Heber's. Heber rolled onto his back and scooted a bit closer. He could now feel where Alan's thigh broadened, and where their skin touched. Alan's breath remained unchanged.

Heber had never been stirred like this. He knew it was wrong to lie this close to a woman before marriage, let alone a man, but he couldn't make himself move to the edge of the couch where he belonged.

Alan's arm fell across Heber's chest. He still slept, his breathing deep and even. Was he dreaming of Lydia? Could it possibly be Heber?

Heber lay mesmerized, his nostrils filled with Alan's scent, musky and warm. Moonlight floated through the window and played on their shoulders.

Alan hardened and Heber grew hard in response. He wouldn't weaken. He'd move away now. Then all thoughts blurred. Everything felt so natural. Heber grazed his fingers along Alan's *garments*. His hand crept toward Alan's thigh, cupped so his palm pressed Alan's thinly clad shaft, his fingers lingering.

He pumped once. Twice. Alan's eyes flew open, and he bolted upright, knocking Heber from the couch. "What the hell!" he shouted as Heber staggered to his feet. He lunged at him, his face purple with rage.

Heber jumped back, stunned. "But you—"

"Faggot!" Alan slammed him against the wall and pinned him there. "Don't–ever–touch–me–again."

Alan released him and Heber crumpled to the floor, his eyes squeezed shut, expecting a rain of blows.

"Get out of my sight," Alan snarled. "Go sleep in the john. Better yet, throw yourself in the river."

"But you … your arm …"

Alan grabbed his pillow from the couch and hurled it at Heber. "Out! Now."

Trembling, Heber rose, drew on his bathrobe, and shuffled into the kitchen. Through the open doorway he saw Alan drop to his knees and pray loudly. "Father, help me with Lydia. And get rid of my sick, twisted companion."

Heber knelt too, resting his forehead against the cold stove. His stomach ached and his mind turned slowly as if finding its way through a thick fog. Maybe he should turn on the stove and put his head in the oven. Alan had made the first move and the heat had consumed him. Wasn't that right?

A tremor shook his body. He was here in the service of God whom he'd sworn to love and serve with all his might, mind and strength. He'd been strictly taught not to touch himself that way, let alone another man. It would never happen again, no matter what. Alan had called him a faggot, but he wasn't one. He'd prove it.

3

Blois, France, August 1938

Standing at the kitchen window, unable to sleep, Heber watched the night lighten into dawn. His entire being felt like a steamroller had flattened him against the cobblestone street below.

He gripped the windowsill so hard his knuckles grew white. Passion had carried him to a dark place. Alan hated him. Maybe Heavenly Father too. He'd prayed now for hours for forgiveness from both Alan and God.

A panic caught in his chest. What if Alan told the mission president and Heber got sent home? He could picture his mother opening a letter from President Hays and crumpling onto a chair. If Heber showed up at home, he'd be greeted by his father, belt in hand, determined to drive the demons out of his oldest son. Heber well remembered the lashings that cut into his legs and back as a child if he even left a gate open. Everyone would shun him.

But Alan couldn't tell. He was part of it and would be sent home too. Heber's heart skipped with relief. Last night would be their secret.

A memory of Alan's thigh against his abruptly filled Heber with renewed desire. He straightened and squared his shoulders. He would keep his promise to the Lord. Penitent and exhausted, he wadded a dishtowel for a pillow and lay down on the plank floor to finally sleep. He dozed fitfully until he heard Alan up, moving about in the other room, then got up too.

Early morning light brightened the kitchen as he and Alan took turns pouring water from a pitcher into their shared porcelain washbowl, brushing their teeth and shaving. Their backs to each other, they silently dressed for the day.

Heber's hands shook as he dressed. He paused, fingering the symbol of a square embroidered on the right breast of his *garments*. The square represented exactness and honor in keeping the commandments and covenants of God. He'd broken the law of chastity. Had made himself unclean and unworthy to wear the *garments*. Should he take them off? He'd sincerely repented. Maybe he could leave them on.

How clever Satan was. Last night had promised to be the best night of Heber's life. Before he ruined it.

Heber finished dressing and walked into the kitchen. Determined to steady himself, he began to spread *conserves d'apricot* on bread for their breakfast.

Alan followed him in. "We should fast," he said, his voice tight. "Show the Lord how sorry we are."

"You're right." Heber set the bread and *conserves* aside. He and Alan already planned to fast two meals once a week for guidance in their missionary work and once a month to save money they could donate to church members in need. He'd gladly fast today for forgiveness. It should have been his idea.

"About last night." Alan's tone was scornful. He narrowed his eyes. "You're a little different, but I didn't think you were like that."

"I'm not. You … I … it just happened. Nothing I planned."

"You ever done that kind of stuff before?"

"Never, I swear. I prayed all night for God to forgive me. I hope you forgive me too."

Alan drew in a breath and let it out slowly. "I don't get it. You're smart. You've been raised in the church." He wagged his finger at Heber. "I know men that look a lot swishier than you. They're leading regular lives. Married in the temple and raising families. You've told me that's what you want."

"It is. But then … you put your arm around me. I was half asleep. Confused. Let's pretend nothing happened."

"Now you're blaming *me*?" Alan took a menacing step toward Heber, eyes smoldering. "You knew I was dreaming about Lydia, and you tried to tempt me. I'm normal. Not like you."

Heber stepped back.

"You pathetic jerk." Alan spat out the words. "I won't turn you in, but I'll have you transferred as soon as I can. 'Til then, you sleep on the floor." He turned on his heel and left the kitchen.

Heber watched him go. Alan would never forgive him. The sharp pain in Heber's chest must be how a broken heart felt.

How could he make peace?

"Let's tract a new section of Blois today," Heber suggested, edging into the living room.

"Get this straight. I'm not doing anything with you. Ever. Don't even ask."

That scorn again. "We have to keep our hours," Heber persisted.

Alan sank onto a chair and stared up at him. "First Lydia, then you. Why me, Lord?"

Heber held his breath, waiting.

"Okay," Alan said at last, "we'll tract. You take one side of the street and I'll take the other. If someone invites you in, whistle for me. Otherwise, stay on your own side."

"Got it." Grateful for even this concession, Heber put on his suit jacket and picked up his *Livre de Mormon*. He grabbed a handful of pamphlets and waited at the door while Alan gathered his things, then stayed a careful two steps behind him as they descended the stairs.

In twenty minutes, they were in a part of Blois Heber hadn't yet seen. "You go over there." Alan pointed to the north side of the street. Heber obediently crossed and approached the first two-story house. *Dear Heavenly Father, please open someone's heart to us,* he prayed. A success might mollify Alan.

He rapped on every door in the first block without a response. In his attire, he knew he was easily identified as a missionary. Maybe people peered out their windows, saw him coming, and ignored his knock.

In the middle of the second block, he approached a wooden door painted the color of a sunflower and gave it a half-hearted tap. A middle-aged woman dressed in a painter's smock spattered with purples and greens opened the door.

"*Bonjour, Madame,*" Heber said, silently thanking God. He handed the woman a sheet of paper titled *Rayons de Lumière Vivante*, a message of living light. "May we take a few moments of your time?" he asked in well-rehearsed French. "We have an important message for you. My companion is right across the street."

"You are Mormons, *oui*? Please come in."

Hope flooded Heber's chest as he whistled for Alan. Missionaries seldom had success in more well-to-do neighborhoods like this one.

Alan hurried across the street but kept an arm's length from Heber while they removed their shoes and walked into the apartment.

A pungent smell of oils filled the room. "*Vous êtes une artiste!*" Heber exclaimed, striding to an easel that held a canvas in process. The painting portrayed a busy, outdoor café with tables spilling onto the sidewalk. "It's the left bank of the Seine in Paris. I saw it when I first came on my mission."

"*Oui, c'est correct.*"

Alan cleared his throat.

"Your painting is wonderful. Another day may I see more?" Heber reluctantly turned from the easel, hoping he hadn't offended the woman. "Today we want to tell you about the restored gospel of Jesus Christ."

"*Mais oui, bien sûr.*" She motioned them to a love seat before settling into an ornate armchair across from them.

Alan sat at one end of the love seat and shot Heber a warning look. Heber sat at the opposite end and pressed his arms against his sides to widen the space between them.

Alan talked about the appearance of God the Father, and his son Jesus Christ, to the prophet Joseph Smith, then a boy of fourteen. How God's true priesthood, the power to act in the name of God, had been lost on earth for generations but was now restored.

The woman asked him to explain more about the priesthood. Caught up in Alan's fluent response, Heber accidentally shifted closer to him and got a sharp jab in his ribs.

Thank goodness the woman seemed not to notice. Heber leaned into the walnut arm of the loveseat.

Alan wound up the lesson and asked the woman if she'd like a second discussion. She agreed after a moment's hesitation, and they set a date and time. Then Heber offered a prayer for her household.

As the two men left the apartment, Heber unintentionally brushed against Alan in the doorway. The moment they reached the street, Alan wheeled around, his eyes glinting steel. "I told you. Don't touch me," he growled.

"I didn't mean to."

"You were sidling over by me in there. Then when we were leaving ..."

"I—" Heber interrupted.

"Not another word."

Both men were silent until they reached the apartment. "I need some time alone," Alan announced when they walked in the door. "I'm going for a swim." He picked up his bathing suit and casual slacks and for the first time went down the hall to the washroom to change his clothes.

Heber followed him and knocked on the door. "Can I go swimming with you? We aren't supposed to go alone."

"No!"

Heber sat on the couch and picked up the book of missionary lessons, his stomach rumbling from his fast. Studying had always focused his mind, but now he kept envisioning Alan in his bathing suit, his broad chest, his well-formed muscles, the bulge. He'd prayed. He'd fasted. He'd found someone interested in learning about the church. But no matter what he did, the Devil continued to haunt him. *Dear Heavenly Father, heal my immoral thoughts*, he pleaded.

Alan exited the washroom without a word or a glance at Heber and headed down the stairs.

Heber's mind kept wandering to the day before. They'd had such a genial swim. If they swam together again today, maybe Alan would relent.

Without a clear plan, Heber changed into his swimsuit under casual street clothes and walked quickly through town. At the Quai St. Jean he found Alan almost to the swim zone.

Alan turned as he approached. "You again?" he snapped. His face clouded with anger.

His reaction sent a punch to Heber's gut. "I know. I shouldn't have come. I'm an idiot." Heber turned to go. Joining Alan at the river had seemed like a good idea when he sat in the apartment, frantic to make amends. But he obviously wasn't wanted here. Besides, the river looked different than it had yesterday. A storm somewhere must have riled it. The water churned a muddy red, and the level had risen at least three feet, almost obliterating the small beach. Even the musty air smelled ominous. There were no other bathers.

"Wait," Alan commanded.

Heber turned back.

"Tell you what," Alan said. "If you beat me to the barge, you can stay in Blois. Otherwise, you're transferred out of here as fast as I can arrange it." He stripped to his swimsuit, secured his clothes in a tree well, and plunged in.

Stay in Blois with Alan instead of being transferred? Heber's heart quickened. He doubted he could make it to the barge in such a strong current, let alone beat Alan, but it was his only chance to make amends. He set his jaw, stashed his shirt and slacks next to Alan's, and jumped in.

Recoiling at the cold water, he steeled himself and struck out against the choppy waves.

With astonishing strength, Alan blasted through the water to the dredge and doubled back, passing Heber fifteen yards outside the swim zone. Heber turned toward him, already fatigued from fighting the swift current. "Hey," he called.

Alan swam on to shore without a glance his way.

Maybe Alan hadn't heard him. "Alan! Help!" Heber shouted.

His heart pounded and his breath came in gasps as the water pushed him further downstream.

Arms and legs throbbing, he fought to cross the current and return to the quieter waters of the swim zone, but he made no progress. Alan must realize he wasn't behind him. Was he going to let him drown?

The river swept Heber past the beach like a scrap of wood tossed in the water, past the embankment where he and Alan had climbed out the day before, toward the St. Jacques Bridge. Soon, walls of stone would make an escape from the river impossible.

The horizon rose and fell. When Heber took a breath, water rushed into his nose and mouth.

Approaching a part of the bank where a tangle of brush and smaller trees bordered the water's edge, he mustered his last bit of strength and grabbed for a branch. It broke off in his hands.

"Help!" he screamed.

Fueled by panic, he lunged for another branch. It, too, broke, and he slipped back into the churning whitecaps. Water closed over his head and he tasted slime on his lips. Sputtering, he raised his face from the river and saw the bridge only a few yards away where stone walls replaced the vegetation. Walls that would be his tomb.

His arms and legs were weights too heavy to lift. He sank in the water. Blackness engulfed him.

So, this was the way he would die. He'd lost his chance to make things right.

No!

Somehow Heber flung his head from the river, lungs burning, gulping water and air. He stiffened against the current, clawing the water and beating it with his legs. With a crack his hand hit against the trunk of a sapling that had been swallowed by the high water. Pain shot up his arm as he grasped it and held on. His foot found a root and he came to a stop, the wall of the bridge less than three feet away.

Heber floundered toward the shore, rocks and branches scraping against his feet. Panting and shivering, nose and eyes running, he dragged himself up the hillside. Dense nettles lashed him, and jagged rocks scratched his bare arms.

At the top of the embankment, he collapsed on the harsh grasses, gasping and wheezing. When his body stilled, his mind churned into action. How had he come to this spot, filthy, shivering, and nearly naked?

He struggled to his feet and slogged his way the half-mile to where he'd laid his clothes beside Alan's. Alan's were gone; Heber's had been kicked into a heap. He pulled his slacks and shirt onto his gritty body and stumbled toward home. Memories of his near drowning and fears of the blackness of his soul filled his mind. He scarcely noticed the sights and sounds of people passing him on the street and milling in the little shops.

Maybe he'd been born with some defect invisible to the world but much worse than his cousin Jesse's harelip. A moral defect. Or Alan could be so mad he'd tried to drown him.

Back at the apartment, Heber stood in the doorway staring at Alan casually reading in an armchair.

Alan looked up. "I see you made it," he said matter-of-factly.

Heber had hoped he might see relief on Alan's face, but he saw only a mix of anger and revulsion.

Alan pointed to Heber's steamer trunk. "I expect you to have your things packed within the hour."

Alan was sending him away.

The unease settling on Heber's shoulders felt as heavy as a wool coat on a summer afternoon. Natalie's words, *'a leaf for every love,'* came back to him. Suppose the loves were men, and he was indeed like that, a vile creature in the eyes of God and of every person he knew? *'As a man thinketh in his heart, so is he.'* His very thoughts must be purged.

4

Orléans, France, August 1939

Immediately after the closing prayer on the Sunday service, Heber headed toward a cluster of men and women gathering at the back of the room. As mission secretary to President Hayes, he'd brought the president's greetings as well as supplies sorely needed by the local missionaries. His companion *Frère* Monroe had come down with the stomach flu at the last minute and President Hays had decided to bend mission rules and allow Heber to make the trip alone.

A tall Frenchman with piercing blue eyes and a shock of dark blond hair approached him. *"Bonjour, monsieur. Je m'appelle André Benoit. Votre service était très intéressant."* The man's voice had a throaty quality, and his lips were full and sensuous beneath a carefully trimmed mustache.

An alarm went off in Heber's head, even as his body tingled in response to the man's greeting.

Heber had carefully monitored himself in the year since the incident with Alan, working hard to live as an honorable man. He felt fortunate to be assigned to work directly with the president, living in the mission home and serving there as mission secretary. Daily he crowded out every impure feeling by focusing on a rigorous schedule of prayer, scripture study, and mission office work. When thoughts of

Alan intruded—the memory of Alan's body somehow stronger than that of his possible duplicity—Heber instinctively pleasured himself and then repented in disgust.

Those times were coming less and less often.

He'd made such strides; he was sure he was over his problem. So why was he magnetically drawn to this man? He mustn't betray President Hays' trust.

Yet President Hays often reminded the missionaries that they were emissaries of God's true church and needed to be courteous to everyone they met. *"Bonjour M. Benoit. Je m'appelle Frère Averil."* Heber shook the man's proffered hand.

André searched Heber's face. "I would like to know more about your church."

"Ah bon. I'll give your name to the missionaries here. They'll be happy to talk with you." The electric current racing through Heber from André's lingering touch was unmistakable. He needed to make the conversation with this man as brief as possible.

"Yes, but days I am so busy," André said. His lips formed an exaggerated pout. "I am preparing my shop, you see, for its opening. Perhaps you could come to my home tonight and teach me."

"I … I …" Heber stepped back.

André took a step forward. "I would like to learn more about a church that inspires such feelings of devotion among its young men. I see you all about the city, always well dressed, always in pairs."

"I'm taking the five o'clock train back to Paris tonight," Heber said, both sorry and relieved. "I work for the mission president there, and he'd be concerned if I didn't return on time. The missionaries here in Orléans can make an evening appointment with you."

"There is a later train, I think about eight o'clock." André put his hand on Heber's arm. "Please come. I would like *you* to teach me."

Suppose André was a sincere seeker of God's word? It would be wrong to miss the opportunity to teach him. Maybe Heber could present a missionary lesson, then leave immediately and get to Paris before midnight.

"Please," André implored again. "I have so much to learn about your church. We can have a little supper first and then you can tell me all about your beliefs."

"*D'accord*," Heber agreed. "But I have to make the eight o'clock train." Good company, good food, and a chance to teach André about the gospel. This was an opportunity to seize, wasn't it? Although it would be much better if *Frère* Monroe was with him. He'd bring André a *Livre de Mormon* and some pamphlets.

"*Très bien*. Five o'clock then." André took a brochure from a display nearby, pulled a pen from his shirt pocket, and printed his address on the front page. With a warm smile, he handed Heber the paper, touched his arm, and walked away.

Heber gathered his jumbled wits as best he could, then found the Orléans branch president and discussed church affairs with him for fifteen minutes. As they talked, images of André crowded his mind. Five o'clock seemed a long way off.

His hand trembling, Heber lifted the knocker on André's door. He'd had all afternoon to try to think of something besides the curve of André's sensuous lips, the tight fit of his slacks, the pressure of his hand. He'd changed his mind about coming here a thousand times as he joined the Orléans missionaries for a bowl of spicy haricot bean soup at a restaurant along Rue de Bourgogne. He changed it another thousand times as he visited the Sainte Croix Cathedral with its magnificent stained-glass windows of Joan of Arc, and the Place du Martroi with a statue of Joan of Arc riding into battle. Now here he was at André's apartment building in a gracious old quarter of the city, a *Livre de Mormon* tucked under one arm, still conflicted.

André answered the door immediately.

"*Bonjour, Frère Benoit.*" Heber handed André the book.

"Please come in." André set the *Livre de Mormon* on a small table in the entry and led Heber to an elegant sitting room where cream-colored drapes edged with gold tassels hung in large windows. An upright piano hugged one wall, a gold-embossed couch, another. In the center of the room a mahogany drop-leaf table was set for two with crystal goblets, delicately flowered china, and silver candlesticks flanking a silver vase that held three pink rosebuds. A heady bouquet of aromas drifted from the kitchen.

Heber studied the exquisite place settings. This was a little supper? And what of the burgundy liquid in the goblets?

"Do not worry." André rested a hand on Heber's shoulder. "It is grape juice. I know you Mormons do not drink wine."

Heber's skin quivered under André's touch. Not good. "Could we have the lesson before dinner?" he asked, hoping he didn't sound rude.

"As you wish." André shrugged and motioned Heber to the couch. Then he retrieved the *Livre de Mormon* from the table and sat beside him.

Heber looked at the buffed sheen of his shoes, at the elegant room, at anything but André's face. He stumbled through a lesson about Joseph Smith's discovery and translation of the gold plates that became the Book of Mormon.

André asked a few questions, listened intently to the answers, then nodded toward the table.

"Now for dinner, yes?"

Heber drew his watch from his pocket. Enough time for a quick dinner and he'd be on his way.

André lit the candles, pulled out a chair for Heber, and took the seat across from him. Heber unfolded the linen napkin next to his plate and smoothed it across his lap. Grape juice. How considerate of his host.

A woman with a neat bun of graying hair and a black dress trimmed in lace knocked, entered, and set a silver tureen and matching ladle between them. André introduced her as his *patronne,* his landlady. When she withdrew, her eyes downcast, he lifted his wine goblet toward Heber. "To us."

Heber paused before lifting his glass in response. The evening had somehow become like a scene from a Hollywood movie. Except instead of Bogart and Bacall, they were two men. He should go now. But if André were offended, and lost interest in the church, it would be his fault.

"Thank you for teaching me these things." André clinked glasses. "I will read your *Livre de Mormon.*"

Heber willed his heart to steady. Maybe André was simply the consummate host. Whenever Heber entered a French home, he was offered something to eat, if only a cookie that might have taken the family's last *centime*. André obviously had the means to entertain in this sumptuous way.

When André lifted the lid of the silver tureen, Heber saw mushrooms floating in a clear broth. His host ladled them each a generous serving. Heber raised his soupspoon to his lips and slurped. Blushing, he apologized. "I've never seen such a fancy table," he admitted.

André frowned. "You must have been in many French homes."

"People interested in the church don't usually have much money."

"I'm lucky to have these things from my parents."

"You *are* lucky."

Heber found himself spilling his story about growing up on a farm outside Ogden. How he had trudged through snow in the dawn's first light to milk their cow, stripping the teats to pass any dirt or bacteria so it didn't get into the milk. How he cared for his three younger sisters and four younger brothers, tying their shoes and zipping up jackets whenever he wasn't in school himself or doing his studies or chores. He even told André how he devoured every book he could find the two years he was at Weber College: fiction, history, biography. Caught movies when he could pinch together enough pennies. Wrote poems and stories that appeared in local newspapers.

In turn, André told him about growing up in Orléans, part of a family of merchants who had once been well-to-do but now felt the strain of the Depression.

Heber relaxed, laughing easily as he and André visited like they'd known each other for years. They came from two different worlds. Their backgrounds differed in every respect. Yet, Heber had never felt so immediately comfortable with a new friend.

The *patronne* brought a *poulet de Provence* and then a *salade*. They finished with a course of varied *fromages* and *tarte aux pommes*. Everything had a delicate, delicious flavor. Heber patted his lips with his napkin. He hated to go, but it must be time. He looked at his watch and jumped to his feet in a panic.

"I must go!" If he missed the last train, he'd have to sleep at the train station.

"*Non,* please don't go. The night has just begun."

"The train!" This time there was no doubt about André's intentions, nor about what the Lord wanted Heber to do.

André reached for Heber's hand. "Soon we might be soldiers in another great war. We must find pleasure in all we can."

Heber froze, images forming in his mind of André in an officer's uniform beside him in a trench, rifles in their hands, both men bloody. The world was turning upside down and he was literally standing in the center of the coming maelstrom.

"I heard you sing at church today," André said, his thumb pressed into Heber's palm. "A fine voice, yes? Will you sing for me?"

Heber's resolve drained away. He dreamt of singing in musical theatre. One song with André, and then he'd go.

André led the way to the piano bench, then sat beside Heber. He played a popular French song, their bodies lightly touching. It felt as natural as their conversation.

Heber sang lyrics he'd heard on the radio, his voice strong and clear.

"Superb," André cried, and played two more songs. "Now it is your turn at the piano." He sat back and turned to Heber.

"I've never had lessons. I just play around if there's a piano in sight."

"*C'est a toi.*" André joined his palms in an attitude of prayer.

"*D'accord.*" Heber shrugged and grinned. Sleeping on the leather-clad benches at the train station wouldn't be so bad. He put his fingers on the keys and magic suffused them as André hummed an improvised harmony. They played and sang, searching out melodies they both knew. When the mantle clock chimed eleven times Heber flinched as if struck. He hadn't heard the strokes of ten. He scrambled to his feet. André stood too, reaching for Heber's hands. "What will the evening bring next?" he asked, his tone suggestive, his eyes twinkling. Before Heber could reply, he led him to a bedroom with an oversize bed draped in white muslin. "This will be much more comfortable than the train station, *n'est-ce pas?*"

Heber looked at the bed and shivered. What would it be like to lie in André's arms? Alan had pushed him away, but André would draw him close.

His conscience stirred. Determined, he jerked his hands free, shoved them in his pockets, and turned from André. "I have to go."

André took his shoulders and turned him back. "Don't you like me?"

"Yes, I like you very much. But no, I can't do this."

"Do what?" André looked perplexed.

"Sleep here. With you." Heber mumbled the shameful words.

"You sleep with your missionary companion, yes? Especially you, such a handsome man. Missionaries are always two by two."

Heber frowned. What if all their French friends believed that? "We share a couch or bed at night, always back-to-back. That's it."

"I do not understand." André sounded genuinely puzzled. "Why wouldn't you sleep together if you get along well? Like you and I do."

"It's an abomination in the sight of the Lord."

"Ah. Your church. The Catholic church teaches the same thing. It's a very old idea. The priests make certain there are children to fill their pews and their coffers. I believe if we are happy, God is happy."

André sounded so confident that Heber wondered for a moment if he could be right. No, absolutely not. That's how the Devil worked.

"We like the same things. We laugh together. I am not so very ugly, am I?" André's full lips curved in a smile. "Why should we not enjoy our time together?" He put his arms around Heber.

Heber tensed. He could smell André's piquant aftershave and feel warmth radiating from his body. *You have to go,* his conscience tried to remind him. Then André's arms tightened around him, and Heber's mind drowned in desire. Their lips met. André's kiss alone existed. Helpless to stop the heat coursing through him, Heber returned the kiss greedily.

André unbuttoned and removed his own shirt and pants, then Heber's clothing, and led Heber to the bed. The wonder of André's mouth kissing his neck, shoulders, eyes, and ears, banished any thought.

Heber's inexperienced body grew frenzied as André stroked his arms, then shifted his body so that he could kiss Heber down the center of his chest and belly. Heber lifted his hips to the Frenchman's warm, wet lips. Wild with an animal heat, he spasmed.

"What an early surprise!" André rocked back on his elbows. "You must really like me."

"I do." Heber's delight lasted only seconds before it turned to mortification. He sat up and hid his face in his hands. What had he done?

He felt a gentle hand on his shoulder. "What is it, my lamb? You came early, but it is all right."

"None of this is all right." Heber climbed out of bed and yanked on his clothing. "I'm leaving."

André reached out to him. "You will learn. I will teach you."

Heber turned away and picked up his shirt.

André turned him back. "It is all right, *Cherie*. Don't be angry with yourself or me."

"I won't be like that!" Struggling with his belt buckle, Heber ran from André's apartment.

Outside, shopkeepers had drawn folding iron grills across the entries of their shops, and muted lights shone hazily in the apartments above. A horse-drawn wagon passed with its clop of hooves and jingle of harnesses. Heber stumbled on an uneven cobblestone and nearly fell. Wandering through near empty streets, he relived the mixed sensations from the evening. He'd enjoyed the sex more than anything in his life, even his moment with Alan. Could André be right about God approving of men lying together?

No. That couldn't be.

Heber found the train station, slumped down on a bench, and settled in to wait for the morning train. His body quivered at the memory of André's lips and tongue. The moist warmth. The electricity. The release. But the church was never wrong. He had sinned even worse than with Alan. Much worse. Satan had his soul for sure.

By the time the train arrived, Heber knew what he had to do. Fasting and prayer weren't enough to atone for his sin. True repentance required confession. He had to tell the man he most respected in the world what he'd done and endure the shame of disappointing him. He had to confess to President Hays.

5

Paris, France, August 1939

Heber shook himself out of his reverie. His gaze wandered to the confessional booth, then to the altar of E*glise Saint-Nicolas-et-Saint-Marc*. Prompted by the crucifix at the front of the church, he bowed his head in prayer. He'd reclaim his soul; free himself from the bonds of Satan's power. The Book of Mormon promised: *'And if men come unto me, I will show them their weakness — and if they humble themselves before me, and have faith in me, then will I make weak things become strong unto them.'*

President Hays hadn't been disappointed in Heber. He hadn't even blamed him.

He'd counseled Heber that he would be fine if he finished his mission honorably, married in the temple and raised a righteous family. Heber would follow the instructions of the president and the Book of Mormon, beginning now with a prayer so earnest he could feel sweat dampening his shirt.

Remove my attraction to men, he prayed. *Let me serve a mission that glorifies you. When I'm home again, lead me to the woman you would have me marry in your temple. I promise to do your will in all things.*

6

Ogden, Utah, June 1941

"Famous actress, meet world traveler. You two should get to know each other." Heber's good friend Susan nodded first to him, then to Ruth Stone, a young woman perched on a sofa.

Susan had guaranteed that Ruth and Heber would be a perfect match. He hoped so. He'd seen Ruth perform with a local theater troupe and wondered why a woman so talented hadn't gone on to Broadway or Hollywood. He'd read her stories and poetry in the *Salt Lake Tribune*, too. She'd won awards for several of them, once taking a first place when he took second, and another time a second place when he won first. They seemed destined to meet.

Ruth stood and extended her hand. Her touch felt soft and warm, and he caught a whiff of lavender, his favorite scent.

In the last two and a half years, Heber had often recalled President Hays' counsel to find a worthy woman and take her through the temple. Not easy counsel to follow. Shortly after his visit to Orléans, all the missionaries serving in Europe were evacuated. A week later Hitler invaded Poland. Although Heber was able to sail from Cherbourg without difficulty, he'd heard stories of the miracles it took to get all the missionaries out of Germany and Czechoslovakia.

Once home, he got a job at the Norse Debt Collection Agency. It wasn't the job of his dreams, but it was a salary. Badly shaken by the events in Europe, both political and personal, he buried himself in books and his own writing when he wasn't working for Norse.

Now he finally felt ready to keep his promise to President Hays, and to himself, to meet the right woman. He would take her through the temple and erase any doubt about his true nature.

"You were terrific in *Life with Father*," Heber said. "I couldn't stop clapping when you took your curtain call."

"Your poetry and short stories in *The Salt Lake Tribune* are wonderful. Your work is a special treat when there are so many disturbing headlines about the war in Europe."

When Ruth mentioned the horrors abroad, her face clouded, but then a sunny smile broke through. Fashionable in a brown polka dot dress with a wide patent leather belt, she wasn't quite tall enough to reach Heber's shoulder. As they talked, she looked up at him in a way he liked, her auburn hair in waves about her face, and her green eyes lively.

"Congratulations on your prizes. You're the competition." Heber grinned. "You inspire me to write better."

"And you, me."

The aroma of freshly baked bread filled the house, and strains of Mozart reached them from somewhere down the hall. Heber caught another whiff of lavender. Good elements for romance. Specifically, romance with a woman. Encounters with men would never lead him to a temple marriage and eternal family.

"Can we help with dinner?" Ruth asked Susan.

"Happy to slice and chop," Heber added.

"I've got the kitchen. You two go walk in the garden." Susan shooed them toward the French doors that led onto the patio and the manicured lawn and flower beds beyond.

"*Mademoiselle, s'il vous plait?*" Heber offered Ruth his arm with a theatrical gesture.

"*Merci beaucoup.*" Ruth wrapped her hand above the crook of his elbow.

They crossed the lawn, Heber matching his stride to Ruth's, and passed through an arched trellis thick with clematis in a rich maroon hue. Feeling oddly debonair, Heber considered snatching one of the flowers and setting it behind Ruth's ear. But no, she might find that a bit too forward.

The archway marked the entrance to a rose garden, some bushes with crimson blooms as big as his fist. "It smells so lovely," Ruth said.

"So do you." Heber smiled down at her.

A sliver of moon rose in the dusky sky. Anything seemed possible.

"You teach, you write, you're part of Ed Alder's theater troupe. How do you do it all?" Heber stepped in a little, so their hips almost touched as they walked.

"I don't do it all. I don't spend enough time on the novel I'm writing. I did sell a story to *Ladies Home Journal* last week."

Heber whistled. "That's a terrific sale. I bet I'll see your novel in bookstores next year."

"I hope so."

"I started a novel right after my mission," Heber confided. "Writing helped me settle back into life here." Visions of Ruth and him as the next Zelda and Scott Fitzgerald jumped into his imagination. Minus the rumored wild parties. "What's your novel about?" he asked.

Ruth shrugged. "I don't want to bore you."

"I really want to know."

"It's about early settlers in the Salt Lake Valley. Polygamists." She watched his face as if waiting for a reaction.

Heber arched an eyebrow. "Interesting topic."

She hesitated. "My grandfather was a polygamist."

"Ah-ha."

"You probably know the church authorities sometimes asked brethren to take a second wife to see that she and her family were cared for. My grandfather was so devoted to both his wives that he built them houses next door to each other and went back and forth, one night at one wife's house, the next at the other's. When he was sick the families carried him back and forth on a door."

"On a door? Ingenious of them. And so dedicated. Then your novel is inspired by family history?"

"Not exactly." Ruth laughed. "There's a villain after young, pretty women, my heroine included. People like him existed, but they weren't my ancestors. The novel does have minor characters living polygamy as a gospel principle. As I'm sure you know, most members of the church didn't practice polygamy at all. Now it's your turn. Your novel?"

"Wait. That's all you're going to tell me?" Heber protested. "When can I read it?"

"After I finish and sell it." When Ruth smiled, her entire face lit up, making her even prettier. "Now it's definitely your turn."

"Not quite. Make sure I get an advance copy. I'll get reviews of it in some newspapers." He hoped he didn't sound cocky. He had connections in Salt Lake and Ogden because of the writing he'd done before and after his mission. She probably did, too, though. He took a breath. "Mine is the story of a young man who goes to Hollywood and breaks into the movies. I wish it were an autobiography; it's pure fiction."

"It might turn out to be autobiographical. Didn't you study theatre at Weber College?"

Heber nodded. She'd done her homework and was out to please. But then, so was he.

"I'll bet you were good on stage." Ruth turned to him. "Ed is always looking for new talent. I should introduce you."

"That'd be swell. I hear he's a terrific director." Heber hadn't seen any ads for auditions for the troupe. Sounded like Ruth could connect him.

They were quiet for a few minutes as they exited the rose garden and strolled along paths bordered by flowerbeds of columbine, petunias, and coneflowers in a multitude of colors. It was a comfortable silence, not the kind of tense void that demanded superficial chitchat.

"You spent time in Paris," Ruth said after a while. "Tell me about it."

"Ah, Paree. Folks in Ogden don't know what old is. In Europe you see centuries-old art and architecture everywhere you look. So much history."

He glanced at Ruth. He could talk for days about France.

"I'd love to travel," she said simply. "You must have seen the Comédie Française."

"I saw a play by Molière there. What a magnificent theater. Everything about France was amazing." He paused, his excitement fading. "Then Hitler changed everything."

Ruth's expression sobered too. "When the Germans invaded Poland, a newspaper boy ran up and down the street by the high school. He waved his papers and screamed the headlines."

"My mission president was instructed to send all the missionaries home. I haven't heard from any of my French friends since." Were the Romrielles all right? The Bellangers' son? He prayed for them every night. André probably would have been called up. Heber pushed away a physical memory of André holding him.

"Mothers losing sons. Whole villages destroyed. Do you think we should join the Allies?" Ruth asked.

"I don't know." He sensed Ruth's genuine concern and pressed her hand where it lay on his arm. "I wonder about it all the time. I know people there and what they're going through. But my uncle says it isn't America's war, and a lot of people agree with him. Maybe it's better to avoid fights if you can." His mind could spin around and around on her question.

"Pearl Buck says the embargo might be enough. She's been writing articles about it. I'm not sure. Mother voted for Wilke, and Papa voted for FDR." Ruth smiled wanly. "I'm sorry to be gloomy. Isn't the garden lovely?"

Heber straightened his arm and took her hand, knitting their fingers together. "I'm glad to be with someone who cares about the outside world."

Once more they were quiet as they walked.

"Tell me more about France." Ruth broke the silence.

"The Loire Valley where I served is as green as an emerald. Rivers cut through every town. You see palaces and churches with stained glass windows wherever you look." A memory of Alan pierced his mood, a mix of grief and guilt. He willed himself to refocus on his conversation with Ruth, hoping she hadn't noticed.

"The stuff of movies," Ruth murmured. Apparently, she hadn't.

"Speaking of movies ..." Heber turned to face her. Being with Ruth felt right. Enough of those other thoughts. "Would you like to go see a movie Saturday? Gary Cooper's starring in *Sergeant York*."

"You look a lot like Gary Cooper. Everyone must tell you that."

"Nah," Heber replied. In fact, he had been told that before, but he didn't believe it. "So, *Sergeant York?* They always have a good Prologue at the Alhambra."

"With all those Moorish columns and frescoes, we could pretend we were in the real Alhambra."

He wished they were in Spain. What a grand travel partner she'd be.

"Then there's the Lyceum." Ruth's face took on a dreamy quality. "Joan Fontaine is there in *Suspicion*. She's my idol."

"You could pass for her. No, I'd say your twin could be Vivien Leigh. Wasn't she something in *Gone with the Wind?*" Heber sounded an approximation of a drum roll. "And now for the theater's most promising leading lady — Ruth Stone."

"And her leading man — Heber Averil."

"We could jump on the train of a touring company and work our way across the country." With his free hand Heber swept the air in a wide arc. His imagination ran pictures of the stops they would make and the shows they would stage. Denver. Cheyenne. Omaha.

Ruth's eyes sparkled with enthusiasm. His might be their mirror.

"Is Saturday good for you?" Heber asked.

"Perfect."

There seemed no end to the things they had in common, and his heart soared with hope. Maybe he wasn't so broken he couldn't be fixed.

7

Ogden, Utah, June 1941

Heber stepped onto the porch of Ruth's stately, two-story brick home and took in the grandeur. A polished brass knocker adorned the heavy, walnut-paneled door, and a long planter box under the front window offered up day lilies in a variety of hues. He blinked away a vision of the tired wooden door on his own house, dented and scratched over the years by eight pairs of small hands. The rickety porch. No planter boxes. Who would have time to tend flowers? All that sort of work went into the large, flat vegetable garden to the west of the house. Produce fed the family; flowers did not.

He and Ruth had obviously been raised differently. Heber squared his shoulders. So what? Ruth wasn't a bit stuck up, and they shared so many dreams. Still, it was one thing to meet her at their friends' home and another to come courting. With luck, when she looked at him, she'd see Gary Cooper, not a bundle of nerves holding a bouquet of wild blue flax and lupine he'd gathered in the hills near the farm.

When she answered, the way her face glowed told him not to worry. She looked as pretty as she had at Susan's. He was glad she didn't go for the heavy goo some girls were getting into these days, just a touch of red lipstick and a light dusting of powder. He was tempted to tell her so. She'd put on a white, pearl-buttoned cardigan that looked smart with her navy-blue dress. He felt proud to be taking her on a date.

He'd dressed carefully for the evening, too, in a brown V-neck sweater over a freshly pressed white shirt, his hair slicked back with pomade, and his best shoes shined 'til they looked almost new. He imagined the two of them, starry-eyed, on a movie poster: Heber Averil and Ruth Stone starring in *Hollywood at Last.*

"Come meet my parents." Ruth led him into the living room where a Persian carpet of rich red hues set off gleaming hardwood floors. Red damask drapes hung at tall windows.

A man with a round, pleasant face and a generous smile rose from an overstuffed chair, setting aside his book and extending his hand. "You must be Heber Averil. Pleased to meet you. I'm Samuel." He gave Heber a firm handshake.

"And this is my mother, Sarah." Ruth gestured toward a small woman seated in a rocking chair, knitting. Sarah looked up from her handiwork but didn't set her needles and yarn aside. A ghost of a smile brushed across her face and vanished. She didn't look at him long. Still, he could swear she'd checked to see if the pleat in his slacks was perfectly centered.

His chest tightened. Ruth's mother seemed as cold as a root cellar. The sort of woman who didn't like people who actually had root cellars. She didn't even know him. Well, he wasn't impressed with her either, although he wouldn't let it show. He nodded at her. "Pleased to meet you, Mrs. Stone."

He glanced at Ruth and saw her discomfort.

"You had that winning story in the *Salt Lake Tribune* last week," Samuel said, his hearty manner reminiscent of President Hays and a sharp contrast to his wife's.

"Yes, he did," Ruth affirmed.

"Charming setting along the Rhone in France. And very romantic, that love story of a goat-herder and a Parisian artist," her father continued. "Sad though."

"Thank you, sir. Poor Monique. She might have known she couldn't combine the two worlds." He imagined Sarah nodding over her needles. The irony didn't escape him.

"Heber's a wonderful writer." Ruth touched Heber's arm. "I followed his stories before I met him."

"You two have a lot in common." Her father nodded.

Heber caught Sarah's quick frown.

"We need to be going. I won't be home late." Ruth pecked both parents on the cheek, then took Heber's hand and led him out the front door. "Sorry about Mother. She's cordial to her friends and active in the community, but she has a harder time than my father meeting new people." Her voice dropped to a whisper as they walked to the car. "I don't like living at home, but Mother always says nice girls don't live alone in apartment houses, and I hate to argue with her. Besides, I suppose it's true."

"Your father is great."

"He can always make me smile. Once, when I was five, I was crying because my sister wouldn't play with me. Papa came to me with a goldfish bowl." Ruth looked up at Heber, her expression now merry. "'Here you go, Little Miss,' Papa said. 'When you've filled this bowl with tears, we'll get a goldfish.' I tried to cry into it, but I kept laughing instead. I have it on my dresser to this day."

"Great seed for a story. You should write it down."

Ruth's stride slowed and her eyes clouded. "Mother really does a lot of good. She's vice-president of the Civic Club and president of the Relief Society."

Heber wondered how a mother and daughter could be so different. Time to switch the mood. Heber inhaled audibly.

"Mmm. You're wearing that perfume again. My lady of lavender."

Ruth's face brightened.

Heber opened the passenger door to the old family Chevrolet. "Miss Stone, your fans await you. I'm sorry the limousine was unavailable."

Ruth giggled as she tucked her skirt around her legs and settled on the seat.

"We have some time before the movie. Anything you'd like to do?" Heber asked.

"A drive in the country? It's such a pleasant evening."

It was indeed. Heber began to hum "Happy Days Are Here Again," and Ruth made up a harmony as they drove out Washington Boulevard past neighborhoods of large homes on sprawling lawns and then smaller brick houses.

Soon they were passing fields of clover nearly ready to be cut. Young corn sprouts marched single file over dozens of acres. A sorrel horse trotted to the gate of its corral and whinnied a greeting, while a lamb nuzzled its mother for supper. Ruth rolled down the window and breathed in the spring air. A pungent smell of fresh manure reached them, but she didn't wrinkle her nose. "These fields look like a painting in a museum," she exclaimed.

"Like a Constable I saw in the Louvre, only better." Heber glanced over at her, more and more impressed. "Here you get to enjoy a bouquet of country smells to go with the landscape."

"You saw a Constable? I've only seen his paintings in books."

"*Mademoiselle*, perhaps someday we'll go to Paris and I'll take you to the Louvre." Heber gave her an exaggerated wink. He didn't know any other woman who read art books. He'd devoured all he could find before he went on his mission, knowing he'd be able to see the real thing soon.

"And the opera afterward. Perhaps *La Traviata*." Ruth slid closer to him.

The sun dipped below the crest of the Wasatch Mountains, leaving trails of magenta and burnt sienna. Heber parked alongside the irrigation ditch that ran the length of the road and turned off the engine. He felt like he'd known Ruth for years as he took her hand that lay between them on the seat. "Do you see that little heifer? Born late in the season. Look at those stilts for legs. How can she even walk?"

"She's adorable."

"I want to live in a big city someday, but I love the country too," Heber said. "'Glory be to God for dappled things.'"

"'For skies of couple-color as a brinded cow.'" Ruth continued the verse.

"You know Gerard Manley Hopkins!"

"He sees everything as a creation of God, and so do I. That's what the Gospel is really about, don't you think? Not all the little rules."

Heber whistled. "Well said. My sentiments exactly. I get impatient with people who take a narrow view of the church's teachings, although who am I to judge?"

Ruth turned to look into his eyes. "I'm glad we met."

"So am I."

They leaned tentatively toward each other, and his lips brushed hers. Everything felt right. He could imagine a future with Ruth that included a temple marriage, a house, kids. The life he dreamed of that would fix everything.

8

Salt Lake City, Utah September 1941

Heber's arm rested lightly around Ruth's shoulders, and he breathed in the warm desert air drifting in the open windows of the car. The lights of Salt Lake City spreading out below them winked on by ones, twos, then dozens, like the fireflies he'd seen in France. Crickets chirped, and an electric line buzzed overhead.

"I've wanted to see *How Green Was My Valley* ever since I heard they made the book into a movie. They did a good job." Heber let out a contented sigh.

"Maureen O'Hara was splendid, don't you think?" Ruth asked. "I'd love to act that well."

"You already do. I've seen you." He squeezed her shoulder.

She snuggled closer and he breathed in her signature lavender perfume. A sense of pure pleasure filled him; not the inexplicable fire for André or the spurned passion for Alan, to be sure, but nice.

The summer had passed by quickly: mornings working at the agency, evenings rehearsing with Ruth in Ed's company, or going with her to a movie or dancing. Some afternoons they took long, chatty walks through downtown Ogden, past the Ben Lomond Hotel and City Hall, talking about everything from their childhoods to their favorite books. Other afternoons Ruth settled onto the handlebars of his bicycle, and they pedaled along the country roads of the nearby farmlands. They exchanged poetry and short stories they'd written. Ruth was always such good company.

This was one of those rare evenings when he slipped behind the steering wheel of the Model A Samuel had passed on to Ruth when he bought his Packard. Ruth would scoot over close to Heber on the bench seat and hold his hand when he wasn't shifting, while they drove to Salt Lake for a play or film not available in Ogden. Then they'd drive into the foothills and talk about it, snacking on leftover popcorn, cold but still salty and delicious.

Heber had never met a woman he liked as well as Ruth. She was pretty, and sweet too, and so smart and well-read she could discuss everything from classical literature to church history.

If only he desired her. Their relationship was incomplete, like a puzzle with a piece missing. He'd expected passion for her to develop as they grew closer in every other way. Instead, when Ruth raised her face for a kiss, a peck was usually the best he could do.

He'd fasted and prayed to feel more, wanting it for them both. Once, when he was telling her about the incredible experience of attending an opera at the Palais Garnier, she'd asked if he found her too ordinary after his foreign travels. How could she think that? She was extraordinary. Everything a man could want in a woman. A normal man, that is. Despite President Hays' reassurance, he was more and more worried something was wrong with him.

"It's such a lovely night." Ruth kissed his cheek.

"You're lovely too." Enough of his infernal musings. Maybe he needed to jumpstart this passion thing, like he sometimes had to jumpstart the family car. He turned away from the steering wheel to put his other arm around her.

She laid a hand along his face and looked into his eyes. "I wish tonight could go on forever."

"I wish it could too." Great movie, great company, great view of the city. No fireworks, but very pleasant. Life was good. He tightened his arms around her.

Ruth leaned into him, her breasts full against his chest. Then she pulled back to search his face. "Heber, do you mean that?"

"Mean what?"

"Do you really wish this night could go on forever?"

"'Course I do. You're the best company ever."

She cocked her head. "Are you asking me to marry you?"

Marry her? Surprise jolted him, and his arms loosened.

"I guess not," Ruth murmured and moved away, her face flushing.

"Wait." Heber reached for her hands. "We've only been dating a few months. I'm awfully fond of you."

She folded her arms across her chest. "I get so confused when I'm with you." Her voice trembled, and tears welled in her eyes.

He completely understood. They seemed so perfect for each other. Except for that missing piece. "Oh Ruth," he said, offering her his handkerchief. "I do want a temple marriage and a family for all eternity. Kids playing around my feet. You'd be the right partner for sure. I've thought so since I met you." He drew a breath. "It's just happening so fast."

For the millionth time he said a quick prayer for help. Then he looked again into Ruth's face. Her striking green eyes, wet with tears he'd caused, her lips so often smiling but quivering now. "I can't support you yet. I haven't even finished school." He searched for the right words, unable to tell her the source of his reluctance.

Ruth dabbed her eyes with the handkerchief.

"I truly love you. Maybe we should go ahead." He did love her in his way. Why not marry her?

Ruth's expression stayed guarded, and she crossed her arms. "Maybe? I'm sorry I misunderstood you. I'm so embarrassed."

"Don't say that. Sometimes I have rocks for brains. We should get married. I'm sure of it." Heber got out of the car, walked around, and opened Ruth's door with a flourish. When she stood in front of him, he dropped to one knee on the rough ground and raised a hand toward her. "Ruth Stone, will you marry me and make me the happiest man on earth?"

He waited for her answer — ten seconds, twenty seconds — gravel grinding against his knee. He'd never find anyone like her.

She gave him a winsome smile. "You'd make an excellent leading man."

"Please say yes." He waited, watching a dozen expressions flash across her face.

Finally, "Yes, I'll marry you."

Heber exhaled. Time to play the role of suitor. Why hadn't he done it before? If his Hollywood dream came true, he'd be taking lots of actresses in his arms. He stood, pulled her to him and kissed her boldly. He'd never kissed a woman with mouth open, tongue searching. Imagine the spotlights. The background music. It was all fine.

"Oh, Heber." Ruth reached up and pushed her fingers through his hair. Her eyes shone with happiness in the soft moonlight as she leaned toward him for another kiss.

He took his missionary pin from the lapel of his jacket and awkwardly pinned it on the front of her sweater near her shoulder. "Now we're officially engaged. I'll get a ring when I can afford it."

Ruth fingered the pin, then looked at him shyly. "I love you so much. I've wanted to tell you."

"We'll have a glorious time together." Heber gathered her in his arms again, a flush of genuine affection for her growing in him. "We'll turn the world upside down."

"Acting, writing, we'll do it all." Ruth's lips felt warm and nice this time when he kissed her. No play-acting needed.

He held her a moment longer, then released her. "Guess we'd better head back." He opened the car door and she settled back in.

"If we married next summer, maybe I could teach in Salt Lake while you finished school. Daddy has connections at the school district office."

Next summer. The words began to circle uneasily in his mind. Marriage had seemed like such a grand idea only seconds ago.

An owl hooted nearby. Heber started up the car. "You'll be Mrs. Averil soon," he said, catching her eye and pursing his lips in an airborne kiss as they headed back to Ogden.

"Mrs. Averil." Ruth fingered the missionary pin. "We could have the reception at my parents' home in the garden. Wouldn't that be splendid? Who do you think we should invite? We could each make a list. I have a recipe for a fruit punch that would be perfect. And Dora, a friend from school, makes delicious cakes."

Heber kept his attention on the road as Ruth's voice grew more and more remote.

When they reached Ruth's house, he parked the car, opened her car door, and took her hand. They walked together to the porch steps. "Good night, my love," he said with his best Clark Gable imitation.

"Let's wake my parents and tell them."

He put his hand on her arm. "I hate to disturb them. Let's wait 'til tomorrow night."

THE CHOICE OF MEN

"All right." Disappointment replaced the excitement in her eyes. "It's hard to wait." She lifted her face, and he kissed her goodnight, a good kiss for him.

When the door closed behind her, Heber climbed on his bicycle and headed down the driveway. He was sorry to disappoint her, but he needed to gather his courage to face Sarah. She'd broken up Ruth's last engagement. In her book, the guy hadn't been good enough. Her continued coldness toward Heber made it clear he wasn't good enough either. One would think she'd be pleased that her daughter had another opportunity for a temple marriage.

Samuel would be happy for them. He always welcomed Heber into their home, commenting on Heber's most recent story in the *Tribune*. Tonight, he'd asked about Heber's plans to start attending the University of Utah in two weeks.

Ruth found Heber splendid. He would be marrying her, not her mother. Still, tomorrow was plenty soon to talk to them.

By the time he'd reached the street, a seething dialogue had erupted in his head, one voice incredulous, the other insistent.

You're engaged?
I want to marry Ruth.
Want and desire are different. Desire matters.
I love her. The passion will follow.
Has it so far?
We're great friends.
Friends? Remember France? What are you going to do in bed?

Heber's heart froze, and his hands felt slick on the handlebars of the bicycle. Would he be able to make love to Ruth when they married? He tightened his grip on the bicycle and willed his legs to push the pedals.

"I'm supposed to get married," he said out loud. "It's the Lord's plan. Ruth's a wonderful woman. I'll make it work."

His stomach churned more and more viciously. Spilling his bicycle, he threw up in the irrigation ditch that ran alongside the road.

As Heber approached the family farmhouse, he saw a light shining dimly through the muslin curtains in the front room. No way could he talk to anybody right now. He rode past the house to the old tool shed where he could think, climbed off his bike, and went inside. Pushing garden implements out of the way, he dropped down against one wall. His gaze rested on an old sled with rusted runners opposite him.

The sight of the sled sent a shiver through him.

He'd been nine at the time. Heber could remember every detail of his mother's pale, pinched face as he huddled with her in lightly falling snow, his mother's suitcase resting on the sled beside them.

As they waited for the Bamberger streetcar, he held back his tears. The streetcar would take his mother along the curve of the Wasatch Mountains to her relatives in Bountiful, away from their family forever.

He didn't know why she had to go. Sometimes she wept silently as she fixed the family supper. Was it the argument he'd heard the previous night, and many nights before, that made her cry?

His father's voice angry: 'Good God, woman, what more do you want? I work two jobs to put food on the table.' His mother's bitter: 'I want you to leave me alone, you and your filthy hands. This new baby will be the death of me.'

A chill colder than the December air shuddered inside Heber. He wrapped his arms around his mother's waist and dropped his head against her bulging belly, tightening his jaw so he wouldn't cry.

'See that Alice and Katy get to school every day,' Mother said, her hand on his head. He could feel her slight tremble through her glove. 'And see that Father's supper is ready when he gets home. Sister Brown will keep the twins while you're in class.'

'I will.' He pressed against her. How would he care for his father and his five brothers and sisters by himself? He was only a kid.

The streetcar arrived and opened its doors. Heber watched the motorman take his hand from the big lever that opened the door and put it back on the steering wheel.

'Goodbye, Mother,' he said, taking his arms from around her waist and dragging the suitcase from the sled to her side. Still, he didn't cry.

His mother didn't get on right away. She looked at the motorman and at an empty seat behind him. She looked at Heber. She looked at the snow-laden town. Then she wrapped her old, black coat tighter around her and took a deep breath. 'I'm going now,' she said. Gripping the handle of the suitcase, she climbed up one step.

He couldn't be strong any longer and salty tears slid down his face.

His mother paused, staring down the aisle at the rows of empty brown seats, then back over her shoulder at Heber. She waited a long time. Hours it seemed. Finally, she stepped back down. 'I'm sorry to have bothered you,' she told the motorman, squaring her shoulders as she turned away from the streetcar. Her eyes glistened with her own tears as she gave Heber a hug.

Heber wiped snot on his coat sleeve. Together they carried the suitcase to the sled and tugged it home, Heber awash with joy and relief.

All these years later, Heber ran his hand along a runner of the old sled. His mother had never left again, but he remembered spending the rest of his childhood worrying she might. She'd born two more children and kept the whole family fed and clothed. She had taught him well that family is the most important thing, no matter what it takes to keep it together.

Heber left the shed and tiptoed in the back door. He went to his bedroom and took his Patriarchal Blessing from the top drawer of his dresser, the blessing he'd been given shortly before his mission. Along with it had come the assurance that if he lived a worthy life, he was guaranteed its promises. One sentence in the blessing made everything clear: '*The time will come when you will be privileged to enter the Holy Temple with a true and chosen companion, and there be sealed for time and all Eternity.*'

It was God's will that he marry Ruth.

9

Salt Lake City, Utah, October 1941

Heber arranged two sheets of stationery, a bottle of ink, and a fountain pen on the desk that filled the small alcove of his studio apartment. Maybe a letter would fuel his desire for Ruth.

My darling Ruth,
    Rather silly of me, perhaps, to sit down and pen this note when I ought to be getting to work on my paper. But I can think only of you. Soon we will be married and truly one. It seems hard to believe. Your sweet influence enfolds me. Even as I write to you, my love grows constantly greater and brighter.
Yours for eternity,
Heber

Now that he was a student at the University of Utah, Heber missed the lively conversations Ruth and he had often shared. He missed the warmth of her touch when she took his arm as they walked. When he saw a movie or read a book he knew she'd enjoy, and when he heard a song they'd sung together on one of their walks, he wanted to share it with her. When she finished her novel and sent it out, he wished he could give her a big hug. That was it. Not the passionate longing one should feel for a fiancée.

He read over his words. What else could he say? A bit of Shakespeare perhaps? She'd like that. He added an excerpt from Sonnet 29: *'Thy sweet love remembered such wealth brings, that then I scorn to change my state with kings.'* Then he folded the letter into a neat rectangle and slid it into an envelope.

He continued to sit, lost in thought, his shoulders slumping more and more. He'd done everything President Hays counseled. Why was it a male student in his Chaucer class who aroused him every time their eyes met? Why not Ruth? She deserved a good husband and he desperately wanted to be one. A new thought struck him, and he sat a bit straighter. He had no experience with women. He might surprise himself and enjoy intimacy with Ruth.

With new hope, he picked up his pen again to address the envelope. But when he tried to imagine himself lying with Ruth doing his husbandly duty, his hand shook too much to write legibly.

He tapped the pen on the ink blotter. How he wished he could talk to somebody about his struggle. Who could advise him? His mother would be shocked, his father enraged. His bishop would preach repentance. He'd lose any friend he confided in. There was no one.

Disconsolate, he slipped the letter into a drawer. He could work on his *Hamlet* paper. Do some more research on how others interpreted the play, especially the character of Ophelia. That would cheer him.

On his brisk walk to the library, he considered how Hamlet tortured himself with reflections on his flawed nature. Now there was a heroic struggle; how to avenge the murder of one's father. *'Though this be madness, yet there is method in't.'*

In the library's plain plaster rooms, students sat at long oak tables placed along two walls. Heber went to the card catalog drawer marked "H." He meant to look for Hamlet, but the word *homosexuality* suddenly filled his mind. The word no one said out loud. He glanced around to make sure he wasn't being watched, and then searched for a reference on it. Nothing. He checked a second time, then pushed the drawer closed, nearly slamming it.

Where else could he search? Oscar Wilde. Maybe that would help him understand others with the very problem he might have. His search turned up Vincent O'Sullivan's *Aspects of Wilde*. He found the book and settled into one of the overstuffed chairs at the far end of the reading room.

He'd been turning pages for several minutes when he heard a cough and glanced up. A lean, tawny-haired young man smiled down at him.

"That book sure has your attention. I hope it's for our class." The rich tenor of the man's voice quickened Heber's pulse.

"Our class?" Heber surely would have noticed him.

"I'm Brian Hawkins, Steen's new teaching assistant."

"Creative writing."

"I picked up some papers yesterday. You sit in the front row near Steen's desk."

Heber closed the biography and straightened his shirt collar.

"I couldn't catch your eye. You were so focused on your exam." Brian put his index finger on the book. "Ah, Oscar Wilde. He sure had an incredible understanding of the human condition."

Heber looked at the finger on the book and back to Brian's face. "Yes, yes he did," Heber stammered, hating how he became all legs and elbows as he rose to his feet. "I have to be going. Sorry."

"Sure thing. See you in class." Brian nodded, turned, and walked away before Heber could take a step.

Heber's knees buckled and he sat back heavily in his chair. This wasn't the information he'd come for. He'd get the letter to Ruth and mail it right now, then take the bus to Ogden Friday after his last class. Set a firm date for the wedding. His heart thudded against his ribs as he rushed down the library steps.

10

Ogden, Utah, October 1941

The moment Heber climbed off his bicycle, Ruth ran down the porch steps and into his arms. "You look ravishing," he said. "Like a girl in the movies." She did, indeed, look stylish as always in a mauve skirt and a white blouse belted at the waist. Today there was an extra sparkle in her eyes. He gave her another squeeze, then stood back. "Me thinks thou hast some special news."

"Oh Heber, I sold my novel! I wanted to tell you in person."

"Wow, that's great! Good for you!" Heber grabbed her in a sound hug, lifting her off her feet and twirling her around. His heart thumped a dizzy dance of shared delight. He knew she'd gotten up at 4:00 every morning to work on the novel before teaching. That she'd sent out many letters of inquiry and gotten back a number of rejections, but kept on trying. Now she'd found an editor who wanted to publish it.

"You really are my inspiration," he crowed. "I'm so proud of you." When they were married, they'd settle into a writing routine together. There'd be no limit to what they could do.

He held her longer and, for a moment, his mood darkened. He wanted to be aroused when she pressed against him, her excitement fueling his libido. He wasn't.

And yet he'd stiffened in the library without Steen's teaching assistant touching him. Brian Hawkins. That was his name. Never mind. The marital bed would kindle his desire soon enough. "I love you," he whispered in her ear. He did indeed. She could add novelist to her long list of accomplishments. She was amazing.

"Papa can't wait to see you. And my sister Grace and her husband are in town and finally get to meet you." Ruth took his arm and hurried him into the house. His flush of elation over her news evaporated as Heber braced himself for what he always faced.

When they entered the living room, Samuel rose to his feet and took both Heber's hands. "Heber. Glad to see you, son." He always reminded Heber of President Hays. Same booming voice, same cheerful smile, same faith in him.

"Hello, Sarah, you're looking well." Heber forced warmth into his voice as he turned toward the divan where Sarah remained seated, her mouth set in a straight line.

"Hello, Heber." No smile. No handshake.

Some things never changed. He'd tried again and again to win over his future mother-in-law, bringing her corn and tomatoes from their farm and inviting her to accompany Ruth and him to events he was sure she'd enjoy. The night he'd come to pick the two women up for an organ concert, she'd taken one look at him and stepped backward, a shocked look on her face. Heber had looked around him. What was it?

"The men will all be wearing suits," he'd heard her whisper to Ruth.

He'd ground his teeth to hold his temper. The only suit he owned was a heavy wool thing he would have sweltered in. He'd carefully pressed his white dress shirt and added a tie. Wouldn't that do? No, of course not. Nothing was good enough for Ruth's mother.

A woman who bore a striking resemblance to Ruth, but younger, entered the room. She held the arm of a tall, lean man with hazel eyes set deep in an angular face. "Hello, Heber. I'm Grace, Ruth's younger sister. About time we met," the woman said, offering her hand. "Ruth has talked about you so much I feel like I know you already."

"Glad to meet you, too." Heber tried on a natural smile. The cool look in Grace's eyes and her stiff handshake reminded him of Sarah and canceled his effort.

"Ted Fulton." Grace's husband stepped toward him but kept enough distance that Heber had to reach to shake the man's hand. Something in Ted's gaze and the brevity of his handshake made Heber even more uncomfortable.

Grace sidled over to Sarah and whispered in her ear. Both women glanced at Heber, disapproval obvious in their faces. Was it his clothes? Not the highest style, admittedly, but clean, starched and ironed. Were they checking for hay behind his ears? Two complete snobs. He so wished they weren't Ruth's family.

Ruth took his arm. "Don't mind them," she whispered.

How could he ignore the look the women had given him? Heber doubted Sarah would ever change, and it seemed his future sister-in-law might be equally judgmental. Then there was something about Ted. He'd as soon never see any of them again.

Everyone stood in an awkward circle for a full minute before Ruth broke the silence. "We have to go. Toodles." She grabbed Heber's hand, leading him from the room. "Whew," she exhaled when they reached the porch. "I was worried Grace and Ted would tag along."

"They'd need a bicycle too," Heber chuckled, shaking off the sobering effect of the introductions.

"We can go for a ride in the country. I'll get a sweater and scarf." Ruth skipped into the house and returned minutes later with a long black sweater, a blue silk scarf protecting her hair.

"My lady." He bowed, holding the bicycle as she settled on the handlebars.

"On, noble steed."

Pumping for two was hard work and Heber was soon breathless, but he found his rhythm. Fifteen minutes later they were passing the small farms Ruth always enjoyed. "Look how shaggy the horses are," she sang out as they passed a field with two brown and white paints. "They're getting ready for winter."

If she'd spent her life doing farm chores, she might not be so enchanted, but Heber enjoyed her genuine delight. A few chimneys puffed smoke into the afternoon air. The last marigolds and geraniums decorated front yards with a tapestry of color, and the maples offered up a mix of green and gold. The air smelled fresh after an overnight rain.

Married life would be fun. Mornings they would awaken together and chat a bit before getting up. It would be like Ruth to make hot soup for his thermos and sandwiches and cookies for his lunch pail before she left for work. When he got home, they'd talk about their day while they ate a simple dinner they prepared together. Then they might read or write side by side. When they went to bed, they would lie in each other's arms, her head on his shoulder.

Here his imagination faltered. He abruptly pictured, instead, cuddling in bed with Brian. He could even see a sprinkle of hair on Brian's chest. Shame rose in him as he blinked the image away and pumped the pedals harder.

When sticky sweat soaked his shirt, he steered the bike off the road by a grove of aspens. The leaves of the gray-white trees had begun their fall transformation to brilliant gold and offered a pleasant spot to rest.

Ruth took off her scarf, spread it on the ground, and patted a place for Heber beside her.

"Wish I'd brought something to sit on," Heber apologized.

"You didn't know you'd need to. The scarf washes. I wish I'd made you those cookies you like so well."

"With the chocolate oozing out, almost as sweet as you." Heber smacked his lips in mock appreciation.

Ruth traced the lines in Heber's forehead with one finger. "You look like you've been studying hard."

Heber grinned and took her hand. "You're the best sport. Dad needed the car. He's selling life insurance now."

"I like the fresh air."

"At least this way I didn't have to bring along my brothers or sisters."

Ruth leaned in and kissed his cheek. "You're such a good brother. It's one of the things I love about you."

Heber laughed. "Good brother? Did I ever tell you about my beet-thinning business?"

Ruth scooted closer so their shoulders touched. The light pressure felt nice. "Tell me."

"The summer I was fourteen I decided to get a job and help out the family. I figured with more money maybe Mother and Father wouldn't fight as much."

"Fourteen." Ruth put her head on his shoulder. "So responsible."

He shifted to accommodate her weight. "I decided a beet thinning business would be the thing," he began, a memory of the day playing like a movie in his mind. "We'd work for other farmers, pulling out the straggliest beet plants so the stronger ones had room to grow. Our neighbor had lost her husband in the war, and with no children at home she needed the help. Alice and Katy said they'd pitch in."

"Bright and considerate girls, like you."

Heber's grin turned to a frown. "So, there they were, Alice carrying a lard bucket filled with bread and cheese for our lunch, and Katy carrying a shovel taller than she was."

"Long muslin dresses, big sunbonnets." Ruth lifted her head to smile at him. "You must have been a great success."

Heber grimaced. "Hardly. Long muslin dresses, but I forgot the sunbonnets. We thinned a lot of beets, but we all burned and blistered. That time I deserved the tanning Father gave me."

"He beat you for trying so hard to help? Your father doesn't seem horrid when we have dinner at your house. But it seems there's always more to a person than meets the eye."

Heber shrugged away the comment. "You'll see that our daughters wear sunbonnets. I want two girls like Alice and Katy."

"And sons." Ruth put her head on his shoulder again, snuggling against him. "A big family."

"Girls are better. Lots of girls."

"We'll have some of each, and you'll be the best father in the world," she said, patting his leg. "God will decide anyway."

Heber nodded in agreement. "Sure, God will decide." But he worried, sometimes. If he did have a problem, would God allow it to be passed on to his boys? Better to have only daughters.

11

Salt Lake City, Utah, October 1941

Heber yawned as he packed a stack of papers into his battered satchel, buttoned his jacket against the fall snap, and headed out of Steen's class. He'd taken the last bus from Ogden after his date with Ruth, gotten to bed late, and slept poorly, his mind itching with thoughts of the last few days.

Ruth's family remained a challenge. That pretty well said it. He always liked seeing Samuel and his ever-supportive bear hugs. Sarah might forever be a cold fish. Ruth's sister didn't seem a bit like Ruth. More like Sarah, her mouth hard and her eyes critical. Then there was Ted. Heber couldn't put his finger on what was going on there. Maybe Samuel was the only person with whom he'd ever get along well.

And Ruth. They got along brilliantly. He'd enjoyed his time with her, including his arm around her or holding her hand. He felt more confident that desire would develop.

A quote from Plato had come to mind several times during the weekend. *'The first and greatest victory is to conquer yourself; to be conquered by yourself is of all things most shameful and vile.'*

He was conquering himself and in control of his destiny. They'd set a wedding date. June 20th. He was on track for the life the Lord intended him to live.

"Hello there."

Heber startled. He recognized that voice immediately although he'd heard it only once before, in the library. Brian Hawkins. the teaching assistant.

"There's something I'd like to give you." Brian handed Heber a folio. "As a fellow poet."

His heart racing, Heber opened the folio and glanced at the top sheet. *Morning Mists* by Brian Hawkins. "Your work?"

"Yes, although I don't usually pass it around."

"Thanks." He closed the folio carefully. "My evening's reading."

"Walking my way?" Brian asked.

Heber hesitated. He'd be courting temptation. On the other hand, he'd seen Brian's name as a byline for some terrific poetry in the *Tribune*. It would be great fun to know a fellow poet. He could keep anything else from happening.

"No trouble if you're busy," Brian added.

"I'm on my way home. A boarding house on 12th."

Brian grinned. "My way."

As the two men struck out across campus, Heber noticed their strides matched perfectly. Stifling an urge to take Brian's arm, he swapped the dangerous thought for a question. "Could I ask you about our next paper? Some of the allusions in 'The Love Song of J. Alfred Prufrock' have me stumped."

The two men talked about T.S. Eliot's work, then continued on to Ezra Pound and William Carlos Williams as they left the campus and wandered another half hour along the square grid of streets that made up Salt Lake's downtown area.

Brian nudged him as they waited at a streetlight. "I'm glad we're finally getting together. We have a lot in common. We're the two best poets on campus, you know."

The nudge sent an electric current through Heber. Had Brian felt it too?

"The best? You really think so? I don't know about that."

"No question about it. Funny, I've never seen you anywhere except the library." Brian turned, meeting Heber's eyes. "And class."

"I go to Ogden most weekends. My fiancée lives there. We're getting married in June." Heber exhaled. There. He'd told Brian about Ruth. That would keep everything on the up and up.

Brian nodded. "Congratulations." Was that irony in his voice? Or approval?

They stopped to look at the displays in the department store windows of ZCMI, and then moved on to a theater's posters advertising Charles Laughton in *The Hunchback of Notre Dame*. "That's a great movie," Brian said. "Have you seen it?"

"No, but I want to. I see a film whenever I can rub two nickels together. I graduated the two-year theatre program at Weber College, hoping to act one day." He blushed, wondering if he'd revealed too much.

"Leading man, I'm sure." Brian sounded sincere.

Heber shrugged. "Nah. Bit parts in a lot of things, but I never could land a lead. I still remember my audition to play Macbeth."

"Macbeth. A warrior. A man among men. But more villain than hero, don't you think?"

Heber shrugged. "Maybe." Villain or hero, he had desperately wanted the lead. He checked to make sure no one else was nearby, then looked into the space above and to the right of Brian's head, and reached his arm toward it.

Is this a dagger which I see before me?
The handle toward my hand?

Come, let me clutch thee.
I have thee not, and yet I see thee still.

Brian burst into applause. "Bravo. You're good. You should have gotten the part."

"You think so? My teacher said I was wrong for it. Said I should watch the way men walk and imitate them."

"As if you weren't a man yourself," Brian growled. "I have no use for people like your teacher."

"Gosh, thanks." Heber had never told anyone about the audition and felt respected in a new way. He wanted to hug Brian but punched his arm instead.

They'd nearly reached Temple Square when Brian checked his watch. "I've got a study group in a half hour. I hate to go."

The pit of Heber's stomach told him he didn't want Brian to go either.

"How about getting together after class on Thursday?" Brian asked.

"I'd like that."

Brian turned left at the corner. Heber walked on, suffused with the pleasure of the teaching assistant's company.

Guilt, never far away, kicked at his conscience. He'd had too good a time. Maybe he could arrange for Ruth to meet Brian. She'd enjoy him too, and everything would be fine.

Thursday afternoons with Brian became a regular date. A month passed. The last of the leaves clung to the trees, and the moist air hinted at an early snowfall. Then winter arrived with intermittent snowstorms. If the weather allowed, Heber and Brian walked as they talked. If it was too cold and wet, they met in the library and found a secluded spot where they could swap ideas without disturbing anyone. Brian was Catholic, but it didn't bother Heber. He'd known a lot of Catholics on his mission that were wonderful people. All that stuff some Mormons said about the Catholic church being the Great and Abominable church was hogwash.

Occasionally, Heber noticed someone stare at them and then turn away. What did people think they saw? By unspoken consent, both men guarded the space between them and never even touched shoulders.

One Saturday morning, Brian invited Heber to his apartment to share his latest poetry. Preparing to head over, Heber stood in front of the battered boarding house mirror in his room and carefully tied his green wool scarf. Since guests weren't allowed at the boarding house, he couldn't reciprocate Brian's invitation. Maybe he could pick up a small gift on his walk over instead.

When he passed a bookstore, Heber went inside. To his delight he found an edition of *Leaves of Grass* that he could afford if he skipped lunch for a few days. He gave the clerk the requisite coins and slipped the thin book into his coat pocket. Every poet admired Walt Whitman.

He walked on to Brian's apartment and knocked on the door.

"I like your scarf." Brian ushered him in with a welcoming smile.

Their eyes met. Heber muttered a thanks and looked away.

The studio apartment was decorated in wine reds and deep greens, thick with the scent of musk. Manly and comfortable; far nicer than Heber's room. Heber wondered how Brian could afford such a place.

"Here." Heber drew *Leaves of Grass* from his pocket and handed it to Brian. "I hope you don't have it already."

"The best of the greats." Brian leafed through the pages, then, nodding to Heber, began to read.

> I have perceived that to be with those I like is enough,
> To stop in company with the rest at evening is enough,
> To be surrounded by beautiful, curious, breathing, laughing flesh is enough,
> To pass among them, or touch anyone, or rest my arm ever so lightly round
> his or her neck for a moment—what is this then?
> I do not ask any more delight—I swim in it, as in a sea.

Heber's body burned in response to the sonorous words as Brian read. He usually skipped over "I Sing the Body Electric" as too risqué.

"There's your spot." Brian pointed to an overstuffed chair in one corner with half a dozen books stacked beside it.

"That's my reading list?" Heber eyed the books dubiously.

"Relax." Brian pushed an ottoman in front of him. "Only if you run into something that interests you."

Heber settled into the thick cushions and stretched his legs on the ottoman.

"Can I offer you a cup of coffee?" Brian asked. "Um, Postum?"

"Postum's fine." Heber liked the bitter barley drink, although he wished coffee weren't against the Word of Wisdom. The few times he'd smelled it, the rich aroma had made his mouth water. But then, that wasn't the only temptation this morning. Brian looked very good in his yellow sweater and navy slacks. The mustache he'd begun to grow curved above sensuous lips, and the muscles he'd developed boxing with a local club were well defined beneath his sweater.

Heber took the first book from the pile. *Ancient Greece?*

"The beginning of your education." Brian put a cup of steaming Postum on the floor by Heber and straddled a kitchen chair facing him, his arms folded across the top. "You know, the ancient Greeks accepted homosexuality."

Heber's throat went dry. Brian had actually used the word. "Where's your poetry?" he asked.

"Why were you reading Oscar Wilde in the library?"

Heat crept up Heber's neck.

"If *Ancient Greece* doesn't grab you, take a look at the next book."

Heber looked. "The Bible?"

"Interesting to think about different interpretations of the Bible. One person swears it forbids homosexuality; another says the Bible is full of homosexuals. Even theologians disagree."

Heber ran his tongue over his lips.

"I Corinthians 6:9 that's always quoted? The Greek word *malaka* has nothing to do with homosexuality. It means *soft*. Translators have taken it from there to everything from *effeminates* to *sodomites*."

"You're giving lessons on the Greek language today?" Heber tried for a light response, but his voice came out hoarse.

"People have used that scripture to justify castration, imprisonment, even execution of queers. You think we deserve torture and death? To be crushed and annihilated by people who are rigid and self-righteous in their judgment of us because we aren't like them? It's about bigotry, not God's word."

We? "I think it's time for me to go." Heber set the Bible aside, shoved the ottoman away, and stood up.

"Sit down. You need to know this."

Heber didn't agree. He'd heard stories of men getting their skulls bashed in right here in Salt Lake. He wouldn't be one of them. He had a different kind of life all planned out.

"You shouldn't feel guilty for how God created you," Brian insisted. "Remember in high school getting together with other guys? Maybe for a swim or something?"

"Yeah." Heber sank onto the ottoman. He never could be part of that camaraderie, laced as it often was with innuendoes of each other's physiques and lewd comments about girls. He would sweat with shame at his response to a boy's naked torso or leg and arrive at his next class with his shirt clinging to his damp body.

"Think about what it's like when you go to church. Don't people treat you differently? Maybe some of them avoid looking in your eyes or shaking your hand. It isn't just the Mormon church. Same with us Catholics. Probably the Lutherans too."

Heber grimaced. He had noticed how the first counselor in the bishopric always looked over his shoulder, not at him, when they talked. And the elders' quorum president seldom shook his hand. Heber would tense up when he ran into either of them after a meeting, but he'd turn his mind to other matters, figuring they were distracted with bigger issues than greeting him.

Heber straightened, speaking louder than he'd intended. "I'm not that way." Maybe Brian was queer. That didn't mean he was.

"Come on. You know how we make each other feel." Brian's eyes bored into his. "You knew the original Mormon elders did more than pray together. They danced together, right? And they sometimes greeted each other with a kiss. On the lips."

A knot grew in Heber's stomach. No, he didn't know. Brian seemed better informed than him about a lot of things.

He picked up his Postum and ran one finger around the cup's rim.

"There were brethren in high places in intimate relationships with younger men and the church leadership looked the other way. Do the research. God didn't think they were evil, and He doesn't think you're evil. He created you the way you are."

Heber set down the Postum and rubbed his temples. A drumbeat started in his head. Brian sounded so sure of himself. "If I were like that," Heber said, "it would be a test. I'd show my love and obedience to Him by pushing away any wrong feeling."

Brian bolted from his chair, shaking an accusing finger at Heber. "You actually believe a loving God would ask you to deny your most basic desire? Your most essential self?" His voice quivered with the effort to control his fury. "I know life is a living hell for you. If you can't find a home in your own head, where can you live? There's no sanctuary for you."

"He gives us challenges so we can grow." Heber's voice grew shrill, pleading for Brian to see his side.

"You think you're Job or something?" Brian's dark eyes narrowed.

Heber tasted bile in his throat. He did feel like Job sometimes. He didn't need to be reminded. "I have to go."

"You're damn right."

Heber had crossed the room when Brian caught him by the shoulders and turned him around. "Sorry, Heber. I thought you were ready for this conversation." Brian picked up a notebook and handed it to Heber. "Let's get to our poetry. Then I'll treat you to lunch."

Heber set the notebook on a lamp table and turned toward the door. "I can't."

"There's a great Italian restaurant down the street. Come on."

Heber's hand lingered on the doorknob. He'd wanted to go to Italy after his mission, and Brian was simply asking for his company at a meal. The knob turned in his hand. "I'll see you in class on Tuesday." He closed the door behind him.

Brian's words twisted and turned in his mind like colorful patterns in a kaleidoscope as he trudged back to his boarding house. Had God made him different? He was attracted to Brian, but he wasn't attracted to every man who walked by. He hadn't done anything since his mission. He was going to be married in the temple. That must prove he wasn't one of those.

As soon as he got back to his room, he packed a toothbrush and a change of clothes and caught the afternoon bus to Ogden. All he needed was some time with Ruth and his family and he'd be all right again.

12

Ogden, Utah, December 1941

Heber couldn't look himself in the eye as he shaved and dressed for church. What a louse. When he'd called to tell Ruth he was in Ogden, her voice was filled with delight, and her eyes shone as bright as stars when he picked her up for a movie. He'd give anything to love her the way she loved him. She deserved it. Holding hands with her during the show was all right, but his mind kept conjuring up images of Brian. He'd had every plan to give Ruth a real kiss, not a peck, when he took her home, but his intentions didn't hold sway over his reluctant body. She should dump him.

Shuffling into the kitchen, he kissed his mother on the cheek. "Morning, Ma. How can I help?"

"You're awfully pale, son. Do you feel right?" She turned from cutting thick slabs of crusty bread fresh from the oven, the sweet, yeasty smell wafting through the room.

"All I need's some of that bread. Boarding house food's pretty bad." Heber reached for plates to set the table. The house felt lighter with his father on the road selling something-or-other. He wasn't sure what this time.

"Nine places, not ten. Alice just got up," Katy said, her head bent to her job skimming milk. "She'll be in a rush to get ready for church."

Alice must have been out late with her fiancé the night before, making out somewhere, no doubt, like a regular couple. Images of Ruth and Brian intertwined in Heber's head like the surrealistic paintings by Chagall he'd seen in Paris.

The telephone rang, one long, two shorts, his family's ring on the party line. "Would somebody get that?" his mother asked.

Katy grabbed the phone. John, Heber's youngest brother, wandered in, probably hoping it was Rose Brooks, a girl from a farm down the road. John couldn't date Rose yet since he was only fourteen, but he had plenty to say about her. "The gifts God gave her," were John's exact words.

Heber had never been like his brothers. He'd gone deer hunting with them once. They'd taught him to load a gun and shoot it at a line of cans set up in the yard. He hadn't liked any of it, but they teased him all the time about being closer to his sisters than to them, and he wanted to show that he loved them as well. According to his brothers, the hunt was a great success. They brought back a deer that would feed the family for much of the winter. But when the deer was down, Heber had looked in its soft eyes. In that moment, he felt so terrible about being part of its death that no amount of heckling got him hunting again.

Still, that was hunting. One would think he could respond to women the same way his brothers did.

Ruth was pretty enough. Buxom enough. But it was her warm personality, her accomplishments in writing and theater, her curiosity about everything, that drew him to her. He wished he could be as lusty as his brother when he touched the delicate skin of her cheek or held her in a warm embrace. Instead, it was Brian's body that called to him. He'd sinned when he first awakened this morning and pleasured himself to the image of Brian in his head. Passion wrapped in guilt.

"Heber's right here," Katy said, and passed Heber the phone. "It's Ruth," she whispered. "I think she's crying."

She must have sensed something last night. "Hello?" Heber said, his fingers fidgeting with the phone cord.

"It's Papa," Ruth sobbed.

Heber inhaled sharply, picturing Samuel's broad, jovial face. "What? An accident?

"Terrible pain in his chest. The doctor's coming."

Heber sank to the floor beside the phone stand. Not a heart attack. Not Samuel who had treated him more like a son than his own father. Provided the one real link to Ruth's family. "I'll get there as soon as I can," he told Ruth, then hung up the phone, scrambled to his feet, and raced to his bedroom for his suit jacket.

His family needed the car for church, so he'd have to take his bicycle. Heber pedaled furiously through the slush that remained after an early snow. Samuel had to be all right. Without him there would be no wedding and no chance of Heber straightening himself out.

He scolded himself for his selfish thoughts and pedaled harder. Poor Samuel. Poor Ruth.

When he reached Ruth's house a half hour later, Heber wiped the splatters off his pants as well as he could and rang the doorbell.

Ruth opened the door immediately and fell into his arms. He held her until her sobbing quieted. Her bosom pressed uncomfortably against his chest, but he kept her close, wanting to comfort her. "I'm sweaty," he said. "Sorry."

"It doesn't matter." She took his hand and led him down the hall past an arched doorway that led to the formal dining room with its cut-crystal chandelier and the living room where he usually visited with the family. He glanced at the richly varnished baby grand piano that he'd long to played since he first began coming to Ruth's home. He'd dropped hints for an invitation but was never asked. Even though he'd visited his fiancée often here, he felt more like a foreigner in this house than he had in France.

Ruth led him up a wide, carpeted staircase and along the upstairs hall where Sarah sat stiffly on a chair outside a bedroom. Like Ruth, her eyes were red and swollen, and sympathy welled in him for them both.

"I suppose we'll need another chair," Sarah sighed, her voice haughty right through her grief.

Irritation quaffed his compassion. What an insufferable woman. No matter what she had against him, she could at least be civil. He'd ridden like a mad man to reach them and this was his welcome?

"I'm glad you came," Ruth said when they were seated in a solemn row along the hallway wall. She took his hand.

"I belong here with you." He meant it.

Sarah put her finger to her lips. She apparently didn't agree.

Ruth withdrew her hand and twined her fingers in her lap.

Heber knew not to disturb Samuel with loud conversation, but a soft murmur of voices couldn't hurt. How had Samuel stood to share a home with this woman for so many years? What kind of companionship could she possibly offer? Ruth could never be like her. But she'd withdrawn her hand just now.

He stretched out his legs and crossed them at the ankles. It looked to be a very long morning.

The minutes ticked by, quarter hours marked by the gong of a grandfather clock downstairs. Ruth leaned against Heber, her head on his shoulder. "Poor Papa," she whispered. "When will the doctor come out?"

"He's a strong man. He'll be fine." Heber hoped he spoke the truth.

Sarah glared at them, and Ruth straightened like a nervous child. Heber shifted on his chair and crossed his legs the other way. His thoughts wandered to Brian. Despite the issues their friendship raised, he had definitely felt more welcome at Brian's apartment. Would he still be welcome after the way he'd left things? Could he — should he — learn to accept the joy he felt there? Was it true about some of the early church leaders?

He brought his thoughts back to Ruth. What kind of jerk was he to even think about Brian when he was here to comfort his fiancée? And when a man he truly loved could be dying in the next room?

Pulling a handkerchief from his pocket, he dabbed at Ruth's tears. He tapped one foot, quieted it, tapped the other foot; studied the large pink peonies and tendrils of ivy on the wallpaper and the floral pattern of the hall runner. The rich aroma of a beef roast made his mouth water. Sarah must have started it before Samuel fell ill. He'd missed breakfast and it must be nearly lunchtime now. Should he offer to turn off the oven?

Every situation in which he'd seen Samuel circled in Heber's mind. Death came to every man. Didn't all the poets write about it? But to think that anything could fell a sturdy, six-foot body and active mind with no warning. Without Samuel's influence, would Sarah openly oppose his marriage to Ruth? He needed the marriage to prove to others, God, and to himself that he was morally fit. There he was, thinking the same selfish thoughts again.

The door opened and the doctor came out, an older man with stooped shoulders and a kind face. They all stood to hear his report, Ruth gripping Heber's arm so hard it hurt.

The doctor nodded at Heber. "And you are ..."

"Heber Averil, a friend of Ruth's," Sarah said.

A friend? Not her fiancé? Heber glanced at Ruth, but she avoided his eyes. It was no time to make a scene and he checked an angry retort.

"How is Papa?" Ruth asked.

"The pain has passed. His color is good, and his pulse is strong. It was probably a heart attack."

"I prayed it wasn't that." Tears brimmed in Sarah's eyes.

"Seems it was mild. I expect he'll be fine. I'm leaving him nitroglycerin." The doctor took out several small, round pills from a vial. "If he holds one of these under his tongue at the first sign of pain, it can often ward off another attack." He returned them to the vial and handed it to Sarah.

Sarah's hand trembled as she took the vial. "What else should we do?"

"I'll send a nurse to stay the night and I'll drop by again in the morning. When Samuel feels up to it, I'd like him in my office for an electrocardiogram."

"I've heard of those," Ruth said. "The marvels of science."

The doctor nodded. "We might be able to see if there's damage to the heart."

"It was so sudden." Sarah's voice quivered.

"I'll leave a sedative for both of you in case you need something for sleep. You can see Samuel now, but don't stay long."

"Thank you for coming." Sarah nodded to the doctor and walked into the bedroom.

Heber headed in behind Ruth. He hadn't taken three steps when Sarah turned, frowned at him, then frowned at Ruth, shaking her head.

"Maybe only family should go in for now," Ruth whispered. "You could come when Papa's stronger."

That did it. Wordless, he turned and strode from the house. Wasn't he family? Didn't it matter that he loved Samuel too? He wanted to shake Ruth.

Back at his boarding house in Salt Lake by 8:00 PM, Heber tore three phone messages from his bedroom door. They were all from Brian. Thank God. He went to the phone that the boarders shared and dialed Brian's number.

Brian answered immediately. "You didn't call back. If I upset you that much, I'm sorry."

"I've been out of town."

"I missed you. Want to come over?"

"I could use some company right now." The church leaders might not approve, the current ones anyway, but he was sick of trying to please Ruth's hoity-toity mother. And today Ruth had been firmly under her thumb, agreeing to exclude him from seeing Samuel. Suppose marriage to her wasn't the Lord's plan for him. Was it possible God wanted him to be with the person who accepted him most? The idea was too much to hold in his head on a cold night when all he wanted was to be warmed.

13

Salt Lake City, January 1942

Heber shoved his hands in the pockets of his wool overcoat and stared awestruck at the expansive colonial home of Brian's parents. Meticulously trimmed boxwoods stood like sentinels at either side of the front steps, and an elegant brass knocker adorned the lustrous mahogany door. Even Ruth's home paled in comparison. His family's farmhouse wouldn't make it here as an outbuilding.

He turned to Brian standing beside him on the front porch. "Wow."

Brian chuckled. "Don't be too impressed. My dad's in canned foods and sugar cane. We're regular folks, not the Hiltons."

Heber breathed wispy circles in the frosty air. "Regular folks milk cows and gather eggs. I wish I'd got a haircut." He touched the shaggy tendrils on his neck. He'd gladly have skipped a few meals for the money to get that haircut and make a better impression. Brian could never tell his parents how he and Heber spent their time together. Still, he wanted them to like him.

"Relax," Brian reassured him. "It's their winter open house to gather friends and family. I told them I was bringing a fellow student in need of a good meal. Act like a hungry waif and you'll be fine."

A part easily played. Heber had been a hungry waif often enough. He touched the note in his pocket that Brian had handed him that morning. He'd memorized the words of the poem in two readings, his heart hammering in his chest.

Thoughts of you come softly to my mind
And watching there, and knocking, timid, find
A tender spot that throbs and burns with promise.

Over the last two months he'd found himself in Brian's apartment more and more often. The night he went there after his trip to Ogden, he'd allowed himself only a hug. A warm, tight hug where Brian's chest and thighs pressed into him, encouraging him. He stayed strong until the Saturday morning he'd walked over for breakfast and thanked Brian for the delicious omelet with a quick kiss-turned long and hungry. More hugs and kisses followed over the next week, and then one evening what started in front of a crackling fire in Brian's fireplace ended up in Brian's bed. The love-making session that followed far outdid any fantasy he'd previously conjured. Including André.

"You think you're ready for more?" Brian had then asked, running his fingers lightly down Heber's chest and over his stomach.

Heber pulled Brian's face close for a passionate kiss. The exquisite moments that followed left him in silent wonder. Could life really be like this?

"Good?" Brian had asked afterward, holding him as they spooned.

"So good. And you?"

"Nice. Too bad we don't live in ancient Greece."

Being with Brian was more than a pleasure of the flesh. With him, Heber felt whole in a way he never had before. There were times when his conscience crept in and robbed him of the joy he found in Brian's arms. His shame welled up as intense as the night he'd left André and wandered the streets of Orléans to the train station. He saw how corrupted he'd become, choosing carnal pleasures over the creation of an eternal family. Doing things belonging only within the bounds of marriage and with another man at that. But there were other times when he caught glimpses of Brian's point of view that God had created him the way he was and wanted him to be happy.

Somehow, he couldn't bring himself to break up with Ruth. She'd called apologizing tearfully about keeping him from Samuel the day of her father's heart attack. "I know I was horrid," she'd said. "So worried about Papa, and Mother not handling it well." He'd said it didn't matter, but it did. The empty space between them where his passion should be mattered even more.

During the obligatory visits to Ogden at Thanksgiving and Christmas, and during a weekend in between, Heber said nothing about Brian. He and Ruth went to movies, attended church, talked about his studies and her teaching, their easy camaraderie reminding him what a fine partner she'd make. On those visits he recommitted to the promise he'd made to President Hays. Marriage and family were what he was supposed to do and what he wanted.

But back in Salt Lake he soon put issues around the church and Ruth in a virtual box set high on the shelf of his wardrobe, while he took lessons from Brian in self-acceptance as well as the high art of amazing sex. Now and then he took the box down, reviewing its contents and hating himself. But he always returned it to its appointed place without taking any action. Instead, he turned to Brian for affection and the reminder that he was okay.

Now here he was about to meet Brian's parents.

Brian put his hand on the doorknob. "Ready?"

Heber touched the poem again and took a deep breath. "Let's go."

Brian opened the door and put a hand on Heber's back to push him in first.

"Brian!" a tall woman with Brian's good looks cried as they hung their coats on a coat rack in the entry. She gave Brian a hug, then turned to Heber.

"Mother," Brian said, "this is Heber Averil, that student I told you about in my creative writing class. Been trying to live on graham crackers and milk. Heber, my mother, Loretta Hawkins."

"Thanks for including me." Heber shook Mrs. Hawkins' extended hand, reading none of the disapproval in her face that was ever-present in Sarah's.

Mrs. Hawkins led them down a hallway, past a large portrait of a man in a Confederate uniform with dark eyes like Brian's, on to the dining room and a large table spread with several platters of golden fried chicken, a steaming bowl of mashed potatoes, a tureen of gravy, a green bean casserole, and baskets of puffy dinner rolls. "Help yourselves," she said and turned back down the hall to answer a knock on the door.

"Quite a portrait back there." Heber took two green glass plates from the stack and handed one to Brian.

Brian nodded. "My great-grandfather owned one of the larger plantations in Georgia. Father is quite proud of it."

Heber wondered if Brian were proud too. Men who owned plantations in that era owned slaves as well. Every time he studied that period of history Heber was horrified, all over again, that people could treat other human beings like animals because of the color of their skin. He hoped none of his ancestors had owned plantations and slaves.

Heber turned his attention to piling his plate, inhaling the aromas of the delectable dishes before him. He'd been more nervous than hungry on the way, but now his mouth watered. This banquet was a far cry from anything he was accustomed to, especially now that the formal declaration of war had brought on rationing.

The two men balanced plates of food and cups of fruit punch as they moved among the card tables and chairs that filled the living room and den, people of all ages eating and chatting.

"Uncle Brian!" A little girl with long, copper curls jumped up from a table of children and threw her arms around Brian's waist.

Brian knelt to give her a squeeze. "Esther! How's my favorite redhead? Want to meet my friend Heber?"

"Hi, Esther." Heber knelt too. "You look like Shirley Temple. We should put you in the movies."

"I bet that chocolate cake was yummy." Brian took a handkerchief from a pocket of his sport coat and wiped Esther's chin.

"I'm six now. I had a birthday."

"Happy birthday," Brian and Heber chorused.

"Sit with me, Uncle Brian. Please?"

"There isn't room, but I'll see you later." Brian gave her another squeeze before leading Heber to an empty table in the far corner of the den.

As they took their seats, a young man approached them carrying a plate as loaded as theirs. "Heber Averil. Well, hello."

Heber looked into the familiar face. "Rod Nelson, right? From 20th Century Lit. You're the guy with the good questions."

"Can I join you two?" Rod asked.

Brian nodded and turned to Heber. "My parents and Rod's have been friends forever. Looks like you two already know each other."

"Say Heber," Rod said as he unfolded his linen napkin, "did you tell Brian that in our last class the prof read us your paper on *Tender Is the Night?* Great insights."

"'Course not." Heber wasn't sure if Rod was sincerely complimenting him or for some reason poking fun at him. Something in his tone of voice.

"Heber's quite the Fitzgerald fan," Brian said. "He's reading *The Beautiful and the Damned* right now."

"Good old F. Scott." Rod looked around the room. "Brian," he whispered, "look at that guy by the window. Tall, curly hair. Tight slacks."

Brian turned and glanced at the man. "One of my cousins. Visiting for the holidays before he enlists."

"One look and I can tell you he's a long shot for the army. Can you bring him around? I'd love to train him."

"I bet you would, Romeo."

Heber shifted uncomfortably on his folding chair, grateful they were in a remote corner. Did the conversation between Brian and Rod mean what he thought it meant? He'd have rather kept talking about Fitzgerald.

"Haven't seen you in the usual places for a while. Keeping the new kid to yourself?" Rod winked at Heber.

Heber's stomach turned somersaults. Brian must have told Rod about Heber and him. Why would he do that?

Brian grimaced. "Shh. People will hear."

"Nah. Nobody's in ear shot." Rod punched Heber in the arm. "Brian does love educating the new lads. And I must say he has excellent taste."

"That's enough, Rod." Brian's voice was quiet but firm.

Perspiration beaded on Heber's lip. Educating him? Like the morning months ago when Brian brought out that stack of books?

A middle-aged man approached the table. He looked like the portrait in the hall, except that the confederate army uniform had been switched out for a tweed jacket and dark slacks. "Brian? Gentlemen? I hope you're enjoying the afternoon."

"Dad, you know Rod. This is Heber Averil, a student in my creative writing class. Heber, my father."

Mr. Hawkins looked directly into each of their faces. Heber wriggled under the steady gaze. "You boys don't need to be off in a corner like this. Join the party." The man's words sounded more like an order than an invitation.

"We're chatting about school. I'll make sure to touch base with all our guests," Brian assured him, his tone even. When his father had retreated, Brian turned to Heber. "Got to keep up appearances, you know."

Heber had felt the charge in the air between father and son and noticed how they avoided holding each other's eyes when they talked. He guessed there'd been at least one conversation like the talk Heber imagined he might have with his father. But Brian's father did allow him in the house. There wasn't a chance Heber would be granted that leniency.

Rod picked up the conversation as though they hadn't been interrupted. "Come off it you two. Everyone knows you've been rhyming your couplets for weeks. Right through all the talk about war. Pretty callous of you." He grinned at them.

Callous about the war? Heber and Brian had sprinted to Brian's apartment as soon as they heard the news of Pearl Harbor and huddled over his radio in disbelief. They yelled oaths at the Japanese, made fierce love, then held each other in bed, quivering. December 7th. One month ago. They could be called up any time. Brian said he'd get a 4-F for being queer. It had happened to someone he knew. Heber wondered if recruiters would think he was queer. What would be worse, being killed in the trenches or living in disgrace at home?

"Have a good time while you can. Never know the future." Rod winked at him. "Oh, but I guess you know your future, Heber. I hear you're getting married. Clever guy. Got your ticket to the Celestial Kingdom."

The room closed in around Heber. He pushed back his chair. "Time for me to go. Gotta catch a bus."

Rod chuckled. "Relax. Finish eating. You're with the brotherhood. Any friend of Brian's is a friend of ours."

"Sit down, Heber," Brian ordered, then turned to Rod, his eyes smoldering. "You are way out of line, Rod. You need to find another table."

"I really do-have to go." Heber wadded up his napkin and threw it on the table. What, exactly, had Brian told Rod? When? Why? And what was that Celestial Kingdom crack about?

Brian reached out to stop him.

Heber broke free, willing himself to walk, not run, toward the front door.

"Give me a little more time," Brian whispered, close on Heber's heels. "I can't leave yet. It would look bad."

Heber yanked the door open.

Brian followed him onto the porch and closed the door behind them. "Please stay. We can grab another table." He glanced around, then touched Heber's arm. "I broke up with Rod a year ago but tried to keep him as a friend. Families close and all. I guess he's still bitter."

Broke up? The pillars, the shrubs, the street in front of the house all went out of focus. Had Brian been with Rod like he was with him? "Did you write poems for him too?" Tears stung Heber's eyes.

"I have to go back in. We can talk later," Brian said.

Heber had asked a yes or no question.

Heber knew he wasn't the first man Brian had been with. It was one thing to know in his head, like a passage in a textbook, and something entirely different to be sitting across from a tormented ex-boyfriend. Was Brian toying with him? Was he just one of a string of sad, confused men?

Heber's tears overflowed and he fled into the fat, white flakes of a gathering storm.

"Wait, you forgot your overcoat," Brian called after him.

Nothing could make Heber go back.

14

Salt Lake City, Utah, January 1942

Shivering in his damp suit after a long, wet wait at the bus stop, Heber slumped into a seat at the back of the bus, grateful for the warmth and shelter from the weather. The meal that had seemed so delicious at the beginning of the open house now formed a heavy lump in his stomach, and his mouth tasted like spoiled milk. His thoughts whirled and crashed against each other like loose shutters in a storm. He'd half hoped Brian would appear at the bus stop, fleeing the party to comfort him, and half glad he hadn't. Could Heber have feelings for him and still be okay? Maybe he should drop out of school and enlist. If they took him, that would prove he was normal. But what if they turned him down?

As the bus headed downtown, the six granite spires of the temple came into view. The Angel Moroni blowing his trumpet stood erect atop the central spire. Moroni spoke with God. He'd know if Heber was a — why not just spit it out — faggot.

Heber got off the bus at Temple Square and stumbled toward Moroni. A revelation is what he needed, his own personal revelation. As he rubbed his burning eyes and craned his neck upward, his legs bumped against something soft that squealed. A burly arm pushed him backwards. Barely catching his balance, Heber looked into the blazing face of a man who held the hand of a four- or five-year-old girl. A young woman beside him cradled a baby in her arms.

"You ran into my kid, you bum," the man growled.

"What's wrong with him, Mommy?" the little girl asked.

"He might not be well, honey," she said, taking her husband's arm and giving Heber a wide berth as they walked past him.

"Drunkard," he heard the man say with evident disgust.

Drunkard? That would be an easier thing to fix. Heber swiped at his nose with the damp sleeve of his jacket. He'd lost feeling in his fingers and his feet felt like bricks. A vivid memory of the time he'd lain shivering on the banks of the Loire, gasping for breath, played out in his mind. He'd wondered about a stain on his soul when he'd nearly drowned. He clearly saw the stain now. Dense and black. Could anything scrub it out?

He'd taken a lover, a man at that. A mortal sin, he knew. But crazy as it sounded, maybe God had put Brian in his path. Ruth could talk about literature and theater as well as Brian, but she couldn't make him feel understood. One afternoon he and Brian had talked about satire in literature, ending with a shared sensibility about the price Oscar Wilde had paid for being queer. It wasn't Ruth's fault that he could never have that kind of truly free conversation with her.

Brian accepted him more fully than he accepted himself. After they made love one evening Heber had crumpled in tears. "I've had crushes on guys, but I never did anything about it, so I figured I was okay. My mission president blamed the stuff in France on Satan, not me." He dabbed his eyes with a corner of the sheet.

Brian shifted so he could massage the knots in Heber's neck. "You're very much okay," he said. "Either you live true to yourself, or you hurt not just yourself, you hurt everyone who cares about you."

Heber started to relax. "That's not what I've been taught. I think God wants me to marry in the temple. How can I even say that? I'm here with you." His tears started up again. "I'm not worthy to go through the temple. It would kill Ruth and my family if they knew. I *am* hurting everyone who cares about me."

"God loves you the way you are," Brian said, his voice low and soothing. "He created you after all. You'll figure out what to do about Ruth. What to tell your family."

"God can't love me. I'm breaking his commandments. It's gotta be a test."

Brian's fingers stiffened on his neck.

"Sorry," Heber said, sitting straighter. "I'm saying it again. How can you listen to me? I'm a broken record."

Brian stood and stretched. "Someone special listened to me and helped me feel better about myself. I'm hoping to do the same for you."

Heber remembered every word spoken in that moment. Every feeling choking him. As he walked toward the temple, questions filled his head. What exactly had Brian meant? Was Heber some kind of project? Could a morally corrupt man like Heber ever feel good about himself? Was he really part of the brotherhood? Did he look like a queer, or did Rod think that because he was with Brian? Had Heber's theater teacher been right so long ago? Did he walk swishy?

He didn't think like Brian. About literature, maybe, but not about a lot of stuff. In fact, Brian didn't even seem to mind Heber's engagement to Ruth. Heber had never had the nerve to ask him about it. Personally, he would have been jealous.

President Hays had promised that marriage would solve his problem. He'd go to Ogden. There was a bus tonight. No. He didn't belong there either. Sarah had made that clear.

Where did he belong?

A headache crept across the back of Heber's skull. It happened a lot these days. He raised his eyes to the gold statue. As he looked at it, the sun broke through the clouds and gleamed off Moroni. The words Moroni had spoken in the Book of Mormon came to him: *'And if ye shall ask with a sincere heart, with real intent ... he will manifest the truth of it unto you by the power of the Holy Ghost.'* He could trust Moroni to guide him.

"Okay," Heber said aloud, "give it to me straight. Am I one of those?" He waited in the frigid air until his teeth chattered.

He tried to focus on the statue, the icy wind stinging his eyes. As he blinked tears away, he could swear he saw the statue nod. No doubt about it—the answer was yes.

Devastated, he kicked at the snow, then pulled up the collar on his suit jacket and trudged back to the bus stop. He'd trusted Moroni to show him the truth. But how could Heber live with that truth?

15

Ogden, Utah, January 1942

Heber sat on the bus stop bench, head between his knees, stomach churning. When the bus arrived, he stumbled to a back seat once again. Pulling a pencil and a small pad of paper from the breast pocket of his suit jacket, he scribbled furiously.

Men are such fools! Especially young men –
Very young men who steep themselves
In sentimental poetry and romantic fiction
And sigh and yearn and pine for romance
And think at last they've found it.
Poor fools! Poor, romantic pitiable fools!

Was the poem for Brian? He couldn't go back to him much as he burned for him; he had to choose a more righteous path.

Was it for Ruth? A woman as remarkable as Ruth would never want to marry him if she knew the kind of man she'd fallen for. And he would never meet another woman like her.

He was the scum of the earth. Moroni had made that clear.

He tore the poem to shreds, then stuffed the pieces back in his pocket and stared miserably out the bus window.

Redemption depended on repentance. He'd fast more often for longer, pray more ardently, study the scriptures more diligently. He'd lived the teachings of the church before his mission; he could again.

A throbbing ache started behind his eyes. Repentance required confession. Eventually he'd go to his bishop, but he had to tell Ruth first. She'd break up with him and he'd have no one. Served him right.

Back at the boarding house, he changed into dry clothes, then went to the shared wall phone, took the black receiver from its cradle, and dialed Ruth's number.

"Hello?" Ruth, not her mother. Thank God.

"Hello," he said, his voice flat.

"It's you!" she exclaimed with such joy he wanted to wretch, the acrid taste of bile burning the back of his throat.

She had no idea who—or what—she was about to marry. Memories of their good times flooded his mind. The walks, the films, the conversations.

"I need to talk to you," he said.

Her breath caught. "What is it? Oh, Heber. Have you been called up?"

It was the question on everyone's mind. At the moment, the army didn't sound so bad. The Front couldn't be a worse hell than he was living in right now.

"I haven't been called up. I just need to talk to you."

"Are you coming to Ogden? I can pick you up at the station."

"I can catch the late morning bus tomorrow and get in about one o'clock."

After a brief goodbye, he hung up the phone, trudged to his room and lay face down on his bed. If God's design was perfect, why had Heber been cursed with a desire for Brian, not Ruth? She was the last person in the world he wanted to hurt. He had no idea what he'd tell her, but he had to say something.

When Heber stepped off the bus, Ruth ran to him, and he gave her a sound hug. She'd never felt so good in his arms.

"Are you okay?" she asked, stepping back and studying his face.

He must look as bad as he felt, judging from her expression; pale face and hunched shoulders like he had some dreadful disease. In fact, he did. It started with an H.

"Missed lunch, that's all," he said.

"We could stop by my house," Ruth offered.

An image of Sarah came to his mind, the last person on earth he wanted to be around. Then he thought about Samuel. Did Ruth's father have to know about him? How would Heber ever face him?

Ruth would have to tell them. Sarah would click her tongue against her teeth and say, smugly, "I told you he was no good."

Samuel would sink into a chair, shaking his head, awash with disappointment. "He seemed like such a fine young man."

"Why don't you drive?" Ruth handed Heber the key to her Model A. "Take us anywhere you like."

Heber headed up Ogden Canyon, driving carefully on the icy road. Pulling off at a viewpoint overlooking the city, a favorite local spot for necking, he turned toward Ruth. She was used to his arms loosely around her and his perfunctory kisses when they came to this spot. Now she'd understand.

He saw the worry in her eyes as she waited, gathering her wool coat more snuggly around her as the winter air seeped into the car. Heber wished he had his overcoat to offer her.

"What's wrong?" she finally asked. "Have I done something?"

"It's not you. Not at all." Heber clenched his hands trembling in his lap. "It's me." He drew a breath and exhaled. "I'm basically rotten."

"Rotten? What?"

He lifted his head to search her face, desperate for her to understand. "I enjoy you more than any woman I know. I admire and respect you."

Ruth's eyes clouded with confusion. "You admire and respect me? We're getting married in a few months." She clutched her handbag. "What can it be?" He could see thoughts tumbling in her head. Finally, she asked, "Is there another woman? Be honest."

A mirthless laugh caught in Heber's throat. "Another woman? No. Never."

"Then …"

He hunched over the steering wheel, raking his fingers through his hair. "You don't want to marry me," he mumbled.

"The invitations are ordered. I've sewn my dress. What did I do?"

Heber chewed his lip. "I'm not the man you think I am."

She laid a hand on his arm. "Heber, whatever is the matter?"

Should he blurt it out, *I'm one of those?* Instead, he sucked in his breath. "There's something wrong with me," he began.

Ruth gasped. "You're sick? Darling, we can face anything together."

"It's more of a moral disease …."

Frustration edged Ruth's words. "What are you talking about? Drinking? Gambling? Tell me! We said we'd tell each other everything."

"I want to be a good man. But I don't think I can be." Heber stared at the floorboards of the car, his jaw aching from clenching his teeth. Maybe he'd said enough, and she would guess the rest.

Ruth put her hands on his cheeks and tipped his face toward hers. "Heber Averil, look at me. You aren't making any sense."

"I've sinned." He exhaled. "A sin of the flesh."

Ruth shuddered, her eyes wide. "You said there wasn't another woman."

"It was a man." There. He'd said it.

"No." Ruth reared back as though struck. Her handbag thumped to the floor of the car as the color drained from her face. "I don't believe you."

He groaned. "I wish it weren't true."

Ruth slid against the car door, as far from Heber as she could get, folding her arms across her chest, silent, rocking back and forth. Why couldn't she punch his arm or beat on his chest? Anything but look straight ahead with that terrible hurt in her eyes, tears pouring down her face. After several minutes she opened the car door and stepped out into snow over her ankles.

Heber got out, too, and walked around to stand beside her, both of them shivering in the cold. "I've done everything to change. Fasted, prayed, studied the scriptures. I confessed to my mission president."

Ruth turned away from him. "I'm freezing," she said and got back in the car.

Heber slipped back in the driver's seat.

"You've kissed a man and you kissed me." She stared out the window. Heber heard it all in her voice: revulsion, disappointment, anger. "Was it that man in our acting troupe?"

"No." She had noticed. Then why had she wanted to marry him?

Ruth stared out the window, her hands, balled into fists, rigid at her sides. "Grace and Mother suspected it. I didn't want it to be true. Papa didn't either."

They'd all talked about it. Great. He sunk lower on the car seat. "I hate who I am. I know that doesn't help."

She finally turned to him. "No, it doesn't."

More minutes passed. "Someone in France?" she finally asked.

He nodded. He'd hurt her enough. He didn't need to tell her about Brian.

Again silence.

"I guess the wedding's off," Heber said at last.

He could hear her shallow breathing as Ruth strove for composure. She bent over, picked up her handbag, and gripped it in her lap. "We planned such a wonderful life," she said brokenly. And, a minute later, "A home, a family, our writing. I was finally going to have it all. I'd nearly given up hope."

"I know. I'm so sorry." Heber's words were plaintive, useless.

More minutes passed, long and painful. Heber waited, desperate to comfort her, knowing there was no comfort possible.

"Does anyone else know?" she finally asked.

"No."

From the edge of town, a train whistled, probably the same train they'd planned to take to Los Angeles for their honeymoon.

"So, you're breaking up with me?" She glanced at him, then away.

He blinked, stunned by her question. "No. I figured you'd break up with me."

Ruth closed her eyes. Her lips moved and he assumed she was praying. Time stretched out in a painful silence. Finally, she took a handkerchief from her handbag, dabbed at her eyes, and turned to him. "Do you love me?"

He cupped her face in his hands. "Yes, Ruth, I truly love you. I want a temple marriage and family as much as ever."

She drew back from his touch. "Everything's so complicated." A second time she closed her eyes and moved her lips. When she opened them, tears gathered again. "You said you wanted to change."

"I'd do anything to be normal." Heber meant it.

Ruth pressed her lips together, took a deep breath and then another. "On your mission you were alone," she said, her voice growing steadier. "Away from your family, always around men. It will be different when we're married."

Astonishment and hope rushed into Heber's chest. "You'll have me?"

"I think so. It's just …"

"I can change. I promise I can. My mission president said marriage was the answer." He reached toward her, tentatively.

Again, she drew back. A third time she closed her eyes and moved her lips in prayer. When she opened them, her eyes were clear. "We've always said if we were partners, we could do anything. You're a good man with a monstrous challenge. Heavenly Father will help us."

"'True love is not love which alters when it alteration finds.'" Ruth's voice grew stronger as she quoted the lines.

"'Or bends with the remover to remove. Oh no, it is an ever-fixed mark that looks on tempests and is never shaken.'" Would this amazing woman still have him?

"Give me your hand," Ruth said. And when she'd held it a moment, "Let's give it a try."

16

Salt Lake City, Utah, June 1942

Five a.m. Heber reached to silence his shrill alarm clock before it woke the entire family. Had he slept at all?

"Wedding day," he said aloud as he got up. The early morning sun cast a slanted beam across his bed as he pulled up the covers and for the last time fluffed the pillow. "Goodbye, room," he added as he glanced around the tiny bedroom off the kitchen where he'd spent so many solitary nights.

Today he started a new life: a temple marriage, honeymoon in Hollywood, and then he'd finish his senior year at the University of Utah while Ruth taught in Ogden to support them. They'd rented a refurbished carriage house behind a stately home not far from campus. Ruth assured him she didn't mind the hour-long drive to Ogden High for the coming year while he got his degree. Such a good sport.

He stopped at the phone table on his way down the hall to the bathroom and fingered a yellowed wedding photo of his parents, shaking his head. *Never saw them smile at each other that way. It'll be different with Ruth and me.*

The warm water from the bathroom sink felt good when he splashed it on his face. He wished the shaving brush would quit shaking in his hand. As the razor sliced through the stubble on his jaw, he thought about his wedding night. He tried to picture Ruth and him in bed, kissing passionately, his fingers exploring her body, her fingers exploring his. But in his imagined scene not a single button of her clothing came undone. Ah well. If he couldn't immediately warm their marriage bed and bring Ruth pleasure, he'd try his skills at the method acting he'd learned from a careful study of *An Actor Prepares*, a book his drama teacher at Weber College had admired. That would be better than nothing, wouldn't it?

He paused. No, Heber vowed as he cleared the shadow from his chin, he wouldn't resort to stagecraft. As he wiped the last bits of soap from his face, his thoughts turned to Brian and a sigh escaped his lips. How he missed him. When they'd met at the library for Heber to retrieve his overcoat, Brian's cool tone had stung. He'd said he understood Heber's discomfort at the party and his wish to be part of a traditional life. There was no talk of the two of them getting together again.

True, Heber hadn't wanted to spend time with Rod and Brian's cousin, but he often felt desperate to spend time with Brian despite his promise to Ruth, to God, and to himself to change. Nights were the worst, when sleep eluded him, and he could think of nothing but the feel of Brian's body next to his.

"Marriage is the path I want," he said aloud as he buttoned up his best white dress shirt. He'd worried about getting the *temple recommend* required to enter the temple, and during his appointments with the church authorities to obtain it, he felt like the worst kind of hypocrite. But in the end, by luck or design, the brethren hadn't asked him any sticky, probing questions. They'd stuck to the principles of paying a full tithe, obeying the Word of Wisdom, and supporting the general authorities. Then they'd asked him to bear his testimony of the church as the one true church. Everyone stayed pleasant and comfortable, avoiding difficult conversations.

Heber massaged the muscles in the back of his neck, then paused with a new thought. What if he left a farewell note to Ruth and his family and rode his bike to the bus depot? Went alone to Hollywood to pursue an acting career. Or New York. He'd heard there were queer bars and parks in New York City. He could easily picture himself at a café table or on a park bench with Brian. Ruth was, after all, an accomplished writer, a successful teacher, a well-known actress in Salt Lake Valley, strong and self-sufficient, but also beautiful and charming. She'd easily meet a better man.

Giddiness seized him as he imagined the parade of possibilities if he called off the wedding and liberated them both.

Thoughts of his patriarchal blessing pushed aside his crazy fantasy. He squared his shoulders and turned off the bathroom light. He'd prove his faith and obedience, and overcome his problem, no matter what it took.

In his bedroom, Heber flexed his shoulders in slow circles. He glanced at the copy of *Washington Square* he'd left on his small writing table. How lucky Henry James' characters were, eager and quick to conform to society.

Since his parents were giving Uncle Roy and Aunt Jane a ride to the temple, and Ruth's parents were taking a passel of relatives, Ruth was coming by for Heber. He glanced at the clock. She'd be here soon.

He looked in the mirror over his dresser. Not such a handsome groom. Hollow eyes. Mouth turned down. How was Ruth feeling this morning? Confident she wanted to marry him? Maybe she'd be the one to call if off. The bad news and the good news. But she'd never brought up his confession again.

Maybe he'd be more excited if their wedding was going to be like the secular weddings he'd seen in movies. Ruth would be regal in a beaded satin gown with a long train, he dapper in a black tuxedo. They would smile into each other's eyes as they exchanged vows before a minister in a flower-bedecked church. The whole family could be part of the celebration.

Instead, none of his brothers and sisters would be attending the wedding. That really bothered him. Two younger brothers had enlisted in the army and were in basic training. Alice was waiting for her own wedding to go through the temple for the first time, and Katy and John were too young to get the *recommends* that would allow them entrance. He'd feel a lot better having them there.

Going through the temple was a privilege, right? Only adults who were good members of the church could get *temple recommends* and enter its hallowed walls. There they would get their *endowment*s through a series of rituals and covenants between God and the participants. The *endowment* offered guidance, purpose and protection in this life, and prepared people to enter the celestial kingdom in the afterlife as priests and priestesses.

Then he and Ruth would be married, a marriage that was not "until death do us part" like most marriages, but a sealed unity for all eternity. All good Mormons aspired to a temple marriage and the celestial family that followed.

It was what he wanted, what he'd chosen.

Still, the Catholic church in the Ville D'Avray with its incense and art had felt more sacred.

Heber tied his tie carefully and put on the new suit his parents had somehow managed to buy him, then undid the tie and knotted it again. Turning from the mirror, he folded a new white shirt and new white pants for the temple into neat squares and packed them in a canvas bag. Coins jingled in his pocket to rent the ceremonial hat, apron, robe and ankle-length undergarments once he got to the temple. This would be his second time going through the rituals and surely it would be better.

His first time through the temple, before his mission, had been deeply disappointing. Troubling, in fact. How were blood oaths spiritual? He knew many people who found the ceremony inspiring. Could he be so far out of step? Today he'd have a better attitude. Setting his jaw, he picked up the bag and went outside to wait for Ruth.

When Ruth drove up in her Model A, the car polished to a high sheen, her eyes shone with happiness.

"Thanks for picking me up. Car looks great and so do you. Hair perfect. Love that lavender." Heber gave her a quick kiss before she moved over, and he slid behind the wheel.

"I guess you aren't supposed to see the bride on her wedding day. At least you haven't seen my dress." Ruth settled against the back of the seat with a contented sigh.

A comforting numbness settled over Heber as the highway flowed past. Ruth's animated conversation buzzed around him, and he occasionally nodded or added a few words. The sound beating rhythmically in his head must be the car's engine.

"We're here," Ruth cried jubilantly as he pulled into a parking space at the temple.

"So we are," he said, turning to her and grazing her cheek with his lips. He blinked his eyes to bring the granite walls and spires into sharper focus.

She leaned in for a real kiss. "It's happening!"

"It certainly is." Time to come to the party. She was about to be his wife. He gave her a Hollywood style kiss full on her lips, gentle, deep, unhurried.

He took the suitcase from the back seat. Her temple clothing must be inside. Imagine having enough money to own the items that were worn only in the temple. Ruth reached for a garment bag that he assumed held her wedding dress.

As they entered the temple, two temple greeters shook their hands warmly. "You make a handsome couple," one of the men said genially. "What a radiant bride."

"I'm a lucky man." Looking into Ruth's face so full of love for him, he did feel lucky. He couldn't ask for a finer woman to share his life and the kingdom beyond. She looked very pretty in a simple floral print skirt and white silk blouse. She'd be stunning in her wedding dress. How could he have any doubts about their future together? He would pull off this day for her. Their wedding night too. Whatever it took.

"I can't believe we'll be married soon," Ruth whispered when they reached the changing rooms.

"I'm proud to be marrying you," he said, meaning it, and gave her a tight hug.

He watched her disappear into the women's changing room with her suitcase. He couldn't imagine her liking the temple rituals any more than he had his first time through, but they were the gateway to starting the life together he and Ruth planned.

He remembered liking the initiatory rite. The short scriptural stories and lessons acted out in skits in a series of rooms had been interesting, although a bit wooden. But after each play came the *covenants*, along with a series of *signs* and *tokens* supposedly so sacred they were never to be discussed outside the temple. The penalties for revealing said *signs* and *tokens* were chanted blood oaths, *'rather than do so I would suffer my life to be taken.'* The ritual had seemed more Masonic than the deeply personal experience he'd expected. Would his heavenly father agree with such punishment? Death for revealing *signs* and *tokens*? He might have walked out in the middle of the ceremony had his mission not depended on his completing it.

Today, he wondered what the penalty might be for his immoral acts which seemed a lot more sinful.

Since he'd received his own *endowment* before his mission, today he would go through the ritual for one of his ancestors who waited in a spirit prison to hear the true gospel and accept or reject what his living ears had never heard. Was the whole thing a sham? Not the marriage, but temple work for the dead? Surely a loving God wouldn't expect the unenlightened dead to wait in a spirit prison until some descendant went through the temple for their *endowments*.

He'd considered telling Ruth what she was getting in to but decided it would be wrong to color her experience. He'd make it through this time because after they both received their *endowments,* they would be married in the sealing room. Their temple wedding.

Standing in the dressing room in his temple robe, Heber slapped his cheeks to bring in more color. He was heading to his preparatory *washing and anointing,* not an execution. It had been his favorite part of the ceremony when he'd gone through the temple before his mission. Would it be again this time? Ruth would go through the same part of the temple rite in another room, each of them tended to by temple workers acting through the authority of the holy Melchizedek priesthood.

A temple worker led him from the men's dressing room to a simple, windowless space where the ritual washing, a symbolic sprinkling of water to wash away the sins of the generation, took place. Heber was anointed with consecrated oil and received special blessings on different parts of his body.

When Heber's lips were blessed that he might never speak guile, a moment of peace enveloped him. Respect for others, without cunning or deceit—that was a thought he could embrace. But afterward, when the officiator lightly touched each of his eyes, blessing them with the promise that one might see clearly and discern between truth and error, a chill ran through his body. What was his truth? What kind of man could he become, even with all the blessings promised him? He pushed away the painful self-doubt. He had repented. Today would be the start of a new life. He was being sealed to Ruth for eternity. A righteous path lay ahead of them.

The rite ended with the declaration that he was anointed to become a king and priest in the afterlife. Ruth, in the women's rooms, would be anointed a queen and priestess. Although he didn't often dwell on the afterlife, he knew that Ruth would go to the highest degree of glory. Surely, she could help him live this life more honorably. If he wanted to be with her throughout the eternities, he'd need more than a temple ceremony. He'd have to stay on the straight and narrow.

He steeled himself against a painful image of Brian. He was moving beyond his past. His skepticism. His sins. Here in the temple, he could repent of it all. The future would be different. He'd prove himself worthy of God's wonderful promises.

Temple workers clothed Heber in the sacred undergarment he'd rented and gave him a new name that he'd need throughout the *endowment* session, and he repeated it to himself several times. Back in the dressing room he changed into his white shirt and white pants. Samuel and his father joined him there. His packet of ceremonial clothing in hand, he, his father, and his soon-to-be father-in-law joined the line of men who were filing into pews on one side of the Creation Room.

Women were coming in and taking seats on the other side.

When they had taken their seats, Samuel rested an arm across Heber's shoulders. Heber swallowed past a lump in his throat, glad this beloved man had survived his heart attack and was here beside him.

Heber's father sat on his other side and awkwardly patted his knee. The touch, unusual for his father, seemed like an acknowledgement that Heber was a man now, shouldering a man's responsibilities. That's exactly what he intended to do.

Heber broke into a smile when he saw Ruth enter. Her wedding dress was an exquisite thing, all in satin, with a high, lacy neck and puffy sleeves. She looked beautiful despite the required temple veil, a simple, limp thing gathered around her head. He did want to marry her, even if it meant getting through this ceremony. Why did he ever doubt it? She smiled radiantly when he caught her eye, then took a seat between her mother and his.

Both matrons wore rigid smiles, making no pretense of any warmth between them. Heber's mother had felt snubbed when Sarah refused a dinner invitation to their home with an excuse of a prior engagement. She invited Sarah a second time, anyway, and again Sarah refused. She didn't try again. Now Ruth took the hands of both women like they were all three best friends. Nothing seemed able to mar the glow in her face when she caught Heber's eye again and gave him another thousand-watt smile.

Heber smiled back, then looked at the stunning murals of the world's beginnings that decorated the walls of the Creation Room. He was glad to be here.

Then the actors began to deliver their lines so poorly he winced. He glanced across the aisle at Ruth, assuming she would feel the same. Her face was serene. How was that possible? He squirmed in the pew. He *was* out of step. Maybe the Lord hadn't answered his prayers about his struggle because he lacked a sincere heart. How could he come into God's holy building and criticize people who were doubtlessly living far better lives than he was?

Again, an image of Brian flickered in his head. He snuffed it out with a silent prayer. *Heavenly Father, help me live a life that is pleasing to you and help me be a good husband to Ruth.*

As the group proceeded through the rooms, Heber felt the comforting spirit of the initiatory rite evaporate, replaced by a growing revulsion at the swearing of oaths. Really, he thought again, who would give his life for a handshake?

What was Ruth thinking about all this? When they got to the part where he pledged to honor and obey God, she had to pledge to honor and obey him. Obey? Like a dog? Him, not God? He glanced at her and saw the serenity fade from her face. When she caught his glance, she scrunched her face into a frown like she did when they'd seen a bad movie. Her mother put a hand on her forearm and shook her head in rebuke, but Heber smiled. Besides loving her, he really liked his future wife.

At the end of the endowment rite, he and Ruth would pass through the veil into the Celestial Room. They'd kneel at an altar and be sealed to each other. And if they kept their covenants, they, and their children, would dwell with their father in heaven eternally in the Celestial Kingdom. It was the goal of every good Mormon. And Heber intended to be a good Mormon.

Finally, it was time to go through the veil, a symbolic division between this mortal life and the afterlife, and to take Ruth through. A temple worker stepped up beside Heber to assist. It was President Hays! Heber couldn't believe the coincidence. He wanted to grab his mission president in a bear hug but managed to limit himself to a big smile. President Hays wouldn't still be president of the French mission. He would have returned with the missionaries when war broke out. Although he was a temple worker now, he'd always be President Hays to Heber. The older man winked at Heber and nodded his approval.

Heber basked in the approval and grinned back. God couldn't make it clearer that Heber was doing exactly the right thing.

President Hays took Heber through the veil, receiving the series of solemn handshakes and the five points of fellowship — ear to ear, shoulder to shoulder, breast to breast, navel to navel, hip to hip. Then Heber turned and, with his former mission president's prompts on the correct words and movements, brought Ruth through. She burst into a dazzling smile that further reassured him.

"Now we'll be together forever," she whispered.

"The soon-to-be Mrs. Averil." He pressed her hand to his heart.

Ruth on his arm, Heber entered the sealing room. With its white walls and simple white furnishings, it felt sacred the way a temple should. He and Ruth knelt on opposite sides of a rectangular, upholstered altar in the center of the room and joined hands across it. Their parents, other relatives and family friends watched from chairs along one wall. He could see from their faces that the spirit had touched them too.

After a brief talk about the patriarchal order of the home and the need for a righteous posterity, the temple president instructed Heber and Ruth to look in the hallway. A wall of mirrors provided a sense of unending reflections symbolizing the eternal nature of their temple marriage. Heber's heart burned with conviction as he leaned across the altar and kissed his wife. He was sure of his path.

17

Los Angeles, California, June 1942

At last Heber and Ruth were on their honeymoon. Exhausted after the luncheon and reception that followed the temple wedding, Heber was doubly grateful for Samuel's gift of tickets on the overnight luxury train to Los Angeles.

He watched as Ruth wedged into their tiny bathroom wearing her burgundy travel suit. While she was changing, he wondered yet again if he would be able to consummate their marriage. She emerged wearing a flowing peignoir of blue silk that revealed a glimpse of a nightgown in the same fabric. With a quick glance at him, she climbed onto her berth.

Did she hope he would climb up with her on that tiny excuse for a bed? He didn't like disappointing her, but it couldn't possibly hold two people. One more night to postpone the inevitable and learn the truth. Tonight, he could focus on the thrill of Hollywood that lay at the end of these tracks.

When he changed and climbed onto his berth, he couldn't sleep. As the miles clicked by, excitement over actually going to the City of Stars pushed all other thoughts from his mind. Pulling on slacks and a light sweater, he slipped out of their compartment, climbed the steps to the club car, and took a seat that offered a view of gray shapes in the night desert. He shrugged aside the smells of tobacco and someone's late night snack that included a strong cheese. Nothing could mar the moment. His body vibrated to the sway of the train as it traveled south and west. Hollywood would be warm, with palm trees rising into a perpetual summer sky. For two glorious weeks he and Ruth could wander its streets, no church members, parents or professors looking over their shoulders.

The specter of their imminent wedding night appeared again. In a way, he would rather be going to Hollywood alone and doing exactly as he pleased. Nah, if he could manage the bed part, he'd have more fun sharing the city with Ruth. He could fantasize about Brian if need be. What a crazy thing to even consider.

Finally, he dozed and awoke to see Ruth, dressed for the day, stepping into the club car as the sun streaked the sky with reds and pinks. "Good morning, darling," she said, glancing around at the dozen or so other passengers and kissing him discreetly before sitting down. "I can't believe I slept so well. Imagine going to sleep in Utah and waking up in California."

"Wonderful gift from your father. Traveling coach on the regular train would have taken us nearly a day."

"I have the breakfast your mother packed." Ruth handed Heber a cloth bag.

Heber took out an orange, peeled it, and passed half to Ruth, then popped a sweet section into his mouth as they watched the Joshua trees and spiny cacti take form in the dawn. The San Bernardino Mountains provided a dramatic backdrop for what might have been the set of a Western movie.

Soon an oasis of green palms and white stucco buildings with roofs of bright orange tiles came into view. Heber and

Ruth pressed their noses against the train windows, gawking at Los Angeles' Spanish architecture. How different from the omnipresent red brick rectangles of Ogden.

"Look at that." Heber pointed to the clock tower rising into an azure sky as they entered Union Station. Colorful tile mosaics covered the arched entries, and palm trees lined the grounds. The train jerked to a stop, and they clambered down the steps onto the platform, lugging their suitcases with them.

"We'll go to the hotel in style," Heber announced and hailed a taxi. Ruth's father had booked them a room at the Alvarado Hotel. More of his generosity.

"Oh, Heber," Ruth cried when they pushed through the massive mahogany door to the lobby. "Everything is fabulous. I'm in heaven."

"You ain't seen nothing yet, baby." Heber drawled a fair imitation of Tom Mix. "We know how to treat our women out here in Gold Country."

They followed a bellhop to Room 102 where the young man set their suitcases on the tile floor. Heber gave him a nickel tip, turned the key in the door and pushed it open. With exaggerated gallantry, he lifted Ruth into his arms and carried her, giggling, across the threshold. He kissed her soundly, then set her down on the room's plush carpet, and together they reached into the hall to pull in their bags.

"Are you ready for Hollywood?" Heber asked. "Let's go." He grabbed Ruth's hand. The city of his dreams awaited him. They would walk every inch of it.

"Right now?" Ruth hesitated. "You couldn't have slept well in the club car. We could rest a little and, you know ..."

"How can I be tired? We're in Hollywood! We can catch the Red Car to Sunset Boulevard. Think of it! Sunset Boulevard!"

Disappointment flashed in Ruth's eyes, but she grabbed her handbag.

He yanked open the door, took her hand and hurried her through the hotel lobby to the bustling street. She obviously wanted her wedding night now, but finding his way around a new city—the city of his dreams—was too alluring and a lot easier than facing a test of his manhood. He'd gather the necessary courage from the streets of Hollywood.

People jammed the sidewalks. Cars and taxis honked. The warmth of the California sun seeped into Heber's skin, and he wished he'd worn a short-sleeved shirt. "Hollywood," he marveled aloud.

"Look," Ruth whispered, pointing to a gaunt, bearded man with fiery eyes who muttered to himself as he rushed down the street, a large cardboard envelope under his arm. "I'll bet he's a starving artist taking his work to show someone."

"My wife, the story-teller. You'll be penning his story later." Heber raised her hand to his lips, the word *wife* barely catching in his throat. "There's the Red Car. If we run, we can catch it."

At Hollywood Boulevard and Vine Street they got off the trolley and from there wandered the streets for the rest of the morning, stopping to buy doughnuts for a mid-morning snack. Theaters and clubs tantalized them with their advertisements of entertainment. Heber couldn't afford tickets to the fancy shows, but they walked through the courtyard at Grauman's Chinese Theater, studying the handprints pressed into the cement by dozens of movie stars. Heber half-expected to look over his shoulder and see Marlene Dietrich or Melvyn Douglas.

After grabbing a cheese sandwich at a corner café, they bought matinee tickets for gallery seats in a small movie house, and in the darkness inhaled the drama of Douglas

Fairbanks in *Modern Arabian Nights*. On the street again, Ruth gave him an enthusiastic hug. "Oh darling," she said, her eyes sparkling, "isn't this grand?"

Heber stretched his arms wide. "Indeed. Smell the hibiscus and the orange blossoms."

Back in their hotel room, after dinner at a tiny Mexican restaurant nearby, Heber paced while Ruth took a bath. No more procrastinating. Sex had been easy with Brian, but a woman? Through the wide, double-hung window he could see a full moon low in the sky. It was only nine o'clock. Life still pulsed out on the streets of LA.

I'm married now. I have to consider what Ruth wants, Heber reminded himself. Unpacking his new blue-striped pajamas ordered from the Sears catalog, he fingered a button and set them on top of the maple dresser.

Then he had an idea Ruth would love too. He knocked on the bathroom door. "Ruth? When you're dressed, I have a magical place to show you. Be prepared to be whisked away."

"Why now?" she murmured, words he doubted were meant for his ears. Then, "All right. Just a minute." The tremble in her voice surprised him. She sounded as nervous as he felt.

"My lady," he said with a bow when Ruth emerged, straightening her street clothes. "Follow me and we'll dance across rooftops."

"Fred and Ginger," she giggled, offering her hand.

He led her down the hall, through the door marked Exit, and up the emergency stairs that snaked to the roof. There, above the lights of the city, he put his left hand on her back, took her right hand in his, and they began to dance. Sounds of traffic in the street below came to them distantly. Everything was silver and shadow. Heber sang Gershwin's "I Love You Truly" as they glided around the roof.

I love you truly, truly dear
Life with its sorrow, life with its fear
Fades into dreams when I feel you are near
For I love you truly, truly dear.

She followed his lead smoothly, Fred and Ginger like she'd said, two stars dropped from a constellation, twirling and circling, spinning apart and then together.

Tonight, with God's help, he would lead her as easily in the dance that consummated their marriage. He drew her closer, abdomen pressed against abdomen, for a dip.

Ruth executed the move perfectly.

"Oh, sweetheart, you have such rhythm. I love dancing with you," she breathed afterward as they sped across the roof in the long, graceful steps of a fox trot. "Promise me we'll still go out dancing when we're old and gray."

"I promise," he said, as he lifted his arm and led her through a triple turn.

When they neared the fire escape, she looked toward the stairs.

Heber saw the hope in her eyes. "This will be the last round," he promised, and they danced the circumference of the rooftop. Then, stifling a sign, he followed Ruth down the stairs, glancing over his shoulder at the city lights.

When he opened the door to their room, the double bed, draped in white chenille, loomed against the opposite wall. At least they were both novices when it came to the opposite sex. Devout in the church, Ruth would have done nothing more than neck, even with the man she'd been engaged to. Sarah probably hadn't told her anything except 'things come naturally.' Any expectations would come from what she'd seen in films, not experienced in life.

Ruth ducked into the bathroom and came out minutes later in her nightgown, head bowed shyly. Through the nightgown he could see the shape of her *garments*. Despite them, her nipples lifted her nightgown in two hard points. Stirred, thank God, Heber went in the bathroom to change. As he removed his suit and shirt, he looked at himself in the mirror. Nothing less sexy than Mormon underwear. It was supposedly designed to remind wearers of their covenants made in the temple. Maybe what they really did was ensure that men and women stayed faithful to their mates. They'd be embarrassed for anyone else to see them.

Yet his *garments* hadn't deterred André or Brian. *Dear Lord,* Heber prayed, *turn my thoughts from men. Help me to be a good husband.*

When he came out of the bathroom wearing his pajamas, Ruth was perched on the edge of the bed, the covers neatly turned back. Heber sat beside her and put his hands on his knees where the creases of the packaging showed.

Ruth tentatively put her hand on his thigh.

"Good evening, Mrs. Averil." Heber's voice sounded scratchy, and he ran his tongue over his lips.

"Good evening, Mr. Averil." Ruth laughed. "We sound like *Pride and Prejudice.*"

He laughed too. "Ah, but you'll never be the shrew Mrs. Bennett was." He leaned in and kissed her. Not deep enough for his wedding night, but what he could do for the moment.

Ruth returned his kiss, and he sensed the hunger in her.

Her lips felt surprisingly good against his, soft and warm, and her breath smelled sweet, like fresh mint. He stood and took off his pajamas, then sat again. Ruth pulled her nightgown over her head. They looked quickly at each other in their *garments*, then away, then back. He touched her shoulder. "We have matching underwear."

Ruth giggled. "I guess we do."

Heber slowly slid his *garments* to his waist, revealing his narrow, almost hairless chest.

Ruth drew a breath and then reached out to touch his chest, exploring his nipples with her fingertips. Her touch excited him and he moved her hand to his lap, where happily he was hardening.

Usually so chatty, she waited quietly. The only sounds were of other hotel guests turning locks in doors or calling to each other, and of the city, cars, and trolleys, and somewhere a siren.

He stood and took his garments on down to his ankles and stepped out of them, then took both Ruth's hands and raised her to her feet. Carefully, enjoying the smooth suppleness of her skin, the curve of her waist and hip, he removed her *garments* too. Ruth instinctively crossed her arms over her chest, then dropped them to her sides. They faced each other, naked, both looking away, then back, blushing.

Heber lowered her to the bed and burrowed his face in her neck, inhaling her scent. She reached up and stroked his shoulders as he moved his hands to her chest, cupping her breasts. As he kissed one breast, then the other, his tongue playing with her nipples, she moaned with pleasure. Her body arched and he caught her mouth, her eyes, her neck in kisses.

Her breathing grew more rapid, as did his, her hands more urgent as she reached to pull him against her. Was it his heart pounding or hers?

When he entered her, she moaned again, this time a sound not of pleasure but pain.

He jumped and withdrew. "Did I hurt you?"

"I want this," she begged, tightening her arms around his back.

He entered her again and moved on her rhythmically until his excitement grew into frenzy and he spasmed, crying out, then relaxed.

Supporting himself with an elbow on both sides of her head, he kissed her again, more gently. "My love," he said. "You are so beautiful."

He withdrew and rolled to his side facing her, pushing damp hair from his forehead. A wave of relief washed over him. He could do it. Even like it. "Mmm," he said. "So nice." He touched her face. "Are you okay?"

"I feel so close to you."

"It will be better for you next time I think; not hurt as much. I love you, darling." He kissed her deeply.

They spooned; Ruth warm in his arms as she drifted off to sleep. There was pleasure in making love to her. A new closeness. Yet a nagging ache, like something was missing, crept into Heber, an ache he hadn't felt when he lay spent in Brian's bed. He pushed it aside. He could be a normal husband. He'd proven it.

He fell asleep, grateful to be living God's plan.

18

Los Angeles, California, June 1942

On their third evening in Los Angeles, the Alvarado desk clerk handed Heber a piece of paper. "A telephone message for you."

Ruth's eyes widened and she clutched Heber's arm. "Something happened to Papa."

"Not so fast." Heber read the welcome message, keeping it just out of Ruth's reach. "Looks like I have a little surprise for you." He led her to a leather couch in the lobby and took a seat beside her.

"Stop grinning and let me see." Ruth reached for the paper.

We've been invited to watch a variety show rehearsal. Right in the producer's home."

"Is that the message? What fun!"

"And good fortune." Heber had bumped into Ed Brooks two weeks before the wedding and shared their honeymoon plans. A happy coincidence because he and Ruth had both quit the troupe, Heber to return to school and Ruth to her teaching. Ed had told him about an acquaintance in Los Angeles who was a producer, given him the phone number, and assured him he'd send a letter of introduction. If the producer's troupe were appearing somewhere, Ed had said, perhaps Heber and Ruth could meet him after the show or at least wrangle some tickets. Once in LA, Heber had mustered his courage and called to inquire about performances. The producer's assistant had answered and said he'd relay the message. Now this welcome invitation.

"The rehearsal is Sunday." Heber drew a crumpled city map from his shirt pocket. "We planned to attend Sunday School at Wilshire Ward." He pointed to an X on the map. "Here's where the auditions are. We'd have time for a bite to eat after church and then catch a bus there."

"Should we be going on a Sunday?"

Heber frowned. Ruth could show shades of her mother's piety. Thankfully it didn't happen often. "I figure the Lord provided this opportunity."

"You're right," Ruth agreed and broke into a big smile. "Imagine, a real producer."

Sunday afternoon Heber rang the doorbell of a house that resembled a Spanish hacienda complete with balconies, bougainvillea, and tiled front steps. He hummed Cole Porter's "You're the Top," and tapped his foot nervously. Ruth waited beside him, dressed fashionably in a calf-length blue and white seersucker dress cinched at the waist and navy pumps. She shot him a quick smile and he winked back.

The most beautiful man Heber had ever seen opened the door. He couldn't have been more than twenty. With his dark eyes and olive skin, Heber guessed him to be Italian or Greek. His pink silk shirt and skin-tight pants showed a slender but well-muscled physique.

"May I help you?" he asked, looking from Heber to Ruth, then back to Heber.

"We're the Averil's," Heber stammered, his flush of excitement turning to discomfort. "We were invited to watch the rehearsal."

"Ah yes. I'm the one you spoke with when you called. Please come in." The man moved aside, his gaze still on Heber.

Unsure what to do, Heber took Ruth's hand and they stepped into the living room. His eyes widened at the elegance before him. All the furniture was the same rich mahogany as the furnishings of the Alvarado Hotel lobby. A couch and two overstuffed chairs covered in red and navy velvet filled the center of the room. A Victorian love seat stood against one wall with a host of gilded cupids above. On a side table a vase of gardenias and jasmine perfumed the air.

A round, balding man Heber judged to be about fifty glided into the room and immediately extended his hand. "Bernard Jones. Welcome to my home."

The producer was nothing like Heber had expected. Instead of an expertly tailored suit, he wore Levi's and a blue denim shirt, and instead of Wing Tips, cloth house slippers. His voice was husky and inviting, his handshake a little too clinging. Heber shifted his weight from one foot to the other.

"This is my assistant, Robert." Mr. Jones nodded at the young man. "Robert, please see to our troupe downstairs."

Robert bowed slightly to Heber and Ruth and withdrew.

"Please." Mr. Jones gestured toward the couch. Heber and Ruth exchanged a questioning look and took a seat.

"Ed has written about you. You were part of his troupe."

"Yes, we were."

Heber introduced Ruth, then himself. "We appreciate your invitation very much."

"We are always looking for new talent. It will be a pleasure to hear you read."

Heber and Ruth glanced at each other. The afternoon kept getting stranger and stranger. No one had mentioned an audition; they weren't prepared.

"I'm sorry. We must be confused," Heber stammered. "We expected to see a rehearsal."

"The idea of an audition only now came to me. Come along, we're rehearsing downstairs." The producer clapped his hands and stepped so close to them that Heber could smell his pungent cologne. "We have some very talented young people. You'll enjoy seeing them work." He turned. "Come this way."

"Should we stay?" Heber whispered to Ruth.

She shrugged and rose to follow the producer, looking as uncertain as he felt.

Heber stared at the walls of the stairwell as they descended thickly carpeted steps. At least two-dozen men his age flashed stage smiles from silver-framed photographs. They must be actors who had worked with Mr. Jones.

The finished basement was bare except for an upright piano where Robert sat on a round piano stool, legs crossed, jiggling one foot. He caught Heber's eye and winked. An ensemble of fifteen men and women gathered on folding chairs, chatting, and the producer motioned for Heber and Ruth to join them.

All these actors had the same eagerness in their eyes as Ed's troupe. Heber and Ruth leaned forward, watching them work. "They're really good," Ruth murmured.

Mr. Jones was a genuine producer after all, surprisingly nimble on his feet as he showed a group of dancers a new step. "You need to work on your toes," he told a woman, "on your toes, like this, so you'll be ready to lift yourself, to pirouette."

Next, he choreographed movements for a singer, and suggested a variation of her musical arrangement. "Raise your hands in triumph as you sing that line," he coached. "Hold that note. There. Yes, like that."

The performers applauded each other.

After more than an hour, he turned to Heber. "It's your turn now. Ed told me you're very good at dramatic readings."

Ruth smiled encouragement.

"Is there something you'd like me to read?" Heber asked.

"Surely you know something."

"You always like Shakespeare," Ruth suggested.

Heber had memorized a number of soliloquies for his theater classes. He stood, straightened his shoulders, and turned to face the troupe. This could be his first step in an acting career.

Which one should he recite? He tried to sort his thoughts, but his mind went blank.

"You'll be great," one of the women prompted.

"You have the right look," another added.

Reassured, he held out his arms to Ruth, then lifted them toward an imaginary moon.

But soft! What light through yonder window breaks?
It is the East, and Juliet is the sun!
Arise, fair sun, and kill the envious moon,
Who is already sick and pale with grief.
That thou her maid art far more fair than she.
Be not her maid, since she is envious.
Her vestal livery is but sick and green,
And none but fools do wear it. Cast it off.
It is my lady; O, it is my love!
O that she knew she were!

He finished Romeo's soliloquy to a burst of delighted applause.

"Splendid," the producer cried. "A Shakespearean actor."

Heber took his seat and squeezed Ruth's hand.

"You're good," said a woman on the other side of him. "Keep acting. And keep your love alive. You and your sweet wife."

"Well done. Good rehearsal. We'll continue Friday at 7:30," the producer announced.

"Mr. Jones, you haven't heard Ruth," Heber protested, the pleasure of the moment gone. "She's wonderful."

Ruth forced a smile that didn't reach her eyes.

"Another time, perhaps."

The woman who'd praised Heber's performance took Ruth's arm. "Never mind him. Tell me what you've done in Utah." The two fell into conversation as they headed up the stairs. Heber started up behind them.

The producer appeared at his side. "You gave a fine performance. Very fine. Would you consider joining our troupe?"

"Really?" Excitement washed over Heber. Could this be happening? His Hollywood career starting on his honeymoon? He couldn't wait to tell Ruth and looked up the stairs where she and her new friend had disappeared. Surely Mr. Jones would take her on, too, when he saw how good she was. There'd be a thousand details in arranging to stay. And the possibility of the Army calling him up might be stronger if he dropped out of school. But they could figure everything out.

"Such a handsome man we can always use. With your fine physique, I'm sure you will do the company credit." The producer put an arm around Heber's shoulders. "Come alone tomorrow night. We'll talk all about it."

Heber could feel the heat of the producer's body and smell his sickly-sweet aftershave. His excitement turned to dismay. He moved away, his hands angry fists at his sides, and bounded up the remaining stairs.

Robert stepped out of the shadows in the hallway. "Surely your wife will understand. It's your opportunity." He smiled, showing two rows of perfect teeth.

Mr. Jones was at Heber's side again.

Heber glowered at both men and strode to the living room where Ruth was chatting with several members of the troupe. Mumbling a general good-by, he took her arm and hurried her out the front door.

"What is it?" Ruth asked, trotting breathlessly beside him down the sidewalk.

Heber stopped and turned to face her. "He didn't care if I could act. We need to pack our bags and go home."

Her look said she guessed his meaning. "Don't worry, darling." She touched his arm. "That's all in the past."

The producer and his assistant hadn't had that impression. What made Ruth so sure?

19

Pasadena, California, February 1945

The next three years were filled with blessings as Heber and Ruth settled into marriage. When Heber was drafted, but rejected by the army for flat feet, he finished his degree. And breathed a sigh of relief that otherwise the army found him okay.

"Flat feet," he told Ruth after the physical examination. "They won't take me."

"Flat feet and you get to stay home with me," Ruth said with a smile. He hadn't told her his worry, but he thought he heard a stifled sigh of relief from her as well.

When he landed his first teaching job, teaching Freshman English at the local high school, they were thrilled. He and Ruth had great fun when he also took on directing a school play. Ruth became his co-producer, helping design the sets and making the costumes.

"Is there anything you can't do?" Heber had asked one day as he watched her hem a skirt for a dancer.

"I hope not," she murmured without looking up from her work.

Then he secured a teaching position at Pasadena City College. He and Ruth had loved southern California on their honeymoon and were delighted to return.

The only downside was that the long overnight train ride from Ogden made visits from family rare.

He missed Samuel who called now and then with his hearty support. He'd wanted to come the time Sarah visited for a few days but was unable to travel because of his heart condition. Grace came with Sarah instead. Without Samuel as mediator, Heber found the four-day visit long indeed.

He also missed his sisters and brothers dropping by for an occasional chat. And he missed spending an hour or two on the weekend with his mother in their big kitchen at the farmhouse. Happily, his mother and sisters often wrote him long, newsy letters.

If only they had a child. Heber adored his brothers and sisters, and family responsibilities might ensure that his problem was a thing of the past. In the temple he and Ruth had been commanded to raise a righteous posterity and he dutifully went to her at least once a week. Whenever a man caught his eye, he turned away, resolute. There wasn't a woman more valiant than Ruth. Surely God wouldn't punish her for Heber's past sins.

When they lived in Utah, Ruth had miscarried twice, both times when she was in her third month. Here in Pasadena in their neat four-room house they rented near the college, with a front yard that included a big willow tree and a back yard big enough for a rose garden, Ruth had carried a baby for five months. They had been awash with joy, but she miscarried again—a little boy. Although Heber had hoped for a girl, the loss of their son had pushed him to a very dark place.

When Ruth got pregnant a fourth time, and almost immediately got sick, a friend recommended her doctor. Trips to medical clinics with the last three pregnancies had been miserable for Ruth and always resulted in the same recommendation: bed rest. The value of a trip to yet another clinic seemed doubtful. But this new doctor had been willing to make a house call, so she agreed to see him.

Heber was teaching his Freshman Lit class the morning the doctor paid his first visit to their home. He found it an effort to focus on the class discussion of *Great Expectations*. How might the visit be going? He mustn't hope. This pregnancy was following the course of all the others.

When he got home, the stench of vomit in the room made him heartsick. Yet Ruth's eyes looked brighter than they had when he left for school. "What did the doctor say?" He tried for an upbeat tone of voice.

"He thinks he can help us."

"Does he have some kind of magic pill?" Heber didn't mean to sound sarcastic. He wasn't the one throwing up in a bedpan hour after hour. Still, he couldn't bear another disappointment.

"A shot every day. Diethylstilbestrol. It's helping other women." Ruth spoke with new energy.

Something more than bed rest? Heber felt a fluttering in his chest. Hope? He raised Ruth's hand to his lips, his eyes searching hers. "He really thinks that would help us keep the baby? I can give you shots." He'd read about Diethylstilbestrol. A miracle drug some claimed. "I could practice on oranges, like I did on the farm to give shots to the animals. Not that it's the same."

Ruth put her hand on his. "I know what you mean. Just think. Our own little boy."

"Or girl." Heber grinned. "How about twins? Two girls."

"You always want a girl. I thought men wanted sons."

"I'll love either one." He wasn't about to have that discussion again. He expected her to understand why he wanted daughters without him explaining, but she didn't seem to. Maybe she didn't know he'd overheard a conversation between Ruth and her mother during her first pregnancy. He'd been reading in the living room of their apartment in Salt Lake; Ruth and Sarah were talking in the bedroom. He didn't need to listen at a keyhole to hear them plain as day.

"Don't you wonder what kind of father he'll make?" Sarah had asked Ruth.

Ruth's answer had been typical of her. "He'll be a wonderful father. He's very good with children."

"You always defend him. What about his breeding? Or lack of it? Will he see that your children get the right advantages? Not to mention that other thing." And then, after an overly long pause, "We are praying for a girl." Heber had heard the bed creak. Then Sarah, "But never mind. You need your rest."

Sarah had brought dinner and two bags of groceries when she learned Ruth had started spotting and was confined to her bed, declaring she wanted to help. How was that kind of criticism helpful?

Ruth's sister Grace had come to South Ogden every day for a week after Ruth's second miscarriage, and she and Heber had been civil to each other. That was the most either of them could manage.

Happily, the church's Relief Society in Pasadena had pitched in with cheery visits and meals after Ruth's third miscarriage. Sarah had been in the hospital with pneumonia and he and Ruth had encouraged Grace to focus on caring for her mother rather than coming to Pasadena. Alice and Katy had come for a week and filled the house with their laughter and popular songs they found on the radio, "Sentimental Journey" and "Dream."

This pregnancy, when Ruth took to her bed, her mother had a winter cold that threatened to turn into a second bout of pneumonia, and Ruth once again assured Grace she was most needed in Ogden. Ida, the cheerful, bustling Relief

Society president, again came every few days with other sisters from the ward. They raised the windows to freshen the air, dusted, vacuumed, and filled the refrigerator with casseroles while they caught Ruth up on the ward news.

"You've been a godsend," Heber told Ida more than once when he got home from work to find her scurrying about preparing their evening meal. "I don't know how we'd get by without your help."

She would shrug aside his comment and give him an overview of Ruth's day, plus instructions for warming up whatever she'd put in the fridge for dinner. She'd asked what he liked best, but he was as grateful for a simple tuna casserole as a fancy lasagna.

He reflected often on how much the members of their ward had stepped in to help. He felt immensely blessed. Brian's words sometimes sprang up amid those reflections, like unwanted seeds planted in Heber's head. *'You actually believe a loving God would ask you to deny your most basic desire? Your most essential self?'* The church forbade him to love another man with his body and soul, the thing that felt natural to him. But he did love Ruth. He wanted a family with her. He'd do his best to follow the church's doctrine. Unlike Brian, he couldn't believe it was false.

Heber dragged his thoughts away from Brian's challenge of the faith. The most important thing now was his wife, not these nagging questions.

Ruth placed his hand on her belly. "Feel him? We'll finally need that maple rocker we bought. It will be a strain on you, all the extra work."

"I can take it." Somewhere under his hand there was a child growing. His child. Heber allowed himself to hope.

For three months Heber pierced Ruth's skin with cold steel needles. She winced and he hated to add to her misery, but something was working. As long as she lay quietly, she kept food down and the bleeding stopped. A miracle seemed at work in their lives, which to them was greater than the victory of the Allies in Europe.

After work and a swim at the YMCA to relax, Heber would prepare a quick supper, and on Ruth's good days they ate the meal together.

When she was up to it, they talked about ideas for her new novel. The first was selling well and her editor had requested a sequel. "One big difference in the second novel," Ruth explained, "is that the main character, who is polygamous, is a good guy. Not a villain like the last one."

"Showing both sides of the issue," Heber noted.

"He doesn't like the principle of polygamy but struggles to abide by the request of the general authorities to take a second and then a third wife. Imagine. He has to care for all his families equally. Figure out what to do when the wives squabble or the children fight. Find ways to feed them all. He faces some big challenges. I've based the characters in both novels on actual experiences of the early pioneers."

"I can imagine the financial challenge, not to mention trying to keep everyone happy."

"Exactly." Sick as she was, Ruth's eyes would twinkle as she shared her ideas. She knew Great Basin history the way Heber knew Shakespeare and could outline complete sections of the book in her head, telling wonderful stories to enrich each point. Heber sat on a stool next to her bed, enchanted by the tales she spun.

Or Ruth knitted socks while Heber rolled bandages for the war effort.

When she didn't feel well enough for conversation, Heber read to her — the *Pasadena Star News, The Saturday Evening Post*, a book recently published on baby care by Dr. Spock. Occasionally he read her one of his own poems penned at school as a respite from grading papers, love poems dedicated to her. They always brought a smile.

Here is my love –
My first, idealistic youth-love,
Pure in the emotions
Of an unknowing, untutored heart.
Take it and hoard it
Or take it and lose it,
But take it.
I give it to you.
There may be other loves burning with passion.
There may be loves as constant as time.
But this is my first love,
Idealistic, my youth-love.

He'd never tell her that when he wrote or read the poems his mind sometimes wandered back to his days with Brian. He wished it weren't so. Stress always brought out the worst in him. One day early in Ruth's sixth month, when he'd gone for a swim at the Y, lust at the sight of a handsome older man in the showers had consumed him. Without approaching the man, he'd slunk home to Ruth, disgusted with himself. His wife pregnant with his child, and so ill, and this is how he acted.

By her seventh month, Ruth could no longer turn over without throwing up. Heber would come home from work, wipe her face with a washcloth, and empty the reeking pan into the toilet. Then he'd sit with her, holding her hand and giving her sips of water. The shots continued. Day after day, week after week, she lay only on her back except to struggle to the bathroom. Rather than gaining weight with the pregnancy, she lost more each month. Her skin shone transparent over the bones in her hands, and her nightgowns hung loose everywhere except over her growing belly.

Sometimes Heber woke at night and crept from his twin bed to Ruth's to check on her, his neck a mass of knots. He felt so bad for Ruth. Everything ached, especially her left leg.

One afternoon Heber watched intently as Dr. Cobb, on one of his frequent home visits, gently ran his hand along the warm red streak on Ruth's calf. When she flinched under the light pressure, his forehead furrowed.

"I'll check on you again tomorrow," he said, and Heber read the concern in his face. In the hall, the doctor filled him in. "Phlebitis. Inflammation of a vein. It increases the risk of a blood clot, and a large clot traveling to her heart could be fatal."

Heber's knees nearly buckled. He steadied himself and choked out a question. "What if the clot's small?"

Dr. Cobb's forehead smoothed, and he placed a reassuring hand on Heber's shoulder. "She could handle that."

Heber returned to Ruth's side and found her smiling. "I can feel him moving. Here." Ruth put Heber's hand on her stomach.

He grinned. "It must be an elbow or knee. You're doing it, sweetheart." He offered her ice chips. "We're almost there."

Ruth's face clouded. "Sometimes I'm frightened. I feel like I'm floating above the bed."

"The baby will be here soon." He bent and kissed her forehead. "Anything sound good for dinner?"

"No, sorry."

"Maybe some Jello?" He was heading toward the kitchen when the phone rang.

It was Grace's husband, Ted. "I have bad news."

Heber held his breath.

"Samuel had another heart attack," Ted said flatly. "He was sitting in his chair reading the paper. He just slumped over."

"How is ..." Heber couldn't finish.

"He's gone."

The long-distance line crackled.

Heber gripped the heavy black phone, his eyes pooling. "Such a wonderful man. I loved him so."

"We all loved him. Listen, I have a lot of calls to make. Guess you can't come to the service. Love to Ruth." This was a simple duty call. How could the man be so cold?

Heber longed to pour his heart out to someone, but he wasn't sure if he should even tell Ruth. In her fragile condition, would she survive the news?

He hung up the phone and stood in the hallway staring at the oak flooring, running his fingers through his hair. He'd never lost anyone he loved. They had more than a month until Ruth's due date. Could he pretend, until then, that nothing had happened? *Dear God, what should I do?*

"Heber," Ruth called.

He rubbed his eyes on his shirtsleeve and went to the doorway.

She turned her face toward him. "What is it? Tell me."

What could he say but the truth? He moved to her side and put a gentle hand on her arm. "Your father had a heart attack."

"No! He's not—" Ruth bolted upright and immediately vomited into the pan beside her bed. Her face twisted into taut, gray angles. Heber braced her shoulders.

"I'm so sorry."

A low moan ripped from her. "Papa ..." She wretched again, and Heber handed her a handkerchief to wipe her mouth. "I need him." She cradled her belly as convulsive sobs shook her body.

Heber got a second handkerchief from a bureau drawer and dabbed at her tears. He needed him too. Samuel encouraged him and Ruth in all their endeavors. "I felt closer to him than my own father," he said softly.

Ruth grasped a corner of the bedspread and pressed it against her eyes, quieting herself. "Poor Mother. I can't go to her."

"Grace is there."

Ruth stared at the ceiling. After a few minutes she turned her face and searched Heber's eyes. "What will I do without him? Life was already so hard."

"Should I call Dr. Cobb? Get a sedative for you?" He turned to go to the phone.

"No!" Ruth grabbed his arm. "Don't leave me."

He bent and kissed the top of her head, then pulled a chair to her bedside and took her hand. Fear sat like a stone in his chest. He'd lost the only member of Ruth's family who seemed to care about him. Would he lose Ruth now, too? *Heavenly Father, be with Ruth,* he prayed. So far God had preserved her life and the baby's. Four more weeks.

The day after Samuel died Ruth began cramping and spotting. Heber rushed her to the hospital where the hospital staff placed her in a four-person room, far better than a twenty-bed open ward.

"How many little ones waiting at home?" a woman asked as Ruth settled onto her white iron bed.

"This will be our first," Heber answered for Ruth.

"I have three. Lands, they'll keep the neighbors busy while the doctor figures out this infection in my leg."

"Your first?" another patient chimed in. "When I had my first, my milk wouldn't come in, but Tom, he knew to bring me a beer. Wicked, I know, but that did it."

Heber read an appeal in Ruth's eyes. He drew the curtain around her bed and turned to the women. "My wife is too weak for conversation," he said quietly. "We've already lost three babies. She's trying to keep this one." Then, lowering his voice further, "And her father died yesterday."

The room fell silent. He'd probably shared more of their lives than Ruth would like, but now she could rest.

After that, the women became her guardians, never speaking to each other in more than a whisper and insisting that all visitors do the same. The nurses treated her with extra care. The spotting stopped after a few days. Her stomach finally settled, but she could eat little and continued to lose weight.

Dr. Cobb caught up with Heber outside Ruth's room when she'd been there a week. "I'm worried about Ruth. We should do a C-section. His manner, usually so gentle, was forceful, his eyebrows knit with concern.

"A cesarean?" Heber's breath caught in his throat. "When?"

"Tomorrow."

"Will she and the baby be all right? Is she strong enough for surgery?"

"It's the best option for Ruth. We shouldn't wait."

Ruth? Not the baby too? Heber reached for the wall to steady himself. They'd gone through so much and were so close.

Dr. Cobb took both his hands. "Although it might be early for the baby, Ruth has been so sick. If we wait any longer, we could lose them both."

His wife. And the child they longed for. He could almost feel the feather-light newborn cuddled in his arms. His chest

THE CHOICE OF MEN

constricted and he waited until he could breathe again. "I don't know if Ruth will go for it."

Dr. Cobb's face mirrored Heber's distress. In his frequent visits to their home, he'd become as much a close friend as a physician. "You need to convince her."

Oh God, oh God! Where are you? Heber rubbed his temples. "I'll do my best." He followed Dr. Cobb into Ruth's room and they drew the curtain around her bed, then took places across from each other at her bedside. Dr. Cobb repeated his strong recommendation for a C-section, his face and tone grave.

Ruth frowned. "Will my baby be all right?"

"The heartbeat is strong, but it's early. Ruth, you're so sick." Dr. Cobb's voice broke.

"If it's risking the baby, we have to wait." Her tone was unflinching.

Dr. Cobb took her hand and leaned in. "I'm very worried about you."

Heber touched her face. "At least consider it, darling."

"Let me rest, both of you. I lost my father. I can't lose my baby too." Ruth closed her eyes, her mouth set in a determined line.

The men retreated to the hall. "I can't force her to have the surgery. Maybe she'll change her mind." Dr. Cobb started to extend his hand in a farewell handshake, then hugged Heber instead. "Try to get some sleep," he said as they exited the hospital together.

That night Heber slept fitfully. His dreams were tormented fragments of newsreels about the war mixed with images of Brian and André dancing, jeering at him. Every time he awoke, he'd drop to his knees in prayer. *Save Ruth. Save the baby. Punish me for my sins, not them.*

The next morning, he counted the minutes until visiting hours. Had Ruth thought about what Dr. Cobb said and changed her mind? When he entered her room, Ruth's face was radiant.

"You're looking so much better, darling," he said, trying to hide his surprise as he bent and kissed her forehead.

"The baby and I will be all right," she said by way of greeting. "We can wait until the baby is full term. I saw Papa."

Both relief and apprehension filled him. "Your father?" he asked doubtfully. He drew up a chair and put his hand on her forehead. No fever. She couldn't be thinking clearly.

"I was standing on a bridge over a mountain stream. Aspens on both sides so close I could have reached out and touched them." She looked intently into his face. "Heber, he walked toward me just like when I was little, and we took picnics up Ogden Canyon. He took my arm, and we crossed the bridge, chatting."

He could picture the scene exactly.

"Papa promised I would have a healthy baby and live to raise it."

Heber tried to absorb her words. Both the baby and Ruth healthy. Dare he believe she'd had an actual vision like the prophets of old or the founders of the church? Ruth's faith was strong enough to have a vision if anyone could; to pull off a miracle. He'd give anything to have her standing by his side while he held their baby in his arms.

"Darling, don't look so worried. We'll both be fine. You'll see." Ruth smiled with such confidence he could only kiss her and try to share her faith.

Ruth stayed in the hospital, speaking very few words to anyone, conserving energy, clinging to life. Even news of Hiroshima and Nagasaki and Japan's surrender failed to alter her focus. When the baby's due date came and went and she didn't go into labor, she finally agreed to a C-section.

Heber wondered if he'd have either Ruth or a baby when it was over.

The morning of Ruth's caesarean, Heber paced back and forth on the gray linoleum of the waiting room, a cramped space where olive green couches and vinyl chairs lined two tan walls. He took no notice of his drab surroundings, instead glancing often at his watch. How long did a C-section take? If only he were back in Ogden where Katy and Alice could be with him. Ida had offered to come, but he figured he'd be terrible company and declined. Now he regretted it. Visiting with her would have eased the terrible tension.

Heavenly Father, protect my wife and baby, he prayed. Surely, He'd protect Ruth, even if Heber was on shaky grounds. What a magnificent woman. No one had ever loved him the way she did, praising everything he attempted, from pruning the magnolia tree in their back yard to editing the college's creative writing magazine. She'd never once brought up his prenuptial confession. And the way she'd faced her illness and confinement with the baby amazed him every day.

An older couple in the waiting room lit up one cigarette after another, the smoke filling the air and making him cough. What next, cigars?

A man who walked through the door looked so much like Brian that Heber's heart sputtered. Brian had always understood him so well. Heber turned to the school compositions he'd brought along, fighting an insane desire to go to the somehow-familiar stranger and tell him his frantic worries about his wife and child. He took out a red pencil, but the compositions might as well have been written in Hebrew for all the sense he could make of them. Soon he set them aside and paced some more. He picked up a copy of *Newsweek* to read, then tossed it back on the table and dug his fist into his palm.

A doctor came in with an expression on his lined face that announced bad news. Heber stiffened. But it wasn't Dr. Cobb. Not his news. He watched with guilty relief as the doctor walked to a man Heber's age. The man stood to greet the doctor, then fell into a chair at his words, put his head in his hands, and sobbed.

Dear God, let Ruth and the baby be all right. He wished he had Ruth's faith in her vision.

The passing minutes must be hours, the hours days. The ordeal of waiting would never end. Heber's stomach growled for food, but he ignored it. If he went to the cafeteria, he might miss Dr. Cobb.

He picked up another magazine.

"Heber?" Dr. Cobb's smile shouted the good news as he approached him. "Congratulations. You have a healthy daughter and Ruth is doing well in the recovery room."

"Thank God!" Heber dropped the magazine on a chair and grabbed the doctor in a bear hug. Ruth okay! They had a baby girl! Was it possible? Tears that he'd kept at bay streamed down his face.

He had to wait another hour before staff settled Ruth in a maternity ward and he could see her. At the nursery he stared through the plate glass window at the bassinette labeled Averil. His daughter was perfect. Wispy black hair covered her scalp. Her mouth formed a sweet rosebud. Long lashes whispered against her cheeks.

"Oh darling, you're a wonder. You did it!" he crowed when at last he was at Ruth's side. "A splendid baby girl."

Ruth smiled wanly. "I did so want a boy. My own Samuel."

"Wait 'til you see her." He kissed Ruth's forehead. "She's perfect. God answered our prayers."

20

Pasadena, California, August 1945

A pleasant breeze swirled around Heber as he crossed the parking lot to St. Luke's Hospital, his steps lighter now that Ruth's hellish confinement was over. They had a healthy baby as Samuel had promised, a girl at that. He'd never felt prouder than when he held her in his arms, her features tiny like a porcelain doll, and her skin as smooth as honey. Their own daughter, such a sweet little girl, born under the covenant, with them for eternity as promised in the temple ceremony. *All is well*, he marveled, the words of the hymn singing themselves in his head.

Anticipation quickened his steps down hall C to Ruth's room. She would be hugging their daughter to her breast when he entered. He'd take the baby from her when she'd finished nursing and press the tiny thing, oh so gently, to his heart.

Instead, he saw Ruth lying on her side, her arms empty.

In the bed next to her a woman cradled a fussing newborn. "It's all right, little thing," the mother cooed. In the bed across from her a woman nursed her infant. "There, there, my sweet. That's my darling boy."

His heart lurched. "Where's our baby?" he asked Ruth.

"In the nursery until I'm stronger. Why do I still feel so wretched?"

"You'll feel better soon. I called your mother and Grace and all my family. Everyone is celebrating. We've run the race and we're in the victor's circle."

Ruth had been nothing less than heroic. A shaft of light caught a glint of gold in her auburn hair, and Heber bent to kiss the crown of her head.

"Are we in the victor's circle?" Ruth shifted on the bed.

"Yes, my love, we are." Heber stroked her hair. "What about naming the baby Elizabeth? The name came to me when I was watching her through the nursery window."

"Elizabeth remembered of God. Like the mother of John the Baptist, blessed to have a child in her old age. Elizabeth should be my name."

Heber frowned. "Nah. Thirty-four isn't old."

"I feel a hundred and four." Ruth turned her face to the wall.

"I'll go to the nursery and let you get some rest. Be back this afternoon." Heber nodded to the other women and slipped out of the room.

At the nursery, he peered through a large window at five babies in hospital bassinets, their family names prominently displayed on blue or pink cards. When he didn't see Averil on any of them, he knocked hard on the window.

A nurse put an infant back in its bassinet and came out to him. "Where's my daughter?" he asked anxiously. "Baby Averil?"

"She's over there." The nurse pointed to an isolette against a far wall.

"Why is she in there, not with the others?" he asked, his voice shrill.

"The doctor can explain. Here he comes now." The nurse smiled reassuringly, but Heber couldn't stop shaking.

A man in a white coat with a stethoscope slung around his neck walked down the hall toward them. Heber rushed to him. "Is something wrong with my baby?" he blurted. "She's in the isolette."

The doctor gave him a reassuring pat on the shoulder. "She's fine. She lost a bit of weight at first so she's in the isolette for added warmth. It often happens. Her condition is stable."

Heber clasped his hands to steady them. "How long does she need to be in there?"

"A few days to a week. We'd like to raise her weight by half a pound."

"Can I hold her for a minute?"

"She's best off in the isolette for now. Don't worry. We're taking good care of her."

Not worry? Was the doctor mad? Did he have any idea what Heber and Ruth had been through?

Heber peered once more through the window. He didn't want Ruth to read the concern that must be written on his face, so he shuffled through the lobby to the parking lot instead of returning to her room. In the car, he laid his head against the steering wheel. What, exactly, did *stable* mean? Everything had seemed so rosy an hour ago.

He turned on the ignition and headed toward the Y. A brisk swim would calm his nerves.

Stripping off his clothes in the locker room, Heber headed for the empty pool, his mind buzzing with thoughts of Ruth and the baby. His wife so weak; their baby in an isolette. Lowering himself in the water he began his awkward laps, fueled by anger. Where was the justice? The mercy?

One lap. *At last a child. Such perfect fingers and toes. But so small.* Two laps. *Ruth should get stronger now. She looks so frail.* Three laps. *Elizabeth.*

Heber swam until his arms grew too heavy to lift through the water and his chest ached with exertion, his anger at God spent. As he started up the ladder onto the deck, an older man approached the pool, dazzling Heber with his mane of silver hair and startling blue eyes. Heber's body snapped into high alert and he covered himself with one hand, for the first time wishing the Y allowed swimsuits.

"Nice day for a swim," the man said.

Heber nodded, his pulse quickening, his mind slowing.

"Pool temperature's perfect."

"Yes ... yes, it is," Heber stuttered. He didn't need temptation now when Ruth and Elizabeth awaited his return to the hospital.

The man's eyes roved down to Heber's hand and back to his face. "You finished with your swim?"

"Headed for the showers." He'd make it a quick shower.

"A shower might sound better than a swim." A slow, inviting smile spread across the man's face.

Heber's body burned a joyful response to the overture, followed by guilt so strong it entirely swept away the joy. He'd been faithful to Ruth for a long time. Why would he weaken now when he at last had an eternal family? His body paid no heed to his conscience as he walked with the man through the reek of chlorine and locker-room sweat. The man turned on the shower and rotated slowly beneath the spray of water, soaping his hair, his face, each arm, each leg, his torso, his genitals. His sun-bronzed skin shone with vitality. Heber compared the man's appearance to Ruth's pallor and, ashamed, dropped his eyes to the concrete floor.

"Feels good," the man said, vigorously scrubbing his armpits, then his fully erect member.

Desire welled anew in Heber as he first watched, then joined the man in the community shower. He uttered a prayer to God for strength, but in the next moment moved his hands down to soap his own hardness. Then, with a nod, he and the man reached in perfect accord to stroke each other. Heber climaxed within seconds. Blessed relief. The kind of relief he hadn't experienced since Brian.

Brian. Who might he be with now?

Relief morphed into self-loathing. "Thanks," he mumbled and turned from the man to get his clothes and dress.

"Any time," the man said with the same slow smile. "I'll be watching for you."

Bile writhed in Heber's stomach as he drove to St. Luke's, and he choked back the bitter taste. How low could he get? As he entered the hospital he wondered if his face would betray him. He'd go to Elizabeth first. Reassure himself she was all right. Then go see Ruth.

"Mr. Averil!" The receptionist at the information counter jumped from her chair.

Fear seized him. "Our baby?"

"Your wife. We've been calling your home."

"Ruth?"

"Dr. Cobb is with her."

He took the stairs two at a time and tore down the hall to Ruth's room. When he stepped inside and pulled back the curtain that had been drawn around Ruth's bed, he saw Dr. Cobb and a nurse at her side. Ruth panted inside a clear plastic oxygen tent, her face ashen and tense with pain.

"Heber." She turned her face toward him.

Dr. Cobb motioned him into the hall. "What I feared. She's developed a blood clot and it's broken loose."

Good God. Heber remembered Dr. Cobb's concern about a pulmonary embolism during Ruth's pregnancy. How a clot could be life threatening. The hallway began to blur, and he reached out to the wall for support. Their hell was supposed to be over. "What can you do?" he managed to ask.

"Oxygen. Heparin in the IV. Morphine. That's our arsenal against a thrombus. Now we wait."

Heber automatically began to pray, but anger bubbled up in his chest. *Enough! Punish me for my iniquities, not Ruth!*

Dr. Cobb put a hand on his shoulder. "Go sit with her. I'll be with you as soon as I check on another patient."

The anger drained from Heber. He reentered the room and sank onto a chair by Ruth's bed. "I'm here now, darling." Her hand lay outside the tent and he lifted it to his lips. "I won't leave your side again."

"I need you." She fought for breath, her words gasps.

Dr. Cobb returned and put his stethoscope to her chest, then took a seat across from Heber. Long hours passed. Ruth gripped Heber's fingers until they tingled and ached. Nurses came in the room checking her vital signs: blood pressure, heart rate, respiratory rate, temperature. Dr. Cobb listened to her heart every half hour.

"My lungs are on fire!" she sobbed.

"Sweetheart, I'm here."

"My father promised." Ruth forced out the words. "I'll live to raise our baby."

Her hand was as pale as the bedding. Day faded into night.

Dr. Cobb made a final hospital round, then settled back on his chair.

"Thanks for being here." Heber managed a smile.

"I've been with you since the beginning."

A half hour passed. Dr. Cobb checked her heart again. "Your heartbeat is strong. I know you're in pain, but we can't increase the morphine. I wish there were more we could do." And to Heber, in a whisper, "The next hours will be critical."

They waited, not talking, not reading, exchanging anxious glances. Time moved in punishing slow motion.

Ruth moaned, and gasped for breath, over and over, as though she were drowning. Suddenly her body jerked and was still. All color drained from her skin.

Heber jumped to his feet and leaned in. His precious Ruth!

Dr. Cobb grabbed her wrist and searched for a pulse, then leaned close to her chest, placing his stethoscope over her heart.

A nurse approached the bedside ready to assist.

Heber heard his own heart pounding in his chest. He fixed his eyes on his beloved wife's face, willing her to live, pleading with God.

Somewhere down the hall a patient rang for assistance. Heber startled at the shrill sound.

He blinked, caught his breath, blinked again. Was the color coming back into Ruth's face?

Dr. Cobb straightened and took Ruth's wrist again. "She's still with us!" He let out a rush of breath, wiping his forehead with his sleeve.

Heber choked back tears of relief. "Darling, I thought we'd lost you."

Ruth opened her eyes and looked around the room as if confused. "Papa was with me." She strained to speak. "The pain in my chest ... is gone. Like he promised."

Heber closed his eyes and bowed his head. *Thank you, God.*

21

Pasadena, California, March 1949

Always so many dishes! Heber ran a sudsy plate under hot water. If Elizabeth would quit dawdling with her bowl of oatmeal, he could finish up KP duty and be off to the yard work he enjoyed. Made with brown sugar and cinnamon, the oatmeal was sugary sweet the way she liked it, yet she was still taking all day to eat.

Saturdays had become so jam-packed. Meeting the demands of a four-year-old on top of keeping up the house and yard while Ruth nursed her latest flare up of phlebitis was a lot to add to a long week at the college.

He felt plenty bad for Ruth. The phlebitis had changed her life. Every day she had to spend at least an hour with her leg higher than her heart to avoid another thrombus, and she could no longer take the long walks with Heber they both enjoyed. Days like today she was down for most of the day because of the pain, redness and swelling.

It was all wearing. There was never a minute for the things that sustained him: a swim at the Y, a leisurely stroll through the neighborhood or downtown Pasadena, his own writing. Even "Henrietta's Pig Pen," a story he was writing for Elizabeth to help her learn about cleaning her room, never got more than a few minutes in a day, if that. He'd had fun jotting down the first half, but by the time he had a chance to finish the story, Elizabeth would likely be grown with an entire house of her own to clean.

When tensions mounted, he was tempted to hide in a closet and soothe himself, although he seldom did. The sexual relief lasted seconds while his shame about the men in his fantasies lasted days.

In the first months after Elizabeth's birth, he and Ruth had enjoyed a new intimacy. He thanked God every day for sparing her life and Elizabeth's and doggedly kept his promise to the Lord. Then, despite his abiding appreciation and love for his family, he began to notice the cleft in the milkman's chin and the muscled pecs under the tight t-shirt of a returned servicemen attending college under the GI bill. He was as disgusted with himself as the Lord must be.

Running the dishrag around the inside of a glass, Heber looked out the window above the sink. He'd mow the lawn first. That would lift his spirits. There was so much to enjoy here at home. In the back yard, a peach tree blossomed profusely, and the camellia bushes and pink magnolia burst with flowers. The lavender he'd planted under their bedroom window when Ruth was pregnant with Elizabeth offered up its calming fragrance. In the living room, a large picture window framed the front lawn, flowerbeds, and foothills of the San Gabriel Mountains.

"Hurry, Lizzy," he prodded.

"Feed me, Daddy," Elizabeth begged. "Play 'truck in the tunnel.'"

"Silly girl. We played that when you were a baby. You'll be four soon."

Heber dried the last glass and put it in the cupboard. He'd agreed to have lunch with Dorothy Wright, his department chair at the college. She and her husband had become good friends to Ruth and Heber, sharing an occasional Sunday dinner, a film at the Colorado Theater, or a play at the Pasadena Playhouse. He especially enjoyed the plays since he and Ruth might not have budgeted for them otherwise. A part of him was still enchanted with the idea of being an actor one day. Dorothy and her husband were as kind and generous as anyone he'd ever met. He was happy to provide the listening ear Dorothy needed when she got riled up about politics at the college. Still, the visits were one more demand on his time and energy.

Elizabeth scooped up a big spoonful of oatmeal and shoved most of it in her mouth, then lumped the rest into patterns in her bowl.

"I said hurry." He flinched at the sharpness of his tone.

"Can I have a piggy-back ride outside?" Elizabeth was as cheerful as ever.

Heber marshaled his tattered patience. "When you've finished."

"All done." She pushed her bowl away and flashed her sunny smile that showed most of her baby teeth.

"We'll call it good." He took her bowl, scraped a blob of oatmeal into the wastebasket, washed the bowl and set it in the dish drainer, then helped Elizabeth wash her hands.

"Goodie," Elizabeth sang out as he bent over, and she climbed onto his back. "Gallop, Daddy," she ordered, wrapping her arms around his neck and her legs around his waist.

She bumped him at every step, both sweet and annoying, as they trotted toward the garage.

"You're getting too heavy for this horse to gallop." Heber stopped to catch his breath.

"Look, Daddy, the trees have flowers too." Elizabeth plucked a blossom from the Magnolia tree, and its lemony fragrance filled his nostrils.

He patted her bare leg. "Good job noticing. Ready to mow the lawn?"

"Yes."

Heber trotted on to the garage. "Time to get off." He stooped on the side lawn and Elizabeth slid off. Her jumper scooched up and he knelt on one knee to smooth it, then yanked up her socks that had slipped down into her sneakers. Where had the baby gone that he had cradled in the crook of his arm? How fragile she had been when they first brought her home, this miraculous child of his own flesh. Now a sprinkle of freckles danced across her nose, and her bobbed hair shone thick and wavy like his. She could play in the yard all day without tiring.

She crouched to study the grass. She might have seen a butterfly or wanted to find a four-leaf clover. Sitting on his heels beside her, he gave her a hug. "Sorry I was a grouch at breakfast."

She looked at him solemnly. "Daddy, when I grow up will you marry me?"

Heber tried to match her serious expression, but a chuckle escaped him. "What about Mommy?"

"Oh, she'll be old like Grandma by then."

"I'll get old too, and you'll want to marry someone else. But thanks for asking."

Heber straightened and went to the garage for the push mower.

Breathing in the fresh smell of cut grass, he mowed up one row and down the next, his mind quiet for a change, while Elizabeth pranced and danced around him. She added joy to every day. And Ruth was a good companion. His best friend, still, after seven years of marriage. His little family was the dearest thing in the world to him. Oddly, on some days an overwhelming emptiness would take over anyway, and he'd ache for all the emotions he'd felt those many years ago with

Brian. Despite those moments, he'd rather live with conflicted feelings than be without his wife and child. He'd been more short-tempered with both Elizabeth and Ruth lately. He'd have to do better.

Finished with the lawn, Heber returned the mower to the garage and picked up a pair of clippers. Pruning the camellia near the front door, he cut three late blooms for the nightstand beside Ruth's bed. As he ran water in a vase for the flowers, he checked his watch. Barely time to make his lunch date with Dorothy. He'd have to finish up in the yard afterward.

Elizabeth followed him into the house. "Water," she ordered.

"Say please."

"Please, Daddy."

Heber handed her a cup of water. "Now play outside while I get lunch ready. Don't leave the yard."

Elizabeth gulped down the water. As she skipped on out, he spread mayonnaise on four slices of bread and added lettuce and cheese. Time Elizabeth learned to like lettuce.

He looked out the window but didn't see her. She must be playing around front under the willow tree. He wished he'd asked her to play in the back yard, so she wasn't near the street alone.

He put the sandwiches on plates, poured two glasses of milk, and arranged it all on a tray. Adding the vase of camellias in the center, he carried the tray to the bedroom.

"Thank you, dear. I hate being such a bother. Why don't you and Lizzy join me here for a sort of picnic?" Ruth suggested.

"I have that meeting with Dorothy, but I'll bring Lizzy in. She'll be company for you while I'm gone."

"Then bring us lots of books to read. It's too bad Dorothy's taking your Saturday for school affairs."

"I don't mind. Weekdays get so hectic at the college." Heber set the tray on her nightstand. "She probably needs to get something off her chest."

Ruth sighed. "We miss you is all. You're gone so much."

He stifled a retort. He gave every waking minute outside work to this family.

Returning to the kitchen, he called out the back door. "Lizzy, time to come in." He waited a full minute for a response, then stepped outside. Dorothy would be waiting for him. "Lizzy," he called again. She loved to hide, then jump out and surprise him. Or she was indeed playing in front.

Heber walked around the side of the house. "Lizzy, no more games. I'm in a hurry."

Still no answer. It wasn't like her to disobey.

He checked his watch, then went to the street and looked both directions, wishing for the millionth time their street had sidewalks. He couldn't see her anywhere. The muscles in his arms and neck stiffened with anger and worry. She had strict instructions not to step off the property alone. "Lizzy! Elizabeth!" he shouted, anger turning to panic. Where on earth could she be? Had something happened to her?

"Daddy." He heard her voice from down the street before he saw her. "Daddy, I'm coming."

Elizabeth, still three houses away, bounced toward him, one foot in the gutter and the other on the curb. "I followed a kitty," she called. "He was black and white and—"

Relief swept through Heber, followed by rage. "I told you not to leave the yard," he bellowed. "What if a car had come?"

"But the kitty—"

"You could have been killed! You have to obey me!" Grabbing a willow switch from the pile of clippings, Heber whipped it against her legs.

"Daddy!" Elizabeth shrieked and collapsed on the grass, wailing. Red welts rose on her tender skin.

Heber stared at her in horror. His precious daughter. What kind of madman was he? He flung the switch away, dropped to his knees, and hugged Elizabeth against his chest, rocking her back and forth. Memories of his own father pulling his belt from his pants swam before his eyes as her screams quieted into sobs. He'd sworn to himself that he'd never be like him.

"Daddy won't ever hit you again, I promise." Lifting her still crying, he carried her into the house. Ruth limped down the hall toward them.

Elizabeth wriggled from Heber's arms and ran to Ruth, throwing her arms around Ruth's waist. "Daddy hit me," she whimpered.

Ruth glared at Heber as she stroked Elizabeth's hair. "Let me see."

"What's happening to you?" she hissed at Heber when she saw the reddened stripes on Elizabeth's legs. She gathered her child into her arms and carried her to the bedroom, Elizabeth burrowing into Ruth's neck, sniffling.

Heber swiped at his own tear-filled eyes as he shuffled to the kitchen and put the mayonnaise, cheese and lettuce back in the refrigerator. How could he have lost his temper like that? Especially with Elizabeth, so small and innocent. He reeled with the possibility that he was becoming his father after all and sank onto a kitchen chair. He didn't even have the responsibilities of a large family and the impossible financial burdens that his father had born.

As he returned to the bedroom, he kept his face averted from Ruth's accusing eyes. "Can I get you something else?" he asked, his voice choked with strangled sobs.

"Aspirin would be nice. I seem to be getting a migraine."

Which he'd obviously caused. When he brought the aspirin, Elizabeth was sitting beside Ruth, turning the pages of *A Child's Garden of Verses*.

"Daddy's sorry," he said, sinking down by the bed and reaching out to hug her thin shoulders. She scooted even closer to Ruth, her eyes never leaving the book.

"Leave us be." Ruth's voice was hard.

He slunk to the car and looked in disgust at his hands trembling on the steering wheel like those of a palsied old man. What might these hands do next? He had to hang on. Spring break would be here in two short weeks. He needed to relax before he went completely to pieces.

22

Pasadena, California, March 1949

Heber sat back in the booth of Bob's Coffee Shop, stunned. Dorothy had spoken quietly, but he'd heard every word.

"Dr. Brunswick wants you out. And he has the Dean's ear."

Heber had never imagined anything like this bombshell when they met for lunch.

"You've been with us five years and you still haven't been granted tenure," Dorothy continued. "I've done my best to placate him, but he's furious about the winners of the short story contest. He's on the warpath."

Heber took a sip of root beer, fighting down a wave of panic. This day kept getting worse. Wasn't what he'd just done to his own daughter enough?

"He'd oust me because I didn't vote for his darlings? They weren't the best writers."

Dorothy's brow creased in a frown. "You've crossed him two years in a row. He's vice president of the college, with a special interest in the English department. He wields a big stick."

"It's all politics," Heber countered, wadding his napkin.

"Politics matter, Heber. Dr. Brunswick is the one who got local bookstores to give prizes to the winners. The contest is his pet project, and your votes countered his wishes."

Heber groaned. Why should the selection of winners be based on the wishes of some prejudiced VIP? Still, if his job was in jeopardy, he'd have to do something.

Dorothy's frown deepened. She took a sip of her soda, set her glass down, and cleared her throat. "It's more than the short story contest. I'm worried about you."

The concern in her voice shook him more than her words. "Worried? About what?" he managed to ask. He didn't tell her he was worried too. How could he have struck his little girl?

Dorothy put a hand on his arm. "It's your temper, my friend. The way you flare up sometimes."

Heber took a bite of his hamburger, trying to calm himself. She was right. He felt like a pressure cooker about to blow. But there'd never been an incident with his students; there couldn't be any reports against him. Admittedly, once or twice in faculty meetings he'd lost it. He detested some pieces of the curriculum for Freshman English and some of the recommended readings for World Lit. Dr. Brunswick had probably heard about the time he hurled a book across the room in frustration.

"Hey there, Professor Averil." A lanky young man stopped at their table. "Sorry to interrupt."

Students like this gangly, pimply boy, perpetually excited about literature and creative writing, were a teacher's greatest joy. "Hello, Jeff. What's up?" Heber asked, grateful for the intrusion.

"You asked for volunteers to help put out a creative writing magazine," Jeff said. "I'd like to be on the staff."

"Wonderful. You're my first recruit. My wife and I talked about a gathering in our home this Friday evening." Ruth had offered to provide cake or cookies for it. By then she'd be on her feet again and, with luck, would have forgiven him for this morning's outburst.

Jeff's smile faded. "Gee, Professor Averil, Friday evening's the football game and dance."

When he attended Weber College, Heber had often felt lonely, despite his focus on his studies and his active family life. He didn't seem to fit in with the social life on campus, having no desire to dance with the shy girls his few buddies tried to push on him and finding the male camaraderie at the games intimidating. He wouldn't want that for Jeff. "A week from Monday better?" Heber asked.

"Sure, that would be swell. Thanks."

"If you have a girl, bring her along, or anybody else who might be interested. We need all the help we can get."

"I'll do that." Jeff grinned, shook Heber's hand, and left the table.

"You have such good rapport with your students," Dorothy said. "I so enjoy sitting in on your classes. It's like watching a show complete with quotes from some of lit's greatest works."

"It's the ham in me. I always wanted to be an actor."

"So you've said. You'd have been a good one. There has to be a way to keep you at the college." She put her hand over Heber's. "For starters, behave at faculty meetings."

"I promise."

Dorothy sat back and looked intently in his face. "What's really going on? Can you tell me? Are you unhappy here?"

"At the college? Heavens, no! I love PCC." Heber took another bite of his burger but nearly gagged swallowing it. He pushed the plate away and put his hands to his forehead, massaging his temples, then looked up ruefully. "Except maybe Dr. Brunswick."

"Something at home perhaps? I don't mean to pry. You seem fine when you and Ruth go out with us."

Heber could still hear the thwack of the willow switch against Elizabeth's legs. He was snapping, all right. It was the never-ending student compositions, Ruth's phlebitis, his new calling as Sunday School superintendent, the expenses of a family. And always, always, the turning away from men. What could he do about any of those things? How much could he tell Dorothy without risking his job?

He sighed. "To be honest, finances are a worry. Ruth's eager to buy a house before Lizzy starts school. I need that tenure."

"I'll put you on the scholarship committee. They want someone from our department. There might be another committee or two you could volunteer for." It was Dorothy's turn to sigh. "Make yourself indispensable. And soon."

"I'll be a new man on Monday." Heber put some quarters on the table to pay for his lunch. "That's a promise."

"Lunch is on me." Dorothy pushed his change back to him.

"Thanks. Thanks for everything." He forced a smile.

Once outside the coffee shop, Heber checked his watch. Enough time for a walk to quiet his jangled nerves. Yard work could wait another day. He walked west along Colorado Boulevard toward downtown Pasadena, barely glancing in the windows of Grassmuck's music store, a stationery store, and Coronet's five and dime. Was his future at PCC in as much jeopardy as Dorothy claimed? Her concerns about his temper swirled in his head, mixed with an image of Elizabeth's frightened eyes. Frightened of *him*.

He turned north on El Molino and west again along Garfield, taking little notice of the stately magnolias and elms that usually brought him such pleasure. It wasn't until he reached Pasadena's City Hall with its sweep of green lawns, colorful flowerbeds, and graceful, arching trees that he began to relax. He'd always admired the domed city hall and its meticulous landscaping. He bent to smell a fully opened rose, yellow with the faintest tinge of pale pink fluting its edges.

"The Peace Rose. Exquisite, isn't it?" The sonorous voice behind him startled Heber. Turning, he looked into the sun-tanned face of a stocky man about his age dressed in jeans and a white t-shirt.

"The Peace Rose?" Heber noted the man's generous smile that started in his eyes and enveloped his entire face.

The man nodded. "It might be my favorite. Or Mr. Lincoln." The man pointed to a deep red rose, also fully opened. "That one has such a rich fragrance, doesn't it?"

Heber leaned in and filled his nostrils with the rose's perfume, then extended his hand to the man. "Heber Averil."

"Eric Hartman." Eric's hand was rough with calluses, but welcoming. "I'm a gardener, and these grounds are some of my favorites. Haven't seen you around."

"We must have just missed each other," Heber said. Pure chance that he hadn't encountered this man before. He'd remember him.

"Happy to share some of my treasures if you like," Eric invited. "Lovely day for a stroll."

And there it was. The old answer to alleviating his tensions. He hadn't had male companionship in a long time.

They fell into step, Heber slowing to match the shorter man's strides, and chatted about gardening for half an hour as they walked among the flowerbeds. He didn't have enough energy in this damnable day to listen to the warnings of his conscience.

"Say," Eric said after a while, "care to meander a bit downtown?"

Heber looked at the sun, still well above the foothills to the west. He could steal another hour before heading home to make dinner. Eric was a great conversationalist, and he was enjoying himself. He wouldn't let anything happen; just savor the welcome diversion from the strains of the day. "I don't have long, but I'd like to."

They seemed to be heading toward Nash's department store. After several blocks Eric led the way to a short flight of broad cement steps that led down to a public restroom. An acrid odor rose from the dark, stone doorway. Heber hadn't been here before but could guess why Eric had brought him. So much for conversation. He stopped on the first step. He didn't need more complications in his life, already a poor enough excuse of a father and husband.

"You wanna?" Eric asked. "Your eyes have been saying yes since we met." He put his hand on Heber's shoulder.

The touch burned away any resistance. Heber stiffened against his *garments*. "Yeah." He followed Eric into a dimly lit, graffiti-covered room lined with a row of urinals, two sinks, and four stalls. Eric grinned at him and then went into a stall. As if he'd done it all his life, Heber went into the neighboring stall and immediately found the glory hole through which Eric could reach him.

Found, too, a moment of ecstasy.

Steeped with pleasure, he exited the stall, fumbling with the buttons of his pants. Eric washed his hands at a sink, a bare bulb lighting his thinning hair. For a few seconds more Heber was filled with a rare sense of well-being. Then revulsion swept over him. The stench of the restroom grew unbearable, and he hurried toward the stairs and the light above.

Eric followed him outside. "What? Should I apologize?"

"No. I don't know." Heber studied the cement beneath his feet.

"You want to talk?" Eric pointed to a park bench.

Heber's legs threatened to give out. A public bathroom stall! He'd sunk far below the Y even. He dropped onto one end of the bench and sat slumped and silent, his arms folded across his chest. Eric sat a generous space away, watching him. "I'm married, with a family," Heber finally said.

"Lots of men are. The restrooms lack charm, but they do offer privacy."

"I'm a teacher."

"Plenty of teachers down there. Doctors and lawyers too, if that makes you feel any better."

It didn't. "I'm Mormon."

"Yep. Plenty of Mormons too. You can't go to bars, so where else do you meet?"

Heber lifted his head. "I'm still scum."

"Hey, no offense intended. I was trying to help you feel better. Say the word and I'm gone."

Heber thought about Ruth, waiting for his return. What would she do if she knew he had succumbed to temptation again? And in this disgusting place? Church leaders at the highest level were condemning same-sex attraction more openly all the time. What was it like for Ruth hearing their exhortations? God knew she didn't deserve the likes of him. And speaking of God, what was He thinking creating in Heber an attraction to men so strong he'd forsake his wife and child, if only for a moment?

Heber had tried to satisfy his needs with his wife. Gone to her bed several times a month. Once he'd mentioned oral sex, but she wrinkled her face with revulsion. It was total maleness he craved anyway. Fulfilling sex but more than that. He craved the company of someone who knew the torment he experienced trying to fit into a world of normal men.

Heber stole a glance at this man who had brought him the most pleasure he'd experienced since Brian, putrid setting and all. A more intense, more complete pleasure than he could experience with Ruth. He shifted uneasily on the park bench; he'd worked so hard to change.

Eric took a ballpoint pen and scrap of paper from his shirt pocket and scribbled something on it. "Here's my phone number if you want to get together. Or you can drop it in the trash."

Heber took the paper and stared at it. "Thanks," he mumbled and rose to leave. When he came to a trashcan on the street his hand hovered above it. Then he shoved the paper in his pocket.

23

Pasadena, California, April 1949

The Pasadena Rose Bowl provided a stunning setting for an Easter sunrise service. From the bleachers Heber could see the distant chaparral of sumac, chamise, sage and California lilac. What a scene. Live oak, bay laurel, sycamore and willow marched up the mountain ridges. The sky, turning from soft pinks to startling reds, cast craggy shadows on the San Gabriel Mountains to the north and San Rafael Hills to the west.

"Isn't it beautiful?" Heber whispered to Eric, sitting to his left, and immediately regretted it. He should have asked Ruth. How could he have the audacity to be sitting on these bleachers, his family on one side and Eric on the other? What could be more despicable than bringing his new friend to a church service with his wife?

Yet in the two months they'd been seeing each other, Eric had become as essential to Heber as the air he breathed, and he'd begun spinning a fantasy that Ruth would also like the genial, well-read man. Once Ruth and Eric got to know each other, they could all be great friends. Maybe even like family. Ruth had written novels with polygamous themes involving both heroes and villains. Her grandfather had two wives.

This wasn't the same, he knew. But wasn't it kind of the same? Another kind of triangle?

As preposterous as it sounded, what were his options? Eric quieted the voice in Heber's head that so often berated him for being fundamentally defective. The voice that twisted him into a volatile monster at home and work. Since meeting Eric, Heber was more patient and loving with Elizabeth, making time every evening to play a game with her or read her a book. He came to Ruth's bed more often, although his fantasies of Eric and the tag-along guilt of that affair came too. At the last faculty meeting, he'd calmly presented a coherent argument against a proposed textbook adoption instead of another angry book-chucking. He'd joined two committees at the college and had several pleasant conversations with Dr. Brunswick about books they both admired. The dean had assured him tenure would be his by year's end.

In the beginning he met Eric in the gardens of City Hall, and they walked and talked for most of an hour, then went back to the public restroom, disgusting though the place was. Then one day Eric took him to his cottage on the estate where he worked in South Pasadena. What a different world! They followed a path lined with poppies and marigolds to the cottage where wisteria cascaded down whitewashed stone walls, filling the air with its sweet perfume. A mix of spring flowers formed a jumble of color along its front, and camellia bushes bloomed abundantly at both sides of the front door. "What an enchanting place," Heber had exclaimed. "Like an English estate."

The cottage was as charming inside as out, with a high, timbered ceiling and large, four-paned windows that let in a flood of light and provided a generous view of the gardens. A vase of fresh daffodils and tulips graced the pickled pine table. He couldn't remember anything bringing him as much pleasure as the hours spent there with Eric.

Heber shifted on the Rose Bowl's stadium bench, Brian's words coming to mind, as they did now and then: '*You have to live true to yourself or you hurt not only you, you hurt everyone who cares about you.*' When he was true to himself, he hurt Ruth. He loved her dearly and would give everything he owned for it to be her touch that quieted his nerves. But it was Eric's that made it possible for him to meet his responsibilities as a husband, father, and provider.

He and Eric sat far enough from each other on the bleachers that their shoulders didn't touch, but he could still feel the man's energy flowing in his direction. Could anyone else read the terrible disappointment in Ruth's face that she tried to hide with a tight smile? She and Heber had never talked about his struggle since he'd confessed to her before they married, and she had dismissed her mother's and sister's concerns. But he couldn't expect this smart woman to believe his tale about Eric. "I met a man out walking last month," he'd said to her. "His family is in Maine and he's homesick and lonely. Can we invite him to join us for the Easter service?"

Looking him square in the eyes, unblinking, she'd asked, "Is this what our temple vows mean to you?" Anger laced her voice and tears filled her eyes as she turned away to continue folding laundry. And then, "Do as you wish. You always do," she'd murmured as she made a pile of linens she'd later press with the mangle. He imagined she'd like to run *him* through the hulking machine along with the pillowcases.

Truth be told, he hadn't always done what he wanted. Far from it. In the last seven years he'd given Ruth no reason to distrust him. The encounter with the fellow at the Y had been such a nothing, a singular event. He hadn't written letters or made phone calls to any men except family. Paid no special attention to any of his male students. He'd lost track of the number of times he'd turned away from an attractive man who nodded at him.

Terrified of who he had become before meeting Eric, Heber continued his stumbling plea to Ruth, something about this being the time of year to reach out to others in need. Saying nothing more, Ruth began to mate the clean socks.

She hadn't said no. Wasn't that tacit permission?

He knew better. When Ruth said, "temple vows," she was probably considering not only the promises they'd made to each other during the marriage ceremony, but also the part of the *endowment* ceremony where women vow to honor and obey their husbands while the men vow to honor and obey God. It seemed she was going to honor her vows whether he honored his or not.

He felt guilty hurting her but not guilty enough to call off his plan. He didn't think it was okay to get involved with Eric; he simply didn't see a choice. The memory of whipping his beloved daughter was too fresh in his mind to risk his newfound, Eric-induced calm.

Eric had initially resisted. Said he wasn't up to the task of being a *friend of the family.* Really not interested in meeting the wife. But Heber had kept pressing him, refusing to take no for an answer. And here they were, the four of them. Right or wrong, he was glad.

Heber put his arm around Elizabeth, adorable in a pink organdy dress, innocent and oblivious to the tension her father had generated. She hadn't complained once about getting up before 5:00 a.m. to come to the Easter service, and she now sat quietly coloring. She was getting so grown up. When the family had gone to see *Show Boat* at the Music Center in Los Angeles the month before, she'd sat as straight and tall and attentive as a girl twice her age. He gave her a squeeze and she looked up at him, flashing her infectious smile.

The sky was a swath of vermillion and gold above the sandy, sparsely vegetated foothills. A youth choir of the local congregational church marched out on the field in royal blue robes and lifted their voices into the air.

Christ the Lord is risen today,
A-a-a-a-a-le-e-lu-u-ia.

Maybe Elizabeth would be singing here with a youth choir one day.

"Look Daddy," Elizabeth whispered in Heber's ear, showing him the picture of a cat she'd colored orange like their cat at home.

"It's Pumpkin," he whispered back, and she nodded.

He put a finger on the picture and pretended to pet the cat.

Elizabeth giggled.

He passed the picture to Ruth, then to Eric who studied it carefully, nodding. "A true artist," he said loud enough for Elizabeth to hear. She beamed.

A new song rose in the air, an anthem of celebration for Christ's resurrection and salvation for all mankind. Heber caught Eric's eye. His salvation.

A minister in a black suit approached a microphone set up on the football field. "Think what this day means to all of us," the minister extolled. "Take a moment to reflect on the glorious gift of Christ. Through his grace we know no death but have the promise of eternal life."

Heber would have liked more music and less sermon, but he tried to concentrate on the impassioned words. He closed his eyes and thought about the day in the temple when he and Ruth married for time and all eternity. They were so full of dreams then, both believing marriage and a family would make him normal. Apparently, nothing could.

Elizabeth nudged Heber again. This time she showed him a picture of a house and flower-filled yard, every flower a different bright color. Again, he passed the picture to Ruth, then Eric. Eric winked at Elizabeth. "Pretty," he mouthed.

The youth choir sang two more songs, and then another minister gave the closing prayer. "Dear Lord, may thy spirit be with us throughout this new year. A year that begins today, with the glorious resurrection. Help us to remember the great and holy sacrifice of our Savior, the giver of Eternal Life, Jesus Christ. Help us to diligently heed His divine word in all that we do. Amen."

"Amen," Heber repeated with the crowd.

"Nice service. It's been a pleasure sharing it with all three of you." Eric gave Elizabeth a nod and big grin as they all stood.

Elizabeth put up her arms for Eric to lift her and give her a hug. Ruth stiffened, her lips a shallow curve.

The four of them had reached the bottom of the bleachers and were headed for a gate when Heber heard a woman call his name. "Heber, Ruth, good to see you!" Janine Hall, a friend from church, pushed toward them through a throng of people, her husband Harold close behind. When she reached them, she gave Ruth and Heber each a quick hug.

"Hello there. Looks like we have lots of church meetings today," Harold said. "We Mormons certainly ..." He stopped mid-sentence, staring at Eric.

Eric stepped forward and greeted Harold and Janine. "I did some landscaping for the Halls," he explained smoothly.

Harold glanced at Eric, then Heber, then Eric again. Heber stifled a sharp inhale. Eric had said there were other men in his life, and apparently Harold was one of them. When

Heber first met Harold, the man's eyes and handshake had lingered too long. Heber hadn't responded to the overture, if indeed it was an overture, and over the years they'd served together in church callings and become friends without further incident. Today raised Heber's suspicions all over again, although who was he to talk? "Hello, you two," he managed to say.

From the corner of his eye, he saw Ruth arch an eyebrow. Had she and Janine talked?

"Wasn't the service inspiring!" Janine said brightly.

"Especially the choir. Young people have such enthusiasm," Ruth agreed. Her lips smiled but not her eyes.

"What a fetching dress. It must be new," Janine cooed to Elizabeth.

"It is." Elizabeth giggled and turned in a circle, holding the edges of the full skirt. "Mommy made it."

Heber didn't know what to say next.

"Sorry to run." Ruth took over in an upbeat tone. "I'm teaching the Gospel Doctrine class today and still have a bit of preparation."

"Your lessons are always so interesting. What are we learning about this time?" Janine sounded sincerely interested, not taken aback by Harold's response to seeing Eric with them.

"We'll talk about Jesus Christ and his sacrifice for mankind, as always. I also want to tie in people who more recently have made sacrifices that changed people's lives. Like the work Mother Teresa has begun in India." Ruth flashed a smile around the group. "Now we really must get going. See you in a few hours." Nodding to everyone, she took Elizabeth's hand on one side, Heber's arm on the other, and steered them toward the parking lot.

Elizabeth reached for Eric's hand and trotted happily along between him and Ruth.

"Thanks for including me," Eric said when they reached the car. Ruth opened the back door for Elizabeth to climb in.

"Wait. When will we see you again?" Heber asked, unable to stop himself.

Ruth turned to look at him. Her eyes said, "Have you lost your mind?"

"We can go to the beach!" Elizabeth answered for Eric. "We can build a sandcastle!"

Her enthusiasm was endearing, but they couldn't possibly go to the beach. He'd put Ruth through enough already. He wished he'd just said good-bye to Eric and sent him on his way

"It's hot. I love the beach. We haven't been for a long time. Do you like the beach, Uncle Eric?" Elizabeth asked before Heber could think what to say. When had Eric become Uncle Eric? It was all incredibly awkward.

"Can we Daddy? Everybody say yes," she chattered on.

"I need to work this Saturday," Eric said. "But it's a great idea."

That should please Ruth.

"Then we can go the *next* Saturday," Elizabeth announced. "Goodie!"

A mix of emotions tumbled in Heber's chest. What should he and Ruth tell their little daughter? She couldn't possibly understand the complexity of the moment.

Eric looked at the ground.

Where did they all go from here?

24

Santa Monica, California, April 1949

With their palms and knees dug into the sand, Heber and Ruth managed to spread, re-spread, and finally settle the red and white checked tablecloth on the beach despite the late morning breeze. When a few strong gusts threatened to set it sailing, they anchored the corners with a jar of pickled cucumbers, the thermos of lemonade, the picnic basket, and Ruth's sandals.

Eric had been sitting with Elizabeth, entertaining her with stories about seagulls on the coast of Maine where he grew up, while Ruth and Heber set up the picnic. He stood and stretched, and Elizabeth mimicked him, adorable in her red ruffled bathing suit.

Heber had to grin at them both. So close, so fast. Eric was easy to get close to.

"Let's build a sandcastle," Elizabeth said, taking Eric's hand and pulling him toward the ocean.

"Lunch first, Lizzy." Ruth's voice was strained. Heber knew she would never have agreed to this outing if Elizabeth hadn't badgered her from the moment they left the Easter service, finding a way around every reason not to all pile into their old Plymouth and go to the beach with Uncle Eric. It made perfect sense to a four-year-old to invite this nice man along when he'd paid her so much attention.

Ruth had been silent putting together the picnic at home. Now, as she unpacked the sandwiches and chocolate chip cookies from two large grocery bags, everything about her appeared as taut as the braids twined about her head. After today, Heber would drop the fantasy of Ruth and Eric becoming friends. He'd been cruel to let Elizabeth, in her innocence, carry the day.

"Now. Come on." Elizabeth tugged at Eric's hand.

"Your mother's right. After lunch," Eric told her. "Food sounds good right now. I brought a few things too. Want to help me get them out?" He unpacked fried chicken from the wicker picnic basket he'd lugged from the car while Elizabeth pulled out a jar of potato salad. He reached in once more and placed a blueberry pie on the tablecloth, its filling oozing through the golden lattice-top crust. Just looking at it, Heber could taste the mix of sweet and tart in the filling.

"No one's going to want these bologna sandwiches." Ruth stuffed the sandwiches back in one of the bags, blinking away sudden tears.

"Bologna sandwiches and blueberry pie. A perfect combination," Eric declared. "Where I grew up, we raised blueberries. I picked them, eating as fast as I could pick, 'til I had blue on my fingers, blue on my face, blue on my clothes. If something can be made with blueberries, they're still my first choice." He smiled his easy smile as though he and Ruth were getting along fine, but Heber knew he was babbling to fill with words the uncomfortable void between them.

"Can I have a cookie?" Elizabeth reached toward the plate.

"After lunch." Ruth added paper plates, paper cups and silverware to the fare.

"Time to eat," Heber announced, sitting by Ruth and reaching for a piece of chicken. She scooted so close to him their hips touched. She might as well have hung a sign on him, *Mine*. But then again, he *was* hers.

Ruth handed Elizabeth a chicken leg and a cookie on a paper plate, while Heber served himself mounds of potato salad.

"Where'd those bologna sandwiches go?" Eric asked.

Ruth reached into the grocery bag and gave him one without comment.

Elizabeth nibbled at the chicken leg and cookie, oblivious to the tension swirling around her, then set them down. "Now can we make the sandcastle?" she begged. "Please, Uncle Eric?"

"Can I finish eating first?"

"We have to build a sandcastle this big." Elizabeth spread her arms wide. "With a moat and a drawbridge."

"I see. We need a lot of time. Okay with you?" He got a nod from Heber and Ruth, stood up, and took Elizabeth's hand. "The work of a landscaper is never done," he sighed loudly, then picked up Elizabeth's pail and sand shovel and broke into a delighted grin. "Back soon," he called over his shoulder as they trotted to the shoreline.

Heber and Ruth watched them work on the sandcastle, toes mooshing in the damp sand and shoulders turning pink under the rays of the spring sun. Heber could swear Eric's pecs rippled as he helped Elizabeth form turrets and shape castle walls. Next Eric and Elizabeth dredged a deep moat and built a drawbridge of packed sand across it. Their happy chatter as they worked made both Heber and Ruth smile.

"Eric is wonderful with her, isn't he?" Ruth said, brushing cookie crumbs from the bodice of her bathing suit.

"He is," Heber agreed, pleased at her effort to be positive.

"He does seem to enjoy a family so much. I wonder that he isn't married with children of his own." Ruth moved from

Heber's side and he saw that her hands were shaking as she rearranged the plates of cookies and carrot sticks.

Ah, not positive. This definitely needed to be the last outing all together.

"Finished at last," Heber heard Eric tell Elizabeth. "Didn't we do a fine job? Let's go get another cookie."

Elizabeth shook her head "no" and Heber could see her reluctance as Eric led her back to the picnic spread. "It's not done," she pouted. "We need water for the moat."

"Your castle looks good enough for a princess," Ruth said. "But you're both getting sunburned." She turned to the basket and handed Heber a bottle of Coppertone. "You need another coat of this too."

"Maybe we should head home soon." Heber dabbed some of the suntan lotion on his shoulders, then handed the bottle to Eric.

"Put some on Lizzy first. I'll snack on this." Eric reached for a chicken leg, then jumped up and looked around. "Where *is* Lizzy?"

"She was just here! Someone must have seen her!" Ruth scrambled to her feet and ran toward the nearest picnickers.

"She said she wanted more water." Heber sprinted toward the ocean.

"I'll get the lifeguard." Eric raced toward the lifeguard tower.

Heber scanned the ocean, his heart pounding. No sign of her red suit in the tumbling waves. He and Ruth ran to everyone within a hundred yards asking if they'd seen a little girl in a red bathing suit.

They hadn't.

Heber ran back to the shoreline, his eyes never leaving the gray-blue waves. "Lizzy! Elizabeth!" he shouted over and over. Surely, she hadn't gone in the water alone. Had a wave grabbed her?

The tide surged rhythmically toward him and crashed in ankle-deep foam, then receded. To his right, it formed a kind of triangle, spitting broken shells and seaweed on the beach, then sucking sand and driftwood with it on its way out. A riptide could drag his precious child under.

There. A spot of red!

Heber plunged into the water, fighting to keep his head up as he struggled through wave after wave. The panic he'd felt the day he nearly drowned in the Loire River on his mission welled in his chest, but he had to find Elizabeth. He, the lifeguard, and Eric all battled the waves, fanning out, the swells beating them back as they made zigzag patterns toward and away from each other.

Lord, help us find her, Heber prayed, already tiring, frantic that he wasn't a stronger swimmer.

"I think I see her," Heber heard Ruth cry. He turned and saw Ruth throw herself into the crest of a wave and fall, crying out in pain. Heber pushed back toward her, panting, as she tried to stand up on the shifting ocean bottom and collapsed again with a moan. A wave crashed over her head, then another wave.

"I'm coming," he called to Ruth. The lifeguard reached her first, half-carrying her to shore with an arm under her shoulders.

Heber was in shallow water now, almost to her. "Get Lizzy," she screamed, motioning him to dive back into the bruising surf.

The lifeguard charged past him.

Sunbathers formed knots on the beach and looked out over the ocean.

"What happened?"

"A little girl."

"Those riptides. You never know."

Suddenly Eric appeared, pushing through the surf toward Heber, waves slamming his body. Elizabeth lay across his outstretched arms, her legs dangling down one side, her head drooping on the other. She wasn't moving.

Eric laid her gently on the sand and Ruth hobbled to them. The lifeguard tore from the water and in seconds was bending over Elizabeth, carefully clearing her air passages and beginning artificial respiration. Heber joined Ruth and they clung to each other, watching, not breathing, their tears streaming. The gathering crowd was silent, hands covering open mouths.

Dear Heavenly Father, save Lizzy, Heber prayed. *Please save her. I'll do anything you ask.*

Elizabeth shuddered and coughed, then coughed again, gagged, and spit up salty water. The lifeguard turned her on her side, and she vomited her lunch on the sand. "Mommy," she whimpered.

Ruth clutched her daughter's shivering, wet body to her own and slowly rocked from side to side. Heber put his arms around them both. The lifeguard sprinted to his tower and brought back blankets.

"I was so scared," Elizabeth sobbed as the lifeguard wrapped a blanket around her.

"You're safe now." Heber pressed his face against Elizabeth's.

Eric knelt beside them. "You okay, little one?"

"Um hmm." Elizabeth pulled the blanket up around her face.

Ruth looked into Eric's clear, gray eyes. "You saved her life," she said simply.

"I was lucky. I ended up where she was."

"You were a madman out there, diving into the waves," Heber insisted. "We're so grateful."

Tears poured down Ruth's face. "What if you hadn't come with us? I would have lost my only child." Her voice broke. "I can never repay you."

Eric waited quietly as her tears slowed. "You'll always be welcome in our home," she said, putting a hand on his arm. "One of the family."

One of the family. Heber gazed at these two people he loved, trying to grasp what had just happened. The Lord had saved Elizabeth's life. Imagine if they *had* lost her. But why had he chosen Eric as his instrument? Why not the lifeguard who had nothing to do with their crazy triangle?

25

Pasadena, California, July 1950

Even the sight of the abundant flowers in front of Eric's cottage and the sounds of Gershwin's "American in Paris" filling the air couldn't shift Heber's dour mood as he kicked gravel on the path leading to the door. Ruth had set her heart on a thoroughly dilapidated house a realtor at church had christened the 'deal of the century.' Which century? When they'd looked at the 1904 Craftsman on Tuesday evening, Ruth was smitten. Heber could see nothing beyond an infinite number of needed repairs. Not to mention the overgrown jungle of a yard.

The place would consume every minute and every ounce of energy left after work and family chores. If they bought it, when would he have time to do the things he cared about, like his writing, a special outing with Lizzy, or a walk with Eric? He'd recently sold a story to the *LA Times.* He'd penned the piece in a burst of energy following a long afternoon with Eric, and he wanted to send the newspaper something else while the editors still recognized his name.

A big orange cat, like Pumpkin but twice his size, crept out of the bushes and wrapped itself around Heber's legs as he lifted his fist to knock on the door. For a moment he forgot his worries. "Hey, kitty, kitty." He stooped to pet the cat and it turned on its back, purring.

Heber chuckled. A perfect mirror of his behavior at the cottage with Eric.

His thoughts circled back to the house Ruth wanted. Good neighborhood and schools for Elizabeth. Two spacious bedrooms downstairs for the family. Two more bedrooms upstairs: one for Ruth's office, the other a guest room. Ruth would have a better space to pursue her career, now blossoming with the strong sales of her second novel, and they would have a place for visiting family to stay. There was even a studio apartment attached to the garage that they could fix up and rent. He understood why she wanted it so badly.

And he wanted all that for her. She'd drawn the short stick in the marriage and deserved not only the house but new furniture to fill every room and a fine wardrobe to fill every closet. He had yet to get her a gift for their eighth anniversary. What a gift the house would be! Still, the mortgage would be higher than he'd planned, and the amount of work needed to put the place in shape terrified him.

He'd read Ruth's current manuscript with enthusiasm. Attended lectures and films and plays with her, reminiscing about their days in Ed's troupe. To provide a bit more for the family, he'd added two evening classes and summer school to his teaching load at the college. It was the best he could do. He couldn't take on the extra responsibility and work of the old house.

He rapped on Eric's door. No matter what the church touted as gospel doctrine and how persistent his guilt, he desperately needed a large dose of Eric's calming company. Blasphemy maybe—okay, probably—but he thanked God for giving him this tranquil spot away from his responsibilities. He could see no other way to manage life.

He rapped harder, his knuckles smarting against the wood. The music from Eric's Victrola must be drowning out his knock.

The door sprang open and Harold Hall, eyes averted, slunk past, fussing with his clothing. Heber jumped back. So, he'd been right about the scene at the Rose Bowl.

Eric drew Heber through the doorway into a warm embrace. "You're a nice surprise. I wasn't expecting you."

Obviously. Heber's arms stayed limp at his sides.

Eric gave him an extra squeeze before releasing him. "No worries about Harold. He's an old friend."

An old friend still zipping up.

"Hey, you." Eric pushed Heber's shoulder playfully. "You're the one that matters."

Heber exhaled, aware that he was being ridiculous. He didn't own Eric; he was married to Ruth, after all. "Sorry. I was in a rotten mood before I saw Harold." He tried to keep the whine out of his voice.

"Let's talk. Whatever it is, the garden will make you feel better." Eric put his arm around Heber's shoulders, and they walked out along a white rock path to a cement bench tucked against the trunk of a towering Deodar. Bees droned in flower beds of poppies and nasturtiums raucous with color. An orchard of apple trees burst with blossoms.

Eric sank onto the bench and pulled Heber down beside him so close their torsos touched from shoulder to hip. "Better?" he asked.

Heber relaxed into Eric, drawing in the scents of his surroundings and of Eric's aftershave. "Much. You're my *paraclete*, you know."

"Your *paraclete*?"

"The comforter of my soul. You read my moods and shift them in a way no one has before."

"*Paraclete*. Nice. Is it French?" Eric took Heber's hand and kissed it. "I've never been called the comforter of someone's soul."

"Greek. Applied to the Holy Spirit. An intercessor or comforter."

"Always the teacher," Eric teased. "I'll take the compliment. Although, come to think of it, I have heard the word *paraclete*. Supposedly there's a Catholic Order of the Paracletes up in the Jemez Mountains of New Mexico. A monastery with the most beautiful gardens imaginable. It's also a place where wayward priests are sent for 'spiritual retraining.'"

"Wayward priests?"

"Alcoholics, drug addicts, pedophiles."

Heber shrugged. "Never heard of it. I wasn't alluding to anything but the way I feel around you." He kissed each of Eric's eyelids, then his mouth. Gentle. Affirming.

Eric returned his kiss, deeper, more lingering. "*Paraclete* it is. You're mine too, you know."

Heber kissed him again. "I can't believe the difference you make." That was an understatement. He ran a finger along Eric's jaw. "I'm even getting along with Dr. Brunswick, the VP at our college who had it in for me. One of my colleagues asked if I had a good fairy in my life."

Eric laughed. "What did you say?"

"I kept a straight face and said, 'absolutely.' If she only knew." Heber leaned into Eric, feeling the warmth and firmness of his chest, the rise and fall of each breath under his t-shirt. When a ladybug lit on his arm, Heber coaxed it onto his index finger and carefully set it on a nearby branch. "I wish I could stay here always," he sighed.

Eric nuzzled his neck. "So do I."

"You're going to make me forget why I came over."

"I know why you came over." Eric bit his ear.

Heber turned to him for another long kiss, then pulled away to look into the face of this man he'd grown to truly love. He'd nearly told him a few times. He might even tell him now. But Harold had been here. And worry about the damn house muddled his brain. "It's about a house Ruth wants."

"Uh oh, your serious voice. A house?"

Heber stood and began pacing. "A perfect moment and I spoil it. That's what this house does to me. Fixer-upper doesn't begin to describe the work it needs." He managed to still himself and sat again.

Eric frowned. "Maybe Ruth wants you home more. She has to know what's going on between us. She's a smart woman."

"She considers you one of the family."

Eric grimaced. "Because of what happened at the beach. It doesn't mean she likes it."

"You help with the yard, bring meals when she's down with her phlebitis, babysit Lizzy. She's grateful to you."

"You see what you want to see. When I'm over, she usually takes a book to your bedroom as soon as she can. I worry about her." Eric tugged Heber down beside him. "I've never spent time with the wife and kid before. Plus, I like Ruth and Lizzy. Genuinely like them. I don't want them to get hurt. It isn't a bed of roses for me either."

"I guess not." Heber hadn't reflected on things from Eric's perspective. He was more comfortable pretending the "one of the family" thing was working out.

"You and Ruth must have talked about your attraction to men."

"A long time ago. Before we were married."

"And she believed marriage would change you."

Heber nodded. "Like the Catholics try to change those priests in the mountains."

"I had a friend once, Emily. She tried to change me. With my blessing and full cooperation." He grimaced. "Can't be done."

"Ruth and I never talked about it again."

"Your temple marriage was supposed to solve all your problems. Such a handsome Mormon living in a land of make-believe." He shrugged his shoulders. "Enough of that. Tell me about the house."

Heber groaned. "Every wall needs paint, inside and out. The yard is completely overgrown. But Ruth really wants it."

"She's a reasonable woman, so why this house?"

"Good neighborhood, excellent elementary school four blocks away, and cheap for the area because it's so run down. Four bedrooms — enough for Ruth to have an office and we'd have a guest room." It did sound good as he described it, but just the mental picture of it exhausted him.

"The house sounds wonderful. Lizzy and Ruth deserve the best." Eric played with the hair at the nape of Heber's neck. "Tell you what. Suppose I go with you to see the house? If the job seems doable to me, I'll give you a hand fixing it up."

"You'd do that?"

"Let's say it would ease my conscience. I owe it to Ruth."

"More time with you. Sharing the work. What an amazing offer." Heber gave Eric a grateful hug and the deepest kiss of the morning.

"Isn't it a wonderful house, Eric? Thanks for asking to see it." Ruth's face glowed with enthusiasm as she, Heber, and Eric emerged from the realtor's car.

The realtor launched into his sales pitch. "With a little work, this home will be as charming as the others in the neighborhood, and the value will increase dramatically. An excellent investment."

"Sure, if someone has sixteen thousand dollars lying around to invest," Heber grumbled under his breath, overwhelmed all over again at the sight of the vacant house and large corner lot. In the back yard, where the garage and attached apartment sat, wild grasses nearly smothered a struggling apple tree. He doubted the remains of a persimmon orchard on the west side had been pruned since the house was built, and the trees looked barren of fruit. He'd need to buy a gas mower for the spacious lawns.

Eric was more optimistic. "We can remove some of those trees," he said, pointing to a row of gray-green shapeless firs and cypress that competed with overgrown oleander bushes for the strip of earth between the sidewalk and street. "Let in the morning sun and bring the side lawns back to life."

"We'd need to trim the oleander way back. Those pink blossoms smell like urine. And look at the house." Heber pointed to the square columns of the front and side porches where paint peeled off the cement in numerous places. Pine needles formed a thick mat on the roof.

An undaunted Ruth turned to Eric. "Wait 'til you see the inside."

The realtor unlocked the front door and led them into the living room. Their footsteps echoed on the yellowed hardwood floor. "The house has excellent bones," he said. "All it needs is some cosmetics."

A boatload of cosmetics. Heber's shoulders sagged just thinking about the work.

In the living room, a glassed-in bookcase and a scuffed oak settee flanked a brick fireplace. The dining room featured a buffet built into the length of the wall with three long drawers and china cabinets at both ends, equally faded and scuffed. One door from the dining room opened into the outdated kitchen. Another opened into a large room painted a depressing gray but filled with light from a bank of windows that looked out on the wrap-around porch and the Sierra Madre foothills beyond.

"It does have good bones," Eric agreed. "Picture those built-ins refinished. And look at the view of the mountains from both the dining room and sunroom."

Ruth followed his gaze out the east windows. "It is a sunroom, isn't it? Big enough for a couch, comfortable chairs, maybe a writing table. The house is like something in *Sunset* magazine." Her face shone so brightly Heber felt petty in his reluctance.

Eric traced the beveled edge of a china closet's glass doors with one finger. "If we work on the house every weekend, we could have it in good shape in about six months."

Heber had to admit the view was spectacular. All the floors would need refinishing, but they appeared to be undamaged. He'd been raised in cramped quarters, with only a tiny room to himself. He and Ruth had rented small places their first eight years of marriage. Imagine owning a spacious home.

Ruth slipped her hand in the crook of Heber's elbow. "We could put my chaise-lounge out on the side porch as well as a picnic table and benches. Lizzy could play there with friends when you needed peace and quiet."

Heber could easily picture Ruth there for an hour every afternoon with her leg up as the doctor required, Elizabeth playing beside her. Her view would be the houses across the street, one an imposing Spanish two-story with a balcony across the second floor, the other an immaculate Cape Cod, and then the foothills beyond. He wanted that for her and the daughter she'd given him at the cost of her health.

Had he really asked for peace and quiet that often? He'd better watch it.

The realtor led the way to the kitchen, gushing its merits. "The house was built early in the century so you will want to modernize it; but see all the cupboard space."

Rows of cupboards above and below tiled counters lined a long wall, and they appeared to need only a coat of paint. Everything else in the kitchen needed replacing from the cracked linoleum to the dim ceiling fixture.

Then there were the two cotton-candy pink bedrooms off the downstairs hall that would have to be painted immediately, as would the two grimy bedrooms upstairs. Where would he and Eric even begin? The pressure inside him began building again.

Ruth stepped up to him. "Isn't the house wonderful? A big kitchen and a sunroom where we can have a table for family meals and save the dining room for special occasions. Like we had when I was growing up."

She was so happy. How could he refuse her, especially when Eric would be over often to help with the work? Maybe he could manage.

A sudden, stabbing pain cut into his right temple and for a moment the room swam around him. He staggered, and Eric put out an arm to steady him.

"Are you alright?" Concern replaced the joy in her Ruth's voice.

"A bit faint. Hit with a headache. I want you to have this house, Ruth, but I don't know if I'm up to it." He pressed his temple. "I'll have to sleep on it."

Ruth moved to the realtor's side. "We'll let you know tomorrow," she told him, disappointment heavy in her voice. "I see." The realtor eyed Heber. "Another buyer might come along," he whispered to Ruth.

Heber heard him. He doubted anyone else would come along. What fool would take on this project?

The next day was Sunday, and before they headed to church, Ruth slipped a pot roast into the oven. The bribe would have worked for most things—she made a delicious pot roast, tender and flavorful, with carrots and potatoes. But some time during the night, when sleep eluded him, Heber had decided he couldn't handle the pressure of all the work and expense, even with Eric's help. He was going to pieces again, just when he'd been feeling better.

"There must be a house in a good neighborhood that costs less and is in better shape," he began, following her into the dining room where she was pulling a tablecloth from the bottom drawer of the buffet. He fought to maintain a normal tone of voice but sounded cross instead. Hadn't she seen him nearly fall?

"I'll keep looking if that's what you want." She spread the tablecloth on the table with an impassive expression as though she didn't care one way or the other.

Damn it. She cared plenty. "I'd appreciate that," he muttered and went to the bedroom to get his suit jacket. Church and more nice-nice would fill the morning, and already his jaw clenched with tension. When he returned to the dining room, Ruth had their best china arranged in four place settings, and she was putting the silver flatware at each place. "Eric's joining us," she said without looking up.

"Goodie!" Elizabeth danced into the room in a yellow skirt with a puppy appliquéd on the front.

His jaw softened with her sweet presence, then clenched again. Ruth had co-opted Eric into helping her get the house.

Evidently, she wanted it enough to take on more frequent visits from him. That was a lot of want.

All during Sunday School, he made mental lists of house projects. Maybe Ruth and Eric would listen to him if he presented them with some facts about what would be required.

At one o'clock Ruth set the Dutch oven on a crocheted hot pad in the center of the table, and a rich beef aroma filled the small room. Alongside the roast she put a steaming bowl of green beans with crumbled bacon, a matching bowl of mashed potatoes, lime Jell-O molded in a circle, a tossed salad, and a basket of rolls. Heber took his place at the head of the table with Elizabeth on his right and Eric on his left. Ruth returned from the kitchen and took her seat opposite him. "Lizzy, would you say the blessing?" she asked.

They all bowed their heads as Elizabeth said a prayer. "Dear Heavenly Father, thank you for the food, bless it to nourish and strengthen our bodies, bless Mommy and Daddy and all my friends, thank you for Uncle Eric, in the name of Jesus Christ, amen."

"Amen," they all echoed, then opened their eyes and lifted their heads.

Heber caught Eric's eye and managed a weak smile.

Ruth heaped generous servings of pot roast onto everyone's plates.

"Uncle Eric," Elizabeth asked, reaching for a roll, "did you like our new house?"

"It isn't our house yet," Heber said.

"Mommy said we can fix up my bedroom before kindergarten starts."

"I said *if* we buy it, we can fix up your room," Ruth corrected her.

"You said 'when we buy it.'"

Heber believed Elizabeth.

"If we do buy it, we can rent out the apartment in back for $35.00 a month and hire a gardener with the money," Ruth said. "Simplify the landscaping so it's easier on you. Take out those old persimmon trees. I don't like persimmons anyway."

"I like persimmons." Anger rose in Heber's throat. She had it all figured out, as though their conversation before church had never happened.

"I might like persimmons," Elizabeth piped up.

"If you do buy it, I can get a small persimmon tree for the west yard for a house-warming present," Eric suggested. "We can take out the old trees that probably don't produce much fruit anymore and extend the existing rose garden."

"Our first family project," Ruth added.

Family project, he wanted to snort. He did love roses, but they took care. Every damn thing took care. He looked around the table at his wife, his daughter, and his lover. They outnumbered him three to one. "All right. I can't say no to all of you."

"Thank you, Daddy! I want a yellow bedroom!" Elizabeth jumped out of her chair, ran over to kiss his cheek, then skipped around the table, kissing Eric and Ruth too.

"Thank you, dear." Some of the joy he'd seen yesterday gathered in Ruth's eyes.

Eric's knees nudged his under the table. *We'll be together*, the touch implied.

For once he'd made everyone happy. Everyone else, anyway.

26

Pasadena, California, December 1950

Heber's jaw tightened at the pressure of Ruth's hand on his thigh as they drove west on Colorado Boulevard toward Sears. Tinsel snowflakes on silver wires wrapped the telephone poles and stretched across the street under warm sunshine, a true California Christmas. The day before, Ruth and Elizabeth had been busy making Christmas cards and gingerbread houses. He wished he could catch the festive spirit from them and not feel snarly. As it was, he'd rather be home alone than in the Christmas bustle. Who wanted a grump around?

He and Ruth were shopping for mattresses of all things. What an odd Christmas present to give each other. But Ruth had turned up this big sale and reminded him that their current mattresses had been well used before being passed on to them. Anything to do with a bed called up a picture in his mind of the wrought iron double bed at Eric's. For Ruth, it must call up a wish she had married someone else.

He felt sorry for Ruth. And himself. Eric hadn't come around in two months. When they first bought the house, it was summer vacation, and instead of taking their annual trip to Utah, Heber and Ruth had dedicated August to fixing up the place.

Heber and Eric worked long hours every day. They whacked back the oleander and took out two cramped cypress trees, removed the old persimmon trees on the west, extended the rose bed there, and planted several fruit trees around the yard: a plum, a lemon, and a nectarine. At Ruth's request they added mounds of fragrant lavender front and back. They even readied the apartment for a renter and painted the south side of the house that was badly peeling.

Ruth shopped carefully for supplies they needed and for furnishings for the apartment, as well as preparing three generous meals and snacks daily for everyone.

Elizabeth played contentedly in her room, now bright yellow, or at the home of her new best friend, a girl a year older who lived a few houses away.

Heber was glad to skip Utah this year. He much preferred Eric's company to Sarah's, and Ruth seemed content to focus on house projects and her third novel. Elizabeth liked playing dolls or running through sprinklers with her new friend better than visiting relatives she barely knew.

When school started, Heber returned to work, Elizabeth went off to kindergarten, Ruth settled more deeply into her writing, and Eric disappeared. The last Heber saw of him was when he brought by his gift of a new persimmon tree and planted it as promised. By then he had begged off afternoon walks, claiming one of his clients had a big job for him which took up every spare minute. At first, he answered the phone when Heber called but said he was too busy to talk. Then the phone just rang and rang. He hadn't replied to any of Heber's letters.

This morning, before leaving for Sears, Heber had mustered his tattered courage and dialed Eric's number yet again while Ruth was finishing up the breakfast dishes. No answer.

Damn him anyway. Heber didn't know whether Eric was angry about something or had simply grown tired of him. After everything they'd shared, wouldn't he at least tell him what was up?

Heber rolled down the car window and inhaled the fresh air. It must be well into the seventies. No white Christmases in California; fine with him. After they got the mattresses, he'd work in the yard. That always cheered him. Even without Eric's help, the front and side lawns and flower beds were finally taking shape.

"Christmas is kind of a sad time, don't you think?" Ruth murmured. Her words brought Heber out of his reverie. "Wouldn't it be wonderful if we had three more children writing letters to Santa?"

He hadn't thought about Ruth's miscarriages in a long time. Not that he hadn't deeply grieved them all, but the care of his younger siblings had taught him how demanding kids could be. Between Ruth's health issues and his job, raising Elizabeth was enough responsibility. Christmas was a sad time this year, all right, but for a different reason. A two-week break from teaching and apparently not a minute of it would be spent with Eric.

Heber took one hand off the steering wheel and patted Ruth's fingers where they lay on his thigh. "You're a far better mother than the women at Church taking up a full pew with their gaggle of kids. Think how much attention Lizzy gets." He would have brought their daughter on this shopping expedition if she hadn't been playing at the neighbor's and wanted to stay there. She had a way of making Ruth and him smile. They needed her right now.

Ruth's face brightened. "She does get plenty, doesn't she? I'm so grateful for her. She still seems like a miracle in our lives."

"She is that."

"Especially at Christmas. It's such a family time." Ruth moved her hand to her lap. "Except ... well ... you sounded so annoyed when I asked you to come shopping with me."

"It's those stacks of student compositions I have to read over Christmas break. We could have ordered mattresses from the Sears catalog."

"They're having a big Christmas sale. Maybe we could look at other furniture too. We've never had a real bedroom set."

Heber drummed his fingers on the steering wheel as he waited for a red light. "You know there's no money until we pay off the second mortgage." He hadn't meant to sound accusatory. He'd agreed to get the house, and it wasn't Ruth's fault teachers didn't get paid well.

"I have a little bit left from the advance on my last novel," Ruth said. "It didn't all go down the drain when I paid the sewer assessment."

He managed a chuckle at her pun. He could hardly argue about new furniture if she were paying; their current beds and dressers were admittedly shabby. When she first suggested she have her own bank account for the royalties from her writing, the idea had rankled him. He put his full paycheck into the family kitty, keeping back only an agreed on small amount for his personal expenses like lunches with Dorothy. But her account had become a savings account for them both, paying for things like the sewer bills, their annual family vacations to Utah, and now, it seemed, dressers and beds. "Sure, we could look," he said as he drove across the intersection and pulled into a space in the Sears parking lot.

The omnipresent Christmas décor tempered Heber's mood as they walked into the store, Ruth on his arm. Beribboned pine boughs filled the air with a pungent aroma, and red-foiled pots of poinsettias greeted them at every aisle. "I should send one of these to my mother," Ruth said, stopping to admire a rack of white, linen-like blouses. "They'd go well with her winter suits."

"My mother would like one too," he said. "Would packages get to Utah in time?"

"I planned to mail something on Tuesday. Oh, these are cozy. Maybe they'd be better." Ruth fingered a rack of thick, wool cardigans. "What do you think?"

Blouse. Sweater. Heber just wanted to be sure his mother had a gift from him to open on Christmas. "You decide," he said. He watched Ruth admire a pleated skirt and matching jacket on a mannequin and breathed in familiar guilt. He hadn't considered a gift for her besides the mattresses she wanted. Instead, he'd been focused on the perfect thing to leave on Eric's doorstep. Maybe he could come back alone one day soon and get her the suit.

In the furniture department Ruth rested her hand on the back of a couch covered in a deep blue silk. "Isn't this lovely?"

"What about Lizzy and her friends when they play at our house? We could never keep it clean. We need something practical." There it was again, that tone of voice he so disliked in himself.

"It would be nice someday." Ruth walked to a limed oak bedroom set and a maple grouping next to it, then to a mahogany bedroom set. "This was advertised in the *Star News*," she said as she stroked the red-brown polished surface of a chest of drawers. "You could use the highboy and I could use the dresser and dressing table. Aren't they handsome?"

They were indeed. Heber noted the graceful lines and rich tone of the wood as he opened the doors of the slender highboy and pulled out each of the four narrow, smoothly gliding drawers. They'd be perfect for small things like cufflinks and tie clips. Three wider drawers below the cabinet could hold all his underwear, pajamas, and sweaters. He'd never owned anything as nice. "You're sure you have enough money?"

"Oh, darling, I'm thrilled you like it. Merry Christmas." Ruth smiled happily up at him. "Wouldn't the matching headboard be nice too?"

"It's for a double bed."

"We could buy a double bed mattress," Ruth said.

"We sleep better in separate beds. We decided that years ago." Heber tried to sound matter of fact.

"You decided that." Ruth put a hand on his arm. "I'd like to try a change."

Had she hoped in Eric's absence to develop a more passionate relationship with Heber? It couldn't happen. Heber imagined Ruth's body pressed against his every night. She was still an attractive woman, her hair cut in a trendy pageboy, her skin aglow with a pink flush. She was trim and stylishly dressed, and a great conversationalist as always, sharing some idea she'd read or reflected on. He loved her as much as he was capable of loving a woman. Showed her as much affection as he could. But she wasn't Eric, with whom he felt complete. Without him he felt half empty all the time.

Even if Eric were out of their lives for good—an unbearable notion—Heber was still who he was. What he was.

"Why don't you see if they have headboards for twin beds?" Heber suggested as a compromise, the disappointment in her eyes intensifying his ever-present guilt.

"May I help you?" A salesman approached them; a red carnation tucked into the lapel of his dark suit.

"We'd like this bedroom set, but with headboards for twin beds if you have them." Ruth's voice was even, her face empty of expression. "We'll need mattresses too."

"Right this way." The salesman beamed as he showed them several mattresses and explained their construction. Heber chose a firm mattress, Ruth a softer one. Heber refrained from pointing out the difference in their preferences as a good reason to get twin beds.

Heber took Ruth's hand as they walked to the cash register. "The bedroom set is a real luxury. We'll enjoy it. Should we go back to the women's department now?"

"I'll come Monday afternoon." Ruth's voice was subdued. "I know you're eager to get home."

No argument there.

At home, Heber changed into gardening clothes and dialed Eric's number. No answer. He went outside and started planting splashes of red, yellow, and orange nasturtiums along the sidewalk. As he worked, the feel of the soil and the bright colors of the flowers soothed his nerves. There were moments now when he loved this place. Eric and Ruth had been right about buying it.

"Hello there, Professor Averil. Looks like you're working hard."

Startled, Heber glanced up. Paul Westgate, one of his students, stood on the sidewalk.

Heber wiped his right hand on his jeans and extended it to him. "Excuse the dirt. What a nice surprise."

It certainly was a nice surprise. Paul was older than most of his students, about thirty, and one of the smartest. He looked good in his jeans and t-shirts too. On this sunny afternoon, missing Eric as he did, Heber was very glad to see him.

"Must be nice working in the garden after a week in classes," Paul said.

"It is, but there's so much to do."

"Big place like this, I'm sure there is."

"You live nearby?" Heber asked.

"I live with my sister a few blocks from here. Went for a walk to get out of her hair for a couple of hours. She has enough confusion with four kids." Paul grinned. "I could give you a hand if you'd like. I have time."

Paul had often given Heber slow smiles and sometimes grazed his hand when he turned in an exam. A rush of pleasure filled Heber's chest. It also flashed a warning: *Absolutely not!*

"You're sure you have time?"

"I can get the weeds."

"That'd be great. I'll finish the planting."

Paul worked quickly, his fingers strong. As he weeded, he talked about his favorite books. A Hemingway fan, he especially liked *The Old Man and the Sea* and waxed eloquent about Santiago's struggle with the giant marlin. "Don't you think we all have a struggle in our lives that consumes us, body and soul?" he asked, meeting Heber's eyes.

Heber nodded. Truer words had never been spoken from a bed of posies.

After twenty minutes Paul stood and stretched. Sweat glistened on a sprinkle of tawny hair visible above the neckline of his t-shirt.

Heber imagined that tawny hair narrowing into a line down Paul's taut stomach and into his Levi's. He forced his attention back to the plants still in the tray. His wife and daughter were in the house. He needed to get himself in line.

"Good progress," Paul said. "How about a beer?"

"I might be able to offer you lemonade. I'll check." Heber turned away from Paul's lingering gaze.

"That works too." Paul settled on the lawn, propped on his elbows, face to the cloudless blue sky.

Heber took his gardening shoes off at the back door and went into the house.

Ruth turned from the kitchen table where she was wrapping Christmas presents while Elizabeth colored Christmas cards to go with them. "You have a helper I see," she said by way of greeting. A shadow passed over her face before she could force a weak smile.

"It's Paul Westgate, one of my students. I had no idea he lives nearby." Heber chewed his lip. "I appreciate the help. I wonder if I could offer him some lemonade ... and maybe a cookie?"

"Certainly." Ruth kept the smile, but he read suspicion in her eyes.

Elizabeth jumped out of her seat and held up a construction paper snowman. "See what I made!"

"Nice work, Lizzy." Heber ruffled her hair.

Ruth went outside to pick lemons from their lemon tree. Heber followed her out. "It isn't like that," he whispered, stepping close to her.

She stepped away, picked two more lemons, and started for the house, Heber close behind. While she made the lemonade in silence, he watched for a moment, then took four cookies from the cookie jar and two paper napkins from the holder on the table.

"Can I have some lemonade, too?" Elizabeth tugged at Ruth's sleeve.

"Yes, little one." Ruth patted her head then got down her Little Bo Peep mug, filled it, and handed it to her.

Heber took the lemonade and cookies out to Paul. "Homemade," he said. "Chocolate chip."

"What a treat." Paul took them and Heber sat down beside him. "You're a lucky man, Professor Averil," Paul said after two giant bites of cookie.

"That I am. Baking is only one of my wife's talents. She's an accomplished author, an amazing mother, and she puts up with me." All true, he reminded himself, keeping a careful distance from Paul.

A boxy Sears truck turned into the driveway. "Expecting something?" Paul asked.

"My wife's Christmas present," Heber answered as Ruth rushed outside and approached them.

"They got our furniture on the afternoon truck!" Ruth turned to Paul. "I hate to impose further on you, but would you mind helping Heber take the old furniture to our spare room upstairs? I don't know who else we'd ask."

Interesting. She didn't want other men around until she needed one of them. Eric with the house, Paul with the furniture.

"Glad to." Paul took one more cookie, ate it in two bites, and stood. "At your service."

"I appreciate the help," Ruth said, as they all walked toward the house. "I can get the bedding ready for the new beds."

Inside, Ruth went to the linen closet with a quick glance at the two men. Heber and Paul went to the bedroom to get the old furniture.

He saw Paul glance around the room, then take one end of a twin bed while Heber took the other end. Obviously, Heber didn't sleep with his arm around his wife.

When they set the bed down in the upstairs guest room, Paul looked across it at Heber. "What luck I happened by on the same day as your new bed," he said with a wink.

Heber felt a blush rise in his face as he ignored the comment.

"You rent that apartment in back? I need to find a place of my own."

"It's already rented."

"The semester's almost over. Want to get a drink some time?"

Not subtle, this student of his. And not easily discouraged.

Desire stirred. Paul wouldn't be his student much longer. Suppose Eric didn't come back?

An image of the hurt in Ruth's eyes when she handed him the lemonade and cookies arose in his mind. All desire drained out of him. He had no wish to cause her such pain for a fling. "Thanks, but I don't drink."

"I can be good company." Paul took a few steps around the bed toward Heber.

The only male company worth setting off Heber's uneasy conscience was Eric, his *paraclete*. The crazy triangle of Eric, Ruth and him that, until two months ago, everyone seemed to accept.

Or he saw only what he wanted to see. Maybe Eric's absence was God's way of making sure he rededicated himself to his marriage. Certainly, the only thing he and Paul needed to do together was move the rest of the furniture.

Heber stepped away from Paul. "We need to get the rest of the furniture. Ruth will be waiting. Like you said, I'm a lucky man."

27

Pasadena, California, December 1950

The right side of Heber's forehead pounded like a jackhammer. Is this what Ruth's migraines felt like? If so, he needed to give her a boat load of sympathy when they hit. "I can't make it to Sunday School. Bad headache," he said to her as she tied on her bathrobe. "You know how it is."

"Too much time in the garden yesterday?" The question held an unmistakable tinge of sarcasm.

He listened to her rummage in the kitchen, probably setting out cereal and milk for their usual Sunday morning breakfast. Then he pulled the covers over his head. True, he'd resisted Paul, but he could hardly claim moral purity. His thoughts kept drifting back to Eric.

Eric must have found someone without the weighty responsibilities of a wife, a child, and a 3,000 square foot fixer-upper house. Now Heber was stuck with this monstrosity of a place to keep up alone. As quickly as the anger flared, it drained away, leaving only a desperate longing.

He groaned, forced himself out of bed, and stepped into his slippers. Joining Ruth at the sink, he filled the teakettle with water, placed it on the stove, and reached for the instant coffee he'd purchased one day on impulse. He'd come to like its rich flavor, but that wasn't the reason he occasionally broke the Word of Wisdom. He drank it for the pick-up when he lacked the energy to face another day.

Ruth looked at the jar of Nescafé and pressed her lips together but said nothing.

Too bad she had to share her life with a pathetic sinner. Still, he figured he wouldn't go to hell for using coffee as a medicine. The Word of Wisdom had its limits.

He poked at a bowl of corn flakes, swallowing the cereal almost as difficult as feigning an appetite. He couldn't remember when he'd felt this low. Good thing he didn't have a gun closet like his brothers who hunted. That would stop the infernal pounding in his head.

He wouldn't—he mustn't—do that to Ruth and Elizabeth. Or would his family and the world in general be better off without him? If he shot himself, would this headache be locked in place forever, like the sinners in Dante's *Inferno* paying throughout all eternity for their depravities? He conjured images from Dante's text: The Lustful swirling about in an eternal wind, the Gluttonous lying on the ground with sewage raining down on them forever, the Avaricious pushing along weights in anger and pain. If Dante and the church had it right, what was in store for him?

When the teakettle whistled, he poured a steaming cup of water, stirred in a tablespoon of Nescafé, and stared at it for a few seconds before dumping it down the drain. As if denying himself a cup of coffee would make a difference. Eternal damnation surely awaited him. Or was he already there? No hell could be worse than his throbbing headache and his broken heart.

"Look at me, Daddy." Elizabeth danced into the kitchen and turned a full circle in front of him, showing off her ruby red polished-cotton dress with its full skirt and wide white sash.

How he loved his daughter. She never failed to cheer him. "Pretty as a picture."

"I'm the first one ready for church."

"Yes, you are." She'd even given herself a ponytail — almost. Tucking a stray hair behind her ear, he nearly decided to go with her and Ruth. Church was a family affair and this child his abiding light. But when he pictured sitting on a hard pew trying to concentrate on yet another lesson about the Bible or Book of Mormon, he couldn't do it.

The previous week, the bishop had asked him to teach the deacons' quorum. Teach a class of twelve-year-old boys? What kind of example could he set for those young men just given the Aaronic priesthood? President Hays had instructed him to accept all church callings, but he doubted teaching the deacons would be a miracle medicine for what ailed him, any more than a temple marriage had proved to be. He'd told the bishop he had too many responsibilities at work. He wasn't up to a full confession, which would humiliate Ruth as well as him. He deserved it; she didn't.

"I have a headache, sweet pea, so I'm staying home." Heber brushed the tip of her nose with one finger. "You'll be in Junior Sunday School anyway, not with Mommy and me. By the time you get home I'll feel better, and we can do something."

Elizabeth's eyes sparkled. "What?"

"We could take a magic carpet ride to the moon."

She giggled and shook her head. "Daddy."

"Get an ice cream cone?"

"Promise? The special candy cane flavor?"

"Right after lunch."

Elizabeth started on her Cheerios and Heber returned to his bowl of corn flakes. Ruth left the room, probably to get ready for church. How did she do it, week after week, gracious and smiling, never letting on to what she dealt with at home?

Elizabeth had finished her breakfast and was rinsing her own bowl, so grown up, when Ruth came back to the kitchen, her handbag over one arm, the car keys in her hand. "Get some rest," she said with the irritation that Heber found both annoying and understandable still in her voice. "Come on, Lizzy."

Heber listened to the car pull out of the driveway, then pushed back his bowl and put his head on the table. What to do?

He'd call again. Maybe Eric would pick up this time. Give Heber the opportunity to grovel. Unlikely, but he had to try. Heber went to the sunroom and dialed the black rotary phone.

"Hello?"

Eric's voice sent an electric shock through Heber. "You answered."

"I had a feeling it was you."

"What happened?" The words burst out.

Eric offered no response.

"I can't live without knowing."

"Oh, please." Was that scorn in Eric's voice? "Don't be so dramatic. This isn't Hollywood."

"Tell me." Heber waited, putting a hand on the phone table to steady himself. He had to know why Eric had shunned him, no matter how painful to hear. "I can come over. We can talk," he pleaded when Eric didn't respond. "Ruth has the car. I could catch a bus and be there in an hour."

"Not a good idea."

Heber held his breath.

"I'm a fool to let you come." Eric hung up.

Eric would see him! If he opened the door and took Heber in his arms, the world would be right again. At the very least, they would talk, and Heber could address the gaping hole Eric's absence had left in his life.

Heber scrubbed vigorously in the shower and shaved, his hands shaking so much he nicked himself twice. Bloody bits of toilet paper dotted his chin. He debated between khaki slacks and navy. Chose the navy. Grabbed the light blue shirt. Eric liked him in blue. Finally, he took two aspirin, wrote Ruth a quick note that he'd gone for a walk, and hurried to the bus stop.

Another lie to Ruth, he reflected, as the bus wound through downtown Pasadena. He was a louse, but he had to see Eric and try to work things out. He'd be a better husband and father for it.

His fingers tapped nervously on the vinyl bus seat. What if Eric refused to see him once he was there? Or told him there was someone else? Heber's churning mind lit on an image of Eric and settled there. His *paraclete*. Eric's twinkling eyes and broad shoulders. Their hungry kisses. The way Eric understood Heber's struggle.

Then he was at the cottage door, glancing around but barely taking in the abundant holly laden with berries and the poinsettias in full bloom. Smoothing his slacks, he drew a deep breath and then knocked tentatively.

Eric immediately opened the door but offered no welcoming hug. Not even a smile.

Heber's heart sank into his black, well-shined shoes.

Eric motioned him to the couch and sat down at the opposite end. He was dressed casually in jeans and a clean white t-shirt like he'd worn the day they met. But his mood was very different, his mouth set in a grim line.

A heavy silence filled the space between them. "What did I do?" he blurted.

Eric stood and began pacing the room. His face, usually ruddy and smiling, was pale and sad. "You didn't do anything." He stopped in front of the couch and looked down at Heber.

Heber saw his own anguish reflected in Eric's gray eyes. "It's been three months," Heber said.

"You know how hard it is to stay away from you?" Eric asked, his voice not quite steady. "I picture you all the time. You and your moods: Mr. Serious, Mr. Mischievous. When you're worried and relax into my arms. When we're making love."

"Then why ..." Heber pinched off his question and waited.

Eric sat down again and stared at his hands, folded in his lap. "I've always kept a comfortable distance from the men in my life. Harold, for example. Easy to give them up. But you ..."

Harold easy, Heber not so easy.

"I couldn't go on. You and your family. I was falling in love with all of you."

Heber reached across the space between them and took Eric's hands. "I love you, too. We all do. Come back to us."

Eric pulled away. "Come back to all of you? Be *Uncle Eric* again? Are you mad?"

Heber put a hand on his shoulder. "You *are* a member of the family. Lizzy loves you; she misses you. Ruth ..." Heber struggled for the words to convey how Eric's calming effect on him benefitted the whole family. "You've read Ruth's novels. I've been thinking a lot about them. She might look at the three of us the way she looks at the polygamous families in her books. Focus on the ways you add to our lives."

Eric shrugged off the hand and turned to him. "That's ridiculous. Grow up, Heber. We aren't characters in a novel.

This isn't pioneer Utah. And I'm sure Ruth doesn't find polygamy even remotely the same." His tone was scathing. "It isn't fun anymore. Not for me, not for Ruth. Someday Lizzy will see through the lies and be devastated."

Heber pushed aside the niggling part of him that knew Eric was right. "You make our lives better. Ruth and I have problems, but they aren't all about you."

They did have problems. The stress of his job, her health, the pressure of the mortgage, the upkeep of the house. Lack of physical affection, obviously. Eric's absence didn't change any of those. And as things were, Heber's nerves would continue to fray. He'd warned Ruth. He'd tried to change. He wished he didn't need men, but he did. Specifically, he needed Eric.

He sucked in his breath. "Do you want me to leave Ruth?" he asked, shocking himself. He could never leave Ruth. He mustn't. He and Ruth had been sealed in the temple and Elizabeth born under the covenant. He deeply loved them both. His eternal family.

Eric's frown deepened. "I'd never ask you to. No matter how much I want to wake up to you every morning and go to bed with you every night."

"Then ..."

"Our society and your church have strict requirements. Love isn't the issue here. Conformity and obedience are. And my regard for your wife and daughter."

"But—"

"Your family's probably home waiting for you right now."

They would be in a few minutes if they weren't already, Elizabeth expecting to go to the ice cream shop. There was still the bus ride home. Yet somehow, he blundered on, reaching out to touch Eric's face. "We can figure something out."

Eric pushed his hand away. "We can't. You Mormons are a strange lot. You, Harold, the others. You'd stand in the self-lit flames of a living hell to honor some pledge that you break every time you see me." He stood, his expression defiant. "I'm not part of a church, but I seem to be the one with a conscience. I'm through with you, us, this ludicrous part-of-the-family farce."

Heber stood too, tears welling in his eyes. "You don't mean that."

Eric held firm. "Go. Ruth and Lizzy are counting on you." He crossed the room and opened the door.

Heber held his ground. "I love you. You love me."

"In time we'll forget about each other."

"Has staying away helped so far?" Heber held his arms out to Eric, wanting them to hold each other and make all the hurt go away.

"You got what you came for. Now go."

Heber drew a ragged breath, his hope for reconciliation evaporating. "All right," he said quietly. He could ignore Eric's pain only so many times. He willed his legs to walk.

He was part way out the door when Eric cried, "Wait!" reached for Heber, and drew him into his arms.

Heber fell into his embrace, a man saved from the abyss.

28

Pasadena, California, December 1950

A week later, Eric came to Christmas Eve dinner dressed in a red silk shirt, black pants and Santa Claus hat, a sort-of-Santa suit. His muscular arms were laden with gifts.

When Heber had asked Ruth about including him, she had said, "I was planning to have just family," her voice pinched.

Heber considered saying, "He *is* family. You said so yourself." Instead, he said only, "It's Christmas Eve."

Her eyes clouded. "Yes. All right."

"Goodie!" Elizabeth squealed when she heard that Uncle Eric would be joining them.

When he arrived, Eric handed Elizabeth a large rectangular box wrapped in shiny red paper with a glittery bow.

"Thank you." Elizabeth took the box and carried it carefully to the couch. "Can I open it now?"

"Go ahead," Heber said.

Perched on the edge of the couch, her feet dangling, Elizabeth carefully unwrapped the present. "She's so pretty!" she cried, pulling out a doll with shoulder length blonde hair and round, blue eyes.

"She can walk," Eric said. "See? Hold her hands. The hardwood floor works best."

Elizabeth's eyes opened as wide as the doll's as she watched. "She *is* walking!" Taking the doll's hands from Eric's, she walked her back and forth on the floor beside the floral area rug. "I love her!"

"She looks like you," Eric said. "Except you're even prettier." He touched Elizabeth's cheek.

Elizabeth stood the doll carefully against the front of an overstuffed chair, crawled into Eric's lap, and gave him a hug. Heber didn't know which of them looked happier. In contrast, Ruth was kneading her hands in her lap. He so wished she could somehow be happy too.

Next, Eric handed Ruth a thin, square box wrapped in red paper sprinkled with snowflakes.

She opened it in small, deliberate moves, eyes downcast. "The soundtrack of *Show Boat*. The play we saw last week at the Music Center." She smoothed and folded the wrapping paper. "How kind of you."

Heber picked up the card that was included and opened it. "Look at this. Three tickets to the film when it comes to Pasadena, two adults and a child."

"How generous." Ruth turned away before she'd finished the sentence and put the record on to play. The musical score filled the room.

"Jerome Kern wrote a winner there," Heber commented to no one in particular.

"Can I give Uncle Eric our present?" Elizabeth asked.

Heber nodded.

She pulled a long, narrow box from under the Christmas tree and handed it to Eric.

"Must be a tie," Eric said, opening it. He pulled out a pair of fawn-colored leather gloves.

"Your gardening gloves have holes in them," Heber said.

Eric ran his fingers over the gloves. "So soft. These are too nice for gardening."

"The clerk at Sears said they were heavy enough to stop the sharpest thorns." The gift wasn't personal, but he could give it to Eric in front of Ruth.

"Now come eat, everyone." Ruth shooed them to the dining room table, set with their best china and silver, and they all bowed their heads as Heber said a prayer on the food. Then she brought the dinner from the kitchen and passed around ham, mashed potatoes, sweet potatoes, peas, and a green salad. Heber noticed her hands shaking as she spooned small servings of everything onto Elizabeth's plate. Eric must be noticing too.

"Mmm, it all smells delicious," Eric said.

"Nothing fancy like you would have made." Ruth sat down and smoothed her blue jersey dress over her knees.

Heber and Eric exchanged glances. Thank God for the distracting sounds of *Show Boat*. They'd been doing better, the three of them, before Eric distanced himself and Ruth had new hope.

"Compliments to the cook," Eric said warmly, taking a bite of sweet potatoes. "It's as good as it smells."

Ruth stiffened, put her napkin to her mouth, and rushed from the room.

Heber set down his fork. "I'll check on her. Keep eating."

He followed Ruth into their bedroom where she sat on the bench at her vanity, tears streaming down her face.

"Are you alright?" he asked, putting his hands on her shoulders.

"I thought he was gone. Out of our lives." She turned and looked up at Heber. "When you asked if he could come for Christmas Eve, what could I say? He saved Lizzy."

Heber knelt on the floor beside her. "I felt bad for him, alone at Christmas."

As soon as he said the words, he regretted them. How much worse to ask her to share her husband, especially at Christmas.

Ruth took a handkerchief from the vanity drawer and wiped her eyes. "When did you start seeing him again?" she asked, her voice breaking.

"The day I didn't go to church. I'm sorry Ruth. It's just ..."

"I know. You were getting those moods again. He makes you happy and I don't." New tears soaked her face. "You've even been whistling."

"Oh, Ruth." Heber touched her shoulder. "You do make me happy in so many ways. You couldn't be a better wife."

She wiped her eyes again. "You want him, not me. I'm not good enough. It's strange finally saying it out loud."

"Ruth, darling. You aren't lacking in any way. I'm the one who isn't good enough." He kept his voice low, but resolute. "When we talked about it before we married, we both believed I could change. I don't seem able to; I've truly tried."

She inhaled several deep, calming breaths. "I tell myself I have this wonderful house. I have my career. We have Lizzy." She was silent a moment, gathering herself. "You and I enjoy a lot of things together; we're good friends. I try to feel like that's enough."

"They say if you want to change badly enough, you can. It's just not true."

"If I were more—"

"No," he interrupted. "Being normal is not a choice for me. You have to believe me. There isn't a prayer I haven't uttered, an idea I haven't tried." He had no words to comfort her. No promises to make that he could keep.

Ruth looked at her reflection in the mirror and shook her head. "How does Janine do it?"

He put his arms around her and held her close as her breathing steadied. Eric and Elizabeth must wonder what was keeping them, but he and Ruth had needed to have this conversation for a long time.

"We shouldn't have married," Ruth murmured.

"Maybe not. You deserve the best and it isn't me."

"We wouldn't have Lizzy."

He almost said yes, she was worth everything, they were an eternal family. But he wasn't sure how, in the end, he'd be judged. If they would be an eternal family.

"I can't imagine life without Lizzy." Ruth sighed. "Or you for that matter." She took a brush off the vanity and ran it through her hair. "We need to go back out there. I must look a sight."

"Should I ask Eric to leave?"

"Yes. No. I don't know. I don't know how to do this."

"I can tell them you have one of your migraines."

"I'll be all right. At least for tonight." She wiped her eyes a last time, tucked the damp handkerchief through a drawer pull, and headed to the kitchen. Soon, Heber could hear her beating something with the electric mixer.

He returned to the table, patting Elizabeth's shoulder as he passed. "Eat your peas. You like peas. Then you can have dessert and play with your new doll."

"Is Mommy okay?"

Ruth came in and began clearing the table. "I'm fine, dear. I was making brown sugar frosting for the spice cake."

"I love brown sugar frosting." Elizabeth turned to Eric. "I helped Mommy bake a cake and then I got to lick the beaters."

"Licking beaters is the best part." Eric winked at her as he rose to his feet, set his rumpled napkin on the table, and reached for two serving bowls. "Let me help."

"No need, I've got it," Ruth said firmly.

Eric sat back down.

Heber looked from Ruth to Eric to Elizabeth and ran his fingers through his hair. He was such a jerk. But which was worse? Being a jerk that invited his lover to dinner, or being a madman who whipped his daughter with a willow switch? After more than a year, the memory of that morning still gnawed at him.

29

Pasadena, California, August 1951

Somehow, they got through the school year and Heber's summer school stint. When Pasadena City College granted him tenure, Heber treated Ruth and Elizabeth to a rare dinner out at their family's favorite restaurant, Brotherton's, with its three course dinners and homemade buttermilk biscuits. Elizabeth had learned to read the children's menu by herself and read it out loud to them before choosing the macaroni and cheese.

Heber held onto a thin thread of sanity by meeting Eric regularly at his cottage or downtown, never at Heber's. Ruth must have guessed why he came home late from work an afternoon or two every week. She never said anything. Instead, she reserved her words for her writing and teaching. Heber didn't know how she kept on; the air so thick with tension it pooled between them. Sometimes at dinner he caught her looking at him with angry eyes and a withering frown. Those evenings he half-expected her to hurl a china plate at his head, but it wasn't in her gentle nature to do that. A plate to the head would have been easier than watching her silent emotions morph into a terrible hurt that blurred her eyes with tears.

He and Ruth dealt with Elizabeth's queries about Uncle Eric by having Heber take her to visit Eric once a month. Elizabeth always wanted to wear her best dresses for those visits, and she chattered with excitement as she got ready. Neither parent felt it fair to dull her enthusiasm about her hero.

It was quite the complicated dance. A recurring vignette would play in Heber's head at odd moments like a bad melodrama. In it he came home late, and Ruth met him at the door.

"Did you have a good walk with Eric?" she would ask in a voice stiff and sharp as a knife.

"Yes," he would answer, because there was no use denying where he'd been.

"What of your temple vows?" she would challenge, eyes unblinking, arms folded over her chest, the same question she'd raised when he asked about inviting Eric to the Easter sunrise service.

"I think about them every day." He did, in fact. Every damn day. She could never understand the soul-searing tug-of-war that played out relentlessly in his head.

"And you can still live with yourself? How am I supposed to live with you?" Her voice would grow shrill.

Heber's response to her last question was to shrug his shoulders. He had no defense.

In a way he wished she would throw him out. But for Mormons, divorce was unthinkable. Within the holy walls of the temple, wives vowed obedience to their husbands and husbands vowed obedience to God. The Patriarchal Order. Ruth had it down. If the church proclaimed people saints, she would be canonized.

Martyrdom had its price. Her migraines came more and more frequently. He hated himself for hurting her, and if he could breathe without Eric, he would never see him again.

Only another man like himself would understand his guilt and self-hatred, even as he sought solace with Eric.

It was like Eric said: society and the church were harsh taskmasters with unyielding demands. The church offered warnings of what waited for him on the other side if he made the wrong choices, but never any help with his real problem, only guilt and shame. Despite his misgivings, he'd married Ruth hoping she'd change him. How unfair to task her with making him a normal man. It was up to him. And nothing he'd tried had worked so far.

There were good moments when he didn't feel their marriage was a sham and figured Ruth didn't either. Several mornings a week he climbed in bed with her, and they discussed her latest novel, the creative writing magazine he and his students were putting together, Elizabeth's upcoming all-school spring concert. Sometimes he'd put his arm around her, and she'd rest her head against his shoulder. There were even moments of intimacy.

A few weeks before, as they clothes-pinned sheets and towels on the clothesline together, Ruth had sung, "Can't Help Loving That Man of Mine." Heber had shot her a wry smile and invented a harmony while they worked. If they could get through the next day, the next week, the next month, somehow with the passing of time, life would surely get easier.

One evening, as they were eating supper, the conversation turned to Elizabeth's upcoming sixth birthday.

"You can have six friends for the party because you'll be six years old," Ruth told Elizabeth.

"Anybody I want?" Elizabeth's eyes sparkled.

"Anybody you want."

"Susie, Janet, Corinne, David, Jack, Uncle Eric." Elizabeth counted on her fingers. "That's six."

Heber and Ruth exchanged looks. Heber's eyes asked the obvious. "What do we do?"

Ruth chewed her lip. "I was thinking six children from school or church."

"I want Uncle Eric to come. I told my friends how he saved me at the beach. And I want to show him all the flowers I helped Daddy plant."

Heber watched the parade of competing expressions on Ruth's face turn from horror to revulsion and, after a short eternity, acceptance. "All right," she sighed. "You can call him and invite him yourself."

"I haven't been to the house in a long time," Eric said when Heber met him at the door the afternoon of the party. "But I couldn't turn Lizzy down."

"Uncle Eric," Elizabeth squealed, racing into the room. "You're early!"

"I brought your mother a present, too. I thought I'd better give it to her before your friends get here."

"She's in the kitchen. Come on." Elizabeth grabbed his hand and pulled him toward the kitchen

"Not that a peace-offering could change anything," Eric whispered to Heber as Elizabeth tugged him along.

"Hello, Eric," Ruth said stiffly when she saw them."

"Uncle Eric has something for you," Elizabeth announced.

"Something I thought you could use." Eric pulled a set of needlepoint covers out of a thick canvas bag to replace the worn ones on the six dining room chairs.

"Wow," Heber said when Eric handed the covers to Ruth. "They look like they belong in one of the mansions in San

Marino. I can't imagine how many hours you spent on them."

"I can install them for you if you like," Eric offered.

Heber expected Ruth to be thrilled. Instead, she held them at arm's length, and her eyes filled with tears as she searched Eric's face. "You do needlepoint, too?"

Fortunately, the other guests arrived and a house full of six-year-olds stifled any further conversation. When Eric picked up his jacket and said goodnight, he whispered to Heber that the house would now be off-limits. No exceptions.

Heber couldn't blame him or Ruth.

That night, as Heber tossed in bed, a nightmare played out like a movie. In the dream, he rushed out in the street waving a loaded gun. He woke up in a cold sweat. He'd never owned a gun, but if he did, he was far more likely to use it on himself than innocent folks.

He had no idea how to get out of the situation he'd created. He and Eric had reconciled, but life with Ruth was far from a state of bliss. He could only make her happy if he quit seeing Eric. If he quit seeing Eric, he couldn't go on.

Maybe the dream presented the solution. It had seemed so real and clung to him like a sheet of Saran Wrap as he dressed for the day. He knew how to use a gun. He hadn't touched one since that hunting trip with his brothers, but he figured it would come back to him like riding a bicycle. He could get a handgun from a pawnshop in Los Angeles and take it up into the foothills.

He stopped himself, terrified by his own imaginings. He had had the same thoughts the morning he stayed home from church and instead went to Eric's. But this time he'd nearly come up with a plan. His dream wasn't like Ruth's vision when Samuel appeared to her and said she and the baby would be fine. Her vision seemed to have truly come from God. His dream had come from a dark place, the Devil or his own soul.

When Ruth set pancakes in front of him and Elizabeth, she avoided his eyes and quickly left the room. He followed her down the hall to their bedroom. "I didn't ask Lizzy to invite him," he said as she pulled open a dresser drawer.

She turned to face him. "You might have helped me make up a good excuse. I'm a writer, but I've run out of lines."

"You won't need any more lines. He's not coming to the house again. Ever. His decision." Tight-lipped, Heber left the room. He had to get out of the house.

His hand was on the doorknob when he heard Elizabeth. "Daddy, aren't you finishing your pancakes?"

He went back in the kitchen and kissed her cheek. "Sorry, sweet pea. We're out of milk and I'm going to the store for some. I won't be long."

"Can I go?"

"Not this time. Help Mommy and I'll bring you a treat."

Striding down the first block, he wanted in the worst way to head straight to Eric's cottage. Determined, he turned toward Ralph's grocery store. Ruth had every right to be upset with both him and Eric. Eric hadn't taken vows with her, but he knew Heber had.

At Ralph's, Heber put milk in the grocery cart, then headed to the fruit section. Elizabeth expected a treat. He'd make it a healthy one.

He sorted through the apples, looking for an especially shiny, red one.

Or should he get grapes? She loved seedless green grapes if they had any.

Eric liked plump purple grapes. Seeds didn't bother him. Heber caught himself up. He was buying them for Elizabeth, not Eric. They had to be green seedless.

Heber fingered a pile of blueberries, a memory of Eric, the beach, and the blueberry pie he'd pulled from the picnic basket coming to mind. Eric's heroism. Ruth's gratitude. The delicious blueberry pie. He took a berry from the display and bit into it, holding the sweetness in his mouth. Maybe Ruth would make something with blueberries. A pie or tart like Eric's.

He stopped short, nearly gagging on the sweet juice. How could the idea of Ruth making a tart like Eric's even enter his mind? Letting go the sweetness, Heber swallowed, then swallowed again. The berry stuck tight in his throat. Nothing could pass. With a choking gasp he finally coughed it up. Ruth already kept the cookie jar full for her sorry excuse of a husband. *A worthless cheat. A dandy. One of those.*

Abruptly the display of berries blurred. Heber's legs gave way. He grabbed the table for support, then crumpled to the concrete floor, pulling the table over with him.

Heber lay for a few seconds on the cold floor, knees pulled into his chest. *A heart attack? A stroke?*

A clerk rushed up. "Sir, are you alright? Should I call an ambulance?"

A second clerk knelt by him. "Can I call someone for you?"

Numbness crept over Heber from his fingers to his chest, even more frightening than his collapse. He somehow forced slower, deeper breaths. The room quit spinning. He pulled himself into a sitting position, shoulders heaving. "Give me a minute. Knees gave out. No need to call anyone."

He looked at the smashed berries everywhere on and around him, and at the anxious faces peering down at him. He could breathe again. No pain in his chest. *What then? Nervous breakdown? Had to be. It had come to that.*

"Sorry," he mumbled.

A fellow shopper helped him to his feet. He stumbled out the door, leaving his grocery cart and a murmuring crowd behind. Twice, in the four blocks home, he stopped to vomit in the gutter.

When he got home, Elizabeth was playing schoolteacher in the living room, her walking doll and three teddy bears gathered for the lesson. "Where's my treat?" she asked. Then, looking him up and down, "Daddy, what happened to you?"

Heber looked in horror at his empty arms and his shirt stained with splotches of blue, bits of berry clinging here and there. He didn't even have the milk. "We'll go later, and you can choose something," he managed to say and went up the stairs to Ruth's study.

"Yes?" Ruth said when he knocked.

He opened the door a crack. "I need to talk to you."

"I'm working on my novel. And I need to answer my mother's letter."

"It can't wait." Heber went on into the room.

Ruth turned toward him and inhaled sharply, putting a hand to her heart. "What happened? You're white as a sheet. And your shirt. Is Lizzy all right?"

Heber slumped onto a chair. "I can't go on like this."

"Where's Lizzy?"

"Blueberries."

"You're scaring me, Heber."

"Lizzy's playing downstairs. I love you, Ruth." He looked up at her through red-rimmed eyes.

"Whatever is the matter?"

"I've tried so hard, but it's a lie." Heber fingered a scratch on the arm of the chair.

Ruth exhaled. "I see. This is about Eric."

Heber put his head in his hands and began to sob. "I can't go to Utah again," he said when he could speak. "Temple spires everywhere. I know we leave next week for our summer trip." He pointed to the opened letter on the desk. "Your mother. My family. If they knew ..."

Ruth knelt before him. "Shall I call a doctor? We'll be all right. We always are."

Fresh tears poured down his face. "Something is seriously wrong with me. You have to believe me." He steadied himself. "In the store—the room started spinning. I ... I pulled the display down when I fell."

"You fainted?"

"I was standing by the blueberries. Next thing I knew I was on the floor. Berries everywhere."

"I'll call your doctor."

"He can't help me. Even God can't help me."

Ruth reached an arm toward him. "We can face this together. Figure it out. We always do."

Heber pulled back. "No, Ruth. We can't. We've tried and tried." He swiped at his tears.

"I've been difficult. I can do better."

Anger welled in Heber. He reached for her shoulders as if to give her a good shake. "God damn it, Ruth! Quit thinking it's you. Nothing has ever been your fault."

He dropped his hands. "You've tried your hardest. I've tried. It's just what it is."

She patted his hand, her focus somewhere beyond his shoulder. "Yes. All right. What will you do?"

Heber had no idea. Then he remembered that Eric was leaving for Maine in a few days to visit his uncle. He'd invited Heber along, more in jest because Heber could never go.

Or maybe he could.

"Eric is going to Maine Sunday. He's spending August there to visit family. I'll see if I can go with him."

Ruth staggered to her feet as if she'd been struck. "Don't leave us."

Heber looked away from the terror in her eyes. "It's that or a mental hospital."

"A month. There must be another way."

"I have to go. Or I'll do something terrible. I'll be back before school starts."

"Oh, Heber."

"You have your writers' conference. You run things splendidly. Go give them your wonderful keynote addresses. I'm sure our tenant can lend a hand if you need something. You'll hardly notice I'm gone." The words poured out of him.

Ruth put her hands to her face. "Oh, Heber," she said again. "What good can come of a trip with Eric?"

"When I'm with him I don't hate who I am as much." He leaned in, palms up. "How can I make you understand? What if I go for a drive and wrap our car around a telephone pole?" His mind conjured the burning smell of the oil leaking from the wrecked car.

"We can find help for you here. I know we can."

"Help? For being me? If it isn't a car, you'll find me hanging in the shower." His chest ached with the effort to explain himself. "I've been dreaming about guns. It's Maine or a mental hospital. Or worse."

Ruth took a few steps back and went to her desk. She carefully covered her mother's letter before turning again to Heber, her hands clasped. "A nervous breakdown," she murmured. "All right. Do what you have to do." Without meeting his eyes, she walked past him, closing the door behind her. Her footsteps echoed down the stairs.

30

Mt. Desert Island, Maine, August 1951

Eric's cousin Dell met Heber and Eric at the Bar Harbor bus station. After giving Heber a firm, welcoming handshake, he gave Eric a long bear hug.

"So good to see you. Where's Julia?" Eric asked, looking around.

"She's putting up vegetables. Don't worry, she's not going to miss seeing you. She'll run out when you drop me home."

"Good. It's been too long."

Eric and Heber pulled their suitcases from the growing luggage pile beside the bus and the three men headed for a nearby cafe. Heber was certain he smelled as grungy as he felt after three days and nights on a bus, and apologized, but Dell waved the apology away.

Eric had assured Heber that Dell knew about and accepted their relationship. Amazingly, it seemed to be true. Dell didn't give Heber as much as a sideways glance as they chatted about the cross-country bus trip over breakfast. Heber had never enjoyed a meal more.

When they'd finished generous plates of pancakes and eggs, they headed to Dell's house a few miles outside of town. Heber was delighted to see a bit of Bar Harbor, a coastal resort for the rich elite. He was even more delighted when they arrived at Dell's small, neat farmhouse and he met Dell's wife.

When Julia came out of the house, wiping her hands on her apron, Eric put an arm around Heber's shoulders. "This is Heber," he said as she approached them.

Just like Dell, Julia gave Heber a firm handshake and then gathered Eric in a warm hug.

After they all chatted for a few minutes, Dell handed Eric keys to an old Rambler they could use for their three-week stay. "We'll do just fine with the truck," he assured them, and Julia nodded agreement.

Eric waved out the window, then half turned to Heber as he backed out the driveway. "Can't wait for you to meet Dell's folks, Uncle Floyd and Aunt Agnes. They're the ones who raised me. You saw how Dell and Julia are. They'll be the same."

Heber knit his brow. "I did see. Doesn't seem to bother them at all. I don't get it."

"My aunt and uncle raised us that way. If something came up about my *differences*, they'd remind us, 'It's how the Lord made Eric, and the Lord don't make no junk.'

"It wasn't easy for Dell or me. He got bullied just for hanging around with me." Eric's eyes misted as he talked. "When we were younger, we'd get jumped by older kids on our way home from school. They never beat us too bad, but Aunt Agnes and Uncle Floyd would get pretty upset. The day Dell came home with a chipped tooth and a black eye Uncle Floyd gave us our first lesson on how to fight."

"First lesson."

"Yeah. First of many. He hung a grain bag of sand in his garage and taught us to punch and tackle. He taught us to wrestle, too, and after a while we could pin just about anybody to the ground. Those skills have come in handy over the years."

"Me, I stuck close to the farm doing schoolwork and chores," Heber reflected. "I got teased all right. In my town boys were supposed to shoot guns, drive trucks and play football. I preferred poetry and art. About as different as you can get. The other kids called me names — fairy, homo, pansy. I just told myself they were jealous because I did better in school than them."

"Kids are so cruel." Eric took a hand from the steering wheel and laced his fingers with Heber's.

Heber returned the welcome pressure. "Once in a while I was attracted to some boy, but I thought it was a phase." He flashed a wry smile. "How naïve could I get, right? I didn't really begin to question who I am until my mission."

Heber put his other hand over Eric's and watched the forest of tall pines passing by the window. He wondered if his brothers had ever been hassled because of him. They were a scrappy lot, occasionally coming home from school with a black eye or bloody nose. He never knew what the fights were about; he hoped they hadn't gotten hurt because of him. Still, he doubted anyone would have believed he was "like that." Not in their little Mormon community. All these years later, he couldn't imagine asking his brothers what those fights were about. If he were to ask, what painful truths might spill out?

Ruth had married him even after he told her what he was like. She probably still didn't believe it was his basic nature. She'd looked so stricken when he boarded the bus for Maine that he nearly changed his mind about going. But she would be all right. The writer's conference and her own writing would keep her busy and happy. Lizzy was good company, and Grace was coming to visit while Ted was in the East on business.

At the bus station Lizzy had burrowed into Heber's neck the way she did as a toddler. He'd assured her he'd bring her a present from his trip which comforted her. How he missed her already, he admitted to himself, his thoughts sliding into his deep rabbit hole of grief and regret.

Peeling himself from the habitual litany that solved nothing, Heber focused on the lush hemlock and pine forests of Mt. Desert Island. Cranking down the passenger side window, he leaned out. "Smell the air," he crowed, inhaling the citrusy smells of the trees and muskiness of the forest floor.

"Having a hard time smelling anything besides us. A shared shower is the first thing on my list. You in?" Eric grinned mischievously.

"Can't wait."

At last, he and Eric would have a full night together. On the bus ride from California to Maine, they'd sat a careful distance apart, so people wouldn't get the wrong impression. Or, rather, the right impression. They endured three long days and nights of yearning, unable to grab even a quick hug. In bus station bathrooms, where they washed up, brushed their teeth, and shaved in the grimy basins, they were especially careful.

In a small town south of Chicago, they had pressed knees under the bus station's restaurant counter as they perched on stools and ordered lunch. It felt innocent and invisible, but a heavy man in overalls got out of a booth behind them and grunted as he leaned across Heber's shoulder, ostensibly to get a bottle of ketchup. The man's weight was an unmistakable warning that there was a good beating out back for their kind. Another man called out, "Hey Mike, grab some matches while you're up there. I gotta feeling I'm gonna wanna set something on fire later." Their guffaws and stamping of work boots on the linoleum floor sent a river of chills down Heber's spine.

In Boston, where they changed from Continental Trailways to the slower Greyhound for the last leg of their trip, they had a two-hour layover. They set out to explore, and when they cut through an alley that appeared empty, Eric took Heber's hand. "Hey Ed! Got us a couple of Nancy boys down there," Heber heard someone call from a fire escape above them. Soon the iron staircase shook and rattled with heavy footsteps stomping down the steps. Right behind them, a trashcan got dumped, with tin cans clattering and bottles shattering. Heber and Eric sprinted to the sunlight and busy street. At the next corner, they scuttled their walk and hurried back to the bus station.

Hard to believe that now Heber could be himself, something not remotely possible on the bus or anywhere else for that matter. What had Eric's uncle said? *'It's how the Lord made you and the Lord don't make no junk.'* Sunshine broke through the branches of the stolid evergreens and Heber's chest expanded until he nearly burst. Relishing visions of the time ahead, he broke into song.

Oh we ain't got a barrel of money
maybe we're ragged and funny
but we're traveling along, singing a song, side by side.

"Side by side. Nice," Eric agreed.

When they entered the village of Hall Quarry with its little store, some tiny houses, a single pump gas station, and surprisingly, a post office, Eric explained that it had once been a community of miners working a quarry pit. The quarry had been closed for decades, and only these few buildings remained as ghosts of men's past labors. Hall Quarry looked like a movie set and Heber could imagine the men mining the quarry, freeing large slabs of granite, harsh work but real and satisfying.

Eric drove up a dirt road to a shingled cottage. "My aunt and uncle own this place and it's ours for the next three weeks. Ready for the best time of your life?" He took a key from his pocket.

"Absolutely."

Heber helped Eric lug their suitcases into the cozy living room. On the wall hung a photograph of a stooped, white-haired man and a younger version of the man, huskier, with a full brown beard. Probably Dell years earlier. Between them stood a small woman with silver curls and a round, ruddy face that looked like Eric's. "That's Uncle Floyd and Aunt Agnes." Eric's eyes clouded with memories. "Tomorrow you'll meet them. I can't believe I get to share all this with you."

"Looking forward to it. I'm rather fond of the man they raised." Heber looked intently at Eric in a moment of shared intimacy so powerful it burned in his chest. What amazing days lay ahead!

He followed Eric down a short, narrow hallway, careful not to bump the walls with his suitcase. A teen-age giddiness filled him when he saw the double bed in the small bedroom.

Eric followed the direction of Heber's gaze and laughed. "Of like minds," he said, already pulling his t-shirt over his head. "Shower first."

They made love in the shower, frenzied with the heat that had built up between them on the long bus ride. "That was a good start," Eric grinned afterward, lathering soap along Heber's arms.

Heber nodded, catching Eric up in a soapy hug.

After their shower, they carefully turned back the quilt and lay on the bed, naked. Heber often spooned behind Eric in their stolen moments at his cottage, but time and home were always pressing. Today, neither of them would be going anywhere.

Thoughts of Ruth crept in. An awareness that moments like this weren't possible with her. He refocused on the feel of Eric snuggled up behind him, arms wrapped around him, torso and hips pressed into his bare backside. Eric's touch began to excite Heber again, then the exhaustion of the trip settled over him and he fell toward a deep sleep, kissing Eric's wrist as he drifted off.

When he awoke, Eric was dressing. "Up for some blueberries and sunshine kisses?" Eric asked.

"Until my lips are purple." Heber yawned, stretched, and began pawing through his suitcase for clean clothes. What a perfect afternoon: sex, a nap, and a walk in the woods with this dear man. Heaven couldn't get any better. When he got to the neat stack of *garments*, he hesitated.

"Uh-oh. You've got that I'm-a-terrible-person look," Eric said, standing by the bed watching him unfold and refold the underwear. "Wear 'em if you'll feel better. I've seen 'em before."

"I sort of have to," Heber chuckled. "I don't have anything else."

Dressed and ready, Heber took Eric's hand and they headed out, tromping through hemlock and pine. Large slabs of granite competed with the underbrush for space on the sun-dappled forest floor. Heber's uneasy conscience quieted as he admired the mosaic of living greenery and the long-dead stone. Squinting at one gray hulk, he tried to imagine it as a finished mantle or kitchen counter. When he found a tangle of wild blueberries, plump and more purple than blue, he began to pick them, stuffing about as many into his mouth as he put in the small bucket he carried. Eric kissed him, sharing the sweet taste of berries between them before he moved off to fill his own bucket.

"Lizzy would love this," Heber said. A long shard of guilt pierced the moment. He gritted his teeth against the familiar pain and, with a slow sigh, let it pass. Then he joined Eric at a bush heavily laden with the delicious fruit.

"Even better than you expected, right?" Eric asked.

"Yes, you are. How can I be so lucky?"

"Come see this." Eric led Heber to a lush meadow dotted with delicate yellow buttercups and white daisies. One of the great stone slabs lay almost at their feet, a hulk of granite with rich veins of pink and tan running through it, and the wildflowers of the meadow creeping up its exposed angles. Eric took the pail of blueberries from Heber and set it on the ground.

Heber looked around once to make sure the woods would guard their privacy, then slipped off his clothes and yielded to Eric. The slab was surprisingly smooth against his bare skin. Eric's weight on him, his lips on Heber's eager body, were as welcome as the warmth of the sun setting in the west. Afterward, Eric picked a bouquet of bluebells and lupine and handed them to him. "Welcome to my heaven," Eric said.

Heber took the flowers with one hand and Eric's arm with the other. A feeling of pure contentment washed over him, mingling with the lupine's sweet, florid fragrance.

When they returned to the cottage, Eric pulled a book from his suitcase and handed it to Heber. "For you."

Heber looked at the cover. *Leaves of Grass.* The same book he'd given to Brian. How wonderful that relationship had seemed, and yet, how one-dimensional compared to what he had with Eric. He turned to "I Sing the Body Electric," climbed on the bed, and read from the Walt Whitman poem, gesturing at Eric's body parts as he went along.

Gentlemen, look on this wonder
Whatever the bids of the bidders,
they cannot be high enough for it;
For it the globe lay preparing quintillions of years,

without one animal or plant;
For it the revolving cycles truly and steadily roll'd.
In this head the all-baffling brain;
In it and below it, the makings of heroes.
Examine these limbs, red, black, or white,
they are so cunning in tendon and nerve;
They shall be stript, that you may see them.
Exquisite senses, life-lit eyes, pluck, volition,
Flakes of breast-muscle, pliant back-bone and neck,
flesh not flabby, good-sized arms and legs,
And wonders within there yet.

Heber would have kept reading but for the urge to pull
Eric up on the bed beside him and examine his limbs and
flecks of breast-muscle. This moment, void of shame and
guilt, felt miraculous. There'd been dangers on the bus trip.
Gut-ripping attacks of his conscience on this first day in
Maine. But oh, to freely love and be loved!
A gift he'd been denied his whole life.

31

Mt. Desert Island, Maine, August 1951

During their weeks together, Heber and Eric made four trips into Bar Harbor to visit Aunt Agnes. A stroke had paralyzed her left side, and her speech was almost unintelligible, but her eyes shone with love when she saw Eric. He sat beside her hospital bed, his hand enclosing hers, and entertained her with stories of his vacation with Heber.

There was the afternoon Heber had made a succulent blueberry pie with Eric's expert supervision and Aunt Agnes' prize-winning recipe. Heber had never pictured himself as a baker, but when they took a big wedge to Floyd and he declared it 'every bit as good as the Missus' pie,' he felt as proud as the day he'd won the spelling bee in high school.

Then there was Heber's effort to repair a leak in the bathroom sink faucet. He replaced all the washers in both hot and cold taps, but when he put everything back together the sink leaked worse than before. He'd never been much of a handyman. Yet Floyd and Dell fussed over him so much for trying, with Agnes adding guttural sounds of agreement, that he ended up feeling loved instead of foolish.

The days they didn't go into Bar Harbor, Heber and Eric slept late, made a leisurely breakfast together and wandered through the woods or curled up with books, each reading to the other the passages they most enjoyed. Eric taught Heber how to play cards: Gin Rummy, Crazy Eights, a two-player variation of Hearts. Heber's mother had taught her children that cards were the devil's path to gambling, and Ruth considered playing cards a waste of time. But Heber delighted in the novelty of the games and the easy banter between Eric and him as they played. He even worked on the novel he'd begun years earlier, while Eric wrote postcards to friends. Some afternoons they drove to the beach for a cold dip in the Atlantic. Several evenings Eric found the Glen Miller band on the radio, and they danced, their arms locked around each other, their bodies swaying to the rhythms. At night, they counted thousands of stars in the sky.

They made love when they wanted to. In fact, whenever either of them even slightly wanted to. Eric began calling him *sweetie* and Heber hugged the endearment to his heart. Attendance to Eric's needs came as naturally to Heber as walking or sleeping, and affection flowed between them without effort. Heber had always wanted this same easy physical connection with Ruth. But he always had to consciously think three steps ahead about what would bring her pleasure and how he could offer it. The resulting affection often felt forced and contrived.

Sometimes he pictured Ruth back home at the kitchen table, paying the bills he always took care of, or in the yard, frowning at the knee-high weeds he kept at bay. Twice he woke in the night wondering if he heard Elizabeth crying three thousand miles away. Every few days he sent them each a card, chronicling his favorite sights in Maine and reassuring them of his love. It was the best he could do. He never penned a return address.

Two nights before Heber and Eric were to leave for home, Heber dreamt that he was with Ruth in Sears, standing before twin beds. "We'll be fine with these," he insisted.

"I'm getting the double bed," she said. "You *are* my husband. You made vows in the temple."

He startled awake, clammy with sweat. The clock on the nightstand read 3:27 a.m.

He'd promised Ruth he would return. That was impossible. He couldn't go back to her. He couldn't pretend another minute.

He wanted to wake Eric, snoring softly beside him, and tell him at once. "The time has come," he'd say.

"You know it's what I've longed for," Eric would respond, taking Heber in his arms.

3:31 a.m. Only four minutes of calm certainty, and then his conscience asserted itself. *Ruth depends on you. What about Elizabeth? What about the church? You have a job. Responsibilities. You know what they do to homosexuals, don't you?*

Chastened, Heber gave in to his inner voice. He wouldn't leave Ruth. He had a temple marriage and a daughter to consider. A good job. A circle of relatives and friends who would never tolerate this side of him.

3:35 a.m. Shifting restlessly in bed, Heber placed a hand on his racing heart. He had to stop the lies. Conscience be damned.

He lay awake waiting for the sun to cast its first light in the window, then put his arm across Eric and pressed his cheek against Eric's back, nestling into him.

"Mmm," Eric sighed. "You awake?" He turned, his lips moving against Heber's shoulder.

"I need you."

Eric propped himself up with his elbow. "Ah, that look. What's wrong, sweetie?"

"I've been thinking about home."

"And?"

"I can't go back." How could he live without hearing Eric call him *sweetie* every morning?

"I don't want our time to end either." Eric frowned, sat up in bed, and was quiet for several minutes.

Heber waited; his eyes as unwavering on Eric as they had been on the clock.

"You know we can't stay here," Eric said at last. "It's back to the real world. Job. House. Ruth and Lizzy."

"I've never been this happy."

"Vacations are supposed to be better than real life. That's why people don't want them to end." His tone was light, but his expression was serious.

"You don't think we'd get along this well outside of Maine?"

"We'd get along anywhere. That's not the point."

"It's my point."

"I told you, I'm far too fond of Ruth and Lizzy to break up your marriage. I almost canceled this trip a dozen times. I probably should have. I feel nearly as guilty as you do."

Heber watched, surprised and silenced, as Eric got up and pulled on swimming trunks, a short-sleeved shirt, and casual slacks. Eric's eyes carefully avoided his.

"That's all you're going to say?" Heber finally asked.

"We planned on going to the beach today. Want to help me make a picnic?"

Eric wasn't responding at all the way Heber had expected. He listened in disbelief as Eric put the food together, droning on about how it was going to be a hot and humid day and something about Aunt Agnes and Uncle Floyd.

How could he dismiss Heber so easily? Slouching on the car seat all the way to the beach, Heber nursed his hurt feelings.

"I'll set out our things; you go on down to the water," Eric said when they'd parked the car. He put a hand on Heber's shoulder. "It helps."

Eric knew exactly how he felt and did care about him. That reassurance brought tears to Heber's eyes. He wandered past sea-sculpted pines, through marshy grasses, and across clusters of rocks to stand at the gray water's edge. Heaving waves rolled rhythmically into shore while a stiff wind ruffled his shirtsleeves and spattered his face with brine. His nostrils filled with fresh sea air.

The ebb and flow of the waters finally had a calming effect. Tonight, they could talk about everything. Right now, he needed to enjoy this precious time with Eric.

He stripped to his trunks and waded into the ocean, setting his jaw against the cold, the water barely covering his torso as he walked further and further out. Never in California could he go this distance before the waves buffeted him. Frigid, though. The Pacific sure was warmer than the Atlantic.

Once he'd grown accustomed to the cold he headed across the swells in a purposeful sidestroke, then rested in the water, his hands and feet lightly fluttering to keep him afloat as the waves rocked him up and down, up and down. Eric joined him and they swam lazily side by side.

"Couldn't you do this forever?" Heber asked. They were almost the same words he'd used with Ruth; the ones she had taken as a proposal. This time he was clear about his intentions. He would change Eric's mind. Leave Ruth and be with him always. "Hey," he said, splashing water into Eric's face. "You'd be a great father."

"What? I've never been good with kids." Eric splashed back.

"Like Lizzy isn't convinced you walk on water?"

They swam together to shore. Standing on the sand Heber slicked the water from his arms and legs, then from his recently acquired crew cut.

Abruptly, Eric grabbed him in a hammerlock. They went down in the sand shouting with laughter. Eric settled on top of Heber and his hands were gritty as he cupped Heber's face. Heber quieted and closed his eyes, savoring the salty kiss as Eric's tongue slowly moved over every part of his mouth and lips.

"I'm glad I brought you here. It means a lot to share it with you," Eric said.

"I bet you say that to all the boys."

"I never brought anyone here. Only you."

Heber held his gaze. "Do you have any idea how much I love you?"

Eric sat up and brushed sand from his forearms. "So you've forgiven me for not helping more with your new house?"

"Forgiven you?" Heber put his arms around Eric's waist and looked into his beloved's eyes. "This trip. Being here with you. Can't you see that everything between us is perfect?" This time he would not be stopped. "The nights, the mornings, but so much more. The way your relatives treat me. How we finish each other's sentences. Your knack for saying exactly the right words when I get on myself." He looked steadily into Eric's eyes. "No one can do for me what you do. I can't leave you and go back to Ruth."

Eric pulled back from Heber, shaking his head. "You're really serious."

"You don't know what it's like to live in a marriage without passion and without true acceptance. Ruth keeps hoping I can be different than I am, and I've tried so hard. But I can't be what she wants." Heber's voice rose in a plea for understanding. "You and I love each other in a way I've never known. Life could be like this for us all the time."

Eric looked away from Heber's insistent eyes and studied the tops of his feet.

"It doesn't have to end," Heber pressed.

Eric began drawing patterns in the sand with one toe.

"Look at me," Heber said.

Slowly Eric lifted his head. His eyes were wet. Heber laid a hand along his face. "I know it won't be easy, but we should try. Don't you feel it?"

Eric brushed his hand away and wiped his eyes. "I won't let you leave Ruth, remember?" Again, he turned away from Heber's gaze.

"It's not your decision," Heber said flatly.

Eric still faced away, arms crossed, head shaking reflexively back and forth. "It takes more than love to do what you suggest."

Heber took Eric's shoulders and turned him around. "There's nothing more than love."

Eric laughed a short, brittle laugh. "This isn't a movie, Heber. This is life."

"We've been in a movie for weeks. It can keep playing. I'm done trying to change." Heber reached out to Eric, but Eric pulled free. He kept on anyway. "We can move to San Francisco or New York. I can get a job teaching at a high school, if not a college." The words tumbled out. "Or we can stay here. Find some kind of work. Your family accepts you. They'd accept me."

Eric twisted his mouth in a frown. "Ruth?"

"She has her career and lots of friends. She'll be free to meet someone else who's a better husband than I could ever be."

"Lizzy?"

Not seeing his daughter every day would be the toughest, and for a moment Heber wavered, looking out to sea. Then he caught and held Eric's eyes, and it was simple. He had to be with him. "She can spend summers and holidays with us. More quality time than she gets with me now." He'd never told Eric about the time he whipped her legs. He couldn't risk becoming that person again.

"Your family?"

His parents? His brothers and sisters? They'd disown him, but that wouldn't deter him now. He was who he was. "I'll figure it out."

"Your church?"

Heber exhaled. "I've thought a lot about what Dell said. He's right, you know. 'God don't make no junk.' I'm seeing church doctrine in a new light."

"And the people who sit shoulder to shoulder with you in those pews?"

"Mostly they're good people. I don't know how they can be so narrow-minded."

"You've been doing some thinking."

Heber pushed on. "God helped Ruth carry Lizzy. He saved her life after Lizzy was born. Then, last year, through your hands, He saved Lizzy's life. He's looking after our family, and He brought you in to be part of it. Crazy, but true."

"Or coincidence."

"God might even be glad to see me this happy."

"Huh. That *is* a new Heber."

"Happiness is what parents want for their children. There are all kinds of people in the church. Some of them have helped me a lot; some would kick me to China if they knew." He paused. "There are the people and then there's God. They're becoming separate in my head."

Eric trickled sand through his fingers as Heber waited.

"You have no idea how dangerous life as a queer would be," Eric said at last. "Guys in the shadows, waiting to kick in our skulls. McCarthy's men ridding the country of fags and Commies. Everyone hates us."

Heber remembered the man in the bus stop restaurant and how they were followed in Boston. He'd have to be more careful.

A shadow moved across Eric's face. "Did you know I got a dishonorable discharge from the Navy for being queer? Couldn't find a job anywhere after that, so now I'm a gardener with an engineering degree. What do you plan to do if you can't teach?"

Somehow Eric had never told him that story. He wasn't making it easy. Being with Brian was as close as Heber had come to living the life of a queer, and he'd run from it. He could end up naked and bloody in some ditch. But he was ready to take that chance. "There isn't a problem we couldn't solve together," he said. "Isn't that what you want?"

"Damn fool. You really would leave Ruth, wouldn't you?"

"Yes, I will."

"No, you shouldn't."

Heber opened his mouth to respond, but Eric silenced him with a stern look. "Let me think." He turned, heading toward the trees.

Heber wandered down to the shoreline, kicking sand with every step. Wasn't this what Eric had asked for the day they'd reconciled? A few clouds gathered in the distant sky and the water turned a deeper gray. A lone gull screamed nearby. Heber stared at the ocean, torturing himself with memories. Eric's hardness as they spooned in bed. The stubble of his beard in the morning when they first awakened and kissed. The smell of his body, the taste of his lips. The understanding and acceptance Heber always saw in his eyes. What he'd been denied for so long was now fully his for the first time, and the thought of losing it rocked him to his core.

He waited an eternity to learn his fate.

"I won't have you if you leave her." Eric's voice was husky behind him.

Heber whirled to face him. "What?"

"I want to be with you. You know I do."

Heber braced himself.

"I won't break up your marriage. You'd hate me in the end."

"I'd never hate you."

"I'd hate myself. It isn't just Ruth and Lizzy. Living as a queer is a road I won't let you take." Eric's voice was resolute. "I don't advertise my preference for men, and I don't hang out in queer clubs. I've told only a handful of my closest friends, and I look over my shoulder everywhere I go."

Eric dropped down on the sand and hugged his knees. Heber sat beside him, so close he could feel the intensity of Eric's words.

"I've had to break a few jaws. If you can make it as a family man, you're a lot safer. You have a wife, a daughter, a job you like, standing in your church. Hang on to what you have. You're not built to survive as a queer."

Heber doubted he'd win a fist fight if one came his way. The breeze gusted, rifling the caps of the waves. Heber shivered uncontrollably. His new life was shattering before the glass even cooled.

"I shouldn't have gone back to you in Pasadena. And shouldn't have brought you here. I could have guessed it would end like this. When you board the bus to Pasadena, I'll stay here in Bar Harbor. I'm sure Dell will put me up while I find a job."

Heber jumped to his feet and stared down at Eric, a white-hot pain searing his chest. "Stay here? You can't do that!"

"If I go back to Pasadena, we'll keep playing this scene over and over."

"But—"

"Twice is enough."

"When I came to your cottage that day, I wasn't ready to leave Ruth. I am now. I can't live two lives anymore."

Eric said nothing.

"You're a coward," Heber cried, stepping back from Eric's stony face. "Why don't you just kill me?" He stumbled toward the ocean.

Eric made no effort to stop him.

32

Pasadena, California, August 1951

The sweltering return bus ride from Maine to Pasadena seemed a hundred days long. Heber wore the collective grime of forty fellow passengers as he climbed from the bus to a platform overflowing with people. Overweight women in bulging cotton dresses cut across his path, shouting at the children who milled at their feet. Loud teenage girls wearing too much makeup bunched together in doorways smoking cigarettes. Seedy older men with three days' stubble and a stale smell about them wandered toward the station exit.

He spotted Ruth clutching Elizabeth's hand and winced when he saw she wore a new shirtwaist dress and a fashionable hairdo. She was still trying.

"Daddy," Elizabeth called as he elbowed his way to them.

"Hello, dear." Ruth touched her lips to his and he could feel the uncertainty in her kiss. She looked thinner than when he'd left, and dark circles puffed under her eyes. Was she glad to see him? Angry? Hurt beyond repair? All of the above?

"Where's Uncle Eric?" Elizabeth looked beyond Heber to the people still climbing off the bus.

"He decided to stay in Maine." The words caught in Heber's throat. He felt like a man coming home from a funeral. Restroom mirrors during the trip home reflected hollow eyes, mouth a grim line, skin tinged gray. He and Ruth made a sallow couple.

He saw a glimmer of light in Ruth's eyes at the news of Eric. Did she believe that ending things with Eric would change his relationship with her? He pitied Ruth as much as himself.

"You were gone too long. Don't leave again." Elizabeth took his hand and swung it as they walked toward the luggage being unloaded from the bus.

"I worked on my novel," he told Ruth. "I'm eager to show you what I did." Those weren't the words he knew she wanted to hear, but they were what he could offer.

At the jumble of suitcases, Heber grabbed the handle of his bag. Elizabeth took his free hand. "What did you bring me?" she asked.

"It's in my suitcase. You'll have to wait 'til we get home."

Ruth walked a step behind them to the car.

All the way home, Elizabeth chattered about a birthday party she had attended, games she'd played with the neighbors, a movie she'd seen one Saturday. She wriggled in the back seat, standing up, sitting down, standing up, sitting down. "I can play a song on the piano for you." She leaned against the front seat and wrapped her arms around Heber's neck.

A smile tugged at his lips. If anything could bring his grief-stricken heart joy, it was the touch of his daughter. "You'll have to play it for me after dinner."

"Mommy's making liver and onions. Your favorite."

"It sure is." Ruth cooked the dish just the way his mother did, the liver and sautéed onions a more delicate taste than he found in restaurants. The memory made his mouth water, Ruth's culinary talents a salve on his despair.

Maybe...somehow...

As they turned in the driveway, a revolting stench wafted through the car's open windows.

"Peeeyuu! What stinks?" Elizabeth shrilled.

"Skunk." Heber gagged on the odor. Not that he should talk after his long, unwashed bus ride. Ruth had rolled her window down on the way home and he'd done the same. But his body odor hadn't reached skunk level. In his opinion, anyway. "Some homecoming," he muttered.

Without a word Ruth opened her car door and headed for the house. Heber and Elizabeth got out the driver's side. Pumpkin, reeking of skunk, slunk toward them.

"Scat!" Heber stamped his foot and the cat fled into the bushes along the back of the house.

"Daddy!" Elizabeth wailed, watching the shrubs where the cat had disappeared.

"He's a dirty alley cat." Eric's breakup, the long bus ride, the effort to greet Ruth and Elizabeth lovingly, now this. His fists clenched and unclenched in his effort to stay in control.

"Pumpkin isn't a dirty alley cat." Elizabeth's voice quivered as she began searching for the cat, calling him.

"He got too curious when he met another animal," Ruth said evenly. "You of all people should understand that."

"What?" Heber turned and faced her.

"Here kitty, here kitty, kitty, kitty." Lizzy's worried voice reached them from the side yard.

Ruth took her keys from her handbag and unlocked the back door. Taking shallow breaths, Heber followed her in. The stench was even stronger inside.

He began opening windows in the kitchen and sunroom. "It's going to stink for a year," he grumbled, moving on to the dining and living room windows.

When he returned to the kitchen, Ruth had pulled out cans of tomato soup, tomato paste, and stewed tomatoes. "Are you going to bathe an army, or just one cat?" he challenged, eyeing the counters.

"Don't start in." Her voice flat and low, Ruth opened the cans and emptied them into a dishpan. She looked like she wanted to dump the whole thing over his head.

She was right, of course. She was always right. About every damn thing.

"I found Pumpkin," Elizabeth called from the driveway.

"Hold onto him." Ruth added a generous amount of Ivory Liquid to the tomato products and added warm tap water.

The strongest odor seemed to be coming from the basement. Heber pulled open the junk drawer, retrieved a flashlight, and tromped down the basement steps. Beyond the furnace and four shelving units, the basement became a narrow concrete slab between shoulder-high retaining walls of the foundation.

He played the flashlight above him, moving along the foundation walls.

Two eyes stared at him.

Moving the beam to the right, he found one of the windows that vented the basement open a crack. And no screen. Damn it! He'd meant for months to check all the screens. Too much work on this place to keep up. Eric should have come back to Pasadena and helped like he said he would.

Heber retreated cautiously so as not to spook the skunk. He'd go to the hardware store for a screen, wait outside tonight with some food to lure the stinky little beast away, and then install it.

At the foot of the stairs, he paused. How could he climb out of the dank basement and go on with life as if his heart were still beating? Eric was gone, for good this time. Who would ever love and understand him so completely?

A shaft of light cut through the dim stairwell, catching the beveled glass edges of home canned peaches, plums and strawberry jam. While he was off having his affair, Ruth must have been busy visiting fruit stands and filling the kitchen with steam and sweet aromas. She'd canned beans and pickles, too, loading shelf after shelf with her labors and her love for the family. She'd worked so hard to provide for them and live by the church's directive to set by a year's worth of food storage. Unlike him, she was able to balance being open and loving with being devout and obedient to the church's mandates.

He remembered how drawn she'd looked at the bus station and thought back to the days when she perched on the handlebars of his bicycle, the two of them flying and dreaming, planning their future together. He had stolen the best years of her life. And for what? So he could indulge the stubbornly twisted part of his soul that even the church couldn't cure?

Outside, Ruth and Elizabeth held a struggling Pumpkin in a dishpan of the tomato mix, massaging the red suds through his fur.

"I found the skunk," Heber said quietly.

"Can I see it?" Elizabeth squealed, jumping up.

Pumpkin sprang away from Ruth, who caught him by the flank and pulled him against her. Tomato splattered her apron and dress.

Heber looked at the scarlet stain spreading across her chest. None of this was her fault. He'd foolishly created a picture of Eric catching a plane back to Pasadena, surprising him. Instead, he'd come home to a skunk. Quite fitting, actually. He lifted his arms toward Ruth, the anger draining from him. "I'm so sorry, Ruth."

Releasing Pumpkin, she went to him and they held each other, both leaning in a little to balance the other. "Let's give it a try," he said, remembering that long ago they'd both been so hopeful, and it had been Ruth who spoke those words.

Now, tomato juice soaking his shirt as he held her close, he knew it was his turn to commit. To rebuild the relationship he'd badly stained.

33

Pasadena, California, December 1951

Heber held Ruth's left hand in both his as he looked out the window of the doctor's waiting room. An unusual frost had sapped much of the color from the perennially blooming gardens of Pasadena. It was December, after all, and he supposed there had to be a touch of winter, even in Southern California. This latest worry only added to the gray.

Four days earlier Ruth had gone with him to visit two church families they knew well, taking Christmas cards and fresh-baked loaves of persimmon bread. They'd left Elizabeth watching their neighbor's new television, her eyes shining with excitement.

"I have a doctor's appointment next Monday," Ruth had said as they drove home after the visits. "I wonder if you'd go with me."

He'd nodded. "Sure, glad to."

They were working their way toward each other, slowly, carefully, complimenting every small thing, buying each other a favorite sweet, shopping for groceries together, holding hands as they walked from car to store. Sometimes feelings for Ruth he feared had gone forever bubbled up. Whether it was love or desperation he wasn't sure. Beneath the surface, every day was still a challenge he tried to hide from Ruth. The year before, he'd had the near break-up with Eric. This one was for real.

Going with her to the doctor was an odd request, but he'd honor it. Once upon a time he'd helped Ruth through her horrific pregnancy with Elizabeth. She hadn't asked him to go with her to doctors' appointments in years. What could have her worried enough to invite him along now?

"I found a lump in my breast." Ruth spoke so quietly he almost missed her words.

"A lump? Are you sure?" His stomach lurched to his throat. He parked alongside the curb and turned to face her.

She nodded and he watched the fright grow in her eyes.

"Oh, Ruth!" He enveloped her in a hug. "How long ago?"

"A few months. I didn't want to bother you."

Dear God. She must have found the lump while he was in Maine. When he got home, their relationship was so fragile they had talked of nothing but the weather and Elizabeth for weeks. Once she asked, "Tell me about your trip." Then, in the next breath, "No, I don't want to know."

If he were a real husband, *he* would have found the lump. But he'd been focused on Eric, not Ruth, much as he tried to honor his re-commitment to the marriage. Working in the yard, or in bed waiting for sleep, involuntary tears would begin. He'd written Eric letter after letter in those first weeks back home, often pouring out his heartbreak in poems.

I've missed you so.
On summer nights
With moon mist drifting to and fro,
And all the world stretched out below
And speaking tongues I long to know
An answer
Through all the season's whirl
I've groped alone

Among the poignant moments of our past
Too fragile and too fair to last,
Searing once, now fading fast
Into oblivion.

He had torn every one of them into small pieces. Meanwhile, Ruth guarded her terrible secret. He belonged with Ruth and Elizabeth. He should have written poetry to Ruth when he was away in Maine. Loving, faithful Ruth. How happy it would have made her.

Maybe this lump was Heber's letter from God, penance for his wayward heart. But why would a loving heavenly father punish his innocent wife for his sins? It should have been him given some horrible disease.

These past weeks he and Ruth had grown closer. Their future together looked brighter. And now her lump. Probably nothing, he'd told himself a thousand times. Or something; a something he couldn't even get his mind around. He couldn't lose her. Not after losing Eric.

Dear, dear Ruth. And here he was making it about himself again.

He imagined he looked as pale as Ruth as they sat with their magazines, neither of them able to read. "Mrs. Averil?" The nurse's voice was crisper than her starched white uniform and cap.

Heber released Ruth's hand. "Want me to go in with you?"

"I'll be fine." Her voice faltered, but she straightened her shoulders and followed the nurse through a door that closed with a loud click.

Heber tried again to read an article in the current *Time* magazine about the McCarthy hearings. Those reports always made his blood boil. A friend of his and Ruth's had lost his position as president of a small college in the

Midwest because he'd been a member of a communist cell when he attended Berkeley. The man had only been to a few meetings, exploring ideas, as one did in college.

He set the magazine aside and closed his eyes. Nothing mattered today except Ruth's lump. He could picture Ruth in a shapeless hospital gown, perched on an exam table in a small, antiseptic room. The nurse would be asking a few questions as she took her temperature and blood pressure. Ruth might be shivering from the cold room and from fear. He was shivering, too, despite his warm wool jacket.

He drew a long breath. The lump had to be nothing. God, he hoped so.

"Mr. Averil?" A nurse approached. "Dr. Watkins would like you to join your wife in his office."

Heber jumped to his feet, his heart hammering against his ribs.

Ruth was already seated in the office, erect in a straight-backed chair. Heber sat beside her and took her hand, damp with perspiration like his. He curled their fingers together.

When Dr. Watkins spoke, his voice was rich with sympathy. "I'm concerned about the nature of the lump. I recommend a biopsy."

Heber felt Ruth flinch.

"A surgeon will remove the lump from the right breast," he continued. "Examine a frozen section under a microscope, and, if necessary, do a mastectomy."

Dr. Watkins paused and clasped his hands on his desk. Heber glanced sideways and saw Ruth's eyes as wide as a frightened child's, fixed on the doctor as he delivered his terrible words. "If there is a mastectomy, rehabilitation will begin immediately after surgery. It will focus on the muscles of the right arm so you can return to normal life as soon as possible. I wish I had better news."

The room spun. Ruth might go in for a routine biopsy and wake up without her breast. Or worse. He remembered her thrombosis after Elizabeth's birth. What complications would there be this time? *Biopsy. Mastectomy. Rehabilitation.* Dr. Watkins didn't say the word *cancer,* but it ricocheted around the room.

"I was sure it was nothing." Ruth's voice broke. Her hand trembled in Heber's, and he released it to put his arm around her.

"It could be nothing," Dr. Watkins assured her. "These lumps usually are. I'm referring you to an excellent surgeon, Dr. Maxwell."

"Remember my father's promise," Ruth whispered to Heber. "He said I would live to raise Lizzy."

Heber pulled her close and kissed her hair. "Yes, love. You'll be all right."

He offered Ruth his arm as they walked to the car and asked, "What should we tell Lizzy?"

Ruth stopped. "Nothing. She's only a little girl. Don't worry her until we're certain."

Heber bit his lip to avoid arguing. Elizabeth wasn't dumb—she'd know something was up when her mother went to the hospital. But he wasn't about to upset his wife further.

Please, God, let it be a cyst.

With Christmas less than a week away, Heber couldn't focus on the holidays. *Dear Heavenly Father, bless Ruth,* he silently prayed over and over as he went through the motions of addressing Christmas cards, helping Elizabeth set up their ceramic nativity scene, and stringing lights on the

Christmas tree. Elizabeth and Ruth finished decorating the tree with red balls, foil flower reflectors behind colored lights, and tinsel. He praised their efforts as cheerfully as he could. But even the miniature Christmas village with the windup train he'd had since childhood failed to cheer him.

He'd spent hours figuring out something extra-special to get Ruth and Elizabeth for Christmas and had hidden the gifts at their neighbor's. For Ruth, a shawl of the softest wool, a shade of green that almost matched her eyes. She liked shawls. For Elizabeth, a large, stuffed dog. She wanted a real dog, but Pumpkin would have to do until they knew about Ruth, and he felt more stable. He'd also purchased a big surprise for the family.

Grief over the loss of Eric could still wash up in unexpected waves, bringing a physical pain to his chest. But his obsessive thinking was now more often about Ruth. Why hadn't he realized how much he cherished the companionship they shared? He was desperate to have her healthy by his side. What could he do for her in these terrible days of waiting?

Two days before Christmas, the family made their annual pilgrimage to see the animated department store windows in Los Angeles. Elizabeth looked like one of Santa's elves in her red velvet jumper and white blouse, a red ribbon on each pigtail. She bounced with excitement in the back seat of their Plymouth as Heber drove the curves of the Pasadena freeway. "Jingle bells, jingle bells, jingle all the way," she sang in his ear. Ruth joined in, although her clear soprano was thinner than usual. Where did she get her courage? Heber couldn't sing at all as he gripped the steering wheel with clammy hands, weaving through heavy traffic.

Even when Ruth nudged his arm, he couldn't manage a note. How many more Christmases would they have as a family?

"Can we eat first?" Elizabeth begged as they pulled into the underground parking structure at Pershing Square.

"Yes, my love," Ruth said.

Heber locked the car and they headed to Clifton's cafeteria, Elizabeth skipping between them, swinging their hands. Her contagious high spirits lifted his. Enough pessimism.

At Clifton's they descended into a damp, musty, underground cafeteria cum tropical rainforest complete with artificial rocks, plants and cascading waterfalls lit in a rainbow of colors.

The previous April, Eric had brought them all here to celebrate Elizabeth's birthday. The food hadn't compared to the dinners Eric sometimes made them, but Elizabeth had been thrilled, clutching Uncle Eric's hand all the way down. Heber allowed himself one minute of longing for Eric, then touched Ruth's shoulder as she handed him a tray. They selected their meals from an assortment of Jell-O, meat loaf, a breaded something, mashed potatoes and country gravy, two kinds of Mexican casseroles, three vegetables, and an array of desserts.

"Lots of choices," he whispered to Elizabeth as she considered each item. Life seemed so simple for her. Chocolate or regular milk? Red Jell-O or green?

After lunch, they walked the few blocks to Barker Brothers where every year a Christmas tree seven stories high stood in the open lobby. A choir from one of the local high schools gathered on the mezzanine of the furniture store, dwarfed by the tree. Youthful voices filled the air with carols and a spirit of good will. Someday Elizabeth might be singing here with a high school choir. Would Ruth be standing beside him as she was now, sharing his pride in their daughter?

Tears brimmed in Ruth's eyes.

"Are you okay, Mommy?" Elizabeth asked.

Ruth ruffled her bangs. "Sometimes I cry when things are beautiful."

Heber put his arm around Ruth's shoulders, and she pressed against him, steadying herself.

"Can we see the windows now?" Elizabeth begged.

"This way." Heber led his precious little troop to the May Company where each window displayed a scene from a different fairy tale: Snow White sewing doll clothes, birds and mice helping Cinderella prepare cookies and candies for Christmas stockings, black-eyed raccoons and gray squirrels waving their bushy tails while Hansel and Gretel put final decorations on a big gingerbread house. Elizabeth stood transfixed before every scene until Ruth or Heber moved her on.

Next were the windows of Bullocks that portrayed the story of Christ's birth. Elizabeth tugged at Ruth's hand. "Mommy, tell the story of Christmas."

"You've heard it a hundred times. Why don't you tell it?" Ruth suggested.

"I want to hear it from you."

Heber did too.

"You see the star and the little village below it?" Ruth began. "Once upon a time, in a land far, far away, a family had to take a long trip to that village. They didn't have cars or trains, so they had to walk for days to get there. The woman was going to have a baby and she was very tired. Her husband was worried about her ..."

Ruth's voice faltered.

"So he decided to find her a nice bed for the night." Heber picked up the story. "An innkeeper let them stay in his stable. What comes next, Lizzy?"

"The angels on high! Like those angels!" Elizabeth pointed to three robed figures complete with large, silver wings suspended from the ceiling.

Heber put his arms around both of them. "You're the angels, you and your mother."

On Christmas day, Heber prepared Ruth and Elizabeth for their surprise. "Sit on the couch and close your eyes," he instructed.

They sat obediently. "Hurry, Daddy," Elizabeth ordered, banging the couch with her heels.

"Keep your eyes closed." Heber made two trips into the sunroom, groaning under the weight of his gift.

"Okay, open your eyes."

Ruth and Elizabeth both gasped.

"It's a television!" Elizabeth cried, staring at the tabletop television set on a birch stand. "I can watch Howdy Doody."

"I can watch Kraft Television Theater." Ruth sounded just as delighted.

Elizabeth tiptoed to the TV and cautiously touched it. "Daddy, can I turn it on?"

"There's the antenna to put up yet. Want to help?"

"Yes!" Elizabeth clapped her hands.

"Be careful," Ruth warned.

"We will," Heber and Elizabeth chorused, then looked at each other and giggled.

Heber carried the long, awkward contraption up the stairs, Elizabeth holding one end, so he didn't bump anything. Once he had the antenna balanced on the roof, he sent her back downstairs to report on the picture as he turned the thing this way and that until there was clear reception.

"Family project well done," he announced when he rejoined them in the sunroom.

"Happy trails to you," Roy Rogers sang from the black and white screen as Heber took a seat on the couch between Ruth and Elizabeth. Dale Evans came out of a big ranch house, untied Buttermilk from a hitching post, and rode off with Roy.

"My family didn't even have a radio when I was Lizzy's age. Now we have a television. Thank you, darling." Ruth kissed Heber's cheek. "The news might be on now. Do you want to check for us, Lizzy?"

Elizabeth jumped up and turned a knob on the television until she found President Eisenhower crossing a lawn to speak to someone from Europe.

"Nice job," Heber said. He wanted different news than word on the mounting Cold War with the Soviet Union. News that Ruth's lump was nothing. That's what mattered.

Elizabeth snuggled in between Heber and Ruth. "I wish Uncle Eric was here," she said. "He could watch with us."

That was out of the blue. "He always nagged me to get you a television," Heber said, and immediately regretted his words. He glanced at Ruth and saw a shadow pass across her face. By unspoken agreement neither of them had spoken of him since Heber's return, unless Elizabeth asked about him. At those times he or Ruth would remind her yet again that Uncle Eric had a job on the other side of the country and would be gone for a while.

"What's a while?" she asked in the beginning.

"A long time," they answered.

"Why don't you turn the channels and see what else is on, Lizzy?" Heber suggested.

"We could call him and wish him Merry Christmas," Elizabeth insisted.

"I don't have his phone number."

Should he tell her she'd never see Uncle Eric again? That her mother might have cancer? That maybe he'd caused it all? Him and his damnable trip to Maine.

34

Pasadena, California, January 1952

Awake early the day before Ruth's surgery, Heber watched a sliver of dawn slide across the far wall of their bedroom. How far would the light get before Ruth woke up? Part of him wanted her to sleep. To gather her strength for what lay ahead. But another part wanted her to awaken. An intense desire for her grew in him. She looked so beautiful in the early light. As soon as she opened her eyes he slipped into her bed and curled around her, his chest pressed against her back, his hands cupping her breasts, careful of the spot that was sore.

"Lizzy is still asleep," he whispered, his lips against her ear. "Is it okay?"

"Yes," she said, placing her hands over his. "Oh, yes."

Heber eased Ruth onto her back, and she lifted her head to kiss him.

"You're sure you feel like it?" he asked, returning her kiss, deep, slow.

Ruth welcomed his affection like thirsty ground welcomes rain. He had seldom made love to her since he returned from Maine, and when he did, it was more from duty than passion. Now he needed her to feel his admiration, his appreciation, and his deep love for her.

His hands explored her breasts, Rubenesque in their full, pendular shape and their rich flesh tones. Their beauty reminded him of nudes he'd seen in the Louvre. He kissed the nipple of her right breast, hoping it wouldn't be the last time. Its shape was distorted from the lump, oddly flattened, the red areola larger than on her other breast. He kissed it again. How many times had he longed for Eric when he could have been making love to his wife? He'd been a selfish fool.

"Will you want me if I lose my breast?" Ruth asked softly.

"It's not your breasts that I love. I love you."

Heber kissed her forehead, her eyelids, her mouth to reassure her. But was this true passion finally awakened in him, or feelings borne of the fear of losing her? After her surgery, would he turn again to men, or was he finally cured?

"I love you too," Ruth said. Then, in a whisper, "I'm scared."

"I'm here." He ran his hand along the curves of her torso, across her stomach, along the inside of her thighs. He was through being so self-centered. Now he wanted to comfort her and make her happy more than anything in the world.

"I want you," Ruth breathed.

"I want you too." He kissed her mouth, entered her, and moved with her for several minutes as if they were one. Urgency for release and the wish to make this moment last competed inside him.

Ruth moaned with pleasure, her arms wrapped around him, her fingers pressing into his back as she moved beneath him, her rhythm matching his. He climaxed with a stifled cry, bringing her with him, and stayed in her as she quieted. Afterward, their passion sated, they spooned. Impossibly, Heber had experienced almost as much pleasure as he did with men. Their life together would be so much richer once she returned from the hospital.

Lord, if you're up there, give me time to make amends, he prayed.

That night, after taking Ruth to the hospital to await her morning surgery, he lay alone in their bedroom staring at the shapes the streetlight made on the ceiling. He missed her gentle snoring from the other bed. The first night they'd shared a bedroom the sound had kept him awake. Now silence drove sleep away. She had married him knowing his struggle. Given him their daughter at the risk of her own life. Lived with him and accepted his limited affection even when she knew about Eric. He didn't deserve her; he swore he would become more worthy if God gave him time. He wanted her to live into old age by his side.

The next day, he spent several hours aimlessly thumbing through magazines or walking about in the hospital's waiting room. Ruth grew dearer with each passing minute. The way her hair smoothed in a widow's peak when he brushed it back from her forehead. The laugh lines at the corners of her eyes when he made silly jokes. The lips that so often widened into a smile and offered sweet kisses. A mingled smell of antiseptics, cigarette smoke and floor wax dragged his thoughts back to the tortuous day he had waited for Elizabeth's birth.

Dear God, let there be an equally happy outcome today. Shakespeare had said it well: *'This thou perceivest, that makes thy love more strong/To love that well which thou must leave e'er long.'*

Marge Johnson, who had recently replaced Ida as Relief Society president, approached. "Can you use some company?"

"Hi, Marge. I sure can." He moved his coat to make room on the chair beside him. How he appreciated the boundless support of many church members. It was the church's teachings that chafed him to the core. He hadn't sorted that all out yet.

He and Marge chatted about ways the ward might help Ruth and him, and then turned the conversation to goings-on with mutual friends. Still, he checked the clock on the otherwise empty wall every few minutes. He would have gone completely to pieces if he'd had to wait alone for the doctor's report on the surgery.

When the surgeon finally approached, the expression on his face spoke the word *cancer*. Heber's body went cold.

"I'm so sorry." Marge put a hand on his arm, tears in her eyes as well as his, and stayed with him until he had permission to go to Ruth's room.

Someone had drawn a curtain around her bed, and he was glad for the privacy. A pillow propped Ruth's right arm at right angles to her body, and a folded towel pinned to the mattress further supported it. Compression bandages absorbed the drainage, making a mound under her blanket.

He bent and kissed her.

The muscles in Ruth's face twitched and her eyes opened, shut, opened again. She searched his face. "The doctor told me." Tentatively, she moved her hand across her chest and fingered the compresses. "I still have one breast, don't I? Sometimes they take both."

"Yes. You have one."

"That must be a good sign." Ruth rested a moment, then reached for Heber's hand. "You won't leave me, will you?"

"I won't ever leave you."

"I'll be such a bother." Ruth closed her eyes again and drifted into sleep.

Morbid images came unbidden to Heber's mind: Ruth in a hospital bed, thin, pale, too weak to lift a hand. Heber and

Elizabeth alone at the dining room table, unable to eat the food on their plates. A for sale sign in front of their house.

Ruth had survived a dangerous pregnancy and a thrombosis. She always rose to challenges that would stagger even the strongest. Many women recovered from breast cancer; surely, she would too.

A nurse entered to change Ruth's bandages. "Can I offer you some juice and a blanket?" she asked Heber.

"Yes, thanks."

He hadn't realized he was shivering. When the nurse returned, he wrapped the blanket around his shoulders and set the juice on the bedside table. He doubted he could keep the sweet drink down.

Ruth hadn't seemed this fragile the day Elizabeth was born. He felt fragile too. Once upon a time, Eric would have comforted him. Those days were over. He regretted even having the thought.

Ruth roused again. "I wanted it to be a cyst."

"We all did."

She shut her eyes, rested, then looked at Heber. "Remember my dream. Lizzy isn't raised yet."

"I never knew Samuel to be wrong." Heber covered her hand with his. "Marge sat with me through your surgery."

Ruth smiled faintly. "What was she knitting this time?"

"A blue mohair something."

"We'll get it, along with five casseroles. Thank her for me." Her smile faded and her fingers tightened around Heber's.

He leaned over her, nuzzling her hair. The familiar scent enveloped him. "I love you so much," he said.

"I love you too." She shifted on the bed and winced.

"I wish I could do something for your pain."

"The pain will pass. How's Lizzy?"

"Marge is already organizing a calendar for her play dates."

"We didn't know. I might have gone home tomorrow. We'll have to tell her something." Ruth's eyes glistened. "I am going to get well, aren't I?"

"Sure you are." *Oh, God, let it be true. If there even was a God.*

35

Pasadena, California, April 1952

An April breeze ruffled the young leaves of the peach and plum trees near the porch steps where Heber and Ruth sat chatting.

"The roses smell so wonderful," Ruth said, taking Heber's hand. "How thoughtful of them to burst into full bloom and lift my spirits."

"Mine, too." Heber fingered her wedding band as her hand lay in his. How he treasured this time carved out for the two of them each evening since her surgery.

"I never bought you an engagement ring. I'll take you shopping when you feel stronger."

"You've never taken me to Paris either," Ruth teased.

"That too. Show you the places I went on my mission. Lizzy's old enough to appreciate them. Or maybe she could stay with friends and we could have a second honeymoon."

"There's so much I want to do. We always talked about getting involved in local theater. Let's do that when I feel better."

"Agreed." It was definitely time to start living those dreams they'd shared back when they were young and filled with hope. Before his nerves got bad. Before Eric. Before the cancer.

"You look lovely tonight, dear." Heber put his other hand over hers. "The color's coming back to your face, like it is to the garden. The treatment worked."

If prayers were answered — the prayers of family and friends, and her name on the prayer roll in the temple — their cancer scare had safely passed. Even so, Heber lay awake many nights worrying.

"It was nice of Grace and Ted and Mother to come while I was having the cobalt therapy. I loved seeing them." Ruth put her head on Heber's shoulder.

"They were a big help," he agreed.

"I know it's hard on you."

"Nah. Your mom's an amazing cook. Remember that pork roast with mashed potatoes and gravy? And her green salads with carrots and cucumbers diced fancy? Or how about that chocolate cake made from scratch? I haven't tasted anything like it since France."

Ruth giggled. "I know you snuck into the kitchen a couple of nights for a snack."

"She never allowed me in there. Good thing Grace could go in. Now we have a freezer full of casseroles. She's a great cook too."

Ruth flinched as she shifted on the porch steps, but her voice was bright. "I do love the green tile floor Ted laid in the upstairs bathroom when he pulled up that awful linoleum. Right off my study, I so enjoy it when I'm up to working."

"All in all, it was a good visit. Lizzy was thrilled when Aunt Grace read to her at night."

"Or she read to Grace."

Heber chuckled. "You two have been going through a lot of those Little Golden Books lately, haven't you?" It seemed every friend had given Elizabeth a book or toy when they visited Ruth, as though she was the patient.

"It's such fun. She's so eager to learn. I can't do much these days, but I can do that."

"I bet her teacher at school is impressed."

"Mother and Grace were impressed."

"I'm glad they came." Heber kissed Ruth's hair. As annoying as he found them, he couldn't begrudge her a visit. Look what she was going through. He'd tried his best to be cordial the week they were there. Sarah was Sarah, insufferable as always. Her frequent complaints of backaches and exhaustion often made him feel more guilty than grateful. Grace could be more like Sarah than Sarah herself, judging him and finding him lacking. He could hear it in her whispers to Ruth or Sarah and see it in her face when she looked at him, never mind his position at the college or their lovingly restored home. Ted treated him with a kind of disdain, never striking up a conversation and never quite meeting Heber's eyes.

Still, they'd cheered Ruth for the first time in weeks. Daily he watched with admiration and hope as she did the exercises that would restore full use of her right arm. As she bent at the waist and made ever-widening arcs with her arm, the pain on her face reminded him of how far she had to go for a full recovery.

Ruth shifted again. "Lizzy enjoyed helping her grandma and aunt in the kitchen. I'm worried about her. She seems so quiet lately."

Heber had noticed it too. He missed the joyful spray of her laughter and had asked if everything was okay at school and with friends. She said it was. Most likely it was her mother's illness affecting her. How could it not?

One night when he was grading papers at the kitchen table, she'd slid onto a chair beside him. "Maybe I made Mommy sick. I had that bad cold and I didn't cover when I sneezed." Her voice trembled. "Once when we were playing

Four Square, I hit her in the chest with the ball. Not on purpose."

He'd put his arm around her and drawn her to him. "Oh Lizzy, there's no way you could have caused Mommy's illness." Lizzy, absolutely not. Him and his sins, he hoped not.

Heber ran a finger along Ruth's cheek as she lifted her face to look for the first stars. She turned to him, her eyes bright with happiness.

He moved his finger along her neck and opened his hand to caress the smooth skin of her throat. Then he lifted her in his arms the way he'd done the first night of their honeymoon so many years ago and carried her into the house to their bedroom.

"Lizzy's asleep," he crooned as he removed her clothing, admiring the faint blush of her skin and the warmth of her touch on his arms and shoulders. His fingertips and lips moved along her body, comfortable now with her scars, her badges of courage. How valiantly she'd fought before for her life and Elizabeth's. How valiantly she fought now.

Ruth moaned under Heber, a sound not of passion but of pain.

He moved away. "Did I hurt you?"

"I'm sorry. I'm sore if I don't lie just right."

"We can wait." Heber kissed her forehead. "A week, a month, whatever you need. I want it good for you."

"I don't want to wait." Ruth put her hand behind his head to draw him toward her again. "I want you now."

"I want you too." He kissed her deeply.

They made love slowly, carefully, Heber consumed with a desire to give her pleasure. "Don't worry, my love," he assured her. "It'll feel better as time passes. We'll have many more evenings like this."

"We have tonight," she said and pulled him around her like a warm, familiar blanket. Heber held her until they both fell asleep.

They had a year. A year when Ruth could write again and go with the family to movies at the Colorado Theater, to picnics at Brookside Park, to Los Angeles for the Christmas windows and the youth choirs. She felt good enough for the three-hour drive to San Diego to visit Heber's brother Floyd and his family after they moved there and to watch, smiling, as Elizabeth played with a cousin her age. They went to church as a family again, although he preferred staying home with Ruth when she didn't feel up to going. She helped Elizabeth learn to ride a two-wheeler and make a rag doll. They attended Elizabeth's school play and talked about their Hollywood days and dreams of becoming actors, and of a local repertory group they might check out in a few months. They set up an account at the savings and loan for a trip to Paris, collected pamphlets about the city, and met with a travel agent one afternoon to make initial plans.

Then, as the calendar came full cycle, the cancer returned, and she lost her second breast. Less than six months later, x-rays showed tumors in her bones, and her liver swelled in her belly. She spent most of her time in bed.

Heber did his best to keep hope alive for them both. Becoming her scribe as he had so long ago when she was pregnant with Elizabeth, he made notes of ideas for stories and essays she would write when she got better. He put her favorite records on the record player and played love songs for her on the piano. They sat together on the couch watching her favorite shows on the television, their fingers intertwined. "You're going to get well," he assured her. "The ward is fasting and praying for you. I could feel the spirit when the bishop and Marge's husband gave you that blessing last night."

He cheered Elizabeth, too, as much as he could, making sure they did something special together every few days: going to the library for a new armload of books, getting a treat at the soda shop, playing a board game. But she was often subdued. "How can I help Mommy get well?" she asked one day as he washed the breakfast dishes and she dried them.

He leaned sideways to give her a quick hug. "You make her happy just by being you. The doctors are doing everything they can. We're all praying for her."

"Maybe I'm not praying hard enough."

He shook the water from his hands and drew Elizabeth to him. "Oh, honey, sure you are. You're always so thoughtful. Fluffing her pillows, taking her juice. You do everything just right for Mommy."

He didn't tell her he was wondering why the earnest prayers of family and friends and their ward hadn't been answered. Not in a way he could tell, anyway.

It was a hard, hard time and Heber wanted to shake his fist at God. Ruth was such a good person. Her cancer was so unfair.

Each of Ruth's unsuccessful procedures and every bad lab report still brought moments of desperate longing for Eric to help sustain him. His *paraclete*; his comforter. He was as powerless to prevent the unwelcome thoughts as he was to stop the spread of Ruth's cancer. But to contact him again was unthinkable.

36

Pasadena, California, June 1953

"Ted and Grace will be here soon." Heber set a cup of apple juice and bowl of vanilla pudding on the nightstand by Ruth's bed.

"Good." Ruth coughed, the dry cough of cancer.

Heber was glad she had something to look forward to. When the coughing passed, he put a hand behind her back and helped her sit up, then held the cup to her lips.

She took a sip. "Do be nice to them."

"Nice as pie." Heber took a tissue from the box on the nightstand to dab a bit of juice that had dribbled onto her chin, then fluffed two pillows to support her. "They're building one of those fallout shelters in their back yard, aren't they?"

"Avoid politics." Ruth settled against the pillows. "They'll be helpful."

He could use the help all right. Even with everything the Relief Society and neighbors were doing, he felt overwhelmed, always battling a sink of dirty dishes, a hamper overflowing with laundry, a stack of student compositions from his summer school classes.

"I hear their car." Ruth's face brightened.

Heber headed for the back door to greet them.

"It's been a while," Ted boomed, walking in without pushing the backdoor buzzer and grabbing Heber in a firmer-than-usual handshake.

Heber so disliked the man. What happened to using the buzzer? To *hello?* Why the genuine handshake?

"Where's Elizabeth?" Grace looked around the kitchen without greeting Heber.

"Playing with a neighbor."

"How's she holding up?" Grace asked, frowning. "We worry about her."

"Such a lot for a little girl," Ted added.

Heber felt a prickle on the back of his neck. Since when were they so interested in Elizabeth? Grace had read with her at night only twice on their last visit. Ted barely took notice of her at all. Something wasn't right. "It's hard on her, but she's as tough as her mother. Ruth is expecting you, if you'd like to go right in." Heber nodded toward the bedroom, unable to keep the edge from his voice.

Ted cleared his throat. "We need to talk."

"Grace? Ted?" Ruth called.

"She sounds so weak. We can talk later," Grace whispered to Ted as they headed to the bedroom.

Heber ran his fingers through his hair. He'd promised Ruth he'd be nice to them, but they made it hard. Gardening would calm him; it usually worked magic on the tension in his shoulders. He got the lawn mower from the garage and mowed the side lawn and half the front. When he stopped to empty the grass catcher, he heard Elizabeth.

"Daddy," she sobbed as she ran to him and flung her arms around his waist. "Don't let them take me."

Heber knelt beside her. "Who? Take you where?"

"I came home, and they were talking to Mommy. Don't make me go!"

Heber put his arms around her. "Baby, it's okay. You don't have to go anywhere."

"Uncle Ted said ..." She burst into fresh tears.

"Sweetheart," he soothed, holding her close. "It doesn't matter what he said."

When her sobs had quieted, he set her on the ground and took her hand. "Let's go find out what's up."

She clung to him, sniffling, as they entered the bedroom.

"Lizzy, what's wrong?" Ruth reached toward her.

As he walked to the sunroom, Heber pressed his fingers against his temples, his head threatening to explode. What horrible people. Could they in reality prove him an unfit parent and take Elizabeth?

Talking to Ted and Grace his neck had felt like a metal rod caught in a vice. Now some of the tension drained away as he drew his sweet daughter onto his lap the way he'd done when she was little. She reminded him of a colt, gangly and growing taller by the day. She lay back against his chest, and he wrapped his arms around her. No one was taking her away from him.

Elizabeth nestled in his arms, and they watched a Bugs Bunny cartoon together. Then the Road Runner came on, her favorite.

The Road Runner was streaking across the screen when Grace came in. "Heber, I want to—"

"Shh." Heber tucked his chin toward Elizabeth and put a finger to his lips. "It's 'Meep Meep.'"

"Ruth won't hear of it," Ted muttered, striding up to Grace. He took her arm and hurried her toward the back door, but Heber could still hear him. "She's blind to what's happening right under her nose. Elizabeth's exposure to God-only-knows what. And if Heber were here alone with her?"

"Good-bye Ruth," Grace called over her shoulder.

"Long drive for nothing. I despise his kind," Heber heard Ted snarl. Then, so loudly Ruth must be able to hear as well as Heber, Ted shouted, "This isn't over! Not even close!"

Elizabeth pressed against Heber and he tightened his arm around her, breathing a sigh of relief when he heard the car engine start up.

"What isn't over?" Elizabeth asked. "Are they going home?"

"They're going home, but I guess they plan to come see us again."

"I don't want them to."

"I don't either. Should I uninvite them?"

"Yes," Elizabeth giggled.

"Should I lock the door in case they come right back?"

"Yes!" Elizabeth giggled again.

"You okay if I go in and talk to Mommy?"

She nodded. Heber locked the front and back doors, then went on in the bedroom, glad the cartoons would drown out any scraps of the conversation he and Ruth would surely have.

"I wanted to punch Ted," he said soberly as he sat carefully beside Ruth.

"You've never punched anyone." Ruth touched his arm. "You're a good, gentle man. But if you had, he more than deserved it."

"I can take care of Lizzy."

"Yes, you can."

Heber waited while she gathered strength.

"I used to wonder," Ruth said. "But these last years during my illness you've been wonderful, the way you've handled so much and still made time for her."

Heber thought back to the day he'd switched Elizabeth, and the time he'd collapsed in the grocery store. Ruth must have doubted him in the past. They stood united now. Now, and he hoped for years to come.

"I enjoy it all," Heber said. "Bringing her favorite snacks when I go grocery shopping, watching her favorite TV shows with her, reading together."

"I hear her telling you about her day."

"That's my favorite time of all."

Ruth closed her eyes, her breathing ragged.

"You need to rest. Will the mower disturb you if I finish the lawn?"

She shook her head.

Heber kissed her again and returned to the front yard, his mind whirring like the rotary mower. Whatever happened, he and Elizabeth would manage somehow.

37

Pasadena, California, June 1953

Heber finished the lawn and shook the last of the grass clippings into the garbage can, wishing he could dump the threats of his in-laws in with them. He was clipping roses near the bedroom window for Ruth's nightstand, inhaling their delicate, calming fragrance, when he heard Ruth's faint call. He picked up the roses, set the clippers on the back step, and hurried to her bedside.

Ruth panted from the effort of sitting up. Setting the roses aside Heber helped her, then arranged the pillows behind her back.

"I've been thinking," Ruth said when she'd settled.

"That's good 'cause you're the best thinker I know." Heber tossed a wilted bouquet in the wastebasket, replaced it with the fresh roses, and drew up a chair.

"It's about Lizzy."

He stiffened. She hadn't changed her mind about Ted and Grace, had she?

Ruth reached for his hand. "I do know you're a good father. But she needs two parents."

"Lizzy and I are fine." He tried for a normal tone of voice as panic rose in his chest.

"Darling, I'm not talking about sending her away."

She coughed and Heber waited while she caught her breath. "I'm talking about how to keep her here. With you."

"Let me worry about that. You need to rest. It's been quite the morning."

"I can't rest. I heard Ted say he'd be back."

Damn them, worrying her like this. "I know Lizzy needs someone here to take her to piano lessons," he said. "Make her snacks. Supervise when she has friends over, and you aren't up to it. I'll figure it out."

Ruth's face took on the expression of fierce determination he'd seen when she did her exercises after the cobalt therapy. "I want you to remarry … right away."

"Me remarry?" The words burst out of him.

"There's that nice widow at church who moved here last year. She's got a daughter almost Lizzy's age. There must be lots of — "

"Ruth." He tried for a gentle tone. "You're the most amazing woman I've ever met. And you've been the best companion a man could wish for. I could never replace you. Anyway, you're going to get well."

"I'm so tired." Ruth sighed and another fit of coughing seized her. "I don't want you or Lizzy alone," she said when it had passed.

"Oh, Ruth. When I met you, I thought all my prayers were answered." Heber's voice choked up. "I tried and tried to be a good husband to you."

"On our wedding day … how handsome you were. I thought we had it all."

"*I* did have it all. You got gypped. You're remarkable. Your beauty, your intellect, the way you carried Lizzy. So many things." His voice rose in insistence. "Don't you see? Marrying you — the woman of my dreams — couldn't change who I am, as much as we both wanted it to. If I couldn't be a proper husband with you, it's just not possible."

"I've prayed so often to be able to make you happy."

Heber looked at her so ill, so sad. His chest constricted with the pain of his inability to comfort or cure her. Or make her fully understand. "I prayed, too, to be what you wanted. What you needed and deserved. You have to believe me. I truly love you."

"I know. In your way. But I couldn't make you light up the way that ..." Her voice trailed off.

Eric did. Heber bit his lip, horrified that he'd even thought the name.

"Eric." Ruth uttered the word out loud. "Of course. He could protect Lizzy better than anyone."

The room reeled and Heber's heart rose in his throat. Was she suggesting he bring his ex-lover into their home? "Eric?"

"Lizzy loves him. You love him. He's always been kind to me."

Ruth was drawn and shaking from the exertion of the conversation. The last thing in the world he wanted to do was to inflict more pain on her. "You know I haven't heard from him in years. I don't even know if he stayed in Maine."

"Tell him about Ted. Ask him to come."

Heber tried to wrap his mind around the idea. People would talk. Or worse. Surely, he and Ruth could put together a different plan.

As if reading his mind, Ruth gathered her strength and spoke again. "Lizzy is who matters ... more than anything people say."

"I guess he could stay in the apartment."

"Please, Heber. Call him. For Lizzy. For me."

Heber stood, kissed her and pulled the covers higher around her shoulders. "All right, sweetheart. I'll try to reach him. See if he can come 'til you feel better."

Heber leaned against the bedroom doorframe a moment, then went to the phone on the hall table. He picked up the receiver, hesitated, put it back down. His stomach roiled and beads of nervous sweat dampened his forehead.

He had to do this.

His best bet to get Eric's number was Eric's cousin Dell. Steadying himself he picked up the receiver. When the operator answered, he opened his mouth but couldn't speak. He coughed to let her know he was there, worried she'd hang up on the dead air between them. Finally, he found the words. "Do you have a number for Dell Hartman in Bar Harbor, Maine?"

"One moment, please."

Heber waited an eternity until the operator returned to the line. She'd found the number, the first bit of magic.

The second bit of magic was the opening and closing of a series of switches that pushed his voice clear across the country.

Heber's heart pounded in his ears. Acid from his stomach burned the back of his throat.

"Hello?"

The sound of Dell's voice launched a memory of his words: *'It's how the Lord made you, and the Lord don't make no junk.'*

For a moment Heber couldn't speak. Two years ago, Ruth had sat at their kitchen table reading a card he'd sent from Maine, loving him through everything. Now, desperately ill, she was more concerned about him and Elizabeth than herself. What a magnificent, selfless love. He wanted a chance to return that love. Make up for the tortuous years he had put her through. Be with her always.

Yet he was weak-kneed from the onslaught of his emotions ignited by the idea of calling Eric.

He cleared his throat. "Hello, Dell. It's Heber. Heber Averil."

"Heber! Good to hear your voice."

Welcoming words, heartily spoken. So like Dell. Heber stammered on. "How's Agnes?"

"We lost my mom soon after your visit."

"I'm sorry. I didn't know. I'm glad I got to meet her."

"She liked you," Dell said.

"She was a fine woman."

"And your little girl? Lizzy? Eric's talked a lot about her."

"That's actually why I called."

Both men fell silent. Heber chewed his lip and mustered his courage. "Can you give me Eric's number?"

"Afraid not. I can ask him to call you. Can't guarantee he will."

"Thanks. And hello and sympathy to your dad." Heber replaced the phone in its cradle and dropped onto a nearby chair.

Five minutes dragged by. Would Eric call? And if he called, would he come?

The phone rang, two longs, their line. Heber grabbed the receiver. "Hello?"

"You called." Eric's voice was flat and even.

Not a trace of emotion after nearly two years of silence. Heber's hope shattered like a dropped piece of fine china. He forged on, stumbling over the words, feeling like a schoolboy. "It's Ruth ... Ruth asked me to call."

"She asked you to call? How is she?"

"She has cancer and it's spread."

"My God! I had no idea. I'm so sorry."

Heber steadied himself. "And there's more. Ruth's sister and brother-in-law want to take Lizzy away from us to go live with them. They're gone now, but my brother-in-law swore he'd be back." Heber forced out the hideous accusation. "They say I'm an unfit father."

"That—" Eric growled, stopping himself short. "No telling what people like him will do. With Ruth so sick and all. They can make real trouble for you two."

Heber could picture him holding the phone, nostrils flared, his free hand a fist balled at his side.

"And Lizzy," Heber added.

"I'd be happy to meet Ted on a lonely dirt road somewhere if you can arrange it."

"I know where I'd put my money." Heber could be confident of the outcome if it ever came to that fistfight.

"You know," Heber added quietly, "I didn't want to call."

"I didn't either." Eric chuckled; the warm sound Heber remembered so well. "I'll get the first plane out. In case your brother-in-law decides to come back."

Heber managed a raspy, "Thank you," as relief flooded him. Elizabeth would be safe. Eric was on his way.

38

Pasadena, California, June 1953

"When will Uncle Eric be here?" Elizabeth looked out the front window for the hundredth time.

"Patience, Lizzy. It's two bus rides from the airport." Heber understood her anticipation. His stomach had refused even the sight of breakfast and lunch. What would it be like opening the door to Eric without a word from him since Maine until the phone call?

"You told Mommy he left yesterday."

"He's as eager as you are. He had to drive a long way to the airport and stay in a hotel overnight. His plane left this morning while you were still asleep."

Elizabeth looked out the window again. He tugged one of her pigtails. "Want to play Sorry while we wait?" The board game would be a welcome distraction for them both.

He'd managed to put two yellow men to her three red men in Home when the doorbell rang. Elizabeth raced to the door and yanked it open. Eric had barely enough time to put down his canvas bag before she jumped into his arms.

He gathered her up like a long-lost pup and hugged her hard before setting her down and taking a step back. "Look at you, so much taller. Your eyes are as blue and beautiful as I remembered. I'm so glad to see you."

He turned to Heber and extended a hand. "Good to see you, too." Heber caught the hitch in Eric's voice. "Does Ruth feel up to a little visit?"

"I'll take you," Elizabeth said, grabbing his hand. She led him into the bedroom, Heber close behind.

Heber heard Eric's sharp inhale. This wasn't a Ruth he'd ever seen. She'd lost forty pounds and her skin was as pale and drawn as the day she bore Elizabeth. Still, her face broke into a smile as he crossed the room to her bedside. "Ruth. I'm so sorry. I'm here to help any way I can."

Tears welled in Ruth's eyes. Heber didn't know if she was happy or sad. If Eric's presence brought pain or relief. Probably all those feelings.

"Daddy and I have been cleaning the apartment in back," Elizabeth said, stepping up beside him. "It still doesn't look very good."

Eric frowned. "I can stay with friends 'til I find a place."

Ruth opened her mouth to say something but only managed a cough.

"It was Mommy's idea," Elizabeth interjected. "It's logical."

They all laughed, the tension in the room broken. Where had she learned the word *logical*?

"It is logical. We all talked about it and agreed," Heber said.

"We want you here," Ruth affirmed.

"We didn't rent it when the last tenant moved out," Heber explained. "Not the priority."

"I can imagine. I gratefully accept and will pay whatever the rent is."

"The water's brown," Elizabeth warned. "It's yucky."

Eric grinned. "I'm a fair plumber and painter. I'll fix it up, no worries. Let's check it out and leave Mommy to rest."

Ruth closed her eyes, then coughed again. Heber and Eric exchanged worried glances. "She's been coughing a lot the last few weeks," Heber whispered when they were out of the room. "She's already so weak. Pneumonia would ..." He let the words trail off.

Elizabeth had darted toward the back door, leading the way to the garage apartment, when Heber heard Ruth call. "Eric?"

Eric went to her. Heber stayed behind but could hear them.

"Take care of my little girl," Ruth said. "Take care of her always."

"I promise you I will."

"And take care of Heber."

"That too."

Heber shuddered. Her words sounded so final. Surely the doctors would think of a new medicine. Ruth would draw on some hidden strength like she had done when she carried Elizabeth. And afterward, when the blood clot threatened her life. She'd somehow find a way to stay with them.

The next morning Elizabeth took it upon herself to knock on the apartment door and ask Eric to make pancakes. Admittedly, Heber didn't take the time to make pancakes these days. He was happy to hand over the task. Elizabeth not only got her pancakes, but she unwittingly created a comfortable way for Uncle Eric to be in the house.

Ruth's cough built even more during the night. By late morning she was running a fever. Eric stood quietly nearby when Heber called the doctor, then wrangled Elizabeth into helping him work on the apartment while Heber drove Ruth to the hospital.

Despite Eric being at the house, Heber's mouth was dry, and his head ached with worry as the staff checked her in. In the hospital, the pneumonia responded to penicillin, although her cough lingered. The relentless cancer responded to nothing.

Heber called the college for a substitute. Over the next four days he stayed as much time at Ruth's side as the hospital allowed, while Eric and the neighbors watched Elizabeth. Each day, he took with him another vase of roses from the garden—red, pink, yellow—their color offering a stark contrast to Ruth's ashen hue. The antiseptic hospital smell overpowered their fragrance, but Ruth's face brightened every time he set a new vase by her bed.

"Hello darling," he said on the fifth morning, taking her hand from under the bedcovers to hold in both his. Her skin was almost transparent now, the veins a frightening blue. How different from the chic, giggling young woman who had sat astride the handlebars of Heber's bicycle. He'd fallen in love with her then, in his way, filled with admiration and delight in their easy camaraderie. That love, adolescent and self-absorbed, had grown deeper and fuller over the years; their shared experiences a narrow stream maturing into a broad river. His struggles had caused them both anguish, but, in the end, their deep friendship and love for each other had transcended everything.

"Lizzy must be happy with Eric—" A coughing fit stole the rest of Ruth's words. She took her hand from Heber's to cover her mouth, her shoulders shaking with the effort of drawing breaths. When the coughing passed, she sank back against the pillows.

Heber offered a sip of water from the glass on her bedside table. "He made her favorite dinner last night, pigs 'n blankets. French toast this morning."

"Good."

Heber pulled the side chair close and took her hand again. "He plays checkers and Monopoly with her. They talk about the books she's reading, play badminton and croquet. Some of the neighbor kids come around when they're outside; he's good with them too. He fixed the plumbing in the apartment. Oh, and he's got it prepped to paint the exterior. It's needed it …"

He grimaced. He was going on too long about the wonders of Eric. But Ruth murmured, "I'm so glad." She rested a few minutes. Then, "No sign of Ted or Grace?"

"Eric is the dragon at the door. They wouldn't dare come back." Heber didn't tell Ruth that Ted had had the nerve to call as soon as they were back in Utah.

"I trust you and Ruth have changed your mind," Ted had said without preamble as soon as Heber picked up the phone. "You must see we can provide a better home for Elizabeth while things settle out with you and Ruth."

Heber resisted the urge to hang up on him. "We've arranged for additional help here. We're doing well."

"But you, Heber! What you bring into her life. Grace and Sarah and I—"

At that point he did hang up.

That the three of them would further upset Ruth knowing how sick she was, was outrageous. What danger could he possibly pose to his own daughter?

He hadn't told anyone about Eric living out back except to explain to neighbors that a family friend had moved in to help with Elizabeth's care. If those neighbors were whispering over their fences, he didn't have the time or energy to listen in. Ruth was right. Elizabeth was what mattered. Should they found it odd to have a man rather than a nanny lending a hand, so be it.

Grace had nearly got to him when she called the day after Ruth was admitted to the hospital, asking after her sister. When she heard Ruth was in the hospital she started crying. "Please let me see my sister. I'll come alone. I won't say anything about Elizabeth."

"I'll check with Ruth." He did ask as soon as he got to the hospital. Ruth shook her head no, her sorrow obvious. He was relieved. A visit would further drain her energy and he wasn't convinced Grace could leave the topic of Elizabeth alone. Still, he felt bad for both women. He couldn't imagine being estranged from his sisters.

Sarah had called the day after Grace, wanting to visit Ruth. Again, Heber had asked. "Mother isn't well," Ruth had said, though by now speaking at all was a chore for her.

Heber put an ice chip in her mouth.

"We've been happy, haven't we?" she murmured. "Mostly? You and I?"

Heber nodded. "Very happy. And we will be for years to come." He took her hand again, holding it as gently as a butterfly's wing.

They were quiet together for several minutes, then Heber looked out toward the hospital corridor and checked his watch. "We have a surprise for you. Any minute."

"Lizzy?" Ruth's eyes lit up in a way Heber hadn't dared hope he'd see again. "No," she said, her eyes dimming. "You could never get her in. And she'd be frightened."

Ridiculous idea, the policy of keeping children away from parents who were hospitalized. He'd prepared Elizabeth well for the visit. Ruth's nurse, compassionate and kind, was going to help Eric bring her up the fire escape.

Heber stepped into the hall. Eric, dressed in a long overcoat, walked stiffly toward him like a man on stilts.

Heber caught a glimpse of two thin legs in stockings the same color as Eric's slacks pressed against Eric's broader legs, black patent leather Mary Janes resting on black wingtips. He couldn't help chuckling. Even the staff were grinning as they looked the other way. A disguise worthy of Eric and Elizabeth as co-conspirators.

Eric stopped beside Ruth's door, Elizabeth slipped off, and Heber hurried her into the room. "Mommy!" She immediately jumped up on the bed beside Ruth.

"Lizzy. Dear one." Ruth opened her arms to her daughter and her lips brushed Elizabeth's hair. "Clever girl."

"When are you coming home, Mommy?"

"Soon. Daddy and Uncle Eric will take care of you 'til then."

As he watched them, Heber accepted the terrible truth. Ruth would not be coming home. He honored their silence, mother and daughter quietly filling the room with more love than words could ever express.

Someone knocked on the door and opened it a crack. "I have Mrs. Averil's pain medication."

"Do I have to go, Mommy?"

"Yes, my love."

Elizabeth kissed her and whispered, "I'll sneak back in tomorrow." Then she slid off the bed. "Bye."

"I love you." Ruth's voice quivered.

Elizabeth blew her a kiss before taking Heber's hand. Ruth's eyes never left her daughter as he led her out the door.

Heber gave Elizabeth a reassuring hug and handed her off to Eric.

"Ready?" Eric opened his overcoat and she climbed on his shoes, burying her face in his shirt, and wrapping her arms around his waist.

The nurse slipped past them into the room, giving them a sympathetic smile.

When Heber returned to Ruth's bedside, he found her dozing. He bent close to her. "'Ah, fair lady,'" he said tenderly. "'Doubt that the sun doth move, doubt truth to be a liar, but never doubt I love.'"

Ruth roused and looked in his eyes. "I love you too."

"You mean so much to me."

"Heber."

"Darling."

"We'll be together again." She struggled to form the words.

"Yes, we will." He had to believe it.

"God is just." She rested, then, "No open casket."

Heber shuddered away an image of Ruth lying in a coffin, lifeless arms folded neatly across her chest, eyes permanently closed. Mormons traditionally had a viewing and prayer before a funeral service. Ruth wanted to be remembered as her healthier self, which to him was her right. He'd do his best to make it happen.

He leaned in to kiss her forehead. "Remember when we danced on the roof of the Alvarado? I said we'd still go out dancing when we were old and gray. Someday we'll dance across the heavens."

"Lizzy. My father's promise. She must be raised."

Ruth closed her eyes and Heber thought she dozed again, but she roused. "The baptism ... she'll be eight in August ... she can choose when she's older ... she doesn't have to go to church." The words were broken, and Heber leaned in to hear them.

"I'll take her to church if you want."

"You don't have to go. So much intolerance" — she took a breath — "among so many good people."

She'd given him permission to live outside the fold. The idea was too much to absorb right now. Without Ruth by his side—his splendid wife with such a generous spirit—he wasn't sure what he'd do.

Ruth moved restlessly on the bed. Heber mustered his tattered courage. "Prepare a place for us."

Relief flooded Ruth's face. He caught a ghost of a smile. "Can I ... get ... a double bed?"

"Any bed you want."

"Give ... Lizzy ... the missionary pin." Her breathing grew even more labored.

The pin he'd given her when they agreed to marry. He bent and kissed her lips. "I'm staying here tonight, right in this chair."

"Good." Ruth closed her eyes.

Heber sat by her side all night, his hand over hers where it lay on the bed. In the late-morning her hand grew cool, and her skin took on a gray pallor. Her breaths came further and further apart. She drew a final deeper breath, her body relaxed, and she was gone.

He stayed awhile, sensing her spirit strong in the room. She'd been his true and chosen companion of the Lord. He kissed her one last time. Then, in a daze, he walked down the hall to the lobby. He found Eric seated there, his nose in a newspaper. The hospital must have called the house.

Eric looked up. "Oh, sweetie."

Heber fell into his arms. After a moment, he stepped back, his knees so weak they almost gave way.

Eric put out a hand to steady him.

"Lizzy?" Heber choked out the question.

"I took her to the neighbors for the night. She's welcome to stay there until we get her."

"Does she know?"

"Yours to tell her."

Heber stumbled out the double doors of the hospital, Eric holding his arm, supporting his weight.

Outside they sank onto a bench. Heber gulped air as tears poured unchecked down his face. Eric sat beside him, an arm around his shoulders. They ignored the stares of men and women leaving the hospital, claiming their right to grieve.

"She's gone," Heber said finally.

"She's still with us. Always will be."

"I hope so."

Heber's tears eased. "It's so unfair," he muttered. "She deserved better."

"You gave her the best you could."

"I thought she'd beat the cancer."

Eric held Heber close as fresh sobs shook his body. When he finally calmed, he pulled a handkerchief from his pocket and blew his nose. "She wanted you here. I can't get over it."

"She's a grand woman," Eric said.

They sat quietly for a few minutes. Fresh tears slid down Heber's face. "Remember the day you saved Lizzy?" he asked Eric.

"Like it was yesterday."

"Ruth said we were a family. She never forgot."

"None of us did."

Heber wiped his eyes and straightened his shoulders. "I need to get Lizzy. Let's go home."

39

Pasadena, California, June 1953

"Aren't we going to church, Daddy?" Heber looked up from the couch where he and Eric were reading the morning paper, passing sections back and forth. There stood his little daughter in her new black dress she'd worn to Ruth's funeral five days earlier.

"It's Sunday," she insisted.

Heber, still in his pajamas and robe, glanced at Eric who wore his usual Levi's and t-shirt.

"Church it is." Eric jumped to his feet, catching Heber's eye. The look said, *let Elizabeth lead the way.* "I'll be ready in five minutes."

"Daddy?"

"So will I." Heber headed to the bedroom.

Absolutely, Elizabeth planned to go. She'd gone to church every Sunday her whole life, except for these last months when she'd stayed home with Ruth. She must be eager to see her friends in Junior Sunday School, and maybe to see the well-meaning church members who had reminded her at Ruth's funeral she'd see her mother again in heaven.

Heber hoped the church doctrine was true. That God, in His compassion, would forgive Heber's sins, and they would all be together again for eternity. He wished he were one of those devout saints who had the *sure knowledge,* but he wasn't certain what he believed anymore. Ruth had kept all the vows she made to Heber, to the church, and to God. And yet she was the one to suffer and die of cancer. Where was the justice? The mercy?

Eric wasn't even Mormon and here he was willing to go to church, which shouldn't have surprised Heber given Eric's boundless love for Elizabeth. Problems had already surfaced though. People at the funeral had nudged elbows and glanced sideways at Eric and him, probably because Elizabeth had introduced Eric to everyone she knew as 'Uncle Eric who lives with us now.' Technically, Eric lived in the garage apartment, but that didn't keep tongues from wagging. Even at a funeral, bigotry apparently trumped compassion.

Some, but not all, of Heber's siblings had come to honor Ruth and offer condolences to Heber, and he was grateful for that. Heber's brother Floyd had driven up from San Diego; his brother George had borrowed a motorhome to make the trip from Ogden. Alice and Katie had left their children with their husbands and driven together to Pasadena to be with him at this difficult time. If they wondered about the man Lizzy had dubbed "Uncle Eric," none of them so much as arched an eyebrow when they were introduced to him. Maybe they'd all known Heber's basic nature before Heber did and somehow accepted him for who he was, righteous or not. He'd underestimated them.

His parents had sent a telegram with their condolences. Both a comfort and a relief. Heber was confident his father wouldn't have been as gracious about meeting Eric as his brothers and sisters there with him. Two brothers and a sister hadn't come to the funeral. No one had said why. Heber knew the future held a difficult conversation with all of them.

But for now he had some family support, their presence and seeming acceptance of Eric a greater blessing than he had dared hope for.

Sarah, Grace, and Ted had wired flowers. He was so relieved when they'd said they couldn't make it.

There were also friends like Dorothy and Marge whose tears unexpectedly eased his own grief, and Harold who shook Eric's hand and then briefly draped a comforting arm around Heber's shoulders.

Heber wasn't prepared for how much he missed Ruth. For the excruciating grief that consumed him whenever he saw her toothbrush still hanging by the bathroom sink. Unopened pieces of mail addressed to her piled up in a painful stack on the hallway table. The sympathy cards pouring in brought more ache than comfort, every card reminding him she was gone.

Sunday School was about what Heber expected: sympathy mixed with wary glances, and a lesson in the Gospel Doctrine class about Abraham and Isaac, an Old Testament story he'd always abhorred. What heavenly father would ask a man to sacrifice his own son as a show of obedience? When Ruth taught the story, she had somehow built a beautiful lesson around the ways God wanted mankind to treat their children. Downplayed the obedience part. That was doctrine he could embrace.

Eric didn't say a word when the adults' class was over. Heber was quiet as well, his mind occupied with thoughts of Ruth as they walked down the hallway to collect Elizabeth from her class. When they caught sight of her, she didn't have her usual sunny smile, and she was dragging her sweater on the linoleum.

"What is it?" Heber dropped to one knee and searched her face.

"Nothing. Let's go home." She headed toward the parking lot.

As soon as they got to the house, she mumbled that she wanted to read her new comic and headed to her room. Nothing unusual there. Elizabeth often curled up with a book or comic. Maybe nothing had happened, and it was just too soon after the loss of her mother for her to be cheerful.

Heber changed out of his suit and tie. "Ready to help with lunch?" he called out to Eric. No answer. Had Eric gone on out to the apartment? Heber found him sitting in the overstuffed chair in the living room with his head in his hands.

Heber pulled a chair over to him and put a hand on his back. "You look like Lizzy when we picked her up. You okay?"

"I thought I was prepared for it. Everyone staring at us and whispering. Your church sure can grind people up."

"Jennifer asked me what it's like living with queers," Elizabeth piped up from the doorway.

Heber looked at her, surprised. How long had she been listening?

"She made a face when I sat in the chair next to her in Sunday School class. She used to be nice to me."

"Want to come in here with us?" Eric invited. "Stuff like that hurts. Sometimes it helps to talk."

Eric's words pierced Heber's heart. There had been little talk in his life with Ruth about stuff that hurt. Tensions had been left to fester. If they had talked, would things be any different? It wouldn't have changed Heber's desire for men, but maybe Ruth would have better understood the disappointments in her marriage and not blamed herself. She might even have told him about the lump in her breast before it spread and took her life.

Heber dragged another chair close to him and patted the seat. He wouldn't make the same mistake with his daughter. She perched on the edge of it, her Sunday shoes not quite touching the floor, her lower lip quivering. He put his arm around her, anger rising in his chest. Jennifer had evidently overheard her parents' nasty gossip. But they, too, were parroting what they'd been told. Where did it start and where could it end? Christ taught, *'Let he who is without sin cast the first stone.'* Yet the church seemed determined to supply the stones and paint a target on men like Eric and him.

"What are queers anyway?" Elizabeth sniffled.

Eric pulled out his handkerchief and handed it to her. "Queer means unusual. But people use the word to describe men who care about other men and women who care about other women," he explained. "Basically, it's name-calling. When people don't understand other people who seem different from them, they sometimes do that. It isn't kind."

"Like when a kid at school doesn't want to play on the high bars and they call him a fraidy cat?"

"Yes, like that."

Heber noted Eric's calm, simple way of teaching Elizabeth. He had clearly had years of practice navigating a world Heber and his daughter were just entering. At the very least, they'd have a good guide on the road ahead.

"I don't get what's wrong with Uncle Eric living with us." Elizabeth folded her arms across her chest.

"There's nothing wrong with me living with you. A lot of people are afraid of anyone who isn't exactly like they are." Eric's voice was as gentle as a summer breeze. "Sometimes it's the color of their skin. Sometimes it's the shape of their eyes. In this case it's two men who are making a different kind of family with you instead of a man and a woman."

"We were a family before Mommy got sick," Elizabeth huffed, "They don't know what they're talking about."

Good for Elizabeth. So young, so wise, so determined. Girded for battle. "You're right, they don't," Heber said. "I loved your mother very much. I'll always love her. She wanted Uncle Eric to live with us and help me take care of you."

"I loved your mother too," Eric said.

"Somehow you have to ignore the people who don't understand. I know it's hard." Heber did indeed know it was hard. And the hard was just beginning.

"They're so mean!"

"Some of them, not all of them." Heber tightened his arm around her shoulders.

"Do I have to go to church?"

"Hmm. How 'bout we talk about it next Sunday?"

"Okay." Elizabeth unfolded her arms. "Can I go play now?"

"Sure." Heber released her. She was welcome to escape the hurt with one of her books or dolls, or visit her friend down the street.

"Big moment here," Eric commented when she'd left the room.

"I know." Heber kneaded his temples. "I wonder if she's old enough to decide for herself if she wants to go to church again. That last day in the hospital Ruth said something about her choosing."

"I'm old enough and I never want to go again." Eric's tone was light, but his eyes were serious.

"Totally understandable. But I was raised in the church, and we raised Lizzy in the church. It's what I know. And it's what Lizzy knows. It's hard to just walk away. The way she was dressed and ready, I thought she'd be comforted by some of her old Sunday routines." He blew out a breath. "The church does a lot of good, and it does a lot of harm."

"I figure it's what happens when people try to combine the New Testament and the Old Testament," Eric said. "I can wrap my head around what Jesus taught. His message of love. But Old Testament teachings like we heard at church today? What's the lesson there?"

"My thoughts exactly," Heber agreed.

Eric clasped his hands and leaned towards Heber. "All their talk of God's wrath and vengeance on the disobedient is how a culture thousands of years ago saw God. And we're still preaching it today! Power. Control. Rigidity. So different from love."

"You figured it all out!" Heber wished things were as clear in his own head.

"Men like you and me spend a lifetime trying to figure out why society has it so wrong. Good chance we'll never have our answer." Eric stood. "Now about lunch." He headed toward the kitchen.

Heber's head throbbed from all the swirling thoughts. His relationship with Eric, once a dream, was now a reality. With reality came consequences for them and for Elizabeth. Church authorities would never condone the partnership. Nor would many neighbors, friends, and family members.

He and Ruth had made a careful decision when they asked Eric to rejoin the family, confident he'd take good care of Elizabeth. Neither of them had fully realized how much the love within a family would be judged by others.

40

Pasadena, California, August 1958

How could anyone giggle as much as Elizabeth and her four friends now gathered around the kitchen table to watch her blow out the thirteen candles on her birthday cake? Heber set aside his soapy dish rag and Eric his drying towel. The breakfast dishes could wait while they joined the girls to cheer her on.

With one noisy puff she blew out every candle.

"Good job! What did you wish for?" Heber asked.

Her lips pursed with indignation. "You always say if I tell my wish, it won't come true."

Heber and Eric exchanged a glance and grinned. Now officially a teenager, she could theoretically turn into a handful at any moment. But Heber doubted there'd be much drama. With both Eric and him to turn to for comfort and guidance, she'd navigated the five years since her mother's death with a combination of grit, sweetness, and grace.

Eric had outdone himself today making breakfast for the girls after their slumber party, filling the kitchen with the scent of pancakes and bacon. He'd even hand-squeezed orange juice and heated the maple syrup. Afterward, he'd baked the two-layer devil's food birthday cake, from scratch no less, while the girls went to Elizabeth's room and listened to records.

Bless Eric. And bless Ruth for welcoming him back into their lives. Heber and Eric together were a far better family for their daughter than if Heber had raised her alone. And now that Heber no longer needed to struggle to play the part of traditional husband in public and at home, his mind was quiet, and he functioned better in every aspect of his life.

Still, he missed Ruth. Here at the party, he could swear he felt her standing at his shoulder. If any spirit could navigate the afterlife to attend her daughter's birthday party, it would be Ruth. She'd be in that part of heaven where the best people went, doing whatever angels did.

Overall, life was good, even though his father would have nothing to do with him. Maybe when Heber was younger, his father had seen what Heber couldn't, and those whippings were his efforts to beat the devil out of his son. A harsh form of love. Two brothers and a sister limited contact to an annual Christmas card signed, but without a note. At least there were the cards. His mother's love endured and arrived in the form of a weekly letter. His brothers and sisters who had come to the funeral called now and then to hear all about Elizabeth, with an occasional "How's Eric?" thrown in. Alice and Katie had even visited the prior summer. "Taking a break from cooking and laundry," they'd called it. Nothing could have made him happier. He felt grateful to be enfolded in love with much of his family, and, of course, with Eric and Elizabeth.

"'Let the great world spin forever down the ringing grooves of change,'" he said aloud as he returned to the dishpan of mixing bowls and cake pans, although he'd meant to keep Tennyson's words to himself.

Everyone at the table turned to him.

"My dad's a little strange," Elizabeth explained. "He's always quoting stuff."

"Sorry," Heber mumbled to no one in particular. His frustrated actor must be leaking out. He'd be more careful. The last thing he wanted to do was embarrass his daughter. She had enough challenges.

Like the man around the corner that they avoided whenever possible. They'd been taking a stroll through the neighborhood soon after they lost Ruth, Elizabeth walking between Eric and him, an arm through each of theirs. The man turned from watering his garden and hissed *perverts* loud enough for them to hear. The ugly word hung in the fresh spring air like oily smoke.

Heber still remembered how his muscles had tensed and Eric had audibly sucked in his breath, but for Elizabeth's sake they had continued on. Neither of them had expected this problem so soon after Ruth's death.

Without breaking stride, Elizabeth had asked, "what's a pervert?"

"It's a person who leads someone away from good. Eric and I aren't perverts. And you certainly aren't. He's using the word wrong." Heber was tempted to do some name-calling himself. How many hateful terms would eventually fill Elizabeth's lexicon of words used to vilify her father and adopted uncle?

Especially agonizing was watching the loss of some of her friends, at an age when friends were so precious. Heber looked at the four girls plowing through big slabs of birthday cake. These were the four whose parents allowed them to keep close ties with her. Others who had once played here after school hadn't been to the house since Ruth's death.

"Time to open presents," Eric suggested as he picked up their empty dessert plates.

Elizabeth grabbed a gift wrapped in shiny pink paper. "Neat! The new Nancy Drew mystery." She showed Heber and Eric *The Haunted Showboat*. There were also white bobby socks trimmed with lace, a 45RPM record of "Tell Me You're Mine," and a stuffed cat immediately shown to Pumpkin who was winding through the girls' legs.

The doorbell rang and the party guests picked up their sweaters and the party favors Elizabeth had made for them. Heber had watched proudly while two evenings in a row she sat at the dining room table coloring brown paper bags with the name of each of her friends coming to the party. She'd added a special touch for each girl: ballet slippers for the dancer, a tabby for the cat-lover, a basketball for the athlete, a book for her fellow Nancy Drew enthusiast. Inside each bag she'd placed a small bottle of lavender *eau de toilette* — her choice of fragrance brought an image of Ruth to mind — a tube of lip gloss, and three star-shaped cookies covered with sprinkles that Eric had helped her bake.

The last girl to be picked up was Linda. When he saw her mother at the door, Heber quickly joined Elizabeth to say good-bye. Linda had been his daughter's best friend at church, and he appreciated her parents allowing the friendship to continue when he and Elizabeth quit attending services.

"Nice to see you, Sister Collins," he said, extending his hand in a welcoming handshake. "We so enjoy having Linda in our home."

"She enjoys being here. She says you have the best snacks of any of her friends."

"That would be her Uncle Eric," Heber said with just the slightest hitch in his voice. "He's quite the baker."

Heber and Linda's mother had had a dozen similar conversations over the last few years. He didn't expect anyone to be quite comfortable in their home. Sister Collins came close. Like Marge who had remained a good friend, Linda's mother didn't just talk about the teachings of Jesus, she lived them.

Heber still had some guilt about leaving the church. He and Elizabeth had gone for a few more Sundays after Ruth's death. Each time Elizabeth came home with a new story of a snub. So when she asked to quit going altogether, Heber agreed. Ruth in her maternal wisdom had foreseen that this day would come.

More and more Sunday mornings Heber found himself working in the yard, pruning fruit trees and roses, mowing, weeding. As he worked, he felt the presence of his heavenly father who he now knew loved him the way he was.

Or the family went on a hike up Eaton Canyon, a spot nestled in the San Gabriel Mountains an easy fifteen-minute drive from their house. The trail followed a wash with its desert vegetation—coast live oak and sycamore trees, sages, buckwheat, and prickly pear cactus. It then entered a canyon. Elizabeth usually took the lead there, rock-hopping back and forth across a creek that ran between the high rugged walls and led to a pool at the bottom of a forty-foot waterfall.

She had her mother's curious mind, and after their first hike had wanted to get out their Compton's Encyclopedia and look up the geology of San Gabriel Mountains. "Two billion years," she marveled on the next hike, as they ate a snack by the pool. Lizards bathed on the rocks in the warm sun. Two chipmunks checked for any dropped crumbs.

"God took a long time creating the world, but didn't he do a great job!" Heber said, utterly content.

One time when they were walking along the wash, Eric abruptly thrust his arm out and stopped them all in their tracks. A fat snake slithered across the path and disappeared quickly into the underbrush.

"Was that a rattlesnake?" Elizabeth asked, wide-eyed.

"Sure was," Heber answered. "Lots bigger than the garter snakes we see in the yard. Nothing to be afraid of, though, unless they're coiled and rattling. This guy was probably as surprised as we were."

"Have you seen one before?" She scanned the underbrush.

"I've run across a few snakes." Heber's mind went not to a reptile but to his snake of a brother-in-law, although he hadn't thought about him in a while. Initially Heber had jumped every time the phone rang, expecting Ted to be on the line trying to lay claim to Elizabeth. After a year or so he realized the man was just an impotent bully.

Sarah, another viper, hadn't bothered them either, communicating only to send Elizabeth a card and ten dollars on her birthday and at Christmas.

"Thank you for the great party!" Elizabeth interrupted Heber's reflections, hugging both men.

"You're welcome. It *was* a great party." Heber studied his brand-new teenager, her face more like Ruth's every day. She brought him and Eric such delight. The three of them planned to go to France when she graduated from high school. Heber couldn't wait to show her and Eric the towns where he'd served on his mission and take them to the opera and ballet.

He'd talked of taking Ruth to France when they were courting, and again when she seemed to have recovered from her cancer. He so regretted he hadn't made it happen.

As happy as he was with Elizabeth and Eric, he had to be vigilant or endless regrets could consume him. Every blessing in his life seemed to come at a cost—a cost to someone else. Ruth had been a kind, unselfish, like-minded companion, hurt innumerable times in the marriage. Eric had twice refused to break up Heber's marriage, first in

Pasadena, and then in Maine when he had to painfully rearrange his life to stay in Bar Harbor while Heber returned to his family. Then Elizabeth. Their sweet Lizzy. Enveloped in love at home, but beyond the front door buffeted by the prejudices of society.

"What's next, birthday girl?" Eric asked. "It's still your special day."

Count on Eric to keep the celebration going.

"It's early enough to go camping," Heber volunteered. "We've wanted to check out Spruce Grove Campground." The three of them went camping in the Angeles Forest now and then, an interest he had never pursued until now, but Eric had. Heber had ten thumbs when putting up a tent and even Elizabeth beat him at fire-starting every time, but he was learning from them. Somehow Eric always managed to pack one of his blueberry triumphs for dinner or breakfast. As they ate, they talked about everything from Pumpkin's latest antic to the snide remark of a stranger on the street.

"I'm pretty tired," Elizabeth admitted. Understandably, after a slumber party with five girls giggling long after Heber called "lights out."

"Then maybe a movie," Heber suggested. They all three loved going to the movies and grabbing an ice cream cone afterward, sharing favorite scenes between creamy drips of chocolate and strawberry. Elizabeth was becoming quite the movie critic. Her plea for an acceptance of cross-cultural relationships after they watched *South Pacific* was both thoughtful and passionate.

"Daddy, Uncle Eric asked me what I want to do," Elizabeth reminded Heber with such tenderness that he could only smile ruefully. "I kind of feel like staying home. Can we do that puzzle of Paris you gave me last night for my birthday?"

"Perfect," Heber and Eric said in unison.

Eric went to the bookcase shelf in the sunroom where it had been put away with their stack of games and puzzles. Heber set up their card table. Elizabeth poured them each a glass of lemonade from the pitcher Eric kept filled in the refrigerator.

They began sorting the 500-piece puzzle. As they found pieces that fit together in twos and threes, the places Heber remembered well after so many years emerged: Place de la Concorde, the Arc de Triomphe, Sacre-Coeur Basilica. Even a boat full of tourists on a river boat ride on the Seine.

Organizing by color and shape, Heber was struck by the uniqueness of each piece. Some were vibrant, others dark; some had one or two smooth sides, others were jagged. It was only when they were linked together, that the real beauty of the work was revealed.

Suddenly Pumpkin jumped on the table, sending pieces skittering to the floor. Elizabeth and Eric dove to retrieve the ones that had fallen.

"We have to find them all," Elizabeth ordered. "It would wreck the picture to have even one piece missing."

"Did you ever think," Heber mused when they were seated again, "how like people puzzle pieces are? Different colors, shapes and sizes, each piece unique? It's only when they're all joined together—like a puzzle—that we have the most interesting and beautiful society."

"Spoken like a true college professor," Eric laughed.

Elizabeth cocked her head. "Different colors, some kinda odd angles—they *are* like people!"

"You're a bright one, birthday girl. For that I'll give you this corner I've been saving." Eric carefully slid it to her. "Imagine if we treated people like we do puzzle pieces. Never trying to force them to be a color or shape they aren't."

"We'd have a better world, that's for sure." Elizabeth added two pieces to what they could see was becoming the Eiffel Tower.

Heber found the last one the tower needed and leaned back. "Ah. Now that's the Paris of movies."

"Daddy, Paris is a special place to you, right?" Elizabeth asked.

"Yes, it is. Can't wait to show it to you."

"Is it better than here?"

The question surprised Heber. He looked at his little family. "How could it be better?" He wished he could freeze this moment in time, with Eric's gentle presence, Elizabeth's trust and earnestness, and memories of Ruth, sometimes painful but adding texture and depth to the mix. He started humming a hymn he'd often sung at church.

"We sang that all the time in Junior Sunday School!" Elizabeth exclaimed, breaking into a huge smile. In a sweet, clear voice she began to sing. *'In the cottage there is joy/When there's love at home.'*

Heber added his mellow baritone. *"Hate and envy ne'er annoy/When there's love at home."*

They sang all three stanzas, Heber improvising a harmony as he had so many years ago with Ruth. He wished life were as simple as the song. Love had been both his tonic and his torment for most of his life. He and Ruth had loved each other, but not what the poets called a *perfect love*. Words Brian had spoken came to his mind. *'If you can't find a home in your own head, where can you live? There's no sanctuary for you.'* He'd had no idea how prophetic those words were.

At last, Heber was at peace. His home was his sanctuary. Heber knew tomorrow morning's paper would be full of articles about the atomic bomb testing, violent protests over ending segregation in public schools, and maybe an update on a possible political coup in France. He, Eric, and Elizabeth would draw strength from their family bond as they dealt with the struggles and hardships life brought.

So often throughout his life he'd prayed that he could change. Now his prayers were for the world to change; to become a place where people like him weren't made to feel fundamentally defective, and instead, valued for their uniqueness. Where society, like a puzzle, was its most beautiful and complete when every lost piece was slipped into a place it belonged.

ACKNOWLEDGEMENTS

I started this novel decades ago when my father was still alive to read the first draft and see if I'd gotten right the struggle that he and many others like him dealt with their entire lives. His words were, "How did you get it so right?"

Thanks to Margaret Donsbach, Jane Viehl, Terence Schumacher, Willa Holmes, and Margo Bowman, colleagues from three writing groups, who offered weekly critiques at various points in the novel's development Thanks, as well, to Molly Gloss and Cynthia Whitcomb, amazing writers and teachers, who through both instruction and example helped me develop my skills as a novelist.

A shout-out to Herbert Piekow who heard me pitch an early draft. of the novel and became its steadfast champion, inviting me into his writing group of wonderful writers and thinkers, reading many drafts of the book and sharing his experiences as a gay man so I could more fully understand the issues at the heart of *The Choice of Men*.

To Chris W. Higgins, happily married to his movie producer husband, who went through every word of a draft with me, even writing his version of several chapters so I could more successfully capture the complexity of my characters.

To Jay VanDenBogaard who did a close read and critique of the novel from a counselor's perspective and offered invaluable insights about the portrayal of intimacy in the relationships of the main characters.

To B.J. Bateman, fellow writer and dear friend, who opened her vacation home at Cannon Beach as a writers' retreat every summer and offered limitless, good-humored friendship and encouragement back in Portland, even as her health failed. I miss her every day.

To Ron J. Turker who met with me week after week when I felt too burned out to continue work on this project but loved the idea of going to new and different coffee shops to discuss his critiques. His questions and suggestions led me to a significant deepening of the novel.

To Lois Jean Bousquet who lent the excellent eye of a developmental editor to three complete drafts and many individual pieces and cheered me on throughout our work together.

To my beloved daughter Tami Wood who offered expert consultation on all aspects of the book's appearance and my marketing endeavors.

To Colleen Sell, for eleventh-hour consultations on punctuation when Google failed me.

To Ken Stokes whose personal support throughout the last drafts and invaluable assistance in production kept me breathing.

And to Jeanne Silaski and Kimila Kay who had faith in the quality and importance of the novel when I lacked it and held me on a steady course toward its completion and publication. Jeanne examined and reflected on every aspect of the novel from a better organization of the opening chapters to a better scene, sentence structure or word. Kimila Kay not only offered expert editing, but also took over the technical aspects of publication. If it weren't for these two women, *The Choice of Men* might yet again have been slipped into a drawer. Thank you doesn't begin to say it.

FOR DISCUSSION

1. How might Heber's life have been different if he hadn't offered up his confession to his mission president?

2. In what ways does Heber's relationship with Brian change him?

3. Do you agree with Heber that trying to live a way that feels uncomfortable and dishonest can lead to the kind of stress where one might abuse oneself and others?

4. At one point, Heber wonders if Ruth's family's history of polygamy might encourage her acceptance of Heber's affair with Eric. How are those relationships similar and different?

5. Is Eric an interloper or a true friend?

6. At what point in the novel do you feel Heber fully acknowledges his basic nature?

7. Heber often wonders if God is punishing him or his loved ones for his sins. How is that concern consistent or inconsistent with his religious beliefs?

8. *The Choice of Men* is set in the '40s and early '50's. How is a gay man's struggle today similar to and different from Heber's struggle?

9. Who owns the narrative of love between consenting adults, society or the individual?

10. What kept Heber committed to his church and its doctrines through so many years of his struggle?

11. What happens to Heber after the book ends? To Elizabeth? To Eric?

12. In *The Choice of Men* the Mormon Church is the segment of society that most influences Heber. Would the same be true today? What other religious and/or political institutions play a similar role in people's lives?

"A must read. *The Choice of Men* is a poignant and resonant story of one man's struggle between his basic nature and his desire to follow the tenants of his religion. Although the novel is set in the '40s and early '50s, the issues explored in it continue today for many men and women, and for those who love them."

   Herbert Piekow, writer

 Samantha Waltz is the award-winning author of seventy anthologized personal essays and the editor of *Blended: Writers On The Stepfamily Experience*. *The Choice of Men* is her first adult novel.

Of her writing, acclaimed author Molly Gloss notes, "Samantha Waltz writes with scrupulous honesty and compassion, in a voice as pure and clear as a mountain lake."

CPSIA information can be obtained
at www.ICGtesting.com
Printed in the USA
LVHW091941040621
689416LV00001B/5

9 781735 560403